FRUITFUL

by

MAPLE SVENSON

This is dedicated to my friends that "yes, and"-ed me into writing an entire book (and supported me re-editing the whole damn thing once I decided to take this seriously).

I hope you read it and remember that there *is* a limit to committing to the bit… but we haven't found it yet. <3

Love you, guys!

Chapter 1

"Come on," I mutter through gritted teeth. My hands, wrinkled and pale, scrub furiously at a stubborn stain on a delicate tablecloth. The spot mocks me, refusing to yield no matter how hard I press. My face contorts with the effort. But, as to be expected, the stain remains: a bloody red blotch on otherwise pristine ivory.

I dunk the sheet elbow deep into the basin, the water spilling over the edges as it's displaced by my aggression. I imagine holding the fabric underwater until it surrenders, until it *drowns*.

A chuckle echoes off the stone walls of the laundry room. It burrows deep, settling under my skin. I don't need to turn to know who it is.

Lucian.

My eyes roll, metaphorically, of course. I wouldn't *dare* show such disrespect to a guard. The fae thrive on the overt ways they remind us humans of our place here in the Otherworld.

The hairs on the back of my neck rise as he closes in, his presence like a cold draft slipping between my thoughts. I focus harder on the stain, hoping that ignoring him will make him lose interest…But it doesn't.

My body stiffens when his hand comes to rest on my shoulder. His touch is too familiar, too *heavy*. It drags up the memories I've tried to bury: my bed, those hands, his promises to get me out of the lowest level barracks, twisted and fleeting just to get my body beneath his.

It takes every ounce of willpower not to shrug him off while we're alone in this space. No witnesses means no safety.

"Need anything?" he asks in a honeyed tone. But I don't miss the unspoken *"for a price"*. The fae never do anything for us for free.

"No," I reply flatly, refusing to give him an opening to twist my words. "I thought I was alone. Just… airing my frustrations." I chance a glance at him, and his green eyes glint with amusement. He's enjoying this: my discomfort.

His face, once beautiful to me, masks the savagery behind his eyes, as beauty does with all fae. His broad frame and ego were a lure that now just signal the danger beneath.

In my time as a servant to the king here, I've learned that the charm of the guards only works on the naive, newly captured humans. I have grown a hard shell against their low effort word games. Callused against their tricks like my fingers. Lucian can't trick me with pretty words and stolen touches. Not *anymore*.

"I can help you work out those frustrations," he purrs. His fingers, too smooth for the rough life down here, brush the loose hair clinging to my neck. I fail to suppress a disgusted shudder that he must misread for pleasure, because he repeats the gesture.

He doesn't even remember the way he tricked me all those years ago, when I *was* that naive victim pulled from my promising life in the human world…or maybe he *does* remember and just doesn't care. Either way, the message I received was clear from my first year here: never trust them.

It's a lesson I've never forgotten.

"I should get back to work," I say quickly, my voice hasty despite my best efforts to remain casual. "I don't want to get either of us in trouble for slacking off."

He straightens at the disengagement, his mouth hardening into a line for a moment before he forces that sneer of a smile back onto his lips. He pats my head condescendingly, and I fight back the urge to lean out of reach.

"You're such a good girl, you should learn to misbehave a little," he suggests, his tone dripping with unfulfilled want.

"Girl."

The word stings: a reminder of my perpetual state: eighteen years old and fresh faced. I've been eighteen for far too many years now. While I'm grateful to never have to worry about another period, deteriorating joints, or the responsibility of navigating life in the human world, it's left me stunted and mourning a future I'll never get to see play out.

The regret of my choices grows with the distance between us, as Lucian takes lazy steps back out the door. The tension in my shoulders eases, but the silence he leaves behind feels heavier than before, weighed down by reminders of my mistakes. I glance at the door, half expecting him to still be lingering in the entryway, but it's empty.

For now.

I turn back to the tablecloth, my hands aching as I pick up where I left off. The stain is still there, tainted and unchanging. Just like everything else in this cursed place.

Chapter 2

There are countless jobs assigned to humans in the Otherworld, but I only know one: laundry servant. A role originally given to me – I suspect – out of cruel irony.

Back in the human world, I had been studying fashion. It wasn't just some half hearted dream. I was going to college on a full ride scholarship for my talents.

Or so I thought.

That "scholarship" turned out to be a disguised magical bargain, a snare set by a human trapper – a redcap – whose sole job is to bind unsuspecting souls to this wretched place. And while bargains are *technically* breakable, I've seen what happens to the humans who do: the whippings, the screams, the way they disappear for days at minimum, if not forever. And when they come back, they're *never* quite the same.

Bargains are only magical in that they allow both sides to know when it's been broken. And only *one* side ever gets to enforce punishment for breaking them.

Don't start, I warn myself, feeling the familiar sting of "what ifs" creeping in. I shake off the pride threatening to straighten my shoulders, as I scrub the next stain in my endless pile of soiled decor.

Laundry day after fae revelries is always a nightmare. But last night's party seems to have been particularly indulgent. My team may be fully staffed this summer, but the staff consists of perpetual young adults who will *never* outgrow the heightened emotions of our biological age – it leads to grueling days punctuated by heated encounters and frayed nerves. So I stay on my stool and scrub quietly.

Alone.

As a laundry servant, I was given two choices of my eternal servitude. Choice one: sort and carry soiled bedding and table runners from the maid team to the washing team. Once cleaned by the washing team, press them before returning them to the maid team. Or choice two: be on the washing team. Scrub away and mend the evidence of the royalty's debauchery from those gaudy pieces. Neither option is pleasant, and we help out each other when work loads are uneven, but at least this second choice allows me a semblance of solitude and peace compared to the grueling teamwork of the other chore.

Lucky me.

I scold myself, the memory of my deal with the redcap surfacing unbidden again. The pressure of that decision presses down on me, more suffocating than every ornate duvet in this castle combined. I yawn as the endless hours of work get to me. My back is too tense from my perch on the stool; the sudsing water now gone cold.

The sound of footsteps interrupts my self pity. I glance up to see one of the rarest sites in this waking nightmare: a friend.

Maddie enters the laundry room. Her presence is a welcome distraction compared to Lucian's. My hunched shoulders roll to release some tension, but a pop in the joints tells me I've pushed too hard today.

"Hey, Valerie," she greets warmly. "Hope those covers aren't giving you too much grief. Although, based on word from the maid staff upstairs, I doubt that's the case."

I sigh, rubbing the back of a suds covered arm against my forehead to push an errant curl out of the way. My hair is always where it shouldn't be: an untamable mess of copper.

"Afternoon, Maddie. Where's Lilia?" I ask, ignoring her comment about the tablecloth, we both know she's right. Maddie and Lilia are inseparable and always start the daunting day shifts after a revelry together.

Maddie's plump brown skin glistens with a faint sheen of sweat with her effort to bring me a too large bundle of table runners, and I already know the answer about her partner. It's the same as it is every time we're tasked with cleaning the main hall after events: bringing up the rear and ensuring we're not blamed for other teams' missteps.

"She's almost done lugging stuff back from the last load. I carried the bigger pile for us," she confirms, her eyes drifting curiously to the stained fabric in my hands. My attempted smile falls as I reluctantly remember my foe.

"I think this might be fairy fruit," I mutter. "I should have worn gloves."

Maddie grimaces at the words.

"Just make sure you wash your hands extra well before touching your face again. And don't tell Lilia," she cautions. I nod.

My mind conjures a prototype Lilia seeing me handle the fruit stain with bare hands. She's so protective of Maddie and our sanity, I don't think she'd let me back in our room until sure I hadn't ingested any.

I recall the last person down here who dared try a small bit of fruit skin. He'd harvested it from a discarded napkin, only to slowly lose his mind. His words became incoherent, and hallucinations seemed to outweigh reality around him. He was hauled away by guards soon after, never to be seen by anyone still here again.

Maddie's tone is friendly again when she speaks, banishing the cruel example in my memory. "Imagine if you had just a single drop of *real* dish soap."

I laugh, though there's no humor in it. "Right? That would solve all my problems."

Our conversation lulls after we share another weak smile, as it often does. Too much excitement might draw unwanted attention, and we've learned to keep our interactions brief and subdued during working hours.

In the human world, this stain would be gone in seconds with modern detergent.

It wouldn't even exist, there's no fairy fruit back home.

But here, in the Otherworld, their technology is stuck in archaic times. Hard, fat based soap and wire brushes are all they give us to eradicate the grime.

Maybe they give us these poor products on purpose, just to amuse themselves.

They know it makes our work harder, our lives more miserable. After all, the portal to the human world is within a day's journey of my current imprisonment, if my fleeting recollection of arriving here is still correct. A guard could easily disguise themselves with a floppy hat over their pointed ears and pop over to any store to snag some supplies.

But no. Instead, they force us to use these archaic means, laughing as our hands bleed and our spirits break.

Chapter 3

In my old life, I was always surrounded by friends. A more confident person would say I was popular. My true teenage self had potential – had dreams. But here, my personality and looks aren't special. Our imprisoners only seem to take the most hopeful and glowing from upcoming generations, as if watching our bright eyes lose their luster brings them more joy.

I find myself low on both hierarchies: social and professional.

Being a laundry servant makes true friendship a risk I cannot afford to invest in time and time again. So I keep my circle small.

Survival down at my level means blending in, becoming as unremarkable as possible, and sticking to the assigned team at all times, like sheep in a flock. It's a lonely existence that dulls the emotional senses. But it's the only way to avoid drawing attention – or worse, ire – from ill intended guards.

The barracks the laundry team are confined to are a stark contrast to the opulence of the white glistening castle I steal glimpses of through the skylights above.

Underground and windowless, the only light for our daily work comes from those sealed glass panes overhead, which cast shifting patterns of sunlight across the stone floors as we work. I've grown accustomed to them being the only evidence of time passing and a world beyond this dungeon.

Maybe one day, I'll get to see that world... No. Nevermind. Don't entertain the hope.

The cots we sleep on are cramped and utilitarian, four to a room, with more rooms than I've counted in my time here. I once counted up to thirty when I was new, before a patrolling guard gave me a warning whack to get back to scrubbing. I haven't bothered since.

It isn't all completely hopeless, though. I've been so lucky to room with Maddie and Lilia for all of my time here. The revolving fourth post to our room seems to be cursed, never keeping an occupant for more than a year or so at a time. But the three of us guard each other, finding sisterhood in the small moments.

Lilia, Maddie, and Eddie were my first, and still my only, real friends in this place. We watch each other's backs, covering for one another when someone's heaving their guts sick or breaks from exhaustion. It's not much, but it's the closest thing to safety we have here. And for them, I'm grateful.

So grateful, in fact, that I'm often late to breakfast trying to make sure we're all awake on time.

Like today.

"Lilia, get up," I command, shaking her shoulder to raise her. The peaking sun streaming through the skylights paints the room in the golden glow that signals we should have left the room by now, but Lilia remains stubbornly curled under her thin frayed shield of a blanket.

"If you don't get up now, you'll miss your chance to eat before sundown tonight," Maddie teases.

I know we've won, when she groans in response, sliding off the opposite side of the cot with a lack of grace only humans can achieve. Her normally sleek black hair is a mess around her scrunched face.

"Let's just hope they didn't premix the oats and milk today," she mumbles, shuffling out the door toward the communal washroom. Maddie snorts from her spot on the edge of her bed next to us, watching Lilia trudge past with a smirk.

"Let's hope they even have oats left at this point," Maddie sighs. And she isn't wrong. First meal for us dayshifters follows the last meal for night shift. Whatever they leave for us is a gamble at best, and based on the placement of the shadows cast on the walls, we are running behind schedule to get even those scraps.

Once Lilia has returned, washed and brushed with the stagnant water shared by the team, we head towards the dining hall. We flow into the sea of muslin uniformed servants shuffling to the first meal of the day.

We aren't given the courtesy of fitted dyed garments like the guards or higher level maids, our station tucked so far below the glittering levels of the palace that it's seen as waste to give us comfort.

We're expendable.

I shrug off the dehumanizing idea, and prepare for the work ahead today. We will be starching and pressing pleats into tablecloths, based on the fresh loads the night team lugged down the stairs this morning. We will be busy until well after the sun sets tonight. My arms ache preemptively.

Our trio heads into the dining hall together, the scent of overcooked porridge and the low murmur of tired voices replacing the grime of the tunnels. Meal time is the only chance we get to mingle with other teams of servants on a regular basis. Gossip is exchanged for favors, the only currency most of us have down here. For a group of perpetual teens, it's by far the most exciting part of the day to refill our coin purses.

Once inside, Lilia inclines her chin toward a sight that always sinks my heart: a new arrival. They're a wide eyed wallflower, a tray clutched in white knuckled hands as they scan the room for an open seat. My stomach twists in sympathy, something I forget I still possess. Newcomers are a reminder of how easily we can be replaced, and how all our dreams were crushed upon the reality of arrival here. It makes the memories of my own first day too raw, and I look away.

I try to casually scan the room for Eddie, the fourth member of our trauma forged group and the only one I trust with my heart anymore.

The smile she sports makes her easy to spot in a crowd as dull eyed as this. She's sitting at a mostly empty table, a plate of beige food piled too high in front of her. Her eyes catch mine, and her usual smile beams against her dark skin, equal parts mischievous and reassuring. I smile back despite my thoughts stuck on the grim schedule ahead for today.

"Go on," Lilia teases, nudging me with her elbow. "We'll be fine getting our own food."

I nod and step out of the line, leaving Maddie and Lilia to brave the mushy prospects ahead. The dining hall is a chaotic mix of human servants and shoulder height guards seeking exchanges like a black market. But for a moment, all I see is Eddie's smile creased eyes and the small island of comfort she represents.

I make my way to her, matching her smile with a small one of my own as I slide onto the bench next to her. She's grabbed my favorites: bread and a delicacy that normally doesn't survive to day shift: bacon.

"Thank you, Eddie," I say, wrapping an arm around her shoulders in a quick hug. "You must have gotten here so early to get these."

She slides the tray toward me with a shrug that brushes against my emotional calluses, as if she would have wanted to do nothing more than sit at this table and scare off hungry hands. I let my fingers rest on hers for an appreciative moment before I dig in. The food could use some seasoning, especially some salt, but I know better than to mention it. Salt is banned, at least down in the barracks, I'm not sure about anywhere else. It's supposedly harmful for our captors, but I've never had the pleasure of watching them suffer with it.

The cold bread still has some give. I scarf it down with enthusiastic surprise when I realize it's not entirely stale, then break my bacon strips into small piles. Each pile will go to a friend, my stomach can't handle so much gristle anyway.

As we settle into our meal, Eddie nudges me and nods toward the newcomer as Lilia had done. They still stand alone near the entrance, their tray in their trembling hands as they search for a place to sit, frozen against the mayhem of traded secrets. Their arms must be tired by now from the weight.

"We should invite them over," Eddie suggests.

My stomach feels suddenly too full at the idea.

The last time we brought someone new into our group, it ended in betrayal. She'd used our trust to get stories of other teams and ourselves. Exchanging them for better shifts and eventually, climbing the ranks out of these underground barracks and into a more cushy station. She left us vulnerable, backstabbed, and exposed to more dramatics. The memory makes the bread hard to swallow.

"I don't know, Eddie," I mutter, glancing at the loner. "What if they're another climber like Violet? We can't afford to take that risk again."

Eddie's eyebrows knit at my indifference, and she places a hand on mine. "I get it, Val. But look at them. They're alone, and clearly have no idea what they've walked into. If we don't help them, someone else will, and they might not have great intentions."

She's right.

I stop chewing as the idea of Lucian getting his paws on them flits through my mind. I'm torn between caution and compassion, an emotion that leads to more heartbreak than its noble intent. I look for Lilia and Maddie, finding them most of the way through the line. I catch Maddie's eye, and shrug towards the scared newbie. *"What do you think?"*

She and Lilia exchange a few words. They shrug back: *"It's up to you."*

"Fine," I say finally, exhaling sharply. "But we take it slow. No sharing anything important until we're sure we can trust them."

Eddie's eyes soften with pride. "Of course."

She stands and waves them over, her friendly smile immediately making them bristle.

They're skeptical. Good.

I look over Eddie with their new eyes, somehow not only gorgeous like everyone else stuck down here, but also kind hearted enough to take someone new under her wing. She's too perfect with her toned arms and bright eyes.

They approach cautiously, their eyes darting between us in search of a trap.

"Hey," Eddie gestures to the table. "You look like you could use a seat. Join us."

They hesitate – weighing their options – shifting from one leg to the other after standing for too long. Once they nod, I know they've decided there are no better choices down here – their first of many disappointments. They slide onto the bench on her side opposite me, seeming to heed my narrowed eyes as a warning to stay away.

"Thank you," their voice cracks like they haven't spoken in a while. The moment their hands are free of the tray, they find their way to the back of their neck, searching.

"I'm Eddie, this is Valerie. That's Lilia, and Maddie," she points out each of us in turn, introducing the group. Lilia and Maddie smile, unable to hear us from across the room, but understanding all the same.

"I'm Ash," they rasp. "I just got here yesterday."

They rub their neck again.

Stop doing that, I think.

"We know," I say instead, as I look at their hunched posture. "It's rough at first, but you'll get the hang of it." I pause again, my eyes fixated on the way their fingers disappear behind their collar line. "And stop touching the brand, you don't want it to get infected before it heals."

Their hands quickly snap back in front of them.

I can't be too harsh. I remember getting my brand within my first hour in this world. The acrid stench of my own burning flesh never quite left me, but the pain did as it healed.

I was told by the guards that it permanently identifies us as this kingdom's property, and prevents any chance of escaping into the wilds beyond the castle. As if survival out there even seems possible; tales of cannibalistic humans and monstrous creatures in the forests keep us all here and well behaved.

I study Ash warily, searching for any hint of deception as they pick at their plate. But all I see is fear and exhaustion: the same emotions I felt when I first arrived. It's brutal to see them so fresh on a face again. They really seem to be just another lost soul trying to come to terms with their new existence.

"We have an open bunk in my room. Tell the guards you want to be assigned to the dayshift laundry team, and you want to be on the main hall crew. You'll be given that bed." I give them the courtesy to adjust, remembering my first few days and the complete disorientation of entering a new world: one where magic is *real* but we never get to see it. The absolute despair was only cushioned by my now friends pulling me into their group.

"Valerie, Lilia, and Maddie all are in a room. You'll be safer there than random assignment," Eddie explains, her hand finding mine in thanks. They nod, their eyes full of relief at my instruction.

I wonder what the trapper used to lure them here, how they managed to trick them to sign away their beauty and youth like the rest of us.

"What year is it? Back home?" The question slips out.

"2007," they answer carefully.

Seventeen years. I've been stuck down here for seventeen years.

"How'd they get you?" I ask and immediately regret it. It's way too soon. Tears well in their blue eyes, and Eddie pins me with a glare.

Maybe some camaraderie will smooth this over.

"I was promised a scholarship, I was told I'd live without worrying about money again… They were right. I've never been paid a dime for all this work. So whatever they said to get you here, it can't be as embarrassing as my story." I force a laugh at the end, attempting to distract Ash from their own misfortune.

It doesn't work, and they bury their head into their hands as they break into sobs. Eddie's eyes are too wide as they lock on me while she mouths "knock it off."

I grimace at Ash's reaction, and turn back to my plate.

At least we know they're genuine. For now.

Eddie's hand hovers for a moment questioning the best choice to approach their meltdown, before finally draping over them. They lean against her, muffling the cries as they rack their body.

"Perfect," Eddie mutters sarcastically under her breath, just before a paper is smacked down on the table in front of us. The suddenness makes my head snap up.

A creature with curling horns on either side of his head looks pointedly at me. His pastel blue uniform is a silk so fine it drapes over his form, making him look unreal against the stained, bulky wear of the rest of us.

I've heard stories of higher ranking servants and their strange beauty. But seeing one myself straightens me in my seat.

"Valerie Harlow," he addresses me alone, ignoring the other humans at the table. He's far more handsome than the guards that normally surround us: a youthful glow to his angular cheekbones. His brown eyes are cold as they assess me. "Have you been assigned an order for day shift today?"

I shake my head, confused. The conversations around us die down as my neighbors strain to eavesdrop on the suddenly interesting meal. It'll be good gossip to trade; I can't blame them.

I feel Eddie's eyes fix on me as I compose myself, trying to appear relaxed.

"You have knowledge of textiles?" the creature asks.

I nod. My heart begins to thud with the question about my life before this place.

They've never pushed for information before.

"You are relieved of laundry duties for the next twenty four hours. You will report to the Royal Atelier for second sewing shift tonight. A uniform will be in your room when you arrive after second meal tonight. Do not be late." He orders.

"When is that?" I ask, having not bothered to learn the night shift's schedule in my time here. His chiseled jaw flexes with the inconvenience of my simple question. I hold my breath waiting for him to answer.

"That will be when the guards rotate just past midnight. Another servant will be assigned to assure you leave on time. And clean up before you go, there will be important company." He closes his mouth in a hard line as his rectangular pupils drift down the length of my robe. My shocked reaction escapes for only a moment before I recover.

"Yes, ok," I say, my voice too quick with excitement: an emotion I haven't felt in at least a decade.

The goat-man retreats quickly through the parting crowd of teens, and it's only then that I notice he has *hooves* instead of feet that clack against the stone floor. He leaves the sheet of paper on the table before me, its ivory color already smudged with beige slop.

My shaking fingers lift it. It's a map, printed by hand with ink, leading from the barracks to the studio. There's more information here than I've seen in all my years of servitude. Labeled halls and levels far higher than my friends have ventured to on the hauling team are drawn in a neat little blueprint. The castle is larger than I ever dared to imagine, and we've been confined to such a small labyrinth beneath.

"What the hell was that about?" Lilia blurts, skidding onto the bench across from us. Her eyes widen at the crying Ash in Eddie's arms. Eddie shakes her head before Lilia can question the decisions we've already made.

Lilia snatches the map from me, absorbing all the details she can before I take it back.

"I'm working at the atelier tonight. For some guests," I explain, still processing the news. "They must know my background in…" I trail off, not wanting to mention our dead lives again in front of Ash. Eddie offers an appreciative smile.

"Congratulations, Val," Eddie recovers for me. She bumps my shoulder with hers. I smile and place a peck on her cheek, feeling suddenly hopeful as the reality settles in.

"Just don't forget about us while you're up there," Maddie jokes, reaching a hand my way with mock longing.

"They won't be able to keep me away," I reassure them. "Not with all of you here." I grab her outstretched hand, squeezing it tightly, turning her gesture genuine. Lilia holds out her hand as well, though I know better than to presume it's for me. I let her memorize the layout in the paper. The information gleaned is extremely interesting, I can't fault her curiosity.

"This is Ash, by the way," Eddie tilts our new roommate upright, as they finally reign in the wave of emotion with the lightened news of my turning luck. Their puffy eyes are even bluer when they look at the two across from us.

Lilia and Maddie distract them, prepping them in all the unspoken rules of the barracks while they pick at the bacon from my piles.

The other servants are already back to idle chatter, but I know my temporary assignment will be the talk of the dayshift.

Chapter 4

To heed the horned servant's warning, I have taken the time to detangle my hair, letting it flow down my back. It's too long, but I cannot bring myself to cut it shorter, finding it to be one of the only defining features for me among the other servants. And I guard the small rebellion of individuality like a precious gift.

I scrub beneath my nails, seeing the clean half moons for the first time in years. I meticulously pick away the dirt, grime, and filth of my true conditions down here. Though I cannot cover the most overwhelming evidence: the hatred of the fae forged into my face. I practice schooling my features in the reflection of the still basin water, but find it hard to hide the harshness of reality from my eyes.

I'll just have to lay low and stay invisible, like I always do.

The uniform left on my bed clings to my form like nothing I've worn in this world. Instead of the usual muslin sack, I am clad in dyed navy cotton: two separate pieces of it. The tunic has buttons that I misalign once before getting the piece on correctly. The trousers have side laces, so I can draw them up to my waist and secure them over my hips. I even note a small crest on the cuff of the pants, a white deerhead wrapped with flowering vines. My finger runs over the embroidered patch, recognizing it as the same crest displayed on the guard uniforms and the brands on our necks.

It's uncomfortable to be so covered, constricted in a way I haven't been since leaving my old life.

How did I used to wear stuff like this?

The only things not replaced for my role tonight are my boots. The old leather pieces are worn in from my years here, and I'm grateful to take a small piece of humbling reality with me to this new experience. It will keep my expectations in check.

As I finish pinching my cheeks for a little color, Eddie finds her way to my room. Her timing is impeccable, as always.

"You know I'm about to leave, don't you?" I tease her in a whisper, not wanting to rouse the others after Ash finally found the escape of sleep. Before I can say more, she pulls my face to hers in a quick needy kiss.

"Be safe tonight, okay?" Her lips stay connected with mine as she speaks. When I pull back and raise an incredulous brow, she pulls me into the tunnel to speak more freely.

"There are a lot of rules for… *them*," Eddie begins. The "*them*" in place of any given word: fae, captors, *liars*. "You can't make a mistake being around so many. I know you know what you're doing, but just let me remind you of the rules anyway? Please?"

Though I want to bristle at the implication that I might not know these things, I also know she means well. This is a big test disguised as a small assignment. I'd be worried if it were any of the others from our group.

"How about I recite to you what I remember from the gossip circle?" I offer, knowing it will ease both our nerves to find middle ground. She nods for me to go ahead.

"1. Never approach them first. That one's obvious.

"2. Use their title if they have one: 'Sir,' Miss,' 'Your Majesty,' whatever's needed.

"3. Always trust your intuition. Even though they can't lie, that doesn't mean they tell the truth.

"4. Don't look them in the eye, turn your back on them, or do anything that they might view as putting yourself above them.

"5. Don't bargain with them – purposeful or accidental. Which basically means *not* being polite," I rattle off all the rules in quick succession.

Eddie fixes me with a stern look at the last part, and I clarify. "No 'please,' 'sorry,' or 'thank you.' I've got this."

Her eyes soften, and she pulls me into a smothering hug.

"Stay invisible, stay safe. See you in a few hours, I'll try to wait up for you," she murmurs against my hair. I relax into her for just a heartbeat, savoring the warmth of her embrace.

"I'll be so invisible, they won't even remember I was there," I manage to joke, hoping the light mood will keep my growing nerves away… it doesn't. I glance up at the placement of the moon to see it overhead. Out of the corner of my eye, a stumpy woman with a matching pristine uniform to my own appears in the tunnel, though hers is brown to my navy. Her head barely crests my waist, but she manages to pin me with an authoritative eye from beneath the large brown hat she wears.

"I think I have to go now," I mutter.

With that, I pluck the map from Lilia's bed, and hurry out the door. The servant shoos me ahead and up the stairs.

First a goat, now a dwarf? What else is hiding up there?

"For what it's worth, you look beautiful in that blue," Eddie calls after me, risking a raised voice on the chance I'll hear her. I smile to myself as I pick up the pace past my normal territory.

The small servant in brown doesn't follow me as I expect her to – instead drifting into other areas of the labyrinth. The map guides me through mildewed passages I've never ventured into before, up a rickety flight of stairs, until the slabs of stone become more stable underfoot and the mildew is replaced with ammonia. It's unpleasant in a different, equally suffocating way.

I am detained by a bullheaded monster – one that harkens back to Ancient Greek myths – on the other side of a blind turn. It eyes me accusingly, assuming I'm an escapee. I show it my map, the beast barely giving me time to duck, before it swings its horned head away in dismissal – letting me pass.

I take a shaky breath and turn the next corner.

As I creep further down the monster's tunnel, the walls around me shift, like the unreality of dreams: a dream I didn't think I was allowed to have anymore.

The stone walls of my usual captivity, rough and unadorned, give way to smooth marble that glimmers under the light of wall sconces. The air smells different too: cleaner and floral. I catch myself inhaling dreamily, recalling memories of a life I've spent so long trying to forget.

My hand trails along the wall as I climb, the polished surface so unlike anything I've touched since coming to the Otherworld. Another flight up and my fingers find intricate carvings etched *into* the marble; patterns of vines and flowers that lead me up into a new, almost offensive level of extravagance.

This is what they've denied us for decades.

I'm stunned still on the third landing I am to take, absorbing the light above me with disbelief. A chandelier dangles from the ceiling, its crystals refracting a thousand tiny rainbows across the walls. I've seen crystals before, of course, woven in the silken table runners and the embroidered tapestries I've mended.

But never like this. Never so clean and lit. Never so surreal.

It takes all my strength to tear my eyes away as other servants pass: mostly humans in neutral hues and short fae like the woman who ushered me up the stairs. The bolder ones shoot warning glares at my blocking traffic. This sight is so average to them, I feel resentment stealing away some of my awe.

I have to pretend this is all mundane, if I want to remain safe.

The stairs widen noticeably as I ascend even *further*, their edges gilded with exorbitant details that glint as I pass over them. My boots suddenly feel too out of place against such opulence. I glance down at them, self conscious and now wishing the guards *had* provided new shoes with the uniform.

The feeling keeps me from gawking at this new perspective of life in the castle too much. I steal peeks of other servants in blue hues like my own, but none are human this high up. Some flash jewelry and uniquely decorated uniforms of silk and satin. The few humans I do see don't wear any uniforms at all, instead being wrapped in loose jewel toned robes with delicate embroidery. It's so unlike the levels just a few steps below, so full of open windows and freedom.

They probably don't even know what it's truly like down there.

One group of servants catches my eye when I pass them. They aren't human, but close enough to make me double take: taller than the creatures around us. One has translucent skin that I can actually see through, another too wide eyes and cat-like ears. Their lavish uniforms – if they can even be called that – fit like tailored regalia. They hold their heads higher, postures more straight than the others scurrying in the halls.

I keep my distance.

Another sight detours me, when I divert my focus toward a wall. There's paintings of the ruling family in action lining the hall: the king, the prince, their cousins, and allies achieving feats of heroism unknown to me. But what I do know is that whoever painted these was a master of their craft.

I pause on a particularly harsh looking set of eyes at where the paintings currently end, blank canvas stretching far past for future additions.

"Prince Sylas" is written below the portrait.

And I recognize the name. The current prince next in line for the throne behind his father, King Anders, depicted in a more elaborate painting beside him.

I had heard in the barracks they were "high fae" or "fairies". And I'd assumed that meant they'd have wings and pointy shoes like cartoons from my childhood. But the man shown is more like the elves of fantasy novels than any fairies I can remember. Beautiful and serious, nearly human but uncannily different.

The eyes on the prince's painting are icy, brighter than most of the others, and looking at the audience instead of the nondescript enemy he stands against – daring the viewer, *me*, to look away first.

It isn't until a passing guard with a frog's head shoulder checks me, that I lose the challenge and come back to reality. I curse under my breath, reorienting myself with the map as I remember my time crunch. It directs me to take a left down a carpeted hall, thankfully less trafficked than the main thoroughfare. The walls here are adorned with repeating intricate designs. No haunting eyes follow me as I approach a gilded threshold at the far end.

The words "Royal Atelier" are hammered into a filigree sign decorating the doorway. I glance around, confused by the lack of activity.

They must all be inside already.

I steady myself before turning the unlocked handle and step into the space – determined to make it back to my friends safely.

But when I step into the atelier, my jaw drops at the sight before me. The space is empty of any people, but shockingly full of *life*. Rolls of fabric in every imaginable color line the walls, their woven designs studded with gems and metals that catch the light as I move further into the room. Treadle sewing machines sit beside ancient wooden looms, a collection of analog tools in this electricity exempt world. The scent of freshly laundered fabrics fills the air, and for the first time in years, the odor doesn't make me cringe. Instead, it feels… comforting – like my friends have actually made the journey up here with me.

"Hello?" I call out, my voice echoing off the aisle of fabric. Nothing answers, and a real smile tugs at my lips: genuine and girlish.

If I'm already in danger tonight, I'm going to make the most of it.

I creep to the far wall, my fingers itching to touch the treasures. The rolls stretch back into organized aisles, revealing a trove of textures and colors. My smile widens as I begin snooping through the columns.

Less flashy fabrics are propped against each other right in front of a row. I run my fingers over them, marveling at their smoothness, their inherent warmth. It's a luxury I've only ever glimpsed in the sheets I've washed, never something I've been allowed to touch so dry and unstained in this world.

I push my luck and step further back toward a section filled with lace and mesh. The fabrics are delicate sheers, some sparkling with tinsel, others adorned with intricate vignettes. I pause in front of a bolt on the wall. The burgundy lace is a masterpiece, its design so perfect it must have been made by a master artisan by hand like the painting outside. I let my hand slip beneath it, the threads brushing against my calluses as the pattern comes to life.

The braids and weaves are taut and even, creating a scene of woodland creatures against a tree lined horizon. My palm glides under the surface, and I watch as foxes and deer leap in and out of view. A small squirrel sits beside an even smaller acorn. I can't resist running my finger under the critter to pet it.

When was the last time I saw an animal?

For a moment, I forget where I am, lost in the beauty of the craftsmanship. It's a bittersweet reminder of the artistry I once dreamed of pursuing, a life that feels so far away now.

The sound of the doorknob turning makes my heart leap to my throat.

Chapter 5

"Shit."

The word slips out before I can stop it. I'm too deep in the fabric aisles to have any excuse for being here alone and suspicious.

I clasp my hands behind my back, but it's too late. I have to force my eyes not to widen as angelic creatures step inside. Their vibrant skirts and tunics blaze a trail of rich color, their presence filling the room with an almost tangible energy.

High Fae. A lot of them.

Though I've never met one before, the difference is obvious. They're taller than the guards that trail them, even the one I saw at first meal. Their nearly human looks and uncanny grace don't impress me, I'm too used to fae beauty for that. But I am caught off guard at the way the air shifts with their entrance, an intangible quality that puts me immediately on edge.

One steps forward, eyes locking on me as if deciding how best to peel the skin from my bones. He looks surprised when I meet his eyes – but not with the kind of surprise that softens – the kind that sharpens into a challenge.

I recognize him immediately: blue eyes and elven features.

Oh god, I just stared at the prince.

Prince Sylas steps closer. I overcorrect and drop to a knee, my eyes flicking upward for just a moment – just to ensure I really saw him.

Stay invisible. Stay safe. I remind myself as I force my eyes back down.

Other servants in uniforms matching my own quickly file into the room as well, setting about their work with practiced efficiency. I can't help but notice they're all fae.

Some sort through illustrated papers, while others pull chalk and tools from drawers. The previously still studio comes to life as everyone prepares for the night's schedule.

I keep my eyes on the floor, unsure of the proper protocol when meeting royalty.

Eddie, you didn't prepare me for this.

I don't have to wait long. Pristine black leather boots adorned with gold fastenings glide into my field of view. I don't realize I'm trembling until a hand steadies the top of my bowed head. A finger hooks under my chin, tilting my head up. I bite back a wince at the stretch.

I am forced to look directly at the most beautiful face I've ever seen – the same face that had stared back at me from the painted wall in the hallway: though more glowing than any portrait could capture.

Prince Sylas is younger than I expected, or at least looks like it. Then again, I look younger than I should too. I wonder how old he must be, but the question disappears along with every other coherent thought as his eyes bore into mine.

They are the blue of the sky I glimpse through the skylights of the barracks, set against a porcelain complexion that makes them all the brighter. His silver crown sits atop flaxen hair, his ears tipped in sharp points.

He smiles, and my breath hitches in a way it never has before.

"*That* is why humans don't belong here," one of the royals sneers.

"But they look so perfect on their knees," Sylas muses, smooth thumb brushing a crack in my lip. "Don't they?"

A laugh escapes one of the other fae lounging on a desk she's cleared off, watching me kneel before him.

"Leave the girl alone, Sy," she chides, informally.

His eyes hold me for a beat longer, seeming to savor the tremble in my limbs, before he releases me. I let out the caught breath and rise to my feet, unstable and suddenly afraid of my ability to survive the night.

What the hell was that?

The prince turns to another and embraces him.

"Welcome back to the West court, Prince Ciaran. How's your family doing?" he asks the one who sneered, then begins to unbutton his own grey tunic.

My mind races as I struggle to process everything that's happened since being plucked from my laundry duty.

*West Court? **Prince** Ciaran? There's other kingdoms?*

Uncertainty leaves me further off balance as I realize how little I know about the Otherworld outside the barrack walls. It seems so obvious that there must be entire societies outside. But I've been so focused on my own survival, I hadn't even begun to think about those implications.

Prince Ciaran rolls his eyes before responding to Prince Sylas with indifference.

"Lorelei and Moore are letting Liam play king more and more. Ronan and Orla are causing chaos as usual. I'm just happy to be back with more like minded company," he summarizes, shrugging out of his undershirt. Prince Sylas responds with a rakish wink.

I can feel myself staring at the undressing royalty without a trace of subtlety. Some reveal well curved bodies, others lithe frames. All strangely human in appearance. I think of the servants and guards I saw on my way up, and search for antlers, slit pupils, tufts of fur or claws. But the closest I see is a subtle glow, like magic follows them with every movement if I just look hard enough.

My eyes sweep over Prince Sylas's physique that matches his perfect features – lean and long – even if leagues more ethereal than any human's.

I'm finally able to tear my eyes away from their undressing when someone taps my shoulder. I turn my head toward a tiny servant with green skin and translucent wings.

"Help me with these," he orders in an unamused high tone. I spend the next few minutes trying to blend in, carrying bolts of fabric and clearing off tables – trying my best to shove my intrigue with the fae from my mind. It grows easier. And as they discuss their most recent hunts and conquests, I become another invisible servant.

The evening is back on track.

One girl with white feathers braided into her hair motions for me to follow her, and I help pull a large mirror into the open space of the main room. The only other human: a curly haired girl with olive skin, who looks no older than sixteen, hands me a measuring tape and a pair of scissors. My confused expression makes her roll her eyes.

"Go cut three yards of muslin," she clarifies. When I turn my head toward where I'd just come from, she grabs my shoulders with an exasperated sigh.

"King's graces, girl. It's over there, back row," she goads me in the right direction.

I walk past the royals, who are now all comfortably in slips or nothing at all, and keep my eyes glued to the row I've been sent towards. Their voices lower as I sweep by. I strain to eavesdrop on their conversation, but the words are muffled.

"Not *another* child," I hear one woman grumble to the meaner prince. He barks a laugh. And I blush as I walk faster towards the fabric.

Child. Like I'm not thirty five.

After measuring out three yards of the simple fabric, I make a clip in the corner and tear along the grain. The muscle memory from my old life takes over with the easy glide of the fabric beneath my fingers.

This could be a new uniform for me and at least one other friend, I think bitterly, humbling myself before I get too comfortable up here.

The sound is piercingly loud but quick as I rip off the length. It isn't until I'm folding it that I notice the conversations around me have deadened. My nose scrunches as I juggle the fabric and scissors back through the stifling room.

The human girl snatches the scissors from me, waiting for an explanation.

"I always tear along the grain. It's just habit," I defend myself.

She takes the fabric from my hands, unsatisfied with my response. No other tasks are asked of me, whether because they're not needed or because they don't trust me, I'm not sure.

I don't mind the relief from my duties though, and settle myself against the wall near the door, trying to center my nerves about following the rules. My eyes shut to focus.

It's so much easier to remember what to do when it's all hypothetical.

"They tend to just cut the fabric. But ripping it seems so much more fun," the same feminine voice that teased Prince Sylas says to me.

My eyes snap open at the closeness, turning to see another youthful high fae, draped in a gown so sheer it might as well not be there. She's so close, I can feel her warmth. She smells like fresh oleander and fairy fruit and something sharper I can't quite place – magic, maybe?

Her ginger hair matches my own in shade and wildness, but that's where our similarities end. Her eyes are bright gold to my blue. Where I am angular, she is round. Her skin is bright with an inner radiance, glowing through her bronzed skin.

She is sunlight incarnate.

I force a smile at her acknowledgment and curtsy, recognizing her authority, although I'm not exactly sure who she is. I'm grateful that etiquette calls for me to avert my eyes to the floor, so I don't have to pretend I can't see her entire body.

According to the gossip and more *insistent* guards, nudity isn't scandalous in the Otherworld. I never really believed it, but now… I have no choice but to accept it.

There's no shame in the room, at least not for the fae themselves. But I feel my cheeks burn regardless. My eyes grind into the wooden floor before her, and I will them not to wander to any of the other bodies. The woman continues speaking to me, to my despair.

"What's your name?" she asks lightly.

"V-Valerie, Miss," I answer after a beat, almost forgetting to include a formal title.

"Valerie, that's a good name. It means healthy and strong, did you know that?" she continues.

Why is she talking to me?

I nod politely, hiding my face with my curtain of hair as I focus on the ground. "Yes, I remember looking up the meaning as a kid, back before…" I trail off, dismantling any chance of discussing my lost life with one of *them*.

…Before I was coerced into eternal servitude, my mind fills in with rebellious pride.

"Before you came to this kingdom?" she concludes, rephrasing my thoughts in a much more polished way.

I nod again.

"Fascinating. I love learning about humans, especially girls like you. Did you enjoy any hobbies in the human world?" Her voice stays conversationally low, but not so much that the others can't hear us. Even through her kind words, I feel the stab of the crown prince's gaze on us as we talk.

"Yes, I was a designer. Fashion, specifically-" I cut myself off more obviously this time.

This isn't staying invisible.

She grabs one of my calloused hands, and my eyes rise up to her face against my better judgment. She is disarmingly beautiful: the type I've seen displayed in museums. Her bright smile is nearly impossible to keep my guard up against.

But I force myself to think of Eddie – of all of us stuck downstairs – half starved and ghostly without the sunlight she seems to embody.

She's a monster like the rest of them. Don't trust her.

"You seem promising, Valerie. I would like to hear more about your interests," she squeezes my hand gently, oblivious to the war right behind my eyes. I force a smile at her compliment and swallow my pride.

The fae can't lie, and I have survived this encounter – no matter how unwanted it was.

"Mara, Sylas wants to speak to you," a noble with white hair and matching eyes calls from the other side of the room, halting our conversation.

Mara. That's her name.

I commit it to memory, knowing this information could be worth a valuable trade in the barracks.

She straightens, giving me a conspiratorial smile.

"We will continue this conversation another time," she asserts, dipping into a small, elegant curtsy of her own before striding over to Prince Sylas. I bite my tongue and bow back.

With every step she takes away, I find my mind clearer – less overwhelmed by the possibility of offending her.

I chance a look at them under my lashes. Prince Sylas's brow is drawn taut as the two talk in a low tone I can't hear. My eyes skim over their heavenly bodies: so close to human but without a single flaw. Though none of the other servants seem fazed by the high fae's perfection.

Or their immodesty.

Before my incorrigible eyes betray me again, a final figure makes her presence known. All conversations cease as the royals angle towards her, showing a reverence that surprises me.

The shuffling figure who steps in is ancient, her presence commanding despite her small stature. She's magical – that much is clear by the way my instincts flag her uncanny influence on the room – but she's not fae as I had assumed.

Her rounded ears are a sign of humanity. Though her intricate tattoos and black tinged fingers are telltale signs from stories I remember back in the human world.

No. Not a human. A witch.

She's covered in inky runes – at least I assume that's what the symbols are. Her flowing robe is an intricate patchwork of textured greyscale that looks like it took decades to embroider.

My eyes widen for a split second before I recover, forcing my face back into neutrality.

"Welcome all," she says in a voice that crackles like loose pebbles underfoot in the barracks. She bows in a deep, slow show of respect. Prince Sylas steps forward, a smile on his face as she straightens to meet his eyes without apology.

"Your work for the autumn equinox on such short notice will be greatly rewarded," he vows. The words seem to please her, and she playfully shoos off the promise. Though I know fae words are literal and binding.

He must trust her entirely.

"I expect nothing less from my favorite donor," she replies with a twinkle in her dark, wrinkled eye. "But let me show you the designs before you get too carried away with payment."

She gestures to the other human, who nods and disappears behind a wall of fabrics.

The girl returns moments later, pushing a dolly of dress forms into the room. Each one is adorned with a breathtaking garment: half finished but draped dramatically to showcase their potential. The designs are distinct, each representing a different forest creature – not just the usual furs and leathers, but scales and feathers too – bearing the characteristics I expected to find on the high fae themselves.

I have to focus on my dirty boots to contain my reaction, my heart soaring at the chance to be so close to work like this again. The witch moves among the forms, her gnarled hands brushing against the works with a studying eye that mirrors my own.

For a moment, every fear is gone, banished from my mind by the beauty of the designs and the artistry behind them.

Chapter 6

As the evening goes on, it gets easier to exist around the high fae. If I don't look at them, it's almost like being back in a regular studio… almost.

The witch – Belladonna, I've learned – pins the hem of Mara's costume while she stands on a pedestal. I merely keep the pin cushion within reach as the witch works, no one trusting me to take on an alteration of my own.

I keep my eyes averted – my clammy grip tight.

Invisible. Safe.

Even without the makeup or hair, Mara looks every bit the hawk the dress she's cinched in portrays. Gold and brown scraps of fabric have been honed into feathers and stitched together, creating a daring gown that clings to her form before it fans out just below her hips. Belladonna's quick fingers dart out, adjusting pins with unnatural precision reminding me of spiders and their webs.

Mara shifts in the mirror, the golden gown shimmering as she moves.

"Belladonna, you've outdone yourself," Mara gushes.

The witch doesn't smile. "It's not for admiring yet. Stand still."

Mara corrects her posture, and the pinned hem falls perfectly in line with the floor. Belladonna notices something my less experienced eye doesn't and hunches down. I quickly bring the pins to her, now on the floor. Her weathered hands steal a few pins from me and tuck strategic darts along the back of the dress, emphasizing the tail-like effect of the silhouette.

"I simply don't know how you do it. But I am so grateful you do. Make sure Sy gives you a handsome payment for this," Mara beams at Prince Sylas as he steps up to his own pedestal.

"Oh, he knows what I'm owed," Belladonna's smile reveals teeth whiter than I expect.

She turns toward the prince. I don't look up as I follow – not at first. But the room seems to bend towards him, the light catching the silver threads in his white robe like frost on the skylights in winter. Against my will, my gaze lifts.

A mistake.

His eyes – too blue, too bright – lock with mine. For a heartbeat, I forget how to breathe again. Then I quickly drop my gaze back to the floor and suck in the lost breath.

Focus, I scold myself. *Don't make eye contact.*

But it's nearly impossible with some pull to him calling from inside my own body.

He's high fae. He'd rather gut a human than touch one.

"What are you, Sylas?" one of the nobles with skin as dark as the night outside asks, halfway through a glass of wine as she drapes herself over Mara's abandoned spot on the desk.

"The white stag," Belladonna answers for him. "A symbol of nobility and magic… and the hunt."

Sylas's lips quirk into something not quite a smile.

She carefully pinches and tucks at the fabric, shaping it against his elegant form. I let my fascination with her technique override his alarming effect on me – standing on my toes to see better, meditating in the craft.

At this angle, I notice the jacquard's intricate design: a motif of hooves and antlers woven into the fabric. It's ingenious, the way the images seem to pop once I've noticed them.

A throat clears behind me, snapping me out of my study.

I turn, and flinch.

Prince Ciaran stands too close, unamused. His costume is a scaled sinuous piece, the fabric clinging to his broad frame like a second skin.

"Sorry," I blurt out instinctively.

A quiet *tsk* escapes Prince Sylas. I realize he's watching me in the mirror's reflection as Belladonna alters his robe, drawing all color from my face. I feel a clench low in my core at the connection.

"Be careful with apologies, girl," he warns. "Some will take that as an invitation for revenge."

His gaze flicks briefly to Prince Ciaran in emphasis. I hide the grimace that tries to surface at the word "*girl*" behind an appreciative nod.

Prince Ciaran interjects. "I've no interest in bargaining with one of *them*. Direct bargains are below us. But agreed, she should hold her tongue."

Or he'll cut it out, I fill in myself.

Prince Sylas's head tilts slightly at the push back.

"Ciaran," he addresses, casual as he angles himself toward the other prince. "You forget yourself. Even a human bargain can be practical."

His words are calm, but there's an edge to them that makes the room feel colder. Prince Ciaran rolls his eyes but doesn't argue further, turning away to disengage.

"Ciaran is a snake?" Mara lightens the mood, looking over his outfit.

Belladonna is quick to answer again. "An animal that sheds its skin to become anew, like him joining this court as the new ambassador of the South."

"Only if he's a good boy, and doesn't overstep." Another broad shouldered royal grumbles.

"He is all crown and no throne," Prince Sylas explains to my reflection. His attention makes my palms sweaty. "He's a bastard with ego. At least the ambassadorship is a real title."

Prince Ciaran meets the verbal spar head on. "Call me a bastard all you like, but that's not what Lady Seraphine was calling me upon my return."

The broad shouldered fae scoffs in offense, drawing Ciaran's focus her way.

"I know you had your eyes on her too, sister. You can try to win her favor back. But I must say, we've been a bit preoccupied with each other," he says, though his smile is anything but apologetic as his eyes flick between Prince Sylas and...

Prince Ciaran's sister? So she's a princess?

I risk a look at the woman, and I see the resemblance. The light brown of her skin, and the strong tone in her body. She and her brother are similar in more than just appearance- it's in the way they look through me like I'm just a part of the decor.

"I think Seraphine and Ciaran make quite the match, don't you Balora?" A copper haired fae goads the princess on.

"He can have her hand, if he never takes Leona's. I'll have her heart," she shrugs.

"He better not." The dark skinned lady – Leona I decern – seethes.

I don't understand fae relationships, and I don't think I want to.

"I don't recall seeing you here before," Prince Sylas says over his shoulder, shifting his focus back to me as the others continue to discuss matches.

His voice is casual; his eyes are anything but. My mind blanks as he towers over me.

Does he feel the connection too? Is that why he's interested?

The small green skinned servant glances my way at my dumbfounded silence.

"I have been in your kingdom for seventeen years," I force out my backstory with a stammer. "But I have only ever been around guards, not…" I trail off, unsure of how to conclude, my tongue tied with his continuous eye contact.

"Not royalty," Mara finishes for me, sweetly. I'm quick to agree, then look back at the pins Belladonna has tucked into the robe.

Shut up and be invisible if you want to stay safe, I remind myself.

Prince Sylas's dismissive "hmm" suggests he expected a more exciting story. I feel his gaze linger on me for a moment longer before he turns back to the mirror. His expression is completely unreadable when I flick my eyes once to check. Belladonna ignores the conversations overhead and eventually steps away. I follow, eager to put some distance between myself and the fae.

"Sydney, hem the prince's pants," the witch orders the human servant. Sylas ignores her as she kneels before him.

Oh, to blend in so well.

None of them acknowledge my existence again. I breathe easier when the other royals have been fit and they've all changed back into their more casual finery.

The door closes behind them, leaving us to clean up.

I help Sydney lug the dress forms back to the storage area, staying near the only other human in sight. The costumes – now pinned to perfectly mold to their wearers or patterned with the muslin I cut – are delicate works of art that I'll never see finished. I absorb every detail of light and beauty while I'm up here.

The two of us work slowly in the closet, letting the fae servants fill the main room with their own gossip.

"You should be careful," Sydney finally warns, breaking the silence as she pretends to adjust Princess Balora's sleeve on its dress form.

"Hmm?" I ask.

"Around the folk," she clarifies, still not meeting my eyes. Her jaw tenses – upset with herself for speaking.

"Oh, I can handle myself. I've been here for decades. I just haven't been up *here* before," I reply, gesturing to the space around us with a forced smile. Her own smile is just as unconvincing when she finally looks at me.

"I didn't mean to offend," she disengages. "I just know that down in the laundry rooms, you don't have to deal with them nearly as often. The folk are tricky and self-serving. Especially sidhe. I'm just looking out for you."

Her eyes betray a hint of fear that chills me.

*The **what**? Shee? What has she seen?*

"Do you ever feel drawn to them – the sidhe?" I finally ask the question that's been plaguing me since Prince Sylas's arrival.

Concern colors her face.

"No. But some humans have before. There are… safeguards. If you're worried about it," she hesitates on the word, holding up her hand to display a silver band around her middle finger. "Normally, the team here is stitchers who have worked with Belladonna for years. It doesn't seem fair they pulled you here with no preparation."

Wait.

So what's wrong with me?

A sense of unease washes over me as I remember how instant my draw to the prince had been.

"Speaking of, I should be getting back to the barracks. My shift starts at daybreak," I change the subject as we wander back into the studio's main room. Sydney's eyebrows shoot up as she glances out the window beside us.

"That's way too soon. You can't skip a day?"

I forgo my usual gripe – instead, shaking my head.

"Skipping a day means putting my workload on the other laundry crew. And we already have too much as it is. I've survived sleepless nights before. Don't worry," I explain, trying to muster more confidence than I actually feel.

She offers a pity sigh. "Well, your help tonight wasn't terrible. You were very entertaining, if a little talkative."

Her smile is genuine this time. I mirror it.

I wish I could stay up here with her.

The thought is loud in my head, but I don't dare voice it. It's torturous enough to bid this world of color and stimulation goodbye.

"If you ever need me again, you know where I am." I shrug, ignoring my growing despair.

Sydney's smile falls as she watches me gather my things… *thing*: just the map to guide me back downstairs. I leave the heavenly studio the same way I came and descend to the cold, dimly lit hell of the barracks.

Chapter 7

I stroll slowly through the tunnels, enjoying the quiet moment between guard rotations. The absence of leering eyes softens the fall of my descent so much so, I feel almost at ease as the stairways shorten and constrict. The normalcy after such an abnormal night soothes the last of my terror of offending the royalty – the sidhe.

The crew is going to have so much gossip to trade.

I further relax into my stride, thinking about how my story can secure us some new blankets or pillows – maybe even an extra few hours for me to adjust this morning.

My serene acceptance is ruined when a body slams me against the cold stone wall to my side. Her hand clamps over my mouth, but I'm too stunned to make a sound anyway. My mind almost refuses to process what I see.

Her fiery hair is loose and long, framing a human face that practically mirrors my own. She's a half a head shorter than me – otherwise we are eerily similar. Our blue eyes lock as she studies my reaction with primal focus.

"You're not normally allowed outside of the barracks. Way too easy to sneak up on," she concludes.

I shake my head, holding back the flurry of questions that must be obvious in my eyes. Her hand uncovers my mouth, but her body remains tense – ready to silence me again if necessary. "Did anything unusual happen to you tonight?" she asks urgently.

My brow furrows.

"This whole night was unusual. You need to be more specific," my voice matches her whispered haste.

"Have any sidhe talked to you?" she clarifies, angling herself so she fills my vision. Her eyes bore into mine wildly, searching for something I don't understand.

I don't have to answer. The guilt is written all over my face.

"Who?" she demands.

"Prince Sylas and a high fae-"

"*Sidhe*. Do *not* call them fairies unless you want one of these," she asserts, pulling her tunic down just enough to show a scar across her collarbone.

"A… *sidhe*: Mara," I correct.

"Starting again already," she mutters more to herself than me.

She releases me from the wall with a frustrated growl, then steps back, running a hand over her mouth. My eye is drawn to the bruises on her wrists – lower to more cuts and scrapes marring her visible skin. There's a trickle of blood dried on her thigh that she ignores.

But then her eyes meet mine again with the same stoniness as my own. The resemblance is too uncanny to ignore.

"We look alike," I blurt, unable to stop myself.

Rushed air escapes her nose in a semblance of a laugh. "Yeah, the satyr thought so. That's why he grabbed you too. The sick fuck."

Satyr? The word is lost on me.

"Stay away from them. From *all* of them. For your own good." She commands.

"Yeah, not an issue," I agree.

Before she can say more, the sound of heavy hooves echoes down the corridor: the bullheaded monster. The girl's eyes widen, and she grabs my arm, her grip surprisingly strong for the state she's in.

"Listen to me," she barks. "My name is Becca Dawson. If you escape this place, come find me. You can't tell anyone about meeting me tonight. And you need to stay down in the barracks from now on. Do you understand?"

I nod – though, no, I don't understand.

The hoofsteps grow loud enough for me to pick up two distinct sets. She releases me with a shove towards the shadows.

"They might try and use you like they tried to use me. Don't let them," her words are a flurry of hushed tones. "*Go.*"

I don't need to be told twice.

I pivot and sprint down the offshoot, my heart pounding. There's a small corner of sanctuary that my body nestles into, as I watch my double remain in the dimly lit main tunnel.

"There you are," one of the bulls calls in a rumbling voice. "Thought you could run off after the murder you just committed?"

Murder?

"Awwww, is someone upset about their little-"

Becca's words are cut off, thought severed as cleanly as her skin when the blade slides through her throat. The sound is wet, final, and utterly horrifying. Her eyes lock with mine in that last fleeting moment: wide and terrified. Then she drops, her body crumpling to the ground like waterlogged sheets. The monsters quickly haul her away, her lifeless form leaving a trail of crimson in their wake.

I freeze – my breath coming in shallow, ragged gasps that don't quite fill my lungs. The adrenaline coursing through my veins is overwhelmingly unhelpful as I try to remain quiet.

But no one comes back for me, and the bulls' victorious voices fade.

The small knobbly servant who appears eventually to clean the blood only amplifies my terror, their face unbothered as their too long limbs mop up the evidence.

How often do they see blood up here? I think with renewed hatred for the fae… sidhe.

I force myself to move, my legs trembling beneath me as I slip back into the barracks. The sight of Maddie, Lilia, and Eddie, peaceful and unaware, jars me further.

She snuck in here just to make sure I made it back safely, I think as I slide into Eddie's warm arms, seeking comfort. The image of Becca's bruised face and her desperate pleas haunt me anyway. The weight of her final words crush me, and I have to shrug out of Eddie's grip when I struggle for breath again.

She's a murderer. She probably was just crazy and thought I was some twisted mirror.

The decision of whether or not to tell my friends looms like the ceiling above: dark and entrapping. The horror of what I've just seen is seared into my mind – another secret that might be worth a valuable trade one day.

But as the dusty grey of the sky signals the approaching dawn, I don't think there's anything that would be worth sharing this morbid secret for.

Chapter 8

The next sleep deprived day drags on in the laundry rooms.

The endless cycle of scrubbing, rinsing, and folding leaving my hands split open and my mind dulled over. It's a welcome heaviness, though, as it keeps me from overthinking my decision to keep the encounter in the tunnel to myself.

Becca Dawson.

The murderer who looked like me – popping into my life long enough to tell me to forget her. I force her out of my head.

By the time day no longer filters through the skylights, my limbs feel like they're made of lead. The thought of spending the evening with Maddie and Lilia keeps me stumbling to our room, one trudged step at a time.

Maddie is already there, coiled clouds of hair tied back from her face with a scrap of fabric. A red faced Lilia joins us a moment later with a clay pot of fresh water, placing it between us as she collapses next to Maddie. The lingering scent of detergent clings to us all as we settle onto the threadbare blankets of our cots, drinking our fill.

"So," Maddie begins brightly despite the shared exhaustion. "Tell us everything."

I regale them with details of the costumes, Belladonna the *real* witch, and all her beautiful work for the royal family. Shame prevents me from broaching the topic of my attraction to Sylas – that pull I felt towards the prince that sparked conversations I shouldn't have engaged in.

What the fuck could it mean?

I've never been known to be someone so open with that kind of stuff. I swore off ever letting anyone but Eddie near me like that after too many tricks.

"The autumn equinox is in a little over a month, based on what the maid team said. What do you think they'll do with us this year?" Maddie ventures, as I finish describing one of the costumes draped with real fox tails.

Lilia lowers her head into Maddie's crossed lap. "Same as every year, probably. Lock us in the barracks and pretend we don't exist while they party."

"Not necessarily," Maddie counters, her eyes sparkling with an excitement that never truly finds us down here. "Remember a few years ago? A few of the human kitchen staff got to eat leftovers after a winter party. And a few before that, I remember hearing some of the human entertainment got an entire free day off."

"Yeah, because most of them didn't survive the night," Lilia grumbles. "You know what happens at those revelries when they decide to incorporate *us*."

A pregnant pause follows.

We all know the stories. Human guests are known to vanish during the festivities – never to be seen again. Some say they're simply released out into the wilds to die when they're no longer entertaining. More colorful tales have featured mass casualties and conspiracies to use humans for experimental spells.

The reminder extinguishes any excitement Maddie stoked.

"Still," Maddie breaks the chilling silence. "It's not all bad. What if we get lucky this year? What if they need extra hands in the kitchens or the gardens? It could be our chance to move up."

"Move up?" Lilia scoffs. "You mean trade one kind of servitude for another?"

"It's better than this," Maddie gestures to the damp, moldy room enclosing us. "At least in the kitchens, we'd get to eat something other than leftovers from nightshift. And in the gardens, we'd actually see the sky once in a while."

I glance between them, my compassion torn between the hope in Maddie's voice and the bitterness in Lilia's.

They're both right, in their own way. Life for us here is a prison no matter where we're assigned… But some prisons have softer pillows.

"What about you, Valerie?" Maddie drags me into the argument. "What do you think?"

I pick my words carefully. "I think… If we get to move, we go somewhere that stays away from the sidhe. They seem more dangerous than the guards."

Maddie's grin doesn't falter, but I see a new curiosity in her eyes. "That's a good point. If we move up, we want to make sure we all survive."

She sighs. "At least we still have each other if we stay down here."

Lilia rolls her eyes, but there's a hint of a upward tilt to her lips. "You're impossible, you know that?"

"And you're a pessimist," Maddie shoots back, kissing the round tip of her nose. "But I love you anyway."

Lilia laughs – the sound rare – and for a moment, the weight of our eternity feels a little lighter. In moments like this, huddled together in our little corner, I feel like a typical 18-year-old girl.

It's bittersweet: knowing I'll never grow old with such close friends.

We fall into easier conversation again, discussing drama and possibilities after the Equinox. Maddie dreams of sneaking a taste of the feast, her eyes alight as she describes the dishes she's heard about: namely platters of pastries filled with berries and cream. Lilia, ever the realist, warns us not to wish too hard and how it would likely be tainted with fairy fruit, but even she can't resist joining in when Maddie starts planning how we'll stash our leftovers here in the room.

"Do you ever dream about escaping?" Maddie asks absently during a lull.

Lilia and I exchange angled glances. It's a dangerous topic: one we've learned not to speak out loud. But here, in the safety of our little group, it feels acceptable to broach.

"Most days while I'm working," I confess. "But I don't know if I'd be able to make it in the human world, even if I returned."

I recall the pressures to make my mortal life count – to solve the problems caused by the generations before me. It was suffocating in a way that hasn't been an issue with my eternal youth here.

"We could stay in the Otherworld, just not in this castle," Maddie suggests, playing with the ends of Lilia's raven hair.

Lilia's face falls further. "It's not that simple, Maddie. They would hunt us down. We have brands in our necks that say we are property, and we have no knowledge of what's beyond these walls."

My mind flashes to Prince Ciaran. I think about how he didn't use my apology against me, his complete disdain for my kind keeping him above even that much interaction.

Jerk.

"Actually, I met a prince from another kingdom last night," I add.

"What?" Maddie asks, her voice full of hurt at my omission as she drops Lilia's hair.

"There are other lands, other kingdoms." I shrug, trying to remain nonchalant with the reveal. "And from how he spoke about humans, they don't seem to keep us around. Maybe there's even some place where we're free."

Lilia looks back to the ceiling, but I catch the hope that surfaces in her expression before she does. "So you two get a fairy prince with a heart of gold to break us out of here, and I'll start packing."

Maddie's laugh is enough to dispel the tension of my withheld story. I gratefully drift off to sleep as they bicker about our hypothetical runaway.

Chapter 9

Another week of too short nights and too long days pass without fanfare. We are able to trade my stories of the sidhe for some new robes, free of the patched up holes I've mended over and over again.

But other than that, it's business as usual.

We go to bed, the same routine as always: trading the day's gossip until we're too exhausted to stay conscious anymore. Then I'm met with numbing sleep, my body too overused to give my brain the energy to conjure a dream.

Until the fifth night.

I jolt awake to a fist pounding on the door. My heart leaps into my throat as I sit up – disoriented – my only peace slipping away. Everything is cast in silvery moonlight. I see Maddie and Lilia stir in their shared cot with bleary eyes. Ash remains asleep, mercifully. The grueling work hardening their body and mind to disturbances already.

"Valerie Harlow," a voice calls from the doorway, sharp and commanding. I squint through the cool light to see a shadow on the underside of the door. It is backlit by some flickering source. "You're needed upstairs."

The order sends a shiver of dread down my spine, remembering my look alike's warning.

"They'll try to use you like they were planning to use me."

I glance at Maddie and Lilia and regret not asking for their input on the real situation earlier.

"Upstairs again already?" Lilia yawns.

The servant doesn't wait for my response. He pushes open the door, hooves clacking on the rough floor as he steps inside. Then he jerks his chin towards the door, impatient. "Now."

I scramble out of bed, unable to guess what this summons might mean. My hands tremble as I adjust my sleep twisted robe, the fabric still damp from yesterday's work.

Maddie reaches out, her fingers brushing my arm in a wordless gesture of support. I give her a quick, reassuring nod, though I'm anything but reassured when I turn back to the servant. He has antlers like the one who first pulled me to sewing duty.

Satyr.

"Ok, I'm ready," I lie.

He leads me briskly through the catacomb of the barracks. I wonder how long he must have been here to know the layout so effortlessly.

He doesn't glance back to ensure I still trail him, his confidence in my obedience both reassuring and unsettling. The corridors are eerily quiet, the only sound the echo of our steps, my softened boots a stark contrast to the sharp clips of his hooves. My heart pounds from exertion as we climb staircase after staircase, each step taking me further from the familiar confines of the laundry quarters and higher into the opulent upper levels of the castle.

The air changes as we ascend like it did that first night, effortlessly lighter and sweeter – the very atmosphere infused with floral bouquets. The stone walls of the lower levels give way to smooth marble once again, and I know we still have further to climb.

We pass through an open gallery, its arched windows offering a breathtaking view of the castle grounds beyond. My eyes struggle to focus outside, a distance further than the muscles controlling them have exerted in too long. My vision finally clears on a moonlight gilded fountain – on the hedges arranged in patterns so intricate they rival the winding barracks below our feet.

I want to study the layout, see if I can find my bunk portrayed in rose bushes. But the creature doesn't stop, and I fear falling too far behind.

We push up a new flight of stairs into a spacious hall, its walls lined with intricate tapestries that twinkle in the light of the myriad chandeliers. Sidhe nobles lounge on plush divans and ornate chairs, their conversation filling the expanse with an energetic hum… or maybe that's the magic they seem to shed as they glide around the space.

What do they even do all night?

One with long braided hair reclines on a chaise, her gown shimmering like liquid starlight enough to draw my attention. She glances at me as we pass, her eyes a deep brown that seems to see straight through my forced nonchalance. I catch the faint curve of her lips, as if she finds my discomfort as amusing as Lucian does.

There's always a Lucian.

I avert my gaze quickly – my cheeks flush at being caught staring again. The guard continues on, his pace unwavering as he leads me all the way to the end of the hall.

We find ourselves outside a set of large double doors, their surfaces carved with more intricate patterns of vines and flowers. He knocks and waits a beat, then pushes the door open without waiting for a response.

Seems a habit for him.

"In," he orders me ahead.

I step inside, obedience winning out against my fear. I blink back wide eyes at the sight before me. The walls of this room are decorated with more vines matching the ones carved through the rest of the tower.

An obscene bed dominates the space, its blush pink blankets piled beneath a lazy Mara lounging against a mountain of pillows in variations of dusty rose. She's dressed in a flowing sheer gown, her ginger hair cascading over her shoulders like a river of fire. She could be mistaken for a statue of a goddess, until she blinks.

"Ah, Valerie," she greets me, warmly. "I'm so glad you could join me."

I drop into a low bow, suddenly suspicious.

*Why would a noble call **me** specifically up here?*

"Lady Mara," I mumble quickly, unsure of what else to say. Without sleep, I don't know how much etiquette I'll be able to remember.

"No need for formalities," she beams, waving a hand dismissively. The servant closes the door behind him as he leaves us alone in the room.

"Come, sit." She pats the edge of the bed like one would for a dog.

I hesitate, take a steadying breath, then move to perch on the corner of the bed. The mattress yields to my weight much more than I expect after nearly twenty years on a hard cot. It's the most comfort I've felt in ages.

"I've been thinking about our conversation from the other night and couldn't sleep all day," she drawls. "You've piqued my interest. I'd like you to work for me."

My study of the mattress ceases.

Her servant?

"I…" I stammer, voice dying in my throat.

Mara offers a mischievous smile. "You could be very useful up here. Sy told me that he plans to host many revelries; he wants to forge alliances with other kingdoms since he'll be king soon, and when we marry I will be queen. So, I need a new wardrobe."

I refuse to let my loosened jaw drop, learning of her future throne. My eyes find no jewelry on her left ring finger.

They must not have the same traditions that we did back home, I realize.

"I recall you saying you're interested in fashion. I would like to give you the chance to fulfill that interest and be responsible for my dress as my personal attendant," she continues.

Not just servant. Attendant.

"Personal attendant?" I ask cautiously.

Her eyes brighten. "Oh I know you've seen them. The nicer uniforms, folk of more noble blood with status."

But I'm not one of them.

Still, I know exactly who she's talking about: the servants with their heads held higher in the halls, their beautiful outfits adorning their proud shoulders.

"You want *me*. A human, as your attendant?"

"Yes." She nods.

"And what do you want in return?" I ask boldly, looking at my fingers as I trace the quilt line of her bedding.

"You. I need a *human* girl by my side, one who can do something we can't," she remains cryptic.

"*The fae cannot lie*" echoes in my mind.

"You want me, because I am able to lie," I parse out.

"I want nothing outside of your nature. And I think you have potential. So it's a deal?"

I chew on my bottom lip, deliberating.

If I agree, I will be ripped from my only known safety in this entire life. My friends will be forced to pick up my load, maybe incorporate another outsider into the crew to help. And who knows if I'll even survive.

I'll be going directly against the warnings of my murderous look alike and my *own* suggestion to stay away from the royalty…

But if I don't agree, I don't know if any of us will ever get the chance to actually live again. Fate seems to have dropped this opportunity into my lap, and if I can leverage the position to bring my friends with me one day – if I'm clever enough to avoid the worst of the faes' intent with Becca's warning – then it might be worth the risk.

Right?

I am not sure that I actually nod in agreement, until I feel the magic bond snap in place.

It's nothing visible, almost like an extra heartbeat that pulses through me once – twice – then disappears again.

Mara claps her hands together excitedly. "You'll study up here first while you prepare for the job, of course. Your new quarters will be right over there."

She nods her chin at a door across the room, painted to camouflage with the vine decor of the walls.

"I will make sure you get some proper uniforms and you can move in right away. Let him know if you need anything?" She gestures toward a handsome human with sandy blonde hair and a strong jaw. I didn't notice him before, standing opposite the door to my new chamber in his lavish robes.

I rise, still reeling.

"My friends," I blurt. "I need to speak to them before I stay."

Please let me say goodbye, I beg without daring to utter the words aloud.

"That is fine, but I want you back here before morning. You have a lot of learning ahead, and I expect you to start studying tomorrow evening well rested," Mara says to my profile.

I bow. "Understood."

"Chase," she calls, halting the human before he can usher me out the door. "Take her wherever she needs to go. Just have her back here promptly," she speaks into the half empty wine glass that's against her lips.

He responds with a "yes, my lady," before we are out the door.

When it clicks shut behind us, I find myself staring out the large window opposite the door for a moment. It frames a portion of the garden far below like a living piece of art. Servants that seem to be made of the topiaries themselves tend to the sculpted shrubs – honing perfect angles into the plants, even in the waning night.

"Follow me," Chase instructs gently.

My growing regret as I follow him back down the stairs threatens to send me into a panic.

This is too much. Too sudden.

Seventeen years of my life were stolen in the laundry rooms: no hope beyond seeing the next sunrise. Now, I'm being thrust into one of the higher forms of servitude to the sidhe because they want me to *lie,* when this human escorting me is perfectly capable of it himself?

What did I just agree to?

Chapter 10

Chase guides me back to the barracks quickly. The only tunnels I've ever known in this world feel different as we sink lower – colder and rougher – already deciding I don't belong anymore. My chest begins to ache as we approach my room's door, the weight of what I'm about to do settling heavy in my heart.

He stops at the entrance, his eyes apologetic. "Make it quick."

It may not be his fault that I'm being torn from my only friends, but I can't help the ire I feel for him anyway.

I bite back the snark I want to hurl, and nod before pushing open the door.

The sounds of deep sleep are the only tell of life inside. I inhale the permeating laundry, sharpening this memory forever in my mind: a reminder that these seventeen years happened no matter how long we are separated in the future.

Maddie and Lilia are in their separate beds for once, their faces peaceful in sleep again. Ash is in their own bed, turned away from us all.

For a moment, I consider leaving without waking them, sparing them all the pain of saying goodbye. But I don't.

They deserve to know.

I kneel beside Maddie's cot first, gently grabbing her shoulder. She's always been the easiest to talk to, and my cowardice has me hoping she will help me keep Lilia calm.

"Maddie," I hiss. "Wake up."

Her eyes flutter open, and she blinks up at me, disoriented.

"You're back?" she mumbles.

"No. I – I have to go." The words catch in my throat, suddenly real as I voice them. "They're moving me out of here. I'm going to be the future queen's personal attendant."

Maddie sits up abruptly, cot creaking. "What?"

"I was just told," I explain, my voice barely above a whisper to not wake Lilia for as long as I can. "I'm so sorry."

Lilia stirs in her bunk anyway, her pale face peeking out from under the fraying blanket, my heart is suddenly in my throat unprepared for her usual abrasiveness.

"What's going on?" Her eyes scan my grief stricken face with sharp suspicion.

"Valerie's leaving," Maddie says, bewildered. "They're taking her upstairs."

Lilia leaps to her feet, whirling on Chase. "No. They can't just take you. We'll figure something out-"

"There's nothing to figure out," I interrupt, my voice more sure than I feel.

Chase keeps his own focus on the skylight above, ignoring Lilia's challenge. Ash finally snaps their head to the growing noise, but says nothing.

I continue. "I just… I needed to say goodbye. I couldn't disappear, and you never know what happened."

Maddie throws her arms around me, her grip desperate like she can keep me here with enough contact.

"This isn't fair," she whimpers, her tears dampening my shoulder. "We're supposed to stick together."

I hug her back, my own tears spilling over.

"I know." My voice finally breaks with the emotion I can't hold back. "But this might be a good thing. Maybe I can find a way to bring you up there with me. I'll be working under someone named Mara. She seems kind."

Lilia relents in her standoff with the taller boy, and joins our embrace. Her thin arms wrap around both of us protectively. Ash stays still, watching us with silent distress.

I'm grateful they give me this private moment with my friends, and nod in their direction.

"You better come back for us then," Lilia concedes. Tears don't fall from her eyes, but I see the hurt in them.

"I promise I'll be back to visit the moment I'm allowed," I vow, though the words feel hollow. We all know how little control we have over our own lives.

Chase clears his throat from the doorway, his discomfort with our emotional scene palpable. "Time's up, we have to go."

I pull them both an arm's length away, my heart cracking at the sight of their mournful faces.

"I love you both," is all I can say.

Maddie grabs my hand, squeezing it tightly when it lingers on her arm.

"We love you too," she answers, her eyes pleading for more time we can't spare. Lilia steps back, her arms crossed over her chest, physically holding her protest inside.

"We'll be here," she warns. "Waiting for you."

I nod, unable to speak past the growing lump in my throat. With one last look at my friends, I turn and follow the boy out of our room, the door closing behind me with a finality that echoes off the stone.

"You have one more friend to talk to?" Chase clarifies over his shoulder.

"Yeah," I sniffle, knowing this goodbye will be an entirely different pain.

Eddie has been my anchor: my confidant. She is the one person I trusted with my heart here.

I owe her a real goodbye.

She is in the laundry room, at work despite the early hour when we find her. Her shoulders are hunched over a sudsing basin, her hands scrubbing at a stain with practiced efficiency. The sight of her – my safe, steady love – makes the crack in my heart a little wider.

Chase stays back and nods his approval for me to continue alone. I wipe away the tears, and step into the cramped room.

"Eddie," I can barely speak over the sound of sloshing water.

She turns around immediately.

"Val?" Her brow furrows as she takes in my still puffy eyes. "Maddie told me they took you for another job, is it done already?"

I step closer, my hands twisting nervously in front of me. "I am being moved upstairs… permanently," I say the words – forced – like pulling a stuck dirty bandage. "Mara, the next queen, has requested me as her attendant after we met at the atelier."

Her face falls, her composed demeanor gone for one of the few times since I've known her.

"I didn't have much of a choice," I lie, my voice struggling to stay level as I counter her protest in advance.

She wouldn't understand my plan, always pushing for us to stay together.

She sets the fabric aside and wipes her hands on her uniform, her movements slow and deliberate, buying herself time to process the news.

"This is… this is big, Val," she says with sober sincerity. "Is there anything you can do to prevent it?"

"I don't know," I admit, my eyes filling with tears again. "I can't say no, not when there's a chance that I can convince her to bring you guys up there with me."

She steps closer, her hands reaching out to grasp mine. Her touch is warm and grounding, a stark contrast to the cold uncertainty gripping my mind.

"You just focus on keeping yourself safe," she orders. "We've survived this long, and we'll survive this too."

My mind flashes with the blood of Becca spilling onto the ground unceremoniously.

"I'm scared," I confess. "They are *terrifying*. What if I slip up?"

"You won't," she says firmly, her grip on my hands tightening. "You're the brightest person I know. If anyone can navigate the world up there, it's you."

Her confidence in me is both comforting and overwhelming. I feel the tears threatening to spill over, and I blink them away. "I'm going to miss you," I break. "You've been everything to me here."

Her brow softens, and she pulls me into a hug so tight I can't breathe. "I'm going to miss you too," she murmurs into my hair. "But this isn't goodbye forever. Not if we're still breathing,"

"If they let me," I begin, my voice muffled against her shoulder. "I will visit as soon as I can, I promised Maddie and Lilia the same."

She pulls back slightly, her hands cupping my face as she looks into my eyes. "You better," her tone is light but her eyes are serious. "And if they put you in any danger, find a way to tell us. We'll figure out a way to help."

I nod, unable to speak again. Eddie leans in, pressing gentle kisses to my forehead, my cheeks, my lips. I close my eyes, savoring her presence one last time.

The sound of footsteps closing in breaks the illusion of privacy, and we both turn to see Chase in the doorway.

"Ok, that's time," he says with eyes that can't meet either of us.

Eddie's hands drop from my face, and she steps back, her shoulders going rigid. "Watch your back, Val."

"You too."

I turn and follow Chase out of the laundry room before I lose the resolve, my shattered heart held together by nothing but their love and my own determination.

I will find a way to bring us back together, higher in this castle and happier for it.

Chapter 11

The halls as we ascend feel like a mockery of comfort after I leave my friends: the warmth of the chandelier above and gilded steps below too cheerful for my grief.

I have a simple plan: ask Mara to bring them up once she trusts me to do my job. I just need to stick to it.

Chase doesn't lead me to my new room. Instead, I follow him through yet even more new sights – winding through narrow corridors and staircases – until we reach a door tucked beneath an abandoned staircase.

If I hadn't been there to see Mara give him the orders to chaperon me, I would not have trusted him to lead me so far in the wrong direction. The wooden door we stop at is old and warped, the iron handle rusted with age. Chase knocks softly, the sound swallowed by the thick stone walls around us.

"What are we doing?" I whisper, confused.

"Getting you one of these," he says, holding a hand up so the luxurious sleeve slumps. He reveals an identical ring to the one Sydney had shown me at the atelier. "Just don't tell Mara I'm the one who brought you here, if she asks."

The door creaks open before I can ask any more questions, revealing a figure cloaked in shadows. She's not like any of the other magical creatures I've seen yet, and definitely *not* human. Her eyes gleam with an animalistic reflection in the dim light, and her hair falls in wild, silver streaked tufts around her sallow toned face.

Is she even considered fae?

It doesn't matter what she is, she's upset at our presence.

"You're late," she rasps in a voice like the scrape against stone.

"We had some other errands to attend to," Chase replies just as snappily, stepping inside. The room is cluttered with strange objects as I follow: jars of shimmering liquid, bundles of dried herbs, and trinkets that seem to glow with magic. It all reeks of incense and something alarmingly metallic. My senses are too overwhelmed to focus on one area for too long.

She studies me for a moment, her gaze piercing me in place, before nodding toward a small stool in the corner. "Sit."

I do as I'm told, and she rummages through a drawer. Chase remains in the doorway, watching us as though he's seen this play out dozens of times before.

The creature pulls out a small silver ring, lined with runes that shimmer in the candlelight: another detailed replica of Sydney's ring. She places it on the table in front of me.

I don't notice until it's too late that she produces a small needle as well. She grabs my finger with more force than her small frame should carry – faster than I can blink. I yelp more from shock than real pain as she jams it into my finger.

"This will protect you," she explains as she coats the lining of the ring with my blood. The runes inside hungrily siphon the offering. "It'll shield you from their glamour. But it comes with rules."

I nod, sucking the last of the blood off my finger when she releases me. *Glamour?*

"First, you can only remove it when you're alone, in a place you know is safe. And second…" She blinks out of sync, her silver eyes boring into mine before she speaks. "You must never lose it or let someone else have it. If it's lost or destroyed, there's no replacing it: one ring to one body. Do you understand?"

"I understand," I say, my voice steady despite the anticipation coiling in me. I pick up the ring from her outstretched leathery palm, its cool metal smooth as I slide it onto my middle finger.

It fits perfectly over the callused bumps – as if it was made for me.

The effect is underwhelming. I expect reality to shift around me – to feel the oppressive weight of the castle lifting and the veil of magic falling from my mind.

But nothing happens.

I take a deep breath, swallowing my disappointment.

"Does the magic ever wear off? Do I need to… charge it somehow?" I question, turning the ring with my other hand as I try to read the runes. They're indecipherable nonsense to my human eyes.

"The ring will charge itself as long as you stay near the royalty." She shakes her head. "And it will protect you, but it won't make you invincible from your teenage hormones. Be careful, and avoid being too close to any sidhe if you can," she warns.

Chase scoffs at her words, but both the creature and I ignore him as I rise to leave. It feels wrong to not thank her, but I attempt to stick to the rules.

"I will make sure I use this wisely," I pacify my desire to show appreciation as I step back through the door. Her returning smile is missing teeth.

"You're welcome here anytime, sweetie," she says warmly while closing the door in my face. I tilt my head at the mismatch of her words and actions, before pivoting to shadow my chaperon.

We return to the main hall I recognize. The ring feels weighted around my finger, physically heavier with even *more* rules I must follow. But I make myself remember that it's a shield against the world I'm about to enter. I square my shoulders as I keep pace with Chase and head towards my new room.

"So… what was she?" I ask, wincing preemptively if the question is offensive.

"Boggart. They're less civilized than the Seelie hobs you're used to," he replies, uninterested in talking further.

A rush of air escapes my nose at the ludicrous answer.

"Oh yeah, of course," I match his monotone and smother further conversation.

As we finish our loop of the castle, Chase directs me back to Mara's tower, seemingly trusting me enough to navigate the last leg of the journey alone. He shuffles off in another direction, his steps disappearing into the sounds of music and chatter, before I can muster the words to ask where he's going… and if I can come too.

I long to stay near him: a source of wisdom up here. But I think better of it, hearing the wild laughter ring out from the direction he ventured towards.

So, I obey his instructions and make my way toward my new room instead. Just outside the threshold of my new quarters, I'm met with an unanticipated sight. A girl stands waiting, her posture poised and her expression… expectant. She looks to be around my age, though her demeanor carries a quiet confidence that betrays her maturity.

Her big brown eyes sweep over me with a curiosity that mirrors my own as I take her in. She's shorter than me by a few inches, her long brown hair arranged in a simple braid that hides the tips of her ears.

Is she human?

I note the way she barely blinks – the way she possesses that Otherworldly grace – and decide she probably isn't. We study each other for another guarded moment, the silence stretching between us like a taut thread, before she offers a small smile. I find myself returning it despite the exhaustion of my night.

A potential ally.

"Valerie Harlow?" Her voice is high and clear with the address. "That's me," I answer, my voice raspy from the long night of emotion. I cough lightly to clear it, feeling suddenly self conscious against her perfection.

She steps closer when I don't. "I'm Flora. I'll be getting you up to speed on the royalty and your duties." Her tone carries a note of authority that doesn't quite match the softness in her face, and I find myself intrigued by the contrast.

"Oh, I wasn't aware I'd have a guide," I reply wearily. It's been a lifetime since I've been in any kind of schooling, and the idea feels intimidating.

How much will I need to learn to survive up here?

"It was Mara's idea," she explains, her tone matter-of-fact. She angles her head slightly, her braid slipping off her shoulder as she studies me. "I've been her right hand for many years. And if you're as promising for the role as the royalty seem to think you are…" She gives me a once over, her skepticism of their judgement apparent. "Well, she wants to make sure you have a smooth transition up here."

I force my face neutral, determined not to let her see the surprise creeping into my eyes with the responsibility Mara is placing on me.

"She said we are going to start in the evening? I'll be ready to go right at dusk," I change the subject.

"Absolutely," Flora agrees. "I just wanted to welcome you to my chamber before you get settled in." She gestures to the door behind her, and I blink in surprise.

Her chamber?

"Oh, I thought I was staying here," I cringe at the confusion. My mind races, trying to piece together how I got so backwards from Chase's simple directions.

She shrugs, her smile returning – warmer this time. "You are. I haven't had a roommate in thirty years. It'll be… interesting to have one again."

My face relaxes at the clarification.

A roommate. Not a mistake.

The thought is oddly comforting, a single knot in this frayed fabric of a future I've found myself trying to tie back together.

"Well then, I'm ready," I nod, allowing her to lead me inside.

The moment we step into the room, I'm struck by its grandeur. The chambers are spacious, even halved with Flora, and more extravagant than any room I've called my own in any life.

The walls are adorned with intricate tapestries: rich, vibrant scenes of forests and rivers that sparkle as I move further into the space. A large window makes up one wall, its panes framed by heavy velvet curtains that pool elegantly on the floor. The bed – *my* bed, I assume – sits untouched and freshly made. It's a far cry from the cramped quarters of the cots I shared with my friends and even a step up from my fleeting memories of a childhood bedroom in my parents' house.

I crawl into the bed, the mattress caressing me like a solid cloud. The sheets are disgustingly soft against my skin, and I nestle into them with a groan, the night finally catching up to me. My eyelids grow heavy quickly – exhaustion pulling me under like the table runners I drown in the laundry basin.

"I'll let you settle in," I hear Flora laugh as she watches me sink into the downy warmth.

"Mhmm," is all I can muster before I'm out, the world fading away.

Chapter 12

I awake far too early… or late, depending on how you measure time in my new, nocturnal world. Regardless, the sun is high in the sky, its golden light spilling through a small split in the heavy curtains.

For a moment, I lie still, disoriented by the unfamiliar surroundings. The soft sound of Flora's gentle breathing reminds me of my new position. It's comforting, in a way, to have another body in this place: the security of another set of eyes and ears to look out for trouble.

I steal the moment of privacy to investigate my new quarters, my curiosity outweighing my lingering exhaustion. The wardrobe is the first thing I approach, its polished wood gleaming in the sunlight. I open it carefully, half expecting it to be empty. But instead, I'm greeted by a lavish collection of garments in various shades of blue. The sight stuns me.

I get to make choices?

The thought feels foreign, almost like a test itself. I run my fingers over the fabrics, marveling at the variety of textures and cuts. There's everything from deep navy to soft azure, from satin that glides like water to gauze that feels as light as air. The pieces are a mix of pants, skirts, dresses, and shirts. The necklines, sleeve lengths, and details are all different, each one unique. It's overwhelming. And – for the first time in this new life – I feel a flicker of my old personality spark back.

Royal blue.

Memories of the color resurface: my senior prom dress, my first car, my last birthday cake. I vow to make my first outfit one in that color: a small act of defiance against the dull version of myself this world has forced me to become.

After I've pawed through every option, my attention draws to the doorways waiting on the walls. One near Flora's side of the room is ornately painted – its surface adorned with intricate patterns. I assume it leads to Mara's chambers, a direct match to the one found in her room.

I glance at Flora as she shifts in her sleep, noting the blanket she has tucked protectively around herself. It's grey, speckled, and oddly shaped.

Some kind of animal skin? I guess, but think better than to approach and confirm.

My eyes drift to the doorway I entered through last night, and I smile faintly at the wonder that must have brightened my face at the time. But it's the third door, plain and unassuming, that makes me curious enough to approach.

I creep over to it, the foreign texture of the rug tickling my feet with every step, and pull it open slowly. A private washroom is nestled inside – complete with a bathtub, a huge basin of clean water, and a counter top lined with oils and perfumes. For a moment, I just stand there, my jaw slack as I take it all in. A whiff of oleander filters to me, and I step fully inside onto the cold smooth tile floor. The space is a sanctuary of indulgence in a world where I have had none for so long.

My eyes catch something in the mirror above the counter as I move, and my feet stop. I consider avoiding it, as I've tried to do for most of my life here. The girl looking back at me will be different, I know. Not in appearance, perhaps, but in the way she carries herself – in the shadows that linger in her eyes. But I am compelled to confront the person I've become anyway.

I step closer, my reflection coming into crystal clear focus for the first time since my capture. My hair is greasier and longer than I thought, but my features remain otherwise unchanged: rounded with youth.

That hardness in my gaze is more apparent than it was in the laundry basin reflection. The girl in the mirror looks tired, her shoulders weighed down by invisible burdens. But she doesn't look tired *enough* – she's far too lively for my hollow husk.

Tears well unexpectedly in my eyes, but I wipe them away before they can travel down my cheeks.

There's no room for weakness here.

I spin away to the large oval tub near the basin. An unlit bundle of kindling sits beside it, and my palm tests the porcelain's texture. It makes me think of nights as a child when my mother would gently rinse my hair with a cup – of the privacy I found there when we had to move in with my grandparents into a too loud, too cramped space.

"I forgot how much I loved real baths," I murmur.

"Do you want to take one?" The voice behind me is soft, but I startle at the intrusion anyway. Flora stands in the doorway, her eyes squinting in the daylight.

Damn fae and their creepy sneakiness, I think.

"Oh, I would love to. I didn't mean to wake you. I just… I'm so used to the dayshift schedule that I couldn't sleep anymore," I explain, feeling the sting of embarrassment at having been exposed with such vulnerability.

She shakes her head, her still perfect braid swaying gently with the motion. "It's fine. But don't be so quick to claim fault."

"Why? Is that all it takes for a bargain?" The questions slip out before I think better of voicing them, as if they're not the most obvious deduction in the world.

Her answering laugh is tinged with something darker than mere amusement.

"For the folk who bargain, it takes even less. And your fellow attendants are just as dangerous as the royalty when it comes to them. A lot are power hungry… you're going to have a target on your back working with Mara, and they'll use your politeness against you." Her warning is delivered with deadly seriousness.

"Okay. So no taking the blame. No 'thank you' or 'please' either, I assume?" I guess, trying to pacify my sudden unease at the daunting truth.

She nods approvingly. "Exactly."

"Great. Well, just the bath for now, then," I say, deciding to focus on the immediate problem instead of dwell on the dangers lurking outside these walls.

"I love baths too. Reminds me of home," she smiles. Then she shows me how to fill the tub with the basin that's rigged up to collect rainwater. She walks me through setting the fire beneath to warm the water, and then leaves me to undress and bathe alone. I set the protective ring on the counter within sight as I fold my clothes.

The first tub clouds with grime almost immediately. It's humiliating – even completely alone. I dump it out, sponge myself clean, and try again. The second bath is better, though the water still turns murky after a few minutes of soaking.

I allow myself to float, my head tilted back so that only my face remains above the surface.

"Reminds me of home," Flora had said. She comes from somewhere outside of the castle then. From that big scary Otherworld I know nothing about.

The water muffles her movements in the room beyond, leaving only the steady rhythm of my heartbeat and the constant rambling of my thoughts. My eyes drift shut, the weightlessness cradling me.

Until my stomach growls, reminding me that we missed breakfast or any other potential meals I would have gotten during the day. I resurface, cleaner and more awake.

"Hey Flora? What's there to eat around here?"

Chapter 13

My entire life – both before and after being tricked into this world – was spent waking just before the sun and going to bed not long after it did the same. But the court at this level operates on a different rhythm, one that comes alive with the dusk and sleeps by dawn. Forced to flip my sleep schedule entirely, I feel like a stranger in my own body, my mind too foggy to do anything useful.

The first day as Mara's personal attendant is a blur of disorientation and fatigue. I don't even see her after picking out my royal blue uniform. My body rebels against the nocturnal life, my eyelids heavy and my mind sluggish as I stumble through the unfamiliar routine, learning about my peers and the rules of my new position.

Cu sidhe, grigs, pechs, goblins, sylphs: the list goes on, and I have to learn *every* species' preferred name: whether it be Gaelic, Greek, or another regional choice.

"Pooka" are different from "satyrs" the same way "merrows" are different from "mermaids."

It's exhaustingly nitpicky. But I practice every time I'm in the halls, because calling them "fae" is a deeply offensive categorization. So much so that – according to Flora – it's a punishable crime. The proper term is "fair folk" or simply "folk" when I can't remember their names.

I need to warn the others down in the barracks.

Flora, a "selkie" as I've now learned, is a strict and relentless tutor, her patience thin as I struggle to keep up. My only breaks come in the form of sleep and meals delivered to our room on gilded trays by "brownies" I've grown to recognize – easily distinguished by the *brown* hats and uniforms on their small forms. They don't look at me; my attention is as deadly as the royalties' themselves in their eyes. Even if I am just a human.

Smart servants. I pacify my hurt with the logic, thinking of how I'll have my friends up here one day, and then I won't feel so othered anymore.

The food is simple but always fresh: my favorite quickly becoming a slice of crusty warm bread from the bakery a level away and a small dish of seasonal fruit from the gardens below my window. I stop requesting meat

stew, when Flora turns her nose up one too many times at the savory smell
– Seelie being strictly vegetarian. But I don't mind, it's all more flavorful
than any of the "ideal" foods that made their way through the night shift
back in the barracks. Guilt tampers my enjoyment of every heavenly bite I
swallow.

But when meals are carried away or sleep is abandoned, the volume of
information thrust onto me is staggering. I'm handed charts of lineage that
stretch back generations – their intricate branches and names weaving
together into an untangle-able knot. Power dynamics, alliances, rivalries:
each family has its own secret history, and I'm expected to memorize them
all and how they relate to the West Court, South Court, North Court, and
East Court – the four main courts that compose the Cardinal Kingdom.

At least that part's easy to remember.

Flora quizzes me constantly, her sharp tone cutting through my fog of
exhaustion.

"The East Court's ruling family," she prods. "Who are their allies, and
who are their enemies?"

I stare blankly at the parchment in front of me, the names swimming
before my eyes. "I… I don't remember."

And I don't really care, but I think better than to voice the latter part.

Flora sighs, resting a hand on my shoulder. "I know it's your first
week, but we can't take it slow. The autumn equinox is in three weeks, and
this knowledge can actually be life or death if you say the wrong thing to
the wrong guest."

I bite my tongue, preventing a longer lecture. My brain feels too full
for my neck to support, and I slump forward.

I'll be dead of exhaustion if my tongue doesn't get me killed first.

The workload only grows from there. Schedules, friends, hated foods,
preferred music: every detail of Mara's life is cataloged and presented to
me as if it's the most important thing in the world. I'm told to learn it all –
internalize it until I can recite it in my sleep. But the information slips
through my fingers like spilled salt… which it turns out *is* banned along
with iron for their potential to harm the folk.

Remembering the hellish conditions my friends are still trapped in is
the only thing that keeps me from quitting the job and taking whatever
consequence I must for breaking my deal with a sidhe – which *is* the
preferred term for "high fae."

On the fifth night of rigorous study, I'm told to dress in one of my finer uniforms and meet Flora in the common room of Mara's tower at midnight.

I do as instructed, buttoning up a silk set in soft blue, taking the time to detangle my hair and pin it back professionally.

Flora's bed is unattended for once, and I steal the opportunity to touch the seal skin she always guards on her bed: the speckled gray one. It's so soft I have no doubt it is magical in origin.

I wonder if she'll ever show me her seal form.

I decide I'll need to ask her later, and make my way out of the room down the hall towards her.

The sound as we approach the private lounge of the King's tower is striking. It's more cacophonous than the polite ballroom fair we'd imagined down in the barracks. The sounds of laughter and music curl through the air like smoke even before we step inside.

A real revelry.

Flora adjusts my collar and gives me a cutting look. "Tonight is the full moon. Watch. Listen. Do not dance or engage. I'll handle Mara tonight."

My pulse thrums in my throat as I agree.

She pushes the door open.

The space is an explosion of color and movement. Graceful folk dance under the retracted ceiling. The moon and stars shine bright above.

But I can't be bothered to look up, my eyes darting to the smaller groups of sidhe draped over low couches – limbs tangled in ways that make me blush. I've been here long enough to know: nudity means nothing to them.

But neither, apparently, does fidelity.

Mara lounges on the far side of the room, her hair spilling over the chest of a handsome water nymph with navy skin and stormy hair. His fingers trace idle patterns up her soft, full thigh. She tips her head back to accept a sip of wine from another reveler: this one with antlers braided into her blonde hair that gasps as Mara's hand disappears under her skirt.

And yet, no one bats an eye.

Flora nudges me toward the wall where the other attendants stand, silent as shadows in various blues – a mix of folk I still struggle to name. None of them acknowledge me. Their eyes track their assigned royal with precision, waiting for the barest flicker of command. I mimic their stillness, but my gaze keeps drifting.

Mara isn't the only one indulging. And by the way they all feed each other fairy fruit and let the wine slosh over half filled goblets, it's easy to see why they need a laundry staff as large as what we have in the barracks.

I use the party as a chance to study, trying to place faces to names. I see the elegant Princess Eugenia of the East dancing in a circle with two of her own courtiers. The scary Prince Ciaran of the South is engrossed in conversation on the side with King Anders himself. The flashy Lord Rakan of this court nibbles at a blush fairy fruit, offering a taste to a human escort who politely declines.

There's a prickly feeling against my skin: the mingling around the room shedding invisible sparks of magic. And though it isn't entirely visible, it shows in other ways: half lidded smiles, glowing skin, and a lightness in everyone's limbs.

And then I see *him*.

Prince Sylas lounges on a chair that might as well be a throne, the way he commands the space. His blonde hair messed, his pointed features relaxed in a way they weren't at the atelier – he looks *ethereal* like this.

Another radiant sidhe with copper hair is draped in his lap, fingers tracing the collar of the prince's shirt.

Mara's brother, Alistar, I realize quickly. *Another sun.*

He leans in to murmur something in Sylas's ear, and Sylas's mouth curves in a delicious smirk.

He likes gingers, apparently.

But then his gaze lifts… and lands on me.

My heart stutters.

He doesn't look away. Not when Alistar nips at his jaw, not when Mara laughs loudly in the arms of her company. His endless blue eyes hold mine across the room, sending an unasked for shiver down my spine.

Don't even think about it.

Flora's fingers dig into my arm. "Valerie."

I blink, finally tearing my gaze from Sylas's. My face is warm.

Stupid.

"You're staring," she critiques.

"I-" I force my voice low. "I know it's different here than the human world. But Mara and Sylas are *betrothed*. Shouldn't they at least pretend?"

Flora's lips thin. "Why? The alliance is sealed. What they do with others changes nothing."

I swallow hard, my skin still needling with Sylas's stare.

Mara laughs again, bright and unbothered, as the nymph beside her starts tugging at the lacing of her gown. She catches my eye and winks, sharing our own unexpectedly intimate moment.

And suddenly, the room feels far too small.

Flora exhales through her nose when she sees reality refuse to mesh with my mind's logic. "Welcome to the Otherworld."

We continue to stand and watch the revelers, Flora occasionally braving the crowd when Mara calls for her – usually for a reminder of another's name or to confirm some obscure knowledge about an attendee.

We leave when dawn touches the horizon outside the windows. The gossip-fueled walk back to our chambers is underscored by the distant echoes of pleasure still spilling from the lounge. My feet ache from standing so long, my back stiff from holding that damned attendant's posture: spine straight, hands clasped, eyes alert but never *intrusive*.

Flora yawns beside me, her braid fraying at the edges for once. "You did alright," she sighs the closest thing to praise I've gotten yet.

"I stared at the prince like a freak," I grumble.

"You didn't approach him. That's what matters."

The memory of his gaze lingers like a phantom caress. I run a hand over my face where I feel it.

Our room is blessedly dark when we enter, the curtains blocking all morning sun. Flora collapses onto her bed with a groan, already tugging at the buttons on her top as she drags her seal skin around her. "Don't take too long," she mumbles into the pillows. "Mara will be back soon, but you still have to-"

"Prepare her chambers. I know."

I strip off my nice uniform, trading it for a simple linen shift. Then I slip into Mara's adjoining room.

God damnit.

The scent hits me first: wine and oleander mix with the faint musk of sweat and pleasure from the night before. Glasses sit half empty on the side table. A silk shawl is draped carelessly over the mirror. The bed is a tangle of crumpled sheets from this evening, still bearing the imprint of bodies.

I roll my shoulders to wake my exhausted muscles.

Let's get this over with quickly. First, fresh sheets. The ones I pull from the maple chest carry a *clean* oleander perfume. I shake them out with a snap, tucking the corners tight.

Then the water basin in the bathing chamber. Filled, warmed the way Flora taught me. A cloth folded beside it.

Wine. A new decanter, the glasses replaced.

Curtains. Parted just so, to let in daylight enough to warm the space but not enough to disturb their nocturnal eyes.

I'm smoothing the last wrinkle from the duvet when the door to our room creaks.

"You missed a hairpin." Flora jabs her chin to the floor near the wardrobe: a glint of silver half hidden in the rug's fringe.

I pluck it up between two fingers. "How does she lose these so often?"

"She likes when they pull them out." Her smirk is wicked.

I toss the pin into the vanity dish with a clatter, suddenly flustered. "Spare me the details."

She laughs, but sobers when distant footsteps echo down the hall.

Mara.

Flora grabs my wrist. "Out. *Now*."

We're barely through the connecting door when Mara's laughter spills into the corridor: bright, tipsy, underscored by a softer voice teasing in a way that makes her giggle.

Flora bolts our latch. "And that," she says, flopping back onto her bed, "is how you survive your first revelry. Also, don't touch my pelt again. I can feel it – even separated, you know."

I collapse onto my own bed, staring at the ceiling with an abashed smile.

"And they do this like… *every* full moon?" I focus back on the hands-on revelry lesson.

Flora's only answer is a snore.

Chapter 14

The next night, we are back to studying as usual. But I'm close to my breaking point again. My head throbs from more hours of squinting at tiny, cramped handwriting. My eyes feel like they're filled with grit at the low candle light. I flip through yet another stack of parchment, the words blurring together into a meaningless jumble.

I miss my friends. I think.

"Valerie," Flora barks. "Focus."

"I'm sorry, I'm trying to," I yawn, failing to answer yet another question about Mara's favorite foods. My mind drifts every time Flora speaks, her voice nothing but noise. We've been at this for hours, and I swear I can see the moon crawling across the sky as I struggle to stay present.

"If you're sorry, then that means you've slighted me. So in return, I have repayment to ask of you," Flora chides. She sits up in her chair, crossing her arms as she studies me with frustration.

"I get it. I shouldn't have apologized. I'm just exhausted," I snap back.

Despite my irritation, I'm grateful Flora's at least trying to teach me. I've pretended not to notice the lingering glares and dismissive eye rolls of the other attendants as she leads me through the halls, but I know they must be judging her almost as much as they're judging me.

Flora at least is giving me a chance to earn her approval.

She sighs, pinching the bridge of her nose as she weighs her options. "No, I'm going to hold you to this one. Otherwise you're never going to stop slipping up," she begins. "I'll talk to Mara and get you a few more days to get your shit together. She mentioned possibly visiting the North Court for a harvest revelry this weekend. I'll see to it that she attends. And while she's gone, you don't bother me. You do both of our work – you teach yourself – and I get the week off. Okay?"

Relief floods me, though I feel a twinge of guilt for how much the responsibility of teaching me truly weighs on her.

Still, a few days to adjust sounds like a good bargain.

"Before you lecture me, I know not to say this to anyone else. But thank you," I say, gathering my bag before she can change her mind.

Her eyes roll, but there's a hint of amusement in them as we both feel the magic snap the bargain into place.

"See to it you're ready by the beginning of next week," she orders, then sucks in another breath- holding it – debating whether to say more. I cock an eyebrow, encouraging her to continue.

"Come with me, I think I know a way to help. But you *cannot* tell Mara." Her words are rushed with the caught air.

I follow obediently, curious with the conditional help. Together, we leave the library and make our way through the towers of the castle – still too complex for me to know exactly where we're going.

The corridors are busier now; servants and courtiers louder as the night deepens. Flora leads me confidently to the main hall before we climb a staircase we haven't taken before. A defensive hunch settles in my posture as we approach what I think might be Prince Sylas's tower of the castle.

"Starling owes me big time for covering for them yesterday. I caught them stealing some rare flowers from the garden," she explains over her shoulder.

"Starling?" I ask, unfamiliar with the name.

"They're Prince Ciaran's attendant. Arrived a day or two after you, but have a serious collection of potions that have helped them adjust to the role here. They may have some stuff to help you."

Ciaran: the human hating prince… lovely.

We find ourselves way too soon outside a guest door, and Flora knocks softly before I can compose myself. The sound echoes down the hall, making my shoulders hike further.

After a moment, the door opens to reveal a beautiful face at eye level with Flora. Thick black hair frames angular features; their dark skin glows faintly in the candlelight. A pair of red eyes – the only clear indicator of their magical nature in the small crack of the door – narrow as they take us in.

"Yes, selkie?" they say in a smooth, unamused voice.

"It's me, little dunter," Flora matches their tone.

Dunter? She hasn't taught me about those, I think.

"And this is Valerie," she pulls me from my confusion. "She's struggling to focus on her work with her new schedule. I thought you might be able to help her adjust with one of your potions in exchange for my continued silence."

Starling's expression doesn't change, but they step aside, gesturing for us to enter quickly. The room is smaller than I expect for a prince's attendant when compared to my own – though it's neatly arranged with all the finery I've come to associate with this level of the castle. Starling moves to a shelf lined with labeled bottles, their fingers brushing over them as they search among the shimmering potions.

"Assumed I'd have something, did you?" they grumble, more to themselves than to us. I glance at Flora who rolls her oversized brown eyes at their words, but she holds her tongue.

I want to ask what anyone could possibly need with all these bottles – but follow Flora's lead instead.

"You're correct. I do." They pluck a fist sized bottle from the shelf, its contents a deep, oozing red. They rummage around in a drawer beneath and retrieve a small vial. It's brought to the neck of the potion bottle, allowing a thimbleful to splat inside.

"This should help," they say, capping the small portion and holding it out to me. "But be careful with it. Only take it when absolutely necessary: when you can't focus or stay awake any longer. And only a drop at a time. It's potent stuff. Highly addictive for your kind."

I take the vial with overt care. The glass is cool against my palm, the liquid inside flowing thicker than syrup. "Got it," I lilt, still too nervous to be in this room.

"Consider my debt repaid," they say through their sharp teeth to Flora.

Before Flora can respond, a painted door on the other side of the room swings open. To my horror, Prince Ciaran strides in – his strong features set in a scowl, sweeping over the scene with disdain.

"What is a human doing in my chambers? I recall giving your superiors the *simple* order to keep them all out of my room," he clips, ending our almost finished conversation.

Starling steps between us smoothly, composed – like they expected this reaction. "They came seeking help, it's already taken care of."

The prince's gaze narrows, and he steps closer, his harsh green eyes locking onto Flora as he towers over us all. "And what exactly do you need assistance with that *she* had to come into my room?"

Holy shit. What do we say?

I open my mouth, but Flora beats me to it. "Valerie here is learning about the duties of attendants, Your Highness. She's new, Starling was giving her advice for handling the responsibilities." Her voice is calm through the twisted truth, but there's a steeliness beneath it that I admire.

Ciaran's lip curls into a sneer. "Get out. I won't be as forgiving the next time you disobey orders."

Flora grabs my arm and pulls me toward the door we came through. I clutch the vial tightly, my heart racing as we hurry down the stairs. Behind us, I hear the prince's voice, low and threatening, as he speaks to Starling. But the words are lost in the bustle of traffic in the tower.

As we round a corner out of their sight, Flora finally slows, releasing my arm. "That could have gone worse," she says lightly despite the tension still riddling my shoulders.

I whirl on her, gasping. "Worse? He looked like he wanted to skin us alive!"

"You humans are almost as attached to your skin as us selkies." She offers a rare smirk. "Relax. He *didn't*. Perks of being an attendant." She gestures to the vial. "Just remember what Starling said: be careful with that. Don't let any one – human or folk – know you have it."

I nod, the vial and her trust a heavy weight in my hand.

We continue our studies the next two nights as normal, I don't let myself think about the potion – not when I can keep my eyes open and my mind from fogging entirely.

Flora waits until the third night after the revelry to approach Mara about attending the North Court. The queen-to-be relaxes in her room, wrapped in a silk robe, her copper curls still damp from a bath after a long night of meetings about the upcoming autumn equinox revelry – the one she's been charged with hosting.

I hover near the window, pretending to adjust the already perfect drape of the curtains when Flora clears her throat.

"Mara," she begins, her voice carefully neutral. "Queen Penelope's harvest revelry is this weekend."

Mara hums, swirling her wine as she reads over her agenda. "Mmm. I recall."

Flora's fingers twitch at her sides, the only sign of her nerves. "I think you should attend."

Mara's golden eyes flick up, bright despite the lazy sprawl of her limbs. "Oh? Even with preparations for the equinox still to be decided?"

A beat of silence. Flora nods.

Mara sets her glass and the schedule down with purposeful slowness. "And why is that?"

Flora grabs the decanter automatically to top off the tabled glass. "Valerie needs time to adjust. Properly. Without the pressure of your schedule."

Mara's gaze slides to me. My hands still on the curtain ties.

"Is that so?" she questions.

I smile sheepishly. "It's a lot to learn."

Flora cuts in as she pours. "She's drowning. The lineage charts, the preferences, the protocols: it's too much in too short a time. If you go to the North, she'll be able to focus on just studying for a few days."

Mara's brow furrows. "And you agree?"

Whenever you need me to lie, I'll be able to sell it better, I think.

"I want to be ready for whatever you need me to do." I say instead.

Mara's laugh is melodic. Her eyes are alight at my hidden meaning. "Smart girl." She leans back, tapping a finger against her temple. "Very well. I will go."

Relief floods me until she adds: "But when I return, I expect you to know every major house's current heirs, and some knowledge regarding those that will be in attendance at the Equinox."

My stomach plummets. *That's twenty houses. At least.*

Flora nods eagerly. "Done."

Mara reaches for her wine again. "Good. Now, both of you: *out.* I need sleep if I am to travel tomorrow."

Flora drags me from the room before I can process the dismissal. Back in our room, Flora's relief is visible.

I blink. "That... worked?"

She rebraids the silky end of her brown plait, and I catch a glimpse of her pointed tan ears. "Of course it worked. You need help, she wants you to succeed and is offering it. I've bought you four days. *Use them.*"

Then she moves around me toward the door to the hall, talking under her breath about "set up to fail" and "impossible expectations."

I watch the empty threshold as the door closes behind her, thumbing the vial of Starling's potion still in my pocket to remind myself it's still there.

Four days. No time for failure.

Chapter 15

The dawn hour of Mara's departure arrives with a flurry of activity. The entire courtyard buzzes with servants of various species and job titles. They pack trunks, polish carriages, and prepare the caravan of royalty for the journey to the Northern capitol… however far that actually is.

I wonder if I can find a better map in the library.

I linger by the window, my eyes scanning the unfamiliar faces of the servantry below. Despite knowing the truth, I search for my friends among the few humans I see. The guilt I've carried since accepting Mara's bargain grows as I think about how my biggest problem now is that I need to *study*, while they're still cooped in the barracks underfoot.

Many of the West's guests have decided to accompany the sidhe on her journey, leaving behind empty rooms and unassigned attendants. Mara's tower itself feels quieter already, the usual prickle of shed magic absent with them.

I follow Flora through a set of towering double doors, their height dizzying as I step into cooler air. She moves with efficiency, directing the final preparations with the same sharp eye and commanding presence that's kept me focused on my studies. I watch as she pulls supplies from a satchel and runs down some sort of list she's scratched onto parchment.

How will I ever measure up to her expectations?

Mara is already seated in a gilded carriage connected to two winged horses or "pegasi", her expression bored in the waning moonlight. She doesn't glance our way, her attention fixed on some distant point beyond the castle walls. Her disinterest makes me frown for a beat, before I remember myself.

I'm not here to be noticed. I'm here to help my friends.

A sudden gust of wind catches my hair, and it's only then that I appreciate that we've stepped onto a breezy stairway leading down to the courtyard… *outside.* The light from the castle's windows shines onto the stone steps, but it feels wrong – too harsh and orchestrated against the natural glow of the stars above.

Stars?

I tilt my head back, my breath catching in my throat as I take in the endless expanse of black above me. The sky stretches out in every direction – a vast, seamless version of Mara's sparkling wardrobe that seems to go on forever. I feel small – insignificant in the presence of such eternity.

As eternal as the aos si, the folk, themselves.

Even in the couple of days since my promotion to Mara's attendant, I've spent my time indoors or distracted under open ceilings. I've been surrounded by walls and ceilings that felt more expansive than I'd ever need.

But here, *outside*, there's nothing for my eyes to focus on above except the stars: countless and unreachable.

My knees weaken, and I sink onto a nearby bench, my hands gripping the edge to keep me grounded.

Flora's voice pulls me back from the overwhelming exposure. "While I'd love to let you have this moment to stargaze, we need to go," she says teasingly as she checks off the last of her chores for the night in her agenda. "It isn't safe for humans outside of the castle walls. There's creatures lurking in the forests."

I blink, trying to drag my focus from the looming sky. "Creatures?"

She doesn't clarify, just reaches for my arm to tug me to my feet. She guides me back up the stairs and inside. The familiar scent of candle wax bleeds into the crisp fresh florals, soothing away the existential dread inside me.

"I didn't know it would be so overwhelming to be outside again," I voice the thought – to myself or Flora? I'm not sure.

She ignores my shakiness and pulls out another small notebook from her satchel. "Here," she hands it to me. "Use this to keep track of your studies. And write down questions for me if you have any. I'll be enjoying these next few days of relief from duty."

I take the notebook, running my fingers over the smooth leather cover.

"I will," I promise, tucking it into the pocket of my trousers.

"If you need me, *don't*. Or our bargain is off and I'll make your lessons a lot harder." She warns before leading us back towards our room in uneasy silence.

She's an ally. Not a friend. I remind myself. *I don't need more friends.*

By the time we reach our room, the exorbitance of the night – packing Mara's bags, Flora's dismissal, the overwhelming vastness of the sky –

have left me drained. I set the notebook on my desk and crawl into bed, the softness a familiar, welcome embrace now.

As I close my eyes, the image of the stars lingers in my mind. And I sink into a restful sleep through the entirety of the next day.

Chapter 16

I spend the better part of my first night alone trying to sketch a useful map of the castle interior, but my efforts are fruitless. I sit cross legged on the floor of our room, the notebook from Flora open to yet another blank page in front of me. My only company – a single candle – sits next to me.

This should have just been a quick reference to avoid crossing the remaining royalty again before Mara returns.

The first few pages are a mess of crooked lines and smudged ink – with rooms and hallways overlapping in ways that make no sense. Flipping to a blank page, I frown, tapping the quill against my chin as I try to recall the paths I've walked with Flora and Chase for yet *another* time.

The subterranean portion of the castle is a deliberate puzzle, its winding paths and hidden passages designed to disorient those not privileged with learning the layout. But without help from my guides, I still feel entirely lost up here too.

Maybe I should just ask Chase.

My eyes flick to Flora's empty bed with a wince. I know they're both finding pleasure somewhere other than here tonight. It was obvious when I awoke to them both in her bed, ruining whatever was going on with my presence.

I guess everyone at this level really is just that open, I note.

I don't want to burn my few bridges already. So I write in the back of my notes to ask for help next week, and try one last time.

I start with a new approach – drawing a rough outline of the tower I know well. Mara's quarters are here, near the far end of the tower next to our own. I add a few more lines, marking the locations of the kitchen, the library, common lounge, and the pathway to the gardens, making a mental note to visit the latter for a snack once I'm done with the map.

I add the main hall in the center of the page with its doors leading out to the king's courtyard – the one with the fountain and hedges, *not* the smaller one Mara departed from.

I draw the stairs leading to the Minotaur's labyrinth that divides the barracks from the rest of the castle.

I draw Prince Sylas's tower… then pause, my hand hovering over the page. The tower is somewhere to the east of where I am currently, but I can't remember exactly which staircase in the main hall leads to it.

My encounter with the other dangerous prince is still fresh in my mind. *He's staying in Sylas's tower, I need to know where that is.*

But the more I draw, the more I realize how little I actually know.

"I don't even know where the boggart I got my ring from is." I say to myself, devastated.

Frustrated with another failure, I set the quill aside and lean back against the bed. My joints are stiff from hours of hunching beside my candle. I finally admit defeat, groaning as I close the notebook to set on the desk above.

I'll stick to the areas I know, avoid the east of the castle, and keep my head down.

It's not much of a plan, but it's the best I've got for the next four days.

I bring the candle with me as I rise, feeling the hours of strain catch up with me. My body protests with a deep yawn, as if still trying to remind me that sleep should happen at *night*.

"We still have a long time until sleep," I criticize, stretching my arms above my head in an attempt to work out my shoulders. My body answers with another yawn, more insistent this time.

"Okay, fine. Time to bring in some reinforcements," I mutter, fishing the vial from my pocket. I clear a spot on my still messy bed to slump onto. My palm cradles the small vessel like I can absorb its effects through my skin. The potion inside is thick and viscous, the deep red syrup clinging to the sides even when turned upside down. Something about it feels wrong, unnatural, but I'm too tired – and curious about its effects – to care.

"Maybe you shouldn't drink that," a voice warns from the doorway.

My head snaps up to see Chase lingering in the threshold to Mara's room, his arms crossed: knowing. I try to hide the vial, but he's seen too much already. My back slumps further under his leery eye.

He's an escort. A human. Not an attendant, he probably doesn't care enough to use it against me.

"I didn't know you were back already. I just need help adjusting to the schedule. I've worked dayshift my entire life." The explanation tumbles out defensively before I can stop it.

Chase steps into the room with forced casual ease. His brown eyes shift around the space, taking in the scattered failed maps and the flickering candlelight.

"Look, new girl, I really don't care what you do. But Unseelie magic is just… unclean," he grimaces as though he can see the vial hidden in my closed hand.

"Unseelie?" I test the word out, the meaning lost on me.

Chase barks a real laugh before he rubs an exasperated hand over his face. "You were about to down a vial of their potion and don't even know who made it? You're way too hazardous to last as an attendant."

My fingers twitch around the vial, the distraction of his surprise appearance wearing off enough to remind me why I need it.

"Are you going to tell me what that word means or just judge my decision making?" I snark back.

"The second one," he says with a smirk that's more friendly than his tone. "It's Flora's duty to explain basic magic systems to you."

"Then feel free to judge. Although, I feel like I should be doing the same to you. Don't you have your own room? What are you doing in Mara's?" I brush him off, knowing the potion can't be that bad if he hasn't stopped me outright.

"Oh, I do. But I have her favor. I get perks too," he winks.

I ignore the clear implication of his words.

I don't have the energy for this.

My attention returns to the vial – the deeply unsettling, yet alluring vial. I hold it up to the candlelight to inspect, the color shifting like molten garnet. My eyes flick back to Chase's amused face once before I uncork it.

The scent hits me immediately: cloying and metallic, like iron and honey. It's not repulsive, but it's not inviting either. It reminds me of pricking my finger with a pin – the faint tang of blood rising to the surface. I shove that thought away, refusing to entertain it with the potion's color and texture so eerily similar.

Starling's warning echoes in my mind, giving me pause.

It's potent, and it's addictive for humans. Only take it when absolutely necessary.

"It's necessary," I sigh the justification before tilting the vial back. A single thick drop falls audibly onto my tongue. The taste is bittersweet – almost medicinal – with an undercurrent of something sour. I let it marinate on my tongue, waiting for something to happen.

At first, there's nothing. Just the bitter bite soaking in and the faint worry that maybe I've made a mistake in trusting any attendants after Flora's warning.

"Well, that was anticlimactic-" I begin, but the words die in my throat as a slow warmth spreads through my chest. A tingling sensation follows, traveling down my arms and legs – the potion coursing through my literal veins. My fatigue melts away, replaced by a sharp, jarring clarity. My mind feels focused like I've just woken from the deepest, most restful sleep of my life.

I blink, looking around the room. The colors of the fruit on my neglected dinner tray are brighter – the details on the rinds sharper. I can hear Chase's breathing, the distant life of the castle beyond the walls. It's exhilarating.

"You've got to try this," I say with wonder.

"Used to use it for parties. I'm good," Chase shuts down the idea with a wrinkled nose. "That is just to help you adjust and stay awake. Do not get comfortable with it."

"Or what?" I challenge, feeling a confidence that's normally tucked away with the old Valerie.

"I already said I don't care what you do," he chuckles halfheartedly. "But if you become addicted to Unseelie magic in a *week*, Mara is going to rip you a new one when she's back."

"Mara won't know," I answer without hesitation, eyeing the bottle with newfound respect. "You might call this stuff unclean. I call it effective."

"Whatever. Just take it sparingly, I guess," he shrugs, turning to leave. He pauses at the door, glancing back at me over his shoulder.

"Once a night at most, around halfway through. You'll be fine." With that, he closes the door to Mara's room, leaving me alone with the magic of the potion tingling in me.

The urge to ask about his past with this stuff has me almost crossing to the door, but I push the feeling down. Instead, I sit back on the bed, the vial cradled in my hand protectively.

"Just once a day," I murmur to myself, enjoying the newfound energy thrumming through my veins. For the first time in days, I feel like I might actually survive up here.

Now let's go learn some history while you're focused. I challenge myself, popping off the bed again to head for the library.

Chapter 17

It's almost sunrise and I'm still wide awake, the potion's effects not quite out of my veins.

The rows of books around me are lit by my third single candle, its flame flickering as I move through the aisles in search of something, *anything* that seems interesting.

Most of the spines bear symbols I don't recognize, in languages I don't understand.

But after another pass, a small book – its cover worn and faded – catches my eye. The title is embossed in a delicate, curling script: *How The Realm Was Saved*.

Saved from what exactly?

It's tucked away, hidden among dusty tomes and forgotten scrolls. It's a children's book with colorful illustrations and simple language.

I pull the small tale down and flip through the pages out of curiosity. I expect to see colorful folk and smiling faces, but the flashes of dark forms I scan surprise me. I settle crossed legged on the floor with my candle, my back against the row, and begin to read.

Long ago, before humans and Tyrants, magic flowed freely. The Folk took from the land. And the land took from the Folk.

*Wait. Is this implying that **we** do something to the magic here?* I reread the passage, unsure if I'd skipped a line of context, but the page remains unchanged. A glowing circle is painted around the words, with different representations of folk along the rim: a symbolic cycle of power.

Until humans decided to steal magic for themselves, breaking the cycle. In that time of Folk weakness, a Tyrant King rose to power. He closed the portals between worlds to keep all magic to himself.

I pause, my fingers tracing the illustration on the page. It shows a towering figure – his crown glowing with magic – standing before a massive portal as it explodes into a thousand pieces. The folk around him are depicted as small, their faces filled with despair. I frown, my mind racing.

Portals *to the human world? Multiple?*

The idea is both fascinating and unsettling. I've never heard of such a thing, not even in the gossip of the barrack guards.

And the idea that humans may have been stealing magic…

I turn the page, eager to learn more.

The humans were subdued quickly, but the Tyrant was too strong.
Without flowing magic, all Folk became weak. They tired. They died.

The illustration here is darker: the colors muted. The tyrant king sits on a throne of brittle sticks, his face set in a cruel smile. Around him, the folk are depicted as shadows, their forms fading into nothingness. I pull my knees tighter then turn another page.

But hope was not lost. Four brave heroes rose up against the Tyrant King.
They fought with courage and cunning to end his reign.
On one dark winter solstice, they defeated him, breaking his hold on the
magic of the land through their teamwork.

The illustration shows a pale sidhe with long blonde hair, his face noble and resolute, standing over the fallen tyrant. Behind him, the other three raise their hands – their magic flowing into the land. The colors are vibrant again, showing trails of magic transforming the world around them.

With the Tyrant defeated, the realm was divided into four courts, each
ruled by one of the victorious sidhe.
King Anders took the West.
Queen Elora took the East.
King Moore took the South.
and Queen Penelope took the North.
They now rule as allies, together, protecting the Kingdom and its people.

The End

I close the book, my mind reeling. The story is simple, bite sized for a child's mind in its telling, but the implications are staggering.

"If this King Anders is the same King Anders as the one currently ruling," I whisper to myself. "When did this happen?"

But even more pressing ideas flood into my head. The Otherworld wasn't always like this... and there are humans who know magic.

"Until humans decided to steal magic for themselves."

But how? Humans have no connection to the magic of this world. Belladonna flashes through my mind: the witch with her rune covered arms. I look at the ring on my finger, charged with my own blood.

Runes.

I study the book's cover again, my fingers brushing over the title. It's a children's book, meant to teach young folk about their history.

But I've never seen a folk child. Not once.

The realization is jarring.

They must keep them far away from humans, if they think we'll drain their magic.

I set the book aside, my thoughts chasing many rabbit holes.

Did the portal I come through survive all this? Was the Tyrant King even real or just a metaphor for something worse?

More questions come flooding in that leave me stumped, and my hand struggles to keep up with my potion powered mind, jotting all of them down for Flora's lessons.

The candle gutters out as the night comes to an end. The first streaks of dawn grey the sky, and I decide it's time to go to bed… finally.

I sneak back to my room, invisible and safe without the usual courtiers flooding the space. Flora doesn't look up as I slip inside, brushing her seal skin.

I can't wait to ask her about the Tyrant.

Chapter 18

I wake just past golden hour on my second day alone in the room. For a moment, I'm pleasantly surprised by how far my sleep schedule shifted in just a night.

Maybe I really won't need that potion much after all.

But the thought is fleeting, a creeping unease replacing the contentment.

Something's different in here.

My eyes squint around the room, scanning for whatever must be out of place. The furniture is the same; the notebook is still open to my scribbled questions for Flora about the children's book. But then my gaze lands on the door jamb.

There, tucked into the crack along the frame of my door, is a small plant; its leaves jagged and green. I frown, crawling from my nest of pillows to make my way to the door. My hand reaches out to pluck it from the space without thinking.

The moment my fingers brush against it, a sharp, burning pain shoots through my hand. I yank my arm back, hissing through my teeth, but the damage is done. The sprig falls to the floor. By the time it reaches the marble, my fingers are red and angry. I try to scratch them, but it just stokes the fire under my skin hotter.

"What the hell?" I grumble, shaking my hand in an attempt to dissipate the sting. But the pain is insistent. I press my other hand to the wounded one's wrist, then forearm, testing the limits of the static prickling my fingers. It doesn't spread beyond where I touched the leaf.

That's something, at least.

I open the door and peer down the hall. It's empty, aside from a lone guard and a brownie with no interest in my condition. No one's here to witness the assault's fall out, but that doesn't make it sting any less.

Someone put that plant specifically at my door. Was it meant for me? Or for Flora for helping me? Is that why she wants to distance herself this week?

I close the door again, cradling my stung hand against my chest. The

91

pain isn't enough to make me call for help.

It's just my fingers, after all. Just a few pricks. I've endured much worse at the wrong end of sewing pins.

Still, the deliberate nature of the act unsettles me. I squat down, glaring at the offending plant on the floor just inside the threshold. Its stems bristle with tiny, almost invisible hairs that I hadn't noticed until it was too late. And when I look closer at my fingers, I see the few that remained in my skin.

"Hey Chase?" I call, betting that he's still in Mara's room. After some shuffling from the other side of the door, I am proven right. He pokes a disheveled head into my room, unenthused by my call as he ties his ruby robe loosely around his form.

"Yes?" he yawns.

"Did you see anyone come in or out of this room while I slept? There was a weird plant on the door." I toe the bundle of leaves on the ground with my slippered foot.

He shakes his blonde head, brows creasing sincerely as he eyes it. "No, just you and Flora. Need anything else?"

"Nope, that's all," I dismiss.

He closes the door again with a half hearted smile.

What if he left it? A warning to be careful after the potion?

I open the door to the hall again to kick the wicked plant out of my room, and try to ignore the throbbing in my hand.

"I need to talk to my friends," I decide. The thought of seeing them – of hearing their voices and sharing a moment of normalcy – is enough to push the pain to the back of my mind.

I glance at the sun out the window, puzzling out if I have enough time to sneak down to their barracks before they go to sleep tonight.

It's a risk, but one I'm willing to take.

Chapter 19

I spare a few chance minutes, calling a servant for extra portions of potatoes and fresh fruits – as well as a rare request for beef. When the food arrives, I wrap it carefully in linen napkins, knowing my friends will be able to trade any leftovers for whatever they might need in my absence.

I paw through my wardrobe, finding a tan satchel tucked away in the back. It's sturdy and unassuming, perfect for carrying the food without drawing attention from guards or the other servants down there. I toss the wrapped bundles inside, slinging the satchel over my shoulder before heading out.

The halls are dead, the sun casting long shadows that I still recognize as the end of dayshift. My hand pulses quickly in time with my heart – but I push the sensation aside, focusing on the reunion ahead.

I hope they're as excited to see me as I am to see them.

My memory is hazy as I try to recall which stairs and turns guide me to my old life. The entire lower half of this castle twists in ways that frustrate me.

But I eventually encounter a minotaur, offering the bundle of apples meant for my friends in exchange for guidance. She accepts with a snotty huff, showing me to the narrowing stairway – the one with the misaligned stone steps.

A musty odor chokes the clean florals of the upper levels as I descend – replacing them with something far less pleasant. A stench clings to the walls here: sweat, excrement, and the sour tang of unwashed bodies. I hover on a step, my hand gripping the rough stone wall, and I consider turning back as I fight back a dry heave.

But flashes of my friends fill my mind: Eddie's eyes, Lilia's quiet loyalty, Maddie's kindness. I press on, stepping further into the gloom. The walls close in, and the ceiling lowers as I get closer to familiar territory.

Did I really survive 17 years down here?

The barracks are exactly as I left them, though they feel smaller now: grimmer. The rotted wooden doors are crammed too close together. As I peek inside one, the bunks are too small and filthy.

There are no bards nor storytellers, I realize, as the strange hollowness of the quiet unsettles me.

It's a world away from the polished level of the castle I've already adjusted to – the level with laughter and distractions. I feel ashamed of my disgust with the place.

*You're one of **them** down here. Not one of the attendants.*

I find Eddie first, her familiar frame hunched over a tablecloth drenched in red wine, attempting to remove the worst of the discoloration. She does a double take as I approach, her eyes widening in surprise before a grin sprawls across her face.

"Val?" She stands so quickly her stool scrapes against the floor. "What are you doing down here?"

I don't answer with words. Instead, I close the distance between us and kiss her – the kind of kiss that says everything I can't in the few moments we have.

Her steady hands drop the fabric with a *slap* against the stone floor and find my waist, pulling me closer. For a moment, it's as if I've never left. The stench and the mildew fade away – and it's just Eddie and me and our perpetual dream of surviving together.

But reality comes crashing back too soon as a knock sounds on the threshold. I pull away first, my cheeks flushing. The unpleasant surprise of seeing Lucian's leering gaze straightens my spine.

"You're filling out nicely up there," he comments, eyes traveling over my legs and chest. I square myself to him, feeling strangely steady against this low ranking guard I've always tried to appease.

"Not right now, pech. I am on business for Mara," I lie dryly, holding his gaze in challenge as I call attention to the fact that I *know* what he is.

A "pech." A mine working gnome stuck down here just like the humans – with just enough power not to complain about it.

My knowledge seems to unsteady him; his smirk drops as he surveys my face, looking for any falter in my stead. But finding none, he tips his head in acknowledgment.

"Very well, make it quick. And no more distracting the laundry team," he prowls back into the tunnel for more easy prey.

That was surprisingly simple.

"I need your help," I turn back to Eddie and hold up my hand – the tips of my fingers still angry and red. "Do you know what this is?"

Eddie is serious, examining my face instead of my fingers. "You're a lot more sure of yourself up there, it's a good look on you," she turns to my hand. I blink away the wall of authority I had thrown up at Lucian's intrusion.

"Where'd you get this?" Her brows draw together.

"Accidentally grabbed the wrong plant in the garden," I lie, my voice low. "I don't know what it is, but it's not spreading. The pain stops wherever I touched it."

She doesn't need to worry about my petty upstairs drama, I rationalize.

She turns over a few ideas in her mind, before she answers. "Lilia and Maddie might know. They traveled more than I did before this place."

She grabs my intact hand, leading me towards my old sense of safety. Lilia and Maddie are sitting on a bunk together in our room.

Their room.

Their heads are bent together in a quiet conversation. Both look up as we approach, their faces immediately relieved when they see me instead of the expected guard.

"Valerie!" Maddie exclaims, scrambling to pull me into a hug before overcorrecting her voice to a whisper. "What are you doing down here?"

"I need your help," I say again, showing them my hand without a wasted moment. "Do you know what plant could do this?"

Maddie takes my pale hand in her darker one, her callused fingers rougher than I remember as she examines the remnants of the site.

"Stinging nettle." Her voice is certain. "I grew up around this stuff. It's a nasty sting, but it won't kill you. There's an easy fix: baking soda. It'll help neutralize the acid from the needles. How did you get a hold of that plant?"

I nod, committing the information to memory. "It's a long and boring story."

But it might be one they can leverage, I remind myself.

I finally remember the food I brought: the small bundles tucked into my pack that don't require any trade. I pull them out, setting the carefully tied napkins on the bed before us.

"For you," I explain softly.

Lilia unties a bundle, a handful of grapes spilling onto the stained sheets below. She reaches for one, her fingers trembling slightly.

"Thank you."

Then she pops it in her mouth. Her usual shell cracks with the experience of such vibrant flavors, and a smile curves her full lips.

I sit with them as they scarf down the rest of the offerings, wishing I had brought more – vowing to do so next time. The conversation flows easily despite the days that have passed. I tell them about the food up there, the private bathing chamber, and my new forming circle of Flora and Chase.

I move on at the sadness in their eyes – like they think I'd ever *replace* them with new friends.

I explain my plan to seek out Mara upon her return and ask her to bring them all up under my supervision after a few more weeks of proving myself capable in the role. They listen intently, their faces a mix of hope and skepticism.

"It's not perfect up there," I admit, thinking of the daunting learning curve and threat from so many types of folk that come with the perks. "But it's so much better than this. And we'd be together."

The sunlight disappears entirely as we sit there, and I know it's time to go. I hug each of them tightly, promising to return soon. Eddie alone walks me to the stairs, her cracked fingers laced in mine until she has to let go.

"You're looking well, Val. Are you staying safe up there?" she prompts.

"I'm as invisible as I can be to the royalty." I show her the protective ring on my finger but avoid mentioning Sylas's attention at the revelry.

Her brows raise in question, but I shrug off further explanation. I think better than to tell her about any of that.

She wouldn't be able to do anything about it anyway.

"I'll talk to Mara and get you guys up there with me. I'll test the waters with her when she's back in a couple days," I promise before turning to leave.

Her smile doesn't quite reach her eyes as she watches me ascend the stairs. A cleansing sweetness lightens each step up. The relief as I gulp down the freshness adds to my guilt that my friends haven't experienced the true magic of this world.

I am going to impress Mara, and I am going to plant the seeds of my plan.

My friends deserve better than the barracks… everyone down there does.

Chapter 20

I shuffle back up toward my room without navigational help, my load lighter but my thoughts heavier. I attempt to plan how to approach Mara with this major request.

I'm not so naive to mistake her kindness for simplicity. She would definitely know if I tried to lie to bring my friends up from the barracks. So, I do what I know always clears my mind: I head toward the laundry room in Mara's tower.

I pass Starling in the halls, their hands full of old tomes, and they nod once in recognition.

Hey, that's a start.

When I pass Chase, this time hand in hand with Mara's brother, I avert my gaze. They disappear behind doors to rooms I don't know, and I think better than to snoop.

When I reach the laundry room, Mara's gowns are spread out on a table, forgotten in the last minute rush for the North Court. The delicate fabrics shimmer in the single candle I light for my dark blinded eyes. I run my fingers over the intricate embroidery, the threads catching on my callouses. It's strange, handling something so beautiful – so fragile – when my own hands feel so rough and unworthy.

I'm sure the brownie charged with these won't mind the help. I imagine the small servant returning in a few hours, only to find they have one less chore for the night. The thought brings a faint smile to my face as I dip the first gown into the soapy water, careful not to let the fabric snag on the basin edge. The task is familiar, almost meditative, allowing me to spend some of my new waking hours parsing out a way to help my friends.

"It's so much better than this. And we'd be together." But how? How the hell do I approach an almost-queen with a request like that?

It's not like asking for more time to study. That was asking for Mara to go be debaucherous in another region for a few days. This is asking for her to pity humans and do this with no personal gain… in perpetuity.

I scrub at a wine stain, my thoughts churning as fast as the water. My mind feels foggy, my ideas blurring together into nothing productive. I pause, reaching into my pocket for the vial Starling gave me. The deep red liquid swirls as I hold it up to the candlelight, its color less offputting tonight. I hesitate for only a moment before uncorking it and letting a drop fall onto my tongue. The taste is still bittersweet, but the effect overcomes me quicker than the first time.

A sharp clarity washes over me, my thoughts suddenly brighter like the chandeliers in the halls. Ideas flow through my mind, and I snatch a few to study.

Option one: I could be direct. Walk into Mara's chambers, bow low, and simply ask.

"Lady Mara, my friends are hardworking and loyal. They would be an asset to your team. Please, bring them up from the barracks."

I mock the concept before I can even fully finish it. The idea makes me cringe. Mara might be interested in me, but she's still a sidhe. Directness could come across as presumptuous – even disrespectful. I wring out the gown, the water falling back into the basin along with that dud of an approach.

Option two: I could be subtle. Drop hints during our conversations – weave my friends' virtues into stories about my past.

"Did I ever tell you about Lilia? She's the most loyal person I know. She'd do anything to protect those she cares about," I whisper to myself, testing the tone.

It's less whiny – more conversational – but still feels too calculated. And time is a luxury I don't have. Every day I exist up here, chipping away at her resolve, is another day my friends are stuck in the gloom downstairs. This approach would take months, maybe longer, to see results.

I hang the now clean gown to dry and move on to the next. My hands move automatically as my mind races, the potion's effects sharpening my focus.

Option three: I could appeal to her sense of fairness.

"My lady, it's not right that some of us live in comfort while others suffer below. My friends deserve better."

I try out the idea, but it's stupid. What would fairness mean to a sidhe? Would she even see their existence as the suffering it is, or just the natural order of things? She never seemed apologetic about my prior state when she pulled me onto her staff.

The stain on this gown is worse, a smear of something dark and sticky clinging to the hem.

"Mara, what do you do in these?" I groan, not wanting an actual answer and my mind imagining too many anyway. I scrub harder, my frustration bubbling to the surface.

None of these options feel right. None of them guarantee success. If I fail, I'll alienate Mara, and I'll have thrown away my chance to help my friends. I'll probably be left with nothing but regret, and potentially in an even worse position than before.

Calm down. This isn't helpful.

I pause – the gown dripping in my hands – and take a deep breath to center my spiraling thoughts. The potion's clarity is a double edged sword: sharpening my focus but also amplifying my anxiety.

There has to be another way. Something I'm not seeing.

Maybe I don't need to convince Mara to care about my friends. Maybe I just need to convince her that bringing them up would benefit her… maybe as a private team to make her new wardrobe once she's queen.

I hang the next gown to dry, my mind still turning over the potential of framing the request around Mara's interests.

"I don't know what will work," I admit to myself, dunking another stained gown deep into the sudsy water. I keep bouncing around ideas, debating my options as I work my way through her sullied wardrobe.

By the time I finish the last gown, the moon has settled far past its highest point for the night. And all I've come up with is that I should approach Mara toward the end of her night, when she's less energetic and more willing to sit down for a chat.

But what will I say in that chat?

My shoulder pops as I come up short with an answer.

"Fucking great," I laugh, the sound mocking me as it echoes around the empty laundry room.

Chapter 21

As I blow out the candle and head back to my room, the potion's effects are still coursing through me. There's only a small bit of time before sunrise, but my restless energy demands an outlet.

Walk around a bit to get some perspective. Remap the castle.

It's not a bad idea. I just need my notebook.

I'm almost back to the floor with my room when I hear it around the next corner: light footsteps on the main thoroughfare.

They stop when mine do.

Just some servant weary of the new scary human attendant, I tell myself – trying to pacify the instinctual fear clawing at the back of my mind.

But when I turn the corner, the fear grabs hold. Another attendant is there, her light blue uniform unmistakable. I've seen her before – at the revelry and in the towers. Her blonde hair and tall frame match the prince she serves.

Prince Sylas's attendant: Addie.

The sylph prowls toward me, an awful smile sprawls across her translucent face while wide eyed surprise fills mine.

That doesn't seem good.

"Well," she chirps at the chance of our encounter as she takes a step closer. "I don't think we've met properly yet."

She flashes a glint of metal from her pocket: the threatening silver of a blade.

I don't answer. I *can't*. My chest feels tight – my mind overwhelmed by primal fear.

"I'm Valerie," I try to de-escalate, forcing the introduction out.

"I'm well aware of who you are. You're an imposter among us," she snaps.

I take a step back, then another – my eyes darting to the path that leads to safety.

It's so close, but she's closer. *And* she's taller than me – with long arms and legs that show off how much faster she would be – not including her magical strength that all folk inherit.

"Your guard dog isn't here to protect you. I didn't think I'd actually get the chance to find you alone," Addie says delighted.

I don't wait for her to make the first move; I turn and sprint through the trafficked halls toward my room. My heart pounds in my ears in time with my boots as I run for the first time in twenty years, dodging bewildered guards and shocked brownies.

As I round the corner toward the safety of my room, Flora and another attendant await in the threshold of the space. They're relaxed, chatting in low, casual tones. I consider the possibility that their presence might be a boon.

Maybe an audience will keep her in check.

"Hi," I blurt, forcing my voice into a casual lilt as I step closer, making my presence known. The too light footsteps behind me don't slow.

Both attendants turn toward me, their faces calm: no surprise at my intrusion.

It's only when I'm within a few paces that I feel the unsettling pulse of a bargain reversed – the sensation that usually accompanied a pech guard's pleasured release when they had no intention of keeping their end. It feels like another arrhythmic heartbeat, stinging just enough to remind the bargainers that breaking a bargain is inherently *bad*.

My eyes snap to the malicious curve on Flora's full lip. I pause mid-stride, my gaze darting to the door still behind them. The sound of footsteps grows close.

One potential battle is easier than a prolonged war. I'll talk to Flora later and fix this.

My body reacts before my mind can second guess the decision. I twist to bolt back the way I came. Before my weight fully shifts, an arm snakes around my waist, yanking me upward. I suck in a breath – ready to scream – but a gloved hand slams over my mouth, stifling the sound as my head is forced against a chest.

"She did exactly what you two said she would. I guess I lose, I'll take your next few errands," Addie laughs behind me, her tone dripping with smug satisfaction as she hauls me off the ground – my thrashing body nothing for her folk strength.

They planned this. All three of them.

Panic surges through me, mixing with the potion already in my system.

My legs kick wildly, searching for anything to find purchase against.

But there's only air.

I'm dragged toward the open doorway of my own room, her grunts punctuating our diametric struggle as she fights to keep my limbs under control.

I can't let them get me in there. Not where there's no chance of help.

I scream, but the glove over my mouth muffles the sound. Then, all coherent thought leaves me as instinct takes over.

My teeth clamp down on the meat of her palm before I even realize I'm doing it, biting straight through the fabric. The metallic tang of blood floods my mouth. She shrieks in pain, and I bite even harder.

She shoves me away like I'm venomous. I'm free for a split second, before another pair of arms catches me – pulling me chest to chest with a second attendant.

Meadow – a pooka – stands a few inches shorter than me. But he still overpowers me quickly. Blood lingers on my tongue, sharp and coppery, and my mouth waters at the invading taste. I gather what little defense I can and spit directly into his eyes. He barely flinches, using his shoulder to wipe away the mess from his deer brown eyes, his expression darkening to lethal rage.

His forehead slams into mine in retaliation, narrowly avoiding gouging my eye with his antlers. The impact cracks through my skull with a sickening click of bone meeting bone – only thin flesh separating it. Pain reverberates through my head.

I miraculously don't black out, though we both stagger, shaking off the blow – vision swimming.

"Hey, we can't leave any extra marks her uniform won't cover," Flora warns.

Why is she letting them do this?

"Just teaching her a lesson," a spit covered Meadow grits between his teeth. There's a small victory in seeing his deer brown eyes also focus with effort after the headbutt – a river of faintly glowing crimson streaming down his forehead from the impact site. He twists me around to face the others, fingers digging into my arms enough to bruise.

Flora steps closer, her hand reaching for my chest with an aggression that makes me doubt my chances of survival.

"Flora, don't –!" I yell, the sound cut short as a fist drives into my stomach. The air rushes out of me, leaving me wheezing. My body tries to double over in defense, but I'm held upright and exposed.

"You're going to be quiet, and you're going to behave. Because if you draw any guards over here, we might have to silence you before you can talk," Flora orders, her breath hot – tinged with fairy fruit as it ghosts my cheek.

My eyes lock onto her smug, reddening face searching for any hint of her next move. But I'm too panicked to think clearly. The potion surges my worst fears to the surface of my thoughts, drowning any chance of reasoning.

In Addie's bloody gloved hand, she now holds a stinging nettle sprig – its leaves deceptively innocent looking in the rising sunlight. My stomach drops, a phantom sting ignites on my fingers at the memory of the pain.

"You…?" I gasp, head snapping to Flora. My knees threaten to buckle when she tosses her braid over her shoulder with haughty pride, confirming my suspicion.

My eyes dart wildly, searching for an escape – a weapon – anything useful. Flora is already reaching for my uniform again.

No.

The buttons are undone; the top torn away without ceremony. My focus narrows to my too quick breathing, ignoring the sudden chill against my skin as my vision darkens at the edges.

"That's better," Addie comments on my wordless panting.

"This is what you deserve. Human trash. Just remember that you *need* me to succeed up here. So keep this between us," Flora laughs, intoxicated with the power she wields in this moment.

Then I feel the sharp, prickling stab of the nettle against my chest. The sting spreads like wildfire as the leaves are rubbed over my torso – mottling my skin. My body is sent arching backward into the pooka behind me.

I can't stifle the scream that tears from my throat, raw and guttural, as the burning sensation consumes me.

"Shut up," Meadow snarls, shoving me to the ground with his full folk force. My arms catch me before my head collides with marble underfoot. But his weight is on top of me, pinning me to the marble below before I can right myself.

"Help!" I try to call, but emptying my lungs only makes refilling them harder. The nettle's sting on my chest fades into the background as a new, more immediate threat takes hold.

I can't breathe.

My lungs heave, the press against the floor aggravating the sting. A hand grips my hair, yanking me to Flora's lethal eyes.

"What's wrong? That potion not so helpful now?"

I feel another's fingers pat my pockets, before stealing the bloody red vial inside.

"You really *are* obedient. You've left more than enough for us to have some real fun when we're done with you." Addie pockets the vial in her own uniform. "I still cannot believe Starling just gave away the stuff so *easily.*"

It was all a fucking trick. I shouldn't have trusted any of them.

"Stop gloating and do it," Flora commands, gathering my hair away from my neck as Meadow readjusts his weight.

What are they doing?

The thought doesn't even fully form before a blinding pain erupts from the back of my neck. Flora's hands stay tangle in my hair, locking me in place, as a sickening scraping sound fills the hall.

I scream again and again, but every exhale is just a pathetic whistling with Meadow holding me down. My vision whites out as they cut into my flesh – dizziness threatening to finally pull me under. But I do what I've been doing so far and *will* myself to stay conscious. I squeeze my fists and curl my toes, encouraging the remaining potion to pump through my extremities and not out whatever gash they've carved into me.

"All done," Flora coos, bringing a small red morsel into view before me. My stomach almost empties as I recognize the crest of the kingdom on freckled flesh.

My brand.

"You don't belong here. Not anymore," she gloats.

"What the fuck are you all doing?"

A new voice from the corner of the staircase makes everyone go preternaturally still. I want to turn toward the source – to beg for their help – but the gash flayed in my neck makes any movement agonizing.

"Stay out of this, Unseelie," Meadow spits the word like a slur. My mind flashes with Chase's use of the word.

They're not in on this?

"Starling," I manage to call, before the pooka is off of me. I jump to my feet, the potion they gave me forcing my eyes to refocus instead of swim.

Starling is standing on the other side of the group, narrowed red eyes scanning the bloody sight before them. Their fierce gaze locks on the speck of flesh cut away from me.

"Didn't expect attendants to be so sloppy," is all Starling mutters before throwing themselves onto Meadow.

They're helping me?

I don't wait for answers, as their sharp teeth sink hard into the shoulder of their unprepared opponent. I gather up the waistband of my trousers and sprint downstairs towards the main hall in the next heartbeat, curses echoing behind me as the other two give chase.

Chapter 22

I don't know where in the castle I am anymore. My legs carry me with wanton choice up and down dawn lit halls. I take turns at random, trusting instinct over logic. Hoots and laughter follow: a constant reminder that I'm still prey.

The blood spilling down my back scabs over at some point, but the stinging on my chest worsens under the exertion of my muscles. Meadow's hooves never join their boots, and I silently thank Starling – hoping to make their actions worthwhile. The thrill in the voices behind me keeps me at an agonizing sprint.

Flora said they can't leave marks. But if they kill me, would that be more or less trouble for them to explain away?

My escape comes to an abrupt end as my body slams into what feels like a solid wall. My feet keep moving. The rest of me doesn't, and I curse when I hit the floor hard. The cold bite of stone jolts me back upright.

Flora's footsteps are closer than I thought.

A hand clamps around my forearm before I can decide where to hide, anchoring me in place.

How many of them are in on this?

"Give me a fucking break!" I shriek, a mix of panic and fury tearing through me as I twist to face their collaborator. But it's not another attendant.

It is so. much. worse.

Prince Sylas stands before me – furious. My arm goes limp in his hold, paralyzed by shock in an instant. And I do something I've spent so long training myself not to do: I meet his gaze and address him first.

"Help me," I plead.

So much for staying out of the royalty's way.

His eyes narrow at mine as if he can see every horrible fear that conjures behind them. The intensity is too much, and I quickly look away again, my focus dropping to where his hand still encircles my wrist. He must feel my pulse racing beneath his fingers, it's practically visible under my skin.

"And why should I clean up whatever mess you've gotten into?" he demands coldly.

The answer arrives before I can voice it.

Flora and Addie round the corner with the leaves in their gloved hands, their laughter dying as they freeze in place at the sight of us. Prince Sylas and I turn to face them. The power of his presence seems to still everything around us.

He sets an icy glare on the pair. Even though I'm not in its direct line, the look makes the hair on the arm he's holding stand on end. His grip tightens for a fraction of a second before he releases me, and I cradle my arms close to my chest, shrinking behind him out of their line of sight.

"Your Highness, she-" Addie begins after a synchronized bow with Flora, her voice trembling. Prince Sylas cuts her off with a single menacing step forward.

"This was not a part of your duties." The prince's voice is low, each word dripping with venom as he gestures to the plant in the tall one's hand, then to me. The two shake their heads, their faces ghostly pale at his tone. Flora opens her mouth to respond but thinks better of it.

Good choice.

"You'll be punished for your disobedience. Go to the lounge, and await my judgement." Prince Sylas's voice remains even, and they scatter back towards the room as ordered. Once they've disappeared down the stairs and into the morning dawn, my lungs finally remember how to work.

But the sigh of relief dies on my lips as the crown prince turns back toward me. His icy eyes pierce my skin when they glance down the length of my body, before meeting my face again.

Mortification heats my skin from head to toe. My marred chest is bare. The sunlight streaming through the windows leaves no shadows for me to hide in. His attention leaves me feeling more exposed than in front of all three of my attackers.

I cross my arms higher – protectively – over my chest, knowing how futile the gesture must seem to him.

Maybe the folk don't care about nudity, but I do.

The weight of his gaze feels like a physical touch, and I fight the urge to hunch my shoulders.

Another beat passes before the prince turns to the doorway behind us. A key is still in the lock, as it must have been before I careened into him moments before. He doesn't look back at me as he opens the door, the jingling keys the only sound in the hall now. Holding it open, he extends a hand towards the new space.

"Inside. *Now.*"

The command sends a jolt through me as his voice echoes off the empty walls. Without a word, I move around him and through the threshold.

The door latches behind us, and I flinch at the sound. I force myself to take a cleansing breath, but it does little to calm the anxiety suffocating me from the inside – adrenaline, the potion, and pure terror swirling inside me.

My eyes dart around the room, struggling to process the fact that I've been ushered into the prince's private chambers. The space is overwhelming in its opulence: every detail designed to assert dominance and luxury befitting his station. Floor-to-ceiling windows take the full length of one wall, draped in rich velvet curtains of deep blue and shimmering silver. The growing daylight filters through a purposeful part in them, letting the rich colors of the space shine.

I fiddle with the ring on my finger, while my gaze skims over the room's other details. A massive bed sits too close for comfort, carved from dark, polished wood. I scan the rug beneath it for imperfections to distract me from the prince's looming presence. But there's nothing.

Everything here is as perfect as him.

The competing pains on my neck and torso pull me back to my predicament. I uncross my arms to inspect the angry red welts crisscrossing my skin: the result of my own clawing nails during my escape. My fingers twitch with the urge to scratch again. The pain from my neck teeters on unbearable, but I keep my face blank – the thought of the prince discovering my missing brand is far more terrifying than the assault itself.

"Tell me what happened." He prompts.

If I tell him the truth, I'll only paint a bigger target on my back. He will never side with a human over folk.

A lie tumbles out before I can stop it.

"The other attendants and I were just-"

His hand is around my throat before I can blink, pinning me against the door with terrifying speed. Yet, there's no force in his grip – just enough pressure to tilt my head back. He forces me to meet his seething gaze.

The blood caking the back of my neck and hair crunches with the movement; my pulse races beneath his fingers.

"Do not lie to me," he growls. "Ever."

I nod quickly, lip quivering with unrestrained fear. The motion reignites the pain in my neck, searing deeper as the tentative scab splits. He doesn't release me; he doesn't even step back. Instead, he leans *closer*.

"What. Happened."

The scent of mint and lavender punctuates each word, disarming me in a way I don't want to think about.

This time, I don't dare lie.

"The other attendants attacked me in Mara's tower," I confess in a whimper.

His eyes drop to my chest, studying the angry red marks. Shame floods me, but I fight the urge to cover myself – to hide from his scrutiny and provoke further rage while his hand is on my windpipe.

"And that?"

"They used the nettles to voice their disagreement with Mara's choice of new attendant," I joke, attempting humor to dispel the tension. But my voice cracks on the last word, negating my effort.

Tears well in my eyes.

Do not cry. Do not cry.

The mantra repeats in my head, but my mind wars with too many overwhelming needs: to scratch, to cry, to sleep, to scream.

His gaze flicks back to my face, and for a moment, I think I see something surface in his expression: something too close to concern. But it's gone as quickly as it appeared, replaced by the same cold detachment. His hand slowly uncollars me, red coming away with his grip. His ruby coated fingers rub together, testing the consistency.

"You're bleeding," he points out.

Before I can explain, he turns me around, his fingers gentler than before as they brush the blood matted hair away from my neck.

"They cut off my brand," I blurt.

Horror washes over me as I feel him test the skin around the wound.

Will he make me replace it?

I hiss when his finger skims too close to exposed flesh, sparking another round of pain. He releases me immediately.

"An executable offense," he mutters to himself.

I don't know if he's referring to my omission or the attendants' actions.

But by the way he releases me abruptly, I assume it's the latter.

He steps away finally, leaving me gasping for air. I sag against the door, my arms instinctively crossing over my chest again as I stare at the floor.

He shifts in my periphery, noiseless even in his lounging slippers and simple robe. The thought that he must have been about to retire before I careened into him only solidifies my dread at his sudden interest in my well-being.

I can't tell Eddie about any of this.

I remain stationary, not allowing myself to scratch at the marks again. The itchiness numbs slowly into a constant radiant heat as my body adjusts to the toxin.

When the prince steps back into my line of sight, my eyes drift up to his hands. In them is a piece of dark fabric that he extends into my space.

"Put this on," he commands, his tone leaving no room for discussion.

I hesitate.

"I don't like to repeat myself, and you're making it a habit."

The unspoken threat spurs me into motion. I uncross my arms and accept the garment, pretending I'm unbothered by my bare skin or the lingering sting.

It's a simple cotton tunic, I realize as I unfold it. The prince doesn't look away as I pull it over my head, his stare challenging any comfort I might find in the gesture. The cut is oversized, falling shapelessly over my frame, and I can't help but wonder if he's worn it himself.

"Thank-" I curtail the apology.

Do not thank him, idiot.

"You're learning, at least," he sighs as he moves away again.

He remembers me from the atelier. Does he remember the connection between us too?

I catch a whiff of his lavender on the fabric. My eyes dare to wander further up, finding the prince's reflection in the window as he pours tea from a gilded pot into two waiting cups.

I seize the chance to study him with his attention elsewhere. His embroidered white robe is tied loosely, revealing the toned planes of his chest and stomach. His skin seems to glow beneath the fabric, as if he's crafted from moonlight itself.

For a moment, I let myself imagine what it would be like to touch him

– to feel the smoothness of his skin beneath my rough hands. The thought is reckless: dangerous.

Meadow's headbutt must have caused a concussion.

He turns back toward me, cups in hand. I look away quickly, my cheeks burning at my own fantasy. My eyes find the floor again.

"This night has been… eventful, Your Highness," I keep my voice steady despite the turmoil inside me. "I forgot my station earlier in the hall. It won't happen again."

"Mara doesn't return for a few more nights," he says, ignoring my excuse. "A lot could happen in that time."

A pit forms in my stomach.

Is he threatening me?

"Correct," I reply, smothering my fear beneath a veneer of professionalism. My head remains bowed, bracing for the shoe to drop.

"And you have no guard, no personal chaperon," he continues.

"Flora was one of the attackers, I assume that means I don't. Unless you count Chase staying in Mara's room," I answer, matching his coolness.

"Well, if that's the case, you will stay in my tower until my attendant and the others are dealt with," he says like it's that simple.

"What?" I blurt, my eyes snapping up to his.

His face remains impassive – his formal distance unchanged as he hands me one of the teacups. I don't remember reaching for it, but the warmth seeps into my fingers, grounding me.

"I will not repeat myself," he states.

"I understand what you're saying, but-" I begin, a boldness I didn't know I possess overtaking me.

"But nothing," he interrupts. "Mara has plans for you. Plans she barely tells me about. But I know they do not involve you being assaulted with nettles or killed this weekend. Which is why she'd tell you exactly the same as I'm telling you now: you are staying on this floor. At least for today. No one will test you with me present."

He gestures to the room around us. The authority of his words leave me reeling.

*Plans? He knows about her needing me to lie? Is **that** why he's helping me?*

I take a sip of the tea, letting the soothing mint distract me, if only for a moment. The prince does the same. We stand in uneasy silence, the weight of his decision hanging between us. My eyes fix on the teacup in my hands, watching the steeped specks at the bottom like they'll reveal my future.

I see nothing in them.

"Do not leave this floor until I tell you you can. For both of our sakes," he says, his voice returning to that cold formality.

"Yes, Your Highness," I relent.

"Now, go. Three doors to the left. Have him put something on those stings," he says, dismissing me with a wave of his hand.

I set the half full teacup down and excuse myself with a bow, my face still open with shock.

Chapter 23

I glance down the hall, finding the door the prince ordered me towards. It's unassuming, the same paneled wood as all the other doors. But I approach it like a test; I square my shoulders as I knock, reminding myself of my attendant status.

The door swings open instantly, revealing a heavy figure silhouetted against the dim light of the room beyond.

Mara's brother – Alistar – stands there, his close cropped copper hair accentuating the Otherworldly features of his round face. His eyes – a vibrant shade of gold like his sister's – look down the length of me in the prince's borrowed tunic and the blood that's been smeared into his handprint at my neck.

"You must be Valerie," he guesses. There's a knowing smirk playing at the corner of his lips, a glint in his eyes that feels both inviting and disturbing.

He's a courtier. He's Mara's sibling. He probably has to know everyone, I reason before I can wonder if Sylas or Mara warned him about me.

"I am," I confirm. "The prince sent me to get some help with this."

I yank the collar of the shirt low, showing the red welts on my chest. He tsks at the wounds, then steps aside, gesturing me in with a flourish that feels almost theatrical. "Well, come on, then. You're lucky I was studying to become a healer before Mara got swept up with the royalty."

I take a step inside. The room is smaller than mine and Flora's: a desk piled high with scrolls and books, a closed wardrobe… and Chase, half dressed on the bed.

When he sees me, his brown eyes bulge at my bloodied state. He leaps off the bed before I can blink and ties his robe closed.

"I'm gonna go. This is above my duties," he excuses himself, moving around me and out of the room.

Alistar crosses to the cluttered desk once we're alone. "So, you're the human who's caused such a stir. I have to admit, I was curious to meet you."

I shift uncomfortably, unsure how to respond. "I… didn't mean to cause any trouble."

He laughs, the sound bright and warm. "Don't worry, it's been all positive things. Now, why don't you take off that shirt, and let me see what we're dealing with."

My cheeks flush, even knowing how ridiculous it must seem. I avert my eyes from his while I remove the tunic. "I had an incident with stinging nettle. One of the servants downstairs told me that baking soda can help?" I try to remain even toned, clinical in conversation.

"Oh, I'm sure my sister will kill whoever did this to you, if Sy hasn't already." He says confidently. I can't resist gauging his reaction any longer, and find his eyes across the small space. They're curious: studying my face more than my chest. "I can see why Mara chose you. You're striking."

Before I can respond, the door opens, and Prince Sylas fills the threshold. His presence is like a magnet, instantly drawing both our attention.

His expression is as composed as ever, but there's a sharpness in his eyes that makes my stomach twist.

"Get a salve on her stings and stitch up her neck," the prince commands crossly.

Alistar straightens, his smirk fading as he raises a glass jar. "I was just getting to that."

The prince's gaze shifts to me, and I feel it like his hand at my throat again. He doesn't address me – searching for something in my eyes. After finding whatever he's looking for, he spins on his heel, the door closing behind him with a click as he leaves. The stifling silence that descends is heavy.

I glance at Alistar, unsure of what to say or do. He's already turned away, his attention on the jar.

"Let's get you cleaned up," he says warmly – even after Sylas's cold appearance.

The thought of his hands on my chest sends tension right to my shoulders. But knowing Prince Sylas trusts him to do this, I have no room to argue. I lower myself onto the wooden study chair he's pulled out for me.

"I didn't mean to make you uncomfortable," he murmurs. "You've had enough bad encounters today, I was trying to keep the mood light. I'm just here to help."

I force a smile to my lips, failing to calm the spiral inside me with the useless gesture. I meet his eyes again with some effort, and am greeted with genuine apology in them. Knowing he'd never say the words, it's the closest to one I have ever gotten from the folk.

"Okay," I answer, offering to accept the unspoken apology. His grin brightens again, reminding me of how others must view Eddie when she's a stranger.

"This might sting," he warns as he unscrews the lid of the jar. "But it'll help with the swelling and the itch."

I brace myself as he scoops a handful out, catching a whiff of sharp medicinal herbs in the cream. The moment the salve touches my skin, I yelp, my body jerking away instinctively. The coolness of the ointment is a shock, but it's the sting that follows that makes me grit my teeth. Alistar's hand pauses, his eyes flicking up to mine. "You still okay?"

"Yeah," I manage to say, though my voice is tight. "Just… keep going."

His touch is confident and quick as he spreads the salve over the inflamed skin, moving methodically from one welt to the next.

"You're handling this well," he says after a moment, conversational.

"I've had worse," I mutter, my eyes unfocusing on the wall behind him. The memory of steam burns flashes in my mind – of stitching through my hands and other injuries in the barracks that were left to heal organically.

I breathe, my jaw nearly popping out of socket by the time he finishes applying the salve. The worst of the sting fades quickly; a cooling numbness relieves the last of the itch. Alistar sits back on his heels, studying his work with a critical eye before wrapping the spots with bandages.

"Now for the neck." A pause. "This will *definitely* hurt more."

I swallow hard as I tilt my head forward to give him better access. The wound on my neck is brutally sensitive as Alistar prepares it, using a spare bandage to wipe away most of the blood from the sight.

"Whoever did this wasn't messing around," he comments under his breath, tossing the drenched scrap aside. Then he grabs a convenient needle and thread from the desk.

"I'll go as fast as I can," he promises louder when I don't respond. My hands lock around the seat of the chair, and I keep my head angled downward as he leans in with the tools. The first stitch is a blinding pain that makes me gasp, my knuckles bleaching white. Alistar works quickly, but there is no way to make this painless.

The irony of my current predicament isn't lost on me: a designer being stitched back together. I focus on the laughable reality, when the pain reaches a new apex that sends spots through my vision.

I begin to doubt my ability to handle the agony as he pulls the thread taut – the jagged edges of the wound meeting again. A growl fights its way out of my throat as he ties off the knot.

"Done," he says, sitting back. He wipes his hands on a clean bandage, an impressed expression on his face as he watches me slump to my elbows. "You're tougher than you look. That's good for your position."

I let out a shaky breath, my body trembling with the aftermath of the entire ordeal. "That's good to know… I think."

He chuckles warmly. "You should rest," he suggests. "You've had a hell of a night."

I pull the tunic gingerly back over my bandaged chest, not needing any further prompting. But as I stand, my legs wobble. Alistar is there in an instant, his hand steadying my back. His touch is comforting, and I let myself lean into him – enough to smell the same oleander that follows Mara.

"Easy," he murmurs close to my ear. "I've got you."

The knob turns again, and Prince Sylas is there – a filled bag in hand as he looks over the two of us.

"Time to sleep," he orders. I pull away from Alistar, my cheeks flushing as I regain my balance.

"Ok," I agree, though my voice lacks conviction.

Alistar leads me to the prince, his grip suddenly less molded to my body.

"She's in shock," he says quietly. "I'm not sure she'll be able to make it to bed on her own."

The words are muffled behind a roar in my ears. I look away from the two, unsure what to do.

There's something wrong – my blood not reaching my limbs – a cold sweat coating my brow. But before I can voice the concern, everything goes black.

Chapter 24

Consciousness returns in slow, syrupy waves.

First, the scent of lavender – rich and relaxing – woven into the linens pressed against my cheek. Then, the weight of a down filled duvet draped over me: impossibly soft. Finally, the quiet rustle of a turning page near my feet.

My eyes flutter open.

This is not my bed.

My body goes rigid as I take in the unfamiliar ceiling above – its gilded designs more intricate than in my room. There's only one place I've seen them in before.

Prince Sylas's room.

Panic sends me bolting upright: too fast. The room tilts, my vision spotting at the edges again. I suck air through my teeth as I clutch the sheets, waiting for the dizziness to pass.

The rustling page stops.

"Finally awake."

The prince's voice is devoid of its usual ice. I twist toward the sound, my pulse hammering in my ears.

He's sprawled on a chaise at the foot of the bed, one leg propped up to balance a book on his knee that he continues skimming. The nearby fireplace gilds the sloped beauty of his face. His hair is tousled enough to hide the tips of his pointed ears. He looks… *approachable.*

It's unnerving.

"How long was I out?" My voice is rough.

"All day." He flips the page, not looking up. "Alistar said you'd be disoriented. The nettle toxin mixed poorly with the shock."

I only have three nights to study.

My stomach lurches. "I should go-"

"You're not going anywhere." His gaze flicks to me, blue as sky. "You're still under my protection."

I swallow through the dryness in my throat. "But this is *your* bed."

"And?"

"And…" I flounder, heat creeping up my neck. My fingers twist in the sheets. "What if you'd wanted company?"

A beat of silence. Then he laughs – short, quiet, but undeniably *real*. The prince's lips betray a curve before his mask slips back into place. "Do you *want* me to have company?"

"No. I mean-" I stammer, mortified. "I just – I'm in the way."

"You're not." He counters. "I don't usually bring lovers in here."

The admission hangs between us, unexpected. I stare at him, my mind scrambling to reconcile this version of *the* Prince Sylas – the one who reads by firelight while a human hogs his personal bed – with the cold, untouchable prince I've seen up until now.

He watches my confusion with something like amusement. "You expected me to toss you into a guest room."

It's not a question.

"Yes," I admit.

"Guest rooms aren't guarded." He stands, stretching. The movement widens the gap of his robe enough to reveal more skin; I force my eyes away. "And after last night, I wasn't about to leave you exposed for another attack."

Because Mara needs me, I remind myself. *Because I'm useful.*

"Besides," he adds, nodding to the bandages peeking from my collar, "you may have woken in pain."

I blink. *He stayed to make sure I was okay?*

The prince strides to the bedside, his shadow falling over me. Up close, I see the inhuman flawlessness of him clearer: no blemishes – not even a freckle. He reaches for the glass of water on the nightstand between us.

"Drink." He offers it to me. "You're dehydrated."

I take it gingerly, our fingers brushing. A spark jumps at the contact, fleeting but electric. His eyes narrow, but he doesn't comment.

The water soothes my parched throat. I drain the cup, and run through the past night's events again with refreshed clarity. "Is Starling ok?"

He takes the empty glass before refilling it from a nearby carafe. "Ciaran's attendant is fine. You need to focus on your own recovery."

He hands the glass back to me, then makes his return to the chaise. I watch him skim his book, my mind racing with questions I'm too drained to voice. His eyes bounce up once, stern.

I turn onto my side facing away from him, and close my eyes – trying to will myself to go back to sleep as ordered. But every sound from that chaise makes my heart race. I've never been this close to one of *them* before. Not just the two of us, the rest of the world shut out. The unexpected generosity tortures my unsated curiosity, until I can't take it anymore.

"Your Highness?" I wince.

"Yes?" he replies softly.

"Why are you doing this? You don't have to be so… involved."

There's another unbearably long stretch of quiet. And for a moment, I think he's not going to answer at all. But then he finally does. "Because you're under my protection as a subject of this kingdom. And because you're important to Mara."

I swallow hard. *Important to Mara. Not to him. That's good. I need to stay away from his attention.*

"Oh," I reply evenly. "I see."

I close my eyes, trying to quiet my racing thoughts, but it's pointless.

"I don't think I can sleep anymore," I confess after I hear him turn another page.

Sylas snaps his book closed, his gaze lingering on my face before he stands – deciding what to do.

"Come with me." He offers. "There's something I want to show you."

I freeze, reminding myself of every reason I should absolutely *not* go anywhere alone with him. But my curiosity has been poked enough to overwrite my rationale.

"Shouldn't I… head to the library? I promised Mara I would study while she was gone-"

"Mara isn't back yet," he interrupts. "And who better to teach you about the royalty other than someone part of it?"

It's practical, I tell myself, though the voice in my head sounds unconvincing. I slide out of bed, straightening my borrowed, too-big tunic.

He leads me through the castle at a leisurely pace. We walk by a few servants who bow their heads as we pass, but no one seems shocked at the prince's unusual casualness… or mine. I keep my eyes forward, refusing to acknowledge what they all must be assuming happened in his bed today.

This is a bad idea, I think. But my feet keep moving of their own volition. We step outside into the gardens, the moon hanging heavy in the sky – its pale light bathing the gardens in a magical glow. And I try not to cower at the expanse above.

It's ridiculous to be afraid of the sky.

The cool night air is a welcome relief after the stagnant confines of the castle. A mix of jasmine and damp earth welcomes us as we travel deeper into the greenery, lost in easy conversation. Sylas keeps his voice low and measured as he answers my question about the children's book I found in Mara's tower.

"My father *helped* defeat the Tyrant King," he corrects. "No single sidhe could *have* done it alone. Not even him."

I glance up at him. Moonlight catches the sharp line of his jaw: the pride in his eyes discussing his father's work. A smile tugs at my lips as he explains.

"The Tyrant didn't just steal our magic." His tone is insistent. "He consumed it. Left the entire land practically barren under his reign."

A shiver runs down my spine. "Why?"

"Because he believed magic wasn't meant for everyone." The words are too matter-of-fact. "His court was a slaughterhouse. The more magic he took, the weaker we became – until we began to die. There were once thousands of sidhe. Now… maybe several hundred of us on the whole continent."

The image is visceral: a king feasting on his own people's magic, gorging on their power just so they couldn't have it. I swallow hard. "And your father stopped him?"

"He did." Sylas's gaze flicks to me, piercing. "The current rulers of the Cardinal Courts: my father, Margaret's mother, Liam's father, and Eugenia's aunt: they cornered him in his own throne room after forging an alliance with lesser folk." His fingers tighten into a fist subconsciously, like the risk they took still worries him. "It took all of them to tear him apart."

I exhale slowly, the weight of the truth settling over me. *This* is the history they don't put in the lineage charts – the blood beneath the crowns.

Sylas turns abruptly, leading me down a narrow path hedged by towering rose bushes. Their thorns glint like teeth in the dark. "The entire continent was divided into the four cardinal directions after," he continues. "Each of our elders took a segment of the Tyrant's territory – a quarter of his power. The remaining sidhe were titled. The lesser folk granted independence as part of the bargain."

"And the magic?"

"Some returned to the land. Some… didn't." His jaw tightens. "The scars remain."

We venture farther than I've ever gone before – farther than I've ever *seen* before. A sense of unease runs through me as we pass entire mazes with no other souls around.

What the hell does he want to show me?

I can't bring myself to voice the question, knowing it will likely shatter the illusion of whatever fragile thing is between us right now.

Finally, we reach a large, domed structure at the edge of the gardens. Sylas pushes the door open.

I come to a dead stop. "You have an aviary?"

His mouth quirks into an almost smile. "You sound surprised."

"I didn't think you'd keep *birds*," I admit.

"I don't." He gestures for me to enter. "I keep gryphons."

The warmth of the aviary hits me first, humid and sweet with blooming orchids. A chorus of chirps and rustling feathers follows immediately. Gryphons of every color perch on branches, their plumage shimmering like polished gemstones – their catlike ears and hindquarters making them unmistakably magical. Some are no larger than my thumb. Others have wingspans as wide as my arms. They all watch us with keen, intelligent eyes.

Of course they're real too.

Sylas leans against a post, watching me watch them. "I like to surround myself with pretty things."

As if on cue, one dives from its perch – a magnificent creature of cobalt and gold – and lands on his shoulder. It nips playfully at his ear, and for the first time, I see Sylas grin.

I feel myself lean towards him unintentionally.

Dangerous.

"They're also spies," he says, stroking the bird-like crest with a fingertip. "Messengers. Little thieves with excellent hearing and a penchant for repeating what they overhear."

The gryphon chirps, offended, and Sylas chuckles a low, rich sound that quickens my pulse.

I force myself to focus on the aviary and the gryphons, but the way he looks in this moment – relaxed, almost boyish – makes it impossible to avoid admiring him too. "So you… collect them?"

"To an extent." He lifts his arm, and the gryphon takes flight. "Most were rescued or hatched here. They wouldn't survive in the wilds outside."

The blue streak circles once overhead before landing on *my* shoulder. Its claws are gentle; its weight is barely there. It stays just high enough to avoid the wounds on my skin. My stunned wide eyes note the minute color shift of its feathers at this distance – from blue to violet and back again – as it tilts its head, studying me right back.

"She likes you," Sylas murmurs.

I hold very, *very* still. "What do I do?"

"Whatever you want." His voice is softer now, soothing me more than the gryphon. "You've already passed the test, Valerie."

The creature trills, rubbing my ear like a cat, and I giggle: bubbly and way too similar to the old Valerie of the human world.

"They're beautiful," I whisper in awe.

Sylas steps closer, letting the gryphon transfer back to his shoulder. "They're young and beautiful," he adds. "But they're also resilient. Like you."

I turn to him, surprised by the comparison. His gaze is fixed on the gryphon, but there's something in his eyes… something almost *soft*.

Don't fall for it, I warn myself. *He's a prince. He's a sidhe. He's dangerous.*

But the way he looks now – the way his voice wraps around me like the tunic he's let me steal – makes it hard to remember why.

We stand in silence for a while, admiring the creatures as they dart and play. The tension between us is tactile: a quiet undercurrent that grows stronger with each passing moment. I can feel his eyes drift back to me occasionally, and I force myself not to do the same.

But eventually: slowly, *deliberately*: he reaches out and takes my callused hand. His fingers are so careful as they guide me to face him, giving me the chance to pull away.

I don't.

"Valerie Harlow," he says my name like a treasured secret. "There's something I need you to know."

I swallow hard, my heart suddenly in my throat. "What is it?"

He sees the tension overcome me, and his face falls.

"I don't want you to be afraid of me."

The vulnerable admission softens my emotional calluses.

He turns my hand over in his, his thumb spinning the ring on my middle finger. "From the moment I saw you in the atelier, I knew you belonged up here."

My breath catches.

He can't lie.

The words are too heavy – too *intentional* – to be mere flattery.

His gaze locks on mine confidently, the bared truth emboldening him. "You're not just an attendant. You're…" He hesitates, searching for the right word. "Special. To me."

The word settles over me with a comforting weight. *Special.*

Not just to Mara. To *him* too.

I should pull away. I should remind myself of every reason this is a terrible idea. But his touch feels like destiny, his attention a fate I'm not sure I can avoid.

"Why are you telling me this?"

"Because I know you felt it the first time we locked eyes. And I *know* there is something unique about you. Understand?" His voice is low, earnest. "You are safe here while we decide what to do about that… feeling."

The confirmation that he felt the same thing that night lingers between us: fragile and fraught. I think of my friends in the barracks – of the deal with Mara and the vipers' nest of court politics.

"I can't get too close." My voice trembles as I come to terms with the heartbreaking reality. "You're the crown prince. I'm your betrothed's attendant. It's too complicated."

He doesn't let go of my hand. "I forget humans can be so cautious," he murmurs, voice tinged with amusement. "But the truth remains."

I nod, my cheeks burning as he plants a chaste kiss to my knuckle. We stand there a moment longer, the gryphons chirping softly around us, his thumb tracing patterns on my skin.

Then, with a quiet sigh, he releases me. "Come on," he orders, his princely veneer sliding back into place. "Let's get you back to the castle."

I follow him back out to the garden, my mind unsure how to handle tonight's unexpected revelations. The night air feels colder outside as the magic of the moment fades.

I don't know what to make of Sylas's words or his touch. But one thing is clear: nothing about my place here is as simple as I thought.

Getting close to him would be a mistake, no matter if he feels a connection or not, I remind myself.

As we near his tower again, I need space: a moment to think without his presence fogging my mind.

"I'm still not tired, since I slept in so late. I might try to get some more reading done," I chance the request, jabbing a thumb towards Mara's staircase as we come to a halt in the main hall.

Sylas doesn't reply immediately, his face going through too many emotions for me to read clearly. One moment, he looks like he'll argue – his protection order overriding my ask. Then the next, he nods, granting my request.

"If that's what you want."

I freeze, caught off guard by the permission. "You're not going to stop me?" His newfound belief in my safety makes me more uneasy than relieved.

"Your attackers have been dealt their punishment. They won't bother you again," his tone slides back into courtly formality, and I hate that I notice. "I just wanted the chance to show you the aviary – steal a moment alone with you to talk."

My jaw drops.

But instead of asking about what those punishments might be, I offer a half hearted bow – my movements hindered by the bandages.

"Well, in regards to both of those topics: that is good to know," I match his tone.

Then I turn and leave before he can say more, grateful for the reprieve. I jog up the fights to the library of Mara's tower, unable to organize my feelings and thoughts right now.

Better focus on studying instead.

It's quiet when I arrive, the towering shelves like a protective burrow I dig deep into. I find Starling back there sitting at a table, fluffy black hair obscuring a book I can't decipher. I notice for the first time the faint reflection of their red eyes in the dim light.

They're ok. I pacify my resurfaced concern over them, remembering their defense when I was attacked.

They look up – unsurprised as I approach – like they heard my muffled steps on the rug.

"Are you recovering well?" they ask.

I shrug, sinking into the chair across from them at the table. "Physically? Yes. But mentally..."

Starling nods, closing the book and setting it aside. "The Cardinal Kingdom has a way of doing that to people."

I let out a shaky breath, my hands suddenly trembling as I clasp them together on the table – preparing to do something Flora told me never to do. "I just… I wanted to thank you. For saving me back there during the fight. I don't know what would've happened if you hadn't stepped in."

A smile softens their sharp features. "You aren't supposed to thank me. You're giving me way too much leverage. Besides, I did what anyone would've done."

"No," I say, my voice firmer now. "Not anyone. You risked yourself for me. And I… I don't know what to do to repay you for that."

They tilt their head, studying me with those piercing red eyes. "You don't owe me anything."

I laugh without humor, my frustration overwhelming my gratitude. "I just have trouble believing *you*, a folk attendant, would be so willing to risk your safety on my behalf without a catch," I drag the words out, explaining my hesitancy to accept their selfless deed for the surface level kindness they claim it to be.

"If it makes you feel better, I'm fine. Great, even," they reply.

I frown, my gaze dropping to their black clawed fingers. I hadn't noticed their sharpened tips before. "Are you sure? You were hurt, I saw him get a few hits-"

"I heal quickly," they interrupt. "It's part of being Unseelie."

There's that word again.

"Unseelie?"

Starling's head bounces side to side, physically weighing how much to tell me. "We're different from the other folk you've been around. Stronger. Faster. But it comes at a cost."

I want to ask more – to press them about what that cost is and if I can help pay it – but something in their tone stops me.

So instead I relent, accepting their story for now. "Well, I'm glad you're okay. Our attackers were taken care of. Sylas told me."

Their eyes narrow slightly. "Did he now?"

I nod, my stomach twisting at the memory of Sylas's too distant tone when he'd mentioned it. "He basically said they won't bother us anymore."

Starling leans back in their chair, their voice full of more doubt than relief. "You should watch your back around him."

My shoulders deflate. "I know. Everything just feels so complicated. I don't think I can trust myself to know what's right anymore."

They watch me for a moment, studying the way my thumb spins the ring on my finger. "You *should* trust yourself. You've survived however long you had to to get here, didn't you?"

Their confidence feels misguided. "Not alone though. I had my friends down in the barracks. And getting pulled up here was chance. What about you?"

"I don't need friends. Humans and Seelie are too frustrating, and most Unseelie are *worse*." They tip their chair back to balance on two legs.

"No," I smile as they focus on the wrong part of my sentence. "How did you end up working for Prince Ciaran, the South Court's ambassador? He doesn't seem like the easiest person to attend."

The chair thuds back down onto all fours. "Ciaran and I… understand each other. We're both outsiders, in a way. Him, because of his reputation. Me, because of what I am."

I lean forward slightly. "What do you mean 'his reputation'?"

"He's ruthless and self-serving, if you believe the court gossip." They elaborate. "He has no throne he's in line for. His mother bore him before meeting the king in her court and marrying. His title is honorary – kept as long as he proves a fruitful member of the South Court."

I bite the inside of my cheek to keep a smug grin from my lips at the reality of the cruelest sidhe's life. They continue. "He's not trusted. Hence the Unseelie attendant assigned to his station."

My smugness falters. "That's a bad thing? Having an Unseelie attendant?"

Starling snorts, the sound surprisingly warm for the topic. "In the West, there's not a worse option."

I turn their words over in my mind, completely baffled as to what could possibly be wrong with Starling or the creature that gave me my ring.

"He gives me what I need to do my job, and I help him navigate the courts from our level. We're both working to better ourselves, in our own ways." They speak before I can ask any questions.

I am struck by the quiet strength in their demeanor. "You're not like the others around here," I say softly. "You don't... play games."

Starling's smile fades to a grimmer thin line. "Games are for the Seelie. My kind is much more straightforward."

I nod, their words hitting closer to home than I'd like to admit. "I don't like to play games either."

They lean forward to catch my eye. "Then don't play. You're more valuable to them than you think. And you have allies, whether you realize it or not."

The words hang in the air, heavy with meaning I don't fully understand. *Maybe I'm not as alone as I thought.*

But before I can ask for clarification, they're rising from the table. They sling their bag over their shoulder.

"I need to get going. It's close to daybreak," they offer as they turn to leave.

"Goodbye then?" I call to their hustling back. The clawed wave they toss as they jog down the aisle makes the corners of my mouth lift.

Chapter 25

I push open the door to my chambers, pausing at the threshold to take a steadying breath. I know Flora won't be here.

She might not ever be here again.

But seeing her side of the room entirely blank already – no furniture, no seal skin, no mess cluttering the space – is jarring. The emptiness feels like a lesson: a reminder that weeks of trust can be entirely dismantled in a moment.

I use my full body weight to drag the single remaining bed to the middle of the room in an attempt to fill out the space. It helps a little, but it feels too spread out now. I organize my scattered notes of maps and questions that will never be answered by the intended recipient. The sheets are almost too heavy to throw into the garbage, entirely unrelated to their weight. But I manage to drop them into the trash, and the room becomes easier to breathe in.

The less evidence that this place once housed two people, the better.

Pale dawn light filters through the window, reminding me that I've survived the night without Starling's potion.

I should feel relieved. But instead, the changes forced feel burdensome.

*I shouldn't feel bad – **she** attacked **me**.*

I throw myself into bed when the thought doesn't placate my guilt, mentally noting that I'll need to shift it a bit more to the left. But I can't right now. I cover myself in thick blankets, lying there and staring at the plain ceiling.

The silence of the room presses down on me, making it hard to breathe again.

It's strange, being alone.

For seventeen years, the sounds of roommates were a constant presence. Sometimes a comfort, often a torment. I didn't realize how much I relied on the little noises – snores and shifting creaks – to feel safe enough to sleep until they were absent.

Now, the room feels too exposed to be safe. I turn onto my side, pulling the blanket tighter around me, but sleep refuses to come. After hours of faking it, I surrender.

I groan as I get up, settling instead at my desk with a large tome.

A History of Western Fae is embossed in gold script along the spine. I crack open the ancient thing, running my hands through my curls in an attempt to tame them.

The knob turns, and I freeze – fingers still tangled in my hair.

"Valerie?" Sylas's voice is unmistakeable.

I don't turn around immediately, frazzled and unprepared for another private meeting behind closed doors.

What could he possibly want at this hour?

"You didn't come back," he says, stepping inside. "I wanted to make sure you were alright. That I didn't scare you off earlier."

I finally twist in my chair to face him. His eyes brighten in a way that makes my stomach flip when our gazes connect.

"I'm fine, Your Highness," my tone doing little to mask my exhaustion. "Just restless."

He trails a lithe hand over the headboard of the bed I've dragged to the center. His gaze lingers on the empty portions of the chamber where Flora's things once were.

"It's lonely in here now," he observes.

The words hit like a blow.

I shrug. "I'll adjust."

He hums, unconvinced. Then, to my shock, he sits on the edge of my bed, as casually as if he'd done it a thousand times before. The sight is so surreal.

The Crown Prince of the West Court, perched on my borrowed bed like a common visitor.

"What are you reading?" he prompts, nodding to the book.

"A History of Western… Fae."

"Ah." His lips quirk at my use of the word, amused I'd be bold enough to actually say it to his face. "The dry version, I assume. Full of lies by omission."

A startled laugh escapes me. "Is there another version?"

"The one I could tell you." He leans back on his hands. His posture is relaxed, but his eyes – _Sweet Jesus, his eyes_ – are alight with something impish. "If you're interested."

He knows I am.

I turn the book toward him. "The Tyrant King's court. It says here his allies were 'subdued' after his death. What does that mean?"

Sylas's smile widens. "It means they were slaughtered. Their blood watered the soil where the current thrones took root."

"Even the children?"

"Most, though the few surviving ones have long since been reintegrated." His gaze holds mine, unflinching. "Power is inherited here. And my father wasn't about to let rivals grow strong enough to challenge his claim."

I flip to another page, eagerly. "The House of Lord Rakan. Allies or enemies?"

"Both." Sylas shifts, stretching his legs out. "They trade with us but plot with the East. Rakan has a habit of poisoning his escorts."

"Charming."

"Isn't it?" He smirks. "Next question."

And so it goes: page after page, family after family. Sylas peels back the polished veneer of court histories, revealing the rot beneath. He tells me about everything from alliances forged in betrayals to blood feuds disguised as trade disputes.

Hours slip by. The sun outside the window begins its descent, stretching the shadows across the walls in a way my eye still reads like clockwork. My eyelids grow heavy, my head nodding forward despite my best efforts.

"You're exhausted," Sylas murmurs.

"Maybe." I rub my eyes. "But this is… helpful."

"Valerie."

I jolt upright at the sound of my name on his lips again. He's standing over me now, closer than he just was.

"You need sleep." His voice is softer.

"I can't," I admit, the confession pitiful even to my own ears "It's too quiet. Too… empty."

I expect a lecture: a cold reminder that I'm weak and I must thicken my skin if I want to survive.

Instead, Sylas does the last thing I expect.

He bends down and lifts me into his arms.

"Wha-" I gasp, my hands flying to his shoulders. His grip is firm, disturbingly effortless.

"Hush," he carries me to my bed.

He sits beside me, his back against the headboard, one long leg stretched out on the mattress parallel to my stubbier one.

"Ask your questions," he instructs, picking up another book on the nightstand. "I'll answer until you sleep."

I stare at him, my pulse racing.

This is the prince who held me by the throat for lying? The same one who looked at me with nothing but fleeting entertainment in the atelier?

Exhaustion wins. I sink into the pillows, my body giving in finally as I curl onto my side, facing him. "The House of..." I yawn, the name slipping away.

Sylas's voice is a low rumble as he reads from the book aloud instead. His narration blurs into noise, the cadence of his voice weaving through my dreamy thoughts.

Safe. The realization floats through my haze. *I feel safe.*

My eyes drift shut. Just before sleep takes me, I reach out blindly, my fingers brushing his wrist. "Stay for a bit."

A pause. Then his hand covers mine. "As you wish."

Chapter 26

I wake alone, questioning if my memories of yesterday were just a dream.

The bed is cold where Sylas had been sitting, the indentation in the mattress the only proof he'd stayed at all. The book is closed on the nightstand, a single sheet of parchment tucked beneath it.

I snatch the note with trembling fingers.

You ask fair questions. If you have more, my study is open to you.

No signature. No royal seal. Just those words, written by the hand born to one day rule the West. I trace the ink with my thumb.

Why does this feel like a gift?

The door between mine and Mara's room cracks open before I can overthink the offering. Chase leans against the frame, arms crossed, a smirk playing on his lips. "Evening. You were out cold when I checked earlier."

I scramble to tuck the note under my pillow, but not fast enough. His grin widens, "Oho. What's that?"

"Nothing." My voice is too high. "Just... notes. For studying."

"Mhm." He saunters in, dropping onto my study chair like he owns it. "So. You're involved with the prince, huh?"

"*No.* Absolutely not," I pull the blanket up to my chin to shield myself from his prying.

"Could've fooled me." He pushes my notes around on the table. "He doesn't usually take interest in humans."

A flush creeps up my neck. "What's that supposed to mean?"

Chase's eyes glint. "Oh, you know. Late day visits. Private lessons. Letting you sleep in his bed-"

"He was just helping me study!"

"Sure, sure." He grins. "And if he *helps* you into his bed properly, you'll tell me, right? Every detail?"

I hurl one of my many pillows at his face. "We're barely even friends. You can't ask that of me."

He catches it with a laugh. "Come on. It's *Sylas*. Cold, gorgeous, never-looks-twice-at-anyone-who-isn't-sidhe Sylas. And yet..." He gestures at the note peeking out from under my pillow. "You're something special."

The word choice sends a jolt through me. *Special*. The same word Sylas had used.

"I don't know what he sees in me," I mutter.

"You don't have to. He sees it anyway." He rises for the door, tossing over his shoulder: "If you do go to his study, wear the blue bodice. The one that laces up the front. Trust me."

The door shuts behind him before I can throw something heavier.

Alone again, I slump back against the pillows, groaning with my face in my hands.

Chase isn't wrong. Sylas's attention is flattering and *terrifying*. But...

I pull the note out again, rereading it like the words might rearrange themselves.

"If you have more questions..."

As if it's that simple – as if I'm not playing with fire by considering it. I tuck the parchment under my mattress, along with my guilt over doing this behind Eddie's back.

"I won't go," I tell myself. But my own voice doesn't sound committed as the possibilities stretch before me.

Mara returns tomorrow, then he'll lose interest.

I crawl out of bed and change my bandages, wincing preemptively as I expose them in the mirror. My finger tips test the worst areas; they're much less sensitive today. Alistar's salve has encouraged new pink skin to replace the open wounds already.

Good. It probably won't scar.

I throw myself into my duties with renewed energy once I'm dressed, if only to keep from thinking about *him*.

I assist the maid team, scrubbing Mara's chambers until they gleam: fresh linens, polished silver, windows thrown open to allow in the last of the summer's warm breeze before fall fully descends.

I call for a fresh bowl of ripe fairy fruit to finish the scene, letting a dryad – the tree-like creatures who tend the greenery – bring it up so I don't have to go near the trees. Flora may have been more of a snake than a seal, but her advice to never visit the fairy fruit orchard was sound.

Too much risk of exposure.

I pluck a vase of pink oleander from the safe sections of the gardens for her vanity myself.

Her favorite flowers. I tell myself. *She'll be pleased.*

But my hands still when I find a hairpin tangled in the rug: one we all missed: silver, tipped with a tiny sapphire.

I pocket it before I think too deeply about Flora's absence or Mara's tangled hair and decide to study a bit more.

The library is quiet, the few courtiers who usually find their way here absent, likely sleeping off whatever mess I saw some brownies struggling to carry downstairs.

I spread my notes across the table, forcing myself to focus on lineage charts and trade agreements. It's starting to make sense – the drama behind the names making them all more real.

Sylas's voice in the daylight, unraveling histories they don't teach attendants. The way he'd sounded relieved when I asked him to stay-

"Fuck."

I slam the book shut, earning a glare from a passing leprechaun archivist.

I need air.

Chapter 27

The fall leaves are already beginning to show when I make it to the king's courtyard out front, their colors grayscaled in the moonlight. I step on a crunchy one, the sound like a clacking beak… and remember the aviary: the gryphons and the way Sylas had smiled when the cobalt one nipped his ear.

"They're young, beautiful, and resilient. Like you."

A footstep crunches on another leaf behind me.

I whirl, heart in my throat to find Chase grinning at me, a basket of fruit tucked under his lanky arm. "Expecting someone else?"

I scowl. "What do you want?"

"Just delivering a snack to a new friend." He plucks a grape from the bunch, popping it into his mouth. "You missed dinner."

"I've been busy."

"Mhm." His eyes dart to the path leading back inside toward Sylas's staircase. "Busy avoiding someone tonight."

I snatch a handful of grapes from him. "Don't you have a courtier to attend, escort?"

"Most are napping. Which means I get a break." He leans in, lowering his voice less playfully. "So? Are you going to go?"

"Go where?"

"His study." His boyish face lights up.

I throw a grape at him, cross. "Goodbye, Chase."

He laughs, letting my wild shot bounce off his arm. "You're blushing."

"Stop it," I growl.

His usual smirk settles into something more thoughtful as he watches me. Then he digs in the basket for something.

"You think he'll hurt you," he says, not looking up.

I pluck another morsel from the bunch in my palm, answering around the bite. "Isn't that what the folk do?"

"Most of them." He agrees, pulling out the note from my room. I gasp as I snatch it, violated by the idea that he'd go through my belongings behind my back.

"Then why should I just forget about the risk?" I bark. "Because he carried me to bed? Because he left me this note?" I wave it between us.

Chase exhales through his nose. "Because he *cares* about you."

I blink, fist pausing mid air.

"He's not king," Chase presses. "Not yet. But when he is…" He meets my eyes. "Imagine what changes someone like *you* could inspire."

The implication is heavy, dangerous… tempting.

I think of Sylas's hand covering mine.

"As you wish."

Of the way he'd let me sleep in his bed and told me stories that he probably shouldn't have.

"You're saying I should – what? Entertain him for political gain?"

Chase grins, but there's no mockery in it now. "I'm saying the future king is currently *very* interested in a human who isn't afraid to talk back to him. That's a hell of an opportunity."

My hand slaps back down to my side.

An opportunity. Not just for me. For my friends. For every human in the barracks. For the ones who'll come after us.

Chase's brown eyes drift down to my uniform as he steps closer. "Good thing you're wearing the blue bodice," he comments, but his tone has changed.

He isn't teasing anymore.

He's strategizing.

As he passes me, patting my shoulder as he does, I stare at the path to Sylas's study.

I make it to the main hall, and stand at the crossroads of temptation: left to Mara's tower, right to Sylas's.

The note burns a hole in my resolve to stay clear of his attention.

"If you have more questions…"

I glance down at my choice of uniform. *Just one.*

I turn right.

The walk to Sylas's study feels endless, each step heavier than the last. The door is slightly ajar when I arrive, golden firelight spilling into the hallway. I raise my hand to knock, but Sylas's voice calls first.

"Come in, Valerie."

Of course he knew I was coming.

The study is exactly as I expect it to be: walls lined with ancient tomes and a massive oak desk strewn with correspondence.

Sylas stands by the hearth holding his lunch. His sleeves rolled up to prevent the juice from staining them.

"You came," he observes around a chunk of diced fairy fruit.

I lift my chin. "You said I could ask more questions."

At that, he turns. The firelight catches the blue of his eyes, turning them nearly translucent in the glow. "And what does the curious girl wish to know tonight?"

The familiarity in his tone warms me more than the fire.

"Humans. Our place here." I cross my arms. "We're property. And I don't know how you can expect me to think you care for me when you could snap your fingers and have me disappear like Flora."

Sylas's expression shutters. "My father's laws are not mine."

"But you enforce them."

He sets down the bowl. "What do you want me to say? That my father's laws are strict? That the system is unequal?" A bitter smile. "That's nothing new."

"But you're the crown prince," I step fully into the room, my voice shaking as I push back. "You could change things."

"Could I?" His question is sharp, humorless. "You think my father listens to anyone except himself?"

I don't know how to respond, so he does.

"I'll be king one day. And then things might be different. Once Mara and I are wed – once we've birthed an heir – my father plans to abdicate the throne to me," he explains, wiping the last remnants of the red juice from his mouth.

My shock at the openness of his words escapes for a moment.

"And then what? You get to be the one who controls us – controls *me*?"

He flinches like I've slapped him. "You think I'm a monster. But do you want to know what I could be like if I truly just wanted to control you?"

My brow furrows. "What do you mean?"

"Let me give you a demonstration of my power." He lifts his chin, searching my eyes.

I stare at him, waiting for an elaboration that doesn't come. My curiosity wins out against my patience, and I nod before logic can stop me.

"Take off your ring," he commands.

I clutch the silver band to my chest instinctively.

"Never take it off in the presence of the folk."

The rule filters through my thoughts.

"Trust me," he challenges.

It's a terrible idea.

But the way he looks at me – like this means so much more than *just* a demonstration of his power – has me considering it. I slide the ring off before I can think better of it, trusting him in hopes that one day he will trust me too.

The effect is immediate.

Glamour crashes over me like a wave, drowning every thought – every sense of self control. Heat floods my veins and stings under my wounds. He closes the distance between us, and the air becomes a concentrated perfume of his lavender and magic.

"Do you feel it?" His voice is velvet, his fingers brushing my jaw. "The way your body wants me?"

I do.

He leans in, chests nearly touching. "This is what we could do to you all. Strip away your defenses. Leave you begging for our attention." His other hand trails featherlight up my arm, leaving goosebumps in its wake. "And the truth is, you'd love it. You'd stay right here as long as I wish. No collars – no guards needed."

I can't deny it. Not when every fiber of my being is screaming for him. Then his mouth crashes into mine.

The kiss is ruinous: all teeth and tongue and barely restrained hunger. His hands drop to my waist, pulling me flush against him, and I melt into the contact. My fingers tangle in his silky hair. The world narrows to the scrape of our noses, the press of his body, and the way he touches me like I'm the only thing that matters.

I don't realize he's backed me against the desk until the edge digs into my thighs. His lips trail down my neck, nipping at the sensitive skin below my ear. My breath hitches.

"You see?" he purrs. "You'd want nothing more than to please me for eternity."

His hand slides up my ribcage, his fingers searing me through the thin fabric of my bodice as he tugs at the lacing. I arch into him, a moan escaping as his hand skims my collarbone, the sting of my healing wounds mixing with the pleasure of his touch.

Then cold metal presses against my palm.

The ring.

He slips it back onto my finger, and the glamour shatters. The realization of what just happened sends me collapsing on weak knees against the desk. My lips still tingle from his teeth. I press a trembling hand to my mouth. "Why did you stop?"

Sylas watches me process everything, his chest rising and falling as rapidly as mine. "Because I'm not quite the monster you think I am," he says roughly. "If I just wanted you, I'd have had you by now. But I want you to *choose* me."

He looks at me like he's one breath away from pinning me to the desk again – not fully committed to the idea of letting me choose.

"You should go," he dismisses me suddenly.

"I should," I utter mid bow before retreating out the door.

I don't remember the walk back to my room, too busy reliving the rush of his hands on me over and over again. I attempt to throw myself into study to distract from the feel of his lips on mine, but it doesn't douse the blaze that reddens me from freckled cheek to stinging chest at the memory.

As I look over my notes, I realize I've learned all I can for the week. Nothing else sticks no matter how much I try.

I crawl into bed well after sunrise, but it's futile in such an empty room. Sleep evades me again.

Maybe I can drum up a sleepover partner.

I move to the door connecting my room to Mara's.

"Chase? Are you awake?" I hiss.

There's a rustling inside, followed by the sound of footsteps. Chase swings the door open, his hair a mess, robe untied to expose his narrow frame. He blinks at me, his expression shifting from surprise to concern in an instant.

"What's wrong?" he asks, running a probing look over my hunched form.

"Nothing," I say, though the forced lightness in my voice betrays me. "I just… couldn't sleep."

He studies me for a moment, confused. "Do you want me to call for some tea?"

"Oh, I was actually wondering if you wanted to have a sleepover?" My hands fidget with a curl as I wait for his response, bracing for rejection.

This must sound childish to him.

He hesitates, his eyes narrowing slightly as he tries to read me. "Just… us?"

I smile eagerly, nodding.

"Okay, I prefer Mara's bed though," he stretches, stepping out of the way and pulling the door open wider. "Things go okay with the prince?" He pries as he moves toward the bed. Then he begins tossing the rest of the dusty rose pillows onto the floor.

"He kissed me. But then he stopped. Told me he wanted me to choose him." I groan. He hums in acknowledgment, and I continue. "I can't sleep alone after that, after *everything* recently. I'm overthinking it all. I just need someone with me."

"I can do that, stay with you," he chuckles. I gesture toward the sitting area by the window, where a plush chaise too similar to the one I now know Sylas reads on awaits.

"We can chat here for a bit," I offer, but he ignores me, continuing to remove Mara's mountain of decorative bed toppers. "Or – you know – just go straight to bed. Whatever's best for you."

I worked really hard to arrange those nicely, I think with frustration.

He nods, throwing the last pillow onto the pink pile in the corner. He turns back toward me.

"So, Mara's bed is *that* comfortable?" I joke.

"You'll find out soon," he purrs. I step back, my heart racing suddenly as his hands settle on either side of my face.

Oh no. He doesn't think….

"Chase, I'm not trying to sleep with you like *that*," I blurt, covering my face with my hands to get away from any more unexpected lips today.

For a heartbeat, neither of us speaks. The silence stretches between us, heavy and awkward. I peek at him between my fingers to see his brown eyes studying me in turn. Then, to my surprise, he lets out a sigh of relief, pulling me into a hug. The sensation of his laugh shakes both our bodies.

"Thank god." His voice rumbles against my ear. "I thought you were propositioning me or something. I was so confused. You'd never seemed interested before."

I can't help but laugh too, the tension between us dissolving as I pull away. "No," I shake my head. "I'm flattered you accepted, but I really just need a friend."

He smiles, relaxing visibly as he lets me go. "You've got one. But for the record, my job is to keep the court *entertained.* You'll need to be specific with your words if you don't want *more,*" he explains, tone teasing with the attempted jab.

The implications don't miss me. My smile falters with the truth. "If you ever need an excuse to avoid a… job, come back to my room. You can say I'm monopolizing your attention."

"It's not like that most of the time," he's quick to clarify. "The nobles value pleasure over everything else. They don't care for unwilling partners."

"I want you to choose me," echoes in my mind in Sylas's voice.

"Good," is all I can muster.

Chase moves to the bed more animated now, like the friendly hall-mate I know. I follow him, pulling the blanket over us both as we crawl in.

"Well," he says after a moment, his voice suddenly drowsy as he adjusts the pillow behind his head. "I can't remember the last time I slept with someone and meant it only literally."

I roll my eyes, settling in beside him. "Maybe I should've asked Starling instead, if you're going to be like that. We had a really nice heart-to-heart earlier."

He shakes his head, his eyelids already starting to droop. "The Unseelie?" He says the word with disgust, and I feel defensive on their behalf.

"They've helped me, more than once. Jumped on Flora's friend to save my life the other night."

"What?" He turns to face me, suddenly more awake. "I knew those three were gone, but is that why? They *attacked* you?"

As the rays of sunlight brighten the room, I catch him up on every development, extending my stories as an olive branch between us. He accepts, listening wordlessly as I show him my missing brand and the almost healed welts on my chest. I tell him about Sylas's attention and Starling's kindness. But by the time I'm done, he's asleep. His breathing is steady; his face lax in peaceful rest.

"I guess I can tell you it all again in the evening," I joke, turning over.

And as I snuggle into the oleander clinging to the soft pink sheets, I realize that maybe I've found my first true friend up here. The thought is what finally settles my mind enough to sleep.

Chapter 28

When I awake in the evening, Chase is gone. I don't know if he stayed the entire day. Part of me hopes he did – needing proof that our friendship is real. I slip out of bed, smoothing the sheets and fluffing all the pillows to the standards I've been taught.

I move to the door connecting Mara's room to our... *my* chamber, working the tangles out of my hair with my fingers. Deciding to freshen up, I head to the bath to let the fire heated water wash away the lingering tension from my weekend. The sting on my chest is much fainter tonight – almost entirely gone thanks to the salve and time. My hand brushes over the ridge of stitches along my neck, and I'm relieved to find no pain or infectious heat.

As I soak, the muffled sounds of life spill into the hallway, carrying through the walls and into Mara's room. My heart skips a beat.

She's back a bit early.

I drain the tub and dress quickly, checking my reflection for any visible wounds but most are practically gone. I avoid meeting my own eyes, focusing instead on the parts of myself I like: the fuller curves of my body – the shine of my hair. Satisfied, I perch on the edge of my bed, my fingers twisting in the fabric of my sheets.

I want to run to her – to burst into her room and tell her everything that's happened in the few days she's been gone. But that's ill advised, according to my training. Mara is a sidhe, soon to be queen of this region, and even sooner to be married to Sylas. She has more important things to do than listen to her attendant's chaotic weekend.

I force myself to stay put, busying my hands with tidying the room further, though there's little left to do. The minutes stretch, each one longer than the last. Until finally, the door to Mara's chamber creaks open.

I freeze.

"Valerie? Are you in here?"

I straighten my sleeve once more, then step into her line of sight. Mara stands there, her long hair cascading over her shoulders like mine, her golden eyes bright and searching. She's barely eye level with me, yet her sunny presence fills the room effortlessly. She's still wearing her traveling cloak, the fabric dusty at the hem.

"Lady Mara," I curtsy, holding back the relief that threatens to spill into my voice. "I hope the trip was exciting."

She steps toward me, but I keep my eyes low as I'm expected to do. "Not as exciting as what I've heard happened here. I wanted to see you as soon as I could." I glance up to see her scanning the room, taking in the changes: the single bed in the center, the absence of Flora's belongings. Her face softens when she turns back to me, and she reaches out, placing a warm hand on my arm. "Oh, Valerie. How are you healing?"

Her concern catches me off guard. I feel an unexpected lump rise in my throat at the idea and shrug, unable to speak for a moment. Her hand drifts up to my shoulder, squeezing once.

"Come," she orders softly. "Sit with me. Tell me everything."

I let her lead us back into her room, luggage trunks and garment bags now littering the space. She moves us to the sitting area by the window, where the plush couch awaits. She settles onto it, patting the space beside her. I follow, folding my hands in my lap, unsure where to begin.

To her credit, she doesn't push. She simply waits, her eyes filled with enough patience and understanding that I don't feel rushed.

Finally, I take a deep breath and start the story. I tell her about Flora's betrayal, the attack, and how Prince Sylas intervened. Mara listens intently, her expression shifting from shock to fury to quiet relief as I recount that night.

When I finish, she reaches out and takes my hand in hers, holding it tightly. "King's graces," she breathes. "You've been through so much. I should have been here for you."

"It's not your fault," I say quickly. "Who could have predicted Flora turning against me-"

"Against *us*," she interrupts. "You are important to me. More than you realize. Flora was threatened by that."

I feel tears prick at the corners of my eyes and try to blink them away – not wanting to cry in front of her. But she notices and pulls me into a hug, holding me tight as a sob escapes.

Her oleander envelopes me as she alone witnesses my breakdown.

I'm supposed to be stronger than this.

But I lean into her anyway and feel her lips brush the top of my head.

She soothes me with murmured comfort.

"You're alright. Sylas protected you. He won't let anyone harm you."

When I've finally reigned myself in – wiping embarrassed at the tears under my puffy eyes – she pulls me back an arm's length. Her finger hooks my chin, forcing me to meet her gaze.

"You'll need to take on more responsibilities as my attendant with Flora gone. But I trust you to do that." Her gentle fingers move a stubborn curl from my face, removing the last barrier between us. "You may ask for assistance when needed from your fellow staff. I will need you at the autumn equinox, prepared and at my side. Understood?"

"Yes, my lady."

She smiles, the warmth of it spreading through me like sunlight. "Now," she says lighter. "Let's get you something to eat. You look like you haven't had a proper meal in days."

I shrug, the casual gesture surprising myself after so much drama. "I haven't," I admit.

Mara stands, pulling me to my feet with her. "Then we'll fix that. Come on."

As we leave the room together, my hunched shoulders finally unwind. Mara's presence is like its own salve, alleviating the raw wounds of my fear and loneliness.

I can do this, even without Flora's guidance.

Chapter 29

After Mara ensures I've indulged in a rich meal of starches and sweets, I find my way to the library. Studying with relative peace: no attacks by other attendants and no visits from Sylas.

I try not to let the latter bother me.

I sit focused over the table, a pile of parchment at my elbow, my eyes strained from hours of memorizing portraits and descriptions. My own handwriting swims before my eyes, the sloppy letters twisting into illegible shapes if my focus remotely slips.

I wish I had some of Starling's potion, I think begrudgingly.

But I don't. So I change focus to wake myself back up.

I use my growing familiarity with the library to dive into more information on the history and geography of the Otherworld. I stare at a tiny map of the Cardinal Kingdom that I copied: one with a description of the portal to the human world... just in case I ever need it.

The portal really isn't far. A little north of the castle grounds here in the West. I could go home one day.

"Hello?" a voice shatters my focus from behind, and I yelp in surprise. The sound echoes off the stacks at an embarrassing volume. I spin around – my heart in my throat – to see Starling's dark face looming over my shoulder. My fingers quickly tuck the map into the pages of the nearest book before I rise, smiling too widely at their sudden appearance.

"Hey! I was hoping to run into you again," I admit before I can think of a better reason for my excitement.

A smile tugs at the corner of their sharp mouth. "You were?"

"Of course. I don't have many friends around here," I shrug in an attempt to seem nonchalant.

They step closer, dropping their heavy bag on the other side of the table. "Oh, really? We're friends?"

"Unless you think that's too forward," I backtrack. But they let a more genuine smile brighten their face.

"We could be friends," they relent. I catch the distinction.

Could. Not *are.*

"That's good enough for me," I reply, gesturing to the wooden seat across from mine as I lower myself back in front of my studies.

"So, what is my not-yet friend working on tonight?" they ask, following my gesture and sitting in the offered spot.

I yawn, still overwhelmed by the workload. "I'm trying to figure out this world's timeline. I think it would help me grasp the family histories better. It's so much more drawn out here than back home," I admit.

"You're learning quickly. I'm almost impressed," they say under their breath as their red eyes skim my notes.

A small glimmer of pride lightens my chest, but I bury it down to be safe.

They said they don't play games, but do other folk etiquette rules apply to the Unseelie?

"I think the portal here was opened around a hundred years ago," I say, steering the conversation away from their praise as I point to the revelations I've been stumbling upon over the past few hours. They examine the scholar's journals I've been pouring over – references to a portal to my world suddenly an interesting topic of study at the time.

"The same night as Sylas's birth," they comment on my underlined note linking mentions of the newly born crown prince to the night of the portal's appearance.

I don't have time for those implications.

"But if you look *here*, the folk stopped aging before that. Like a hundred fifty years earlier, if this is anything to go by," I add, pulling over the genealogy of Sylas's line. The ages of each noted figure *never* pass two hundred years old for almost a thousand years. And then there's King Anders: Sylas's father. "He was born around three hundred years ago. And he still looks to be the age he was here," I continue, spinning around a striking reference to the current king in a portrait copied to the page from an earlier time. "*That's* when they defeated the Tyrant King and regained magic. The portal came way after. I assumed it was a remaining one, but I was wrong-"

"Did you just say the Tyrant King?" Starling cuts me off, incredulous as they look through my sources. They're face hardens at the children's book that started this entire endeavor.

My face flushes as they pick up <u>*How The Realm Was Saved*</u>.

"That's what they're teaching the next generation here?" Their voice is dejected as they judge the pages, flipping through the illustrations and simple story.

"What's wrong?" I venture, leaning forward.

They've noticed the map I shoved inside, I realize.

"There's just more to the story," they mutter, claws purposefully slow as they better align the map with the pages until it blends, then hand it back to me with a pointed look.

I hesitate before grabbing it.

*They really might be on **my** side.*

"Starling, I was wondering if you would be willing to help me? With studying, I mean. It's a lot to learn on my own."

They raise a thick brow. "You want me to tutor you?"

"Yes," I confirm, trying to sound confident. "You're really smart. And I like hanging out with you."

Starling studies me for a moment, looking for the trick. Then, slowly, they nod. "Alright. I'll help you."

I let out a relieved breath and grin. "Thank you. I'll take whatever bargain you're willing to give at this point."

They lean back in their chair, waving away my words. "You know I don't do bargains, but maybe I'll hold you to that anyway. For now, let's focus on Mara's family history instead of *Sylas's.*"

I blush again, and tuck away my notes on the prince's lineage.

"Good point," I mumble.

"I have some errands to run, so we can start tomorrow. Your room? Midnight?" they offer.

I agree. They turn on their heels and walk back out of the library swiftly. I can't help the smile that surfaces as I pull books and prepare for the next two weeks with my not-yet friend.

Chapter 30

As I walk back to my chambers – tomes in hand – I imagine my
barrack family alongside me. I picture Eddie carrying my books while
Maddie and Lilia debate the significance of date alignments between our
world and the Otherworld.

The idea reignites the promise I made to them: to bring them up to this
level with me as soon as I can. I tune my path towards Mara's chambers,
and take the risk that she's in a good mood tonight.

As I open her door, I find her seated by the window with a sealed letter
in her hands. She looks serene in the calm of her room. I shift my weight in
the doorway, unsure if I should actually approach her tonight.

"Valerie," she addresses without looking up. "You're hovering. Come
in."

I step inside, closing the door softly behind me. "I didn't want to
disturb you, if you were busy."

She sets the letter aside and turns to me. "You're a welcome
distraction, not a disturbance. What's on your mind?"

I take a deep breath, steeling myself.

*This is it. The moment I've been rehearsing in my head for days. Time
to wing it.*

"Mara, I wanted to ask you something. Something important."

She gestures to the spot next to her in invitation. "Sit. You look like
you're about to collapse."

I decline, needing the distance from her to keep my mind clear. My
hands dig into the book spines as I search for the right words. "You know I
came from the laundry team down in the barracks," I begin, my voice
trembling slightly despite my best efforts to sound calm. "I spent almost
half my life down there. There's three people – my only friends – who
helped me survive that long. They've been a family to me."

Mara tilts her head, her gaze attentive and thoughtful. "Go on."

"I was wondering if – after the autumn equinox – you might consider
bringing them up to work here. As your servants. They're hardworking and
extremely loyal. I know they'd be grateful for the chance. I wouldn't ask if

I didn't think they'd be an asset to you."

The room falls into suffocating stillness, the desperation of my request obvious as I hold my breath. Mara leans back after a prolonged moment, resting against the couch. "Valerie, do you understand what you're asking?"

I nod, my throat tight. "I do. And I know it's a lot to ask, especially being so new myself at this high level. But I miss them so much, and I'd take full responsibility for their training."

She sighs, her gaze drifting to the window at the moon beyond. "The barracks are… not like up here. I know that. But bringing *human* servants from there all the way to my tower isn't a simple matter. There's protocols to follow. Folk who would feel slighted… Folk like Flora."

My heart sinks, but I press on. "I know it's complicated. But you are fair and smart. If anyone could make it work, it's you."

A small smile tugs at her full lips. "Flattery won't sway me."

"It's not flattery," I hedge. "It's the truth. You've treated me with respect, even though I'm just a human."

Her smile widens. "You're not 'just a human.'. You're my attendant. One that is *very* important to me."

I struggle to fight back my protest. "Mara…"

She holds up a hand, silencing me. "I'll consider your request. But I can't promise anything. I'll need to ensure they're suited for the work, that we have the space and supplies to keep them here. But if they're as loyal and hardworking as you say, I'm willing to look into it."

I breathe easier with her words. "That's all I can ask for."

Her smile softens into something more thoughtful. "You seem to have a good heart, Valerie. It's one of the many reasons I chose you for your role. Now go get some rest, you look worn out."

I rise from the chair, and offer her a deep bow. "Have a good sleep, my lady."

As I leave her chambers, my heart feels lighter than it has in weeks. She didn't offer a guarantee to save my friends, but it's a start. And I can work with that.

The days that follow are full of brain draining work as I earn her trust enough to bring my friends here. Mara graciously lets me slack on *real* attendant duties – like helping plan the equinox celebration – substituting fresher faces that have been moved up in the absence of Flora and the other two. But I am still expected to run most of her correspondence, ensure her meals are accurate and delivered where needed on time, and continue my studies.

In my midnight sessions with Starling, I don't have the mental space to properly pity my friends. Only the hope for their futures reinvigorates me, when frustration threatens to halt my progress on particularly tough lessons.

Starling and I fall into a rhythm, our sessions a strange but welcome constant in the chaotic preparations as we share meals and trade ideas. They're still guarded – still keeping me an arms length away – but there's security there. Like our goals are completely out in the open without double meaning for once.

I feel like I'm beginning to carve a nice niche for myself in this world, no matter how unexpected my arrival was.

Chapter 31

The room is quiet except for the soft scratch of my pen against parchment as I write notes in the margins of older notes. Starling and I sit on my bed as we pore over the pages spread out between us.

We've been at this for hours. But unlike my frustrating sessions with Flora that needed Unseelie magic to help me parse, the pieces of folk history are clicking into place without force now. It's a small victory, but one that fills me with a quiet pride.

"So, if Mara's mother was cousins with Margaret's father, then that would make the two of them..." I trail off, tapping the quill against my chin.

"Second cousins," Starling finishes. "And if Margaret is first in line for the North Throne..."

I grin, unable to hide my satisfaction. "Then Mara is sixth, after Margaret's sister, and three first cousins."

Starling leans back on their hands. "Exactly."

I pump my fist with victory, but Starling rolls their red eyes. "Don't get too confident. You know we folk love nothing more than catching humans off guard. But you're doing better than I expected."

"Gee, thanks," I retort sarcastically.

Before either of us can say more, an urgent knock at the door interrupts us. It swings open before I can respond – and Chase steps inside – hunched slightly as he winces. His hair is disheveled, his usually warm eyes shadowed. He freezes when he sees Starling beside me.

I haven't seen him all week.

"Chase?" I stand quickly in his worrying state.

He glances at me, then back at Starling, his jaw tightening as he closes the door with deliberate quiet behind him. "I needed a break. Thought I'd come here. Didn't realize you had company."

Starling's expression is composed. They don't say anything, but their disapproval digs against my back as they let me take the lead.

I step closer to Chase, lowering my voice. "Are you okay? You look scared."

He hisses, slumping against the door. "Leona's been rough. She's not taking *their* prince spending his attention on other potential matches well."

My head whips back to Starling, catching the pointed reference to the sidhe they serve. My stomach twists when their eyes narrow on Chase.

"Oh, so Ciaran's entertaining some variety this week?" Starling's voice carries a sharp edge I haven't heard since we started our studies. "Found less stifling company for a bit. And you're the unfortunate one she's taking it out on tonight?"

Chase scoffs. But I notice the way he holds his arms close to his center, as though guarding himself from another attack.

"I'm sorry," I offer. "Do you need anything?"

"You're already doing more than enough – letting me be here," he grumbles as he claims my vacant study chair.

There's a rustling sound from the bed as Starling rummages through their bag.

"This isn't right," I begin, my anger flaring as I notice the handprint of a bruise on his arm. "You're not just an outlet for her-"

"Actually, that is exactly what I am," he huffs.

"Here." Starling's voice cuts off the tense conversation, and we both look to see them holding out a small vial filled with a shimmering, pale blue liquid. "It's a healing potion. It'll help with the pain."

Chase stares at the vial, his brow drawn in suspicion. "I don't need your Unseelie help."

Starling doesn't flinch. "Suit yourself. If you'd rather suffer because of your prejudice, that's your choice."

I shoot them both a look. Chase looks away ashamed. Starling meets my eye in challenge, setting the vial on the bed between the three of us.

Chase's glare levels at it. But then he leans forward and picks it up, studying the small vial with a knowing eye. "What's in it?"

"Nothing that will harm you," Starling says evenly. "It's just a healing potion."

Chase hesitates, then uncorks the vial and takes a cautious sniff. His face relaxes, as if just the scent dulls some of the pain. "Any side effects?"

"Other than healing you? No," Starling replies.

Satisfied, he lifts the vial to his lips and downs it in one swift motion. Almost immediately, most of the tension in his shoulders eases, and he lets out a dramatic sigh. "If it's true you can't lie same as Seelie… thank you," he mutters.

Starling's eyes soften just slightly. "You're welcome."

The room falls silent in the wake of their truce. My focus bounces between them, unsure of how to navigate this uneasy peace.

Chase speaks first. "I didn't think your kind cared enough to help humans."

Starling's lip twitches. "And I didn't think humans would ever give us a chance to prove them wrong. But here we are."

"Fair enough," Chase huffs a humorless laugh.

I relax a little too, wanting to encourage the camaraderie. "Maybe you two aren't so different after all."

"Don't push it." Chase rolls his eyes.

Starling falls back against my pillows. "Yeah, this war isn't over between us."

"Okay, enough of whatever this is," I say, waving my hands. "I really need to study."

But as I sit back down, I can't help feeling a small sense of gratitude. Despite their differences, both of them are here, keeping a peace if only for my sake.

They both remain compliant, offering tips and easing my frustrations with studies until dawn spills through the window. Chase becomes unexpectedly helpful, bringing a more visceral look at some of the courtiers he's entertained. Starling keeps us from gossiping too much about said courtiers.

"Leona's asleep by now, I'll be back tonight," Chase stretches as he stands, the bruise on his arm nearly gone already.

"I'll have another potion ready," Starling mumbles, also moving towards the door.

"See you both tonight, then," I nod, biting back a smile as they both leave.

Chapter 32

The castle is cacophonous with activity before I am even dressed the next few nights. I avoid bumping into other attendants – rushing errands for more and more arriving guests – as I fulfill Mara's own requests. Servants carry loads of decor towards the main hall: huge garlands of fall colors and tablecloths with intricately embroidered details.

My heart is heavy, thinking of how much work my friends in the barracks must be doing on this preparation, out of sight and unappreciated. It makes my packed schedule a much easier burden, remembering the comparison.

The first half of the eve of the equinox, I assist with Mara's final fitting for her hawk dress. Getting to see Belladonna and Sydney again is almost as exciting as getting to see the atelier itself. Their expertise impresses me more, as I finally get to see them work without the fear of that first night.

Midnight, I find myself with Starling and Chase, going over relationships and feuds as we share dinners.

My final morning is spent trying to calm my nerves, looking over maps and journal entries of the Otherworld so I have a better knowledge of the ruling families.

Then, I don't know how, but I manage to sleep.

I *actually* feel prepared when I wake and dress in the fine silk uniform I had worn for the last full moon revelry.

I slip inside Mara's chambers to find them crowded before the sun even fully sets. Hobs of all types flit in and out, carrying trays of jewels, cosmetics, and accessories, while Mara sits at her vanity under the hand of a leprechaun adding real gold flakes to her face.

I keep glancing at the feathered dress laid across the bed. The gown shimmers like molten gold. It's a costume fit for a queen. And with Mara on the horizon of claiming that title, it's perfect.

She dismisses the staff with a kind word, telling them to stay in their rooms tonight and enjoy the break. I remain in the corner, knowing the dismissal doesn't include me.

"Valerie," Mara calls, drawing my attention from the garment back to her. "Would you help me with my hair tonight? We have such similar locks, I trust you know how to tame them."

I smile, setting aside the flashcards of royal lineage I'd been pretending to organize, and move to her side. "Of course," I agree, picking up a comb and running it through her curls. Her hair is soft and vibrant.

Not a single god damn knot in it.

"Do you want it up or down?"

"Up," Mara says decisively. "Something elegant but wild, like the wind is catching it mid flight."

I gather her hair into my hands and twist. The movement recalls a memory I'd forgotten – of my grandmother, who taught me to French twist her hair this way when her joints wouldn't let her do it herself. It brings a bittersweet smile to my lips as I pin the sidhe's hair into a more dramatic shape, pulling out a few strategic pieces to look messier and show off the magical points of her ears.

As I work, I can feel Mara watching me in the mirror, her eyes glued to my face. The room is quiet now, the servants having finished their tasks and bid us goodbye.

"So," Mara says conversationally after a while. "Did you have any children back in your world?"

My hands still for a moment at the surprising question before I resume working. "No," I say with a smile to soften my words. "I was considered way too young for that."

Mara tilts her head slightly, throwing off the work of my fingers as I slot pins into her hair that I know someone's going to pull out later. "What? Don't most humans have children around your age?"

I feel a pang of frustration – anger that the folk steal us away with no understanding of our lives – but I push it aside.

She didn't make my first bargain.

"Not in the culture I come from," I explain carefully. "Many people don't marry or have children for another decade past my biological age. I mean, I wasn't even seriously dating anyone before I…" I trail off, letting my focus shift back to her hair.

I'm rambling, and she didn't ask about half of that.

Mara's expression shifts, her eyes filling with sympathy. "Oh," she says softly. "I didn't know."

I shrug, trying to keep my tone light. "It's not something people really talk about here. It's just the way things were instead of the way things are."

Her gaze drops to her hands in thought, the conversation lulling. Then she speaks again, more somber. "Our people haven't been able to have children for a century. I've been told it was a side effect of bringing humans back into this world," she admits. "My generation is the last, outside of a few exceedingly rare cases."

"Because of the portal that opened when Sylas was born?" I ask, letting her answer questions I've tabled for weeks. She nods in confirmation.

"Yes. His own mother and sibling passed during her next pregnancy – trying to see if the portal could also be reproduced. But she didn't make it. And childbirth for our people has only grown riskier since. It's why Sylas and I… why our marriage is so important. The hope of continuing the royal lines is everything to the ruling families."

My hands come to rest on her shoulders: steadying us both through the harsh implications. "I didn't realize how much pressure there was on you."

I remember the children's book I found in the library, my confusion at the lack of young folk.

I haven't seen any because there aren't any.

She looks up at me in the mirror, her eyes glistening with unshed tears. "We have plans, ideas of how to fix it," she says. "But it's scary, not knowing if everything is going to work out. Especially because…" She reaches up and places her hand over mine, squeezing gently as she trails off. "I am just grateful to have you by my side as I try to resolve this whole mess."

*Maybe my bargain to lie has to do with her future pregnancy? Is she going to **die** for Sylas's heir? What does that mean for me and my friends?*

An ache settles in my chest for the one sidhe in this entire Otherworld who has taken a chance on me. "I can't imagine how hard it must be. I'm grateful to be here too."

Mara takes a cleansing breath, then smiles, her usual warmth returning. "Enough of that. Tonight is about celebration, not sorrow. Let's finish getting ready, shall we?"

I smile back, appreciating the change in subject. I weave in small golden feathers and delicate glass beads into her hair. When I'm done, I step back to admire my work. Mara's locks cascade in twists and curls, with the feathers adding just the right touch of wild elegance.

"Perfect," Mara says, turning her head to admire the updo. Then she stands and turns to face me. She looks like the queen she's destined to be: regal, powerful, and breathtakingly beautiful.

"You're stunning, Mara. Let's get you dressed," I suggest.

She takes my hand in hers for a moment, her tone serious. "You may not have the future you had back in the human world. But with our bargain, you have a meaningful future ahead of you here. Never forget that."

I feel a lump rise in my throat, but I hold back the dramatic reaction to her sentiments. And instead pull her into a hug.

She giggles, then releases me – turning toward the bed where her gown lies. "Now, let me get this dress on, and we can show them what true royalty looks like."

As she removes her dressing gown, she seems to remember something, and turns back towards me. I avert my gaze from her exposed radiant form.

"Oh, I have something for you." She dips down behind the bed, sorting through piles of fabric and dresses. She straightens again, holding an airy gown. It's simple, made of gauzy beige and brown fabric that shimmers as she angles it towards me.

"For you," she says, holding it out. "I thought it would suit you perfectly. I had Belladonna's girl make it. A moth to go with my hawk, don't you think?"

I take the dress, running my fingers over the fabric – only to realize the shimmering details mimic the delicate vein patterns of a moth's wings. It's beautifully made, and the thoughtfulness behind the gift touches me deeply. "It's perfect."

She grins. "Go on, try it on. We'll make quite the pair."

Chapter 33

The main hall of the castle is a dreamy sight for the autumn equinox as I catch a glimpse through the doors ahead. Garlands of dried maple leaves and golden ribbons drape over every surface untouched by enchanted art. The room is electric with laughter and music. The melodies of grig musicians – a green skinned company with too long limbs and endless black eyes – weave through the crowd, tugging at me.

And everyone is surprisingly still dressed, I realize, noting the intricate costumes and fantastical designs around us.

"Alistar was right, a theme really did give this party some new life," Mara whispers to me when she catches me staring at the folk and their guests.

I blink away my surprise and nod enthusiastically. "I didn't expect everyone to take a costume party so seriously."

She laughs as she steps up to the entrance. "We're folk. We take *everything* seriously."

I linger a step behind her, my gauzy moth dress shimmering as I look down the length of myself. I pull at the neckline, uncomfortable with how revealing the garment is, but grateful for it anyway.

"Stand straight, and follow me closely," she nudges me, right before we step onto the staircase.

Guess I'm not on the sidelines tonight.

The herald steps forward, his voice booming through the hall.

"Presenting the Future Queen of the West Court: Lady Mara!"

The room turns toward us as Mara steps forward, her head held high. I follow quietly, my presence unannounced – just another attendant in the shadow of royalty. The crowd parts for Mara as she descends the stairs, their eyes drawn to her with admiration. I stay close, my role clear: to blend in, to observe, and to be ready if she needs me.

As we move deeper into the distinguished crowd, I spot Sylas through the throng of sidhe, satyrs, and other folk. He's dressed in the striking white stag costume, the antler crown he wears crafted from delicate silver filigree. He's surrounded by foreign royalty, I notice Queen Elora of the

East Court and Princess Margaret of the North Court with him – their elaborate costumes and crowns a testament to their status.

"Mara," Sylas says upon our approach. He kisses his betrothed, and I avert my eyes. "You've brought your attendant?"

Mara smiles mischievously. "Valerie is more than an attendant. She's my guest tonight."

His gaze flicks to me, lingering for a moment longer than necessary. "Surely you don't intend to let her on the dance floor? Or partake in the food?"

I don't miss the warning in his tone.

Everything is tinged with fairy fruit tonight.

Mara bats his arm. "She is under my protection. She'll stay by my side: safe and sound."

Sylas's eyes dart over me again, but he doesn't argue before moving on to talk to other guests.

As his distance grows, Mara leans close to me, voice low. "Ignore him. He's just worried about us having too much fun without him."

I smile faintly, though the encounter leaves me off balance.

Does she know that he kissed me? That I almost let him do so much more under the glamour?

I know the folk aren't held to the same rules of intimacy that I remember from the human world, but do they talk about their partners together?

Mara links her rounder arm with mine and leads me toward a bar laden with drinks. She picks up two glasses of sparkling wine, handing one to me.

"Here," she says, her eyes glimmering. "You've earned this night to enjoy yourself. Just stay off the dance floor, alright?"

I take the glass with an "alright."

Will she take me to dance later? I wonder.

My eyes find the bodies moving in perfect synchronization in a circle, and I already feel left out of the flow. But I turn my attention to the glass given to me as a distraction.

At eighteen, I'd had my fair share of parties consisting of cheap beer and stolen liquor back in the human world. But I have never had anything as refined as whatever wine she's just passed to me. I don't want to disappoint her – drinking too much too quickly – so I just take a small sip whenever she does.

The wine is sweet and bubbly. I hum in pleasant surprise. Mara flashes me a real grin. "It's good, right? Let's get you another."

Before I can protest, she's handing me a second glass. I take it, feeling a little overwhelmed but not wanting to refuse.

As the night goes on, Mara keeps the drinks coming. I feed her the names and information about guests as they come to pay their respects. But it's easy – the lessons from Starling, Chase, Flora, and Sylas sticking in my mind.

Each glass Mara hands me is sweeter than the last, and I find myself laughing more easily – the tension in my shoulders melting away entirely.

She seems content to stay at the edge of the party, her laughter mingling with mine as she regales me with stories of past revelries held in the castle.

"You should have seen Sylas," she says, animated. "He tried to dance with the gardening team. It did *not* go well."

I giggle, the sound bubbling up unexpectedly. "I can't imagine him being bad at anything."

Mara shakes her wild hair. "Oh, he's not. It was the human gardeners who were bad. We've paid dryads to tend the grounds ever since."

The realization that I may have heard the other side – the *human* side of this same story – prickles my spine, reminding me again of my precarious position.

But the room feels so warm. The lights are bright and inviting enough that I know nothing will happen if I stay by Mara's side.

I'm not sure how many glasses I finish before my thoughts become delightfully fuzzy. Mara notices my sway to the music and steers me toward a quieter corner, her arm still linked with mine.

"Having fun?" she asks playfully.

I nod a little too enthusiastically. "This is amazing."

Mara's golden eyes study me with a sudden intensity that makes my cheeks flush. "You deserve to enjoy yourself tonight."

Before I can respond, she leans in, her lips brushing against mine. The kiss is brief – almost chaste – but it sends a jolt through me. I freeze, my mind scrambling to process what just happened.

Mara pulls back, her smile coy. "Don't look so surprised," she teases. "You're far too intriguing to ignore."

I open my mouth to say something, but no words come out. My heart races with a mix of disbelief and arousal.

She seems a much safer bedmate than Sylas.

Before I can gather my thoughts, a voice cuts in. "Mara, are you monopolizing your guest?"

I turn to see a stunning sidhe approaching, her intricately woven costume and braids making her look like she is made of fresh foliage. Her gaze slides between Mara and me, a faint smirk playing on her lips.

I can't remember her name with the wine slowing my thoughts.

"Just making sure she's enjoying herself, Leona," Mara replies, her tone edged in challenge.

My heart stutters, realizing *this* must be the one that left those marks on Chase. I settle more into Mara's arms, pretending it's the alcohol.

Leona's dark eyes settle on me, and I feel a shiver run down my spine. "And is she?"

I swallow hard, suddenly aware of how tall she is. "I – I am," I stammer.

Her smirk widens. "Good. Though I must say, you've been neglecting the dance floor." She extends a hand toward me, her gaze unwavering. "May I have this dance?"

"I don't think I'm supposed to," I slur, glancing at Mara, who surprisingly gives me an reluctant nod.

"One dance, then she's back here again," Mara warns.

My heart pounds as I place my hand in Leona's, her grip firm as she leads me to the center of the room, weaving us through the flowing crowd.

The music shifts, the tempo slowing as the buggy grig bards begin a waltz that human masters would struggle to copy. Her hand settles on my waist. I place my other hand on her shoulder, trying to ignore the way my pulse quickens at the contact with someone so cruel.

"You're trembling," she observes, teasing. "Are you nervous to dance?"

"A little," I admit, under the music.

Her brown eyes look irritated as they drift back to Mara. "Don't be. It's insulting."

The words make my face pale.

I realize – once we begin to move – that I don't need to focus on the steps of the dance to keep up with her lead.

The music puppets my limbs, keeping me upright even as my body sags drunkenly into the rhythm. Leona is a skilled dancer, her movements graceful and precise as she guides us around and around. I focus on the gold flecks adhered to her night-dark skin, letting them hypnotize me to avoid stoking her anger with my fear.

I eventually flick my gaze up to gage her mood, only to find her already watching me. Her eyes become endless as they bore into mine with curiosity. "Most humans aren't bold enough to accept a dance with us. You are either incredibly confident or incredibly stupid."

A nervous laugh escapes me.

She smirks, eyes sliding past me to someone else.

I turn my head to follow, my eyes landing on Sylas seated atop a massive, gleaming throne at the far side of the dance floor. It is an ancient tangle of living branches woven together and shaped by decades of careful cultivation. The bark is painted a radiant gold that bends into the form of a regal seat – roots spilling out like gilded tendrils across the dais. The branches bow gracefully, their tips adorned with willow like heaviness in shades of autumn, as though kissed by the season itself.

The throne is *alive*, its branches heavy with fairy fruit: the peaches in varying shades from blush to brown that spell death for my kind. The air this close to it carries sweet nectar.

I've never seen a fairy fruit tree before. It's beautiful.

Sylas presides over the dance floor with detached elegance, his posture relaxed yet commanding all the same. His fingers trail idly along the armrest, where a cluster of fairy fruit hangs within easy reach. With a deliberate motion, he plucks a ripened blush fruit from the lowest branch, his gaze never leaving us. His expression is one of polished indifference, but there's a sharpness in his eyes that feels almost predatory.

I watch – transfixed and craning my neck as the music sends me spinning – when he brings the fruit to his lips to take a slow, indulgent bite. The flesh yields easily, its juices spilling down his chin in a glistening red trail. He doesn't wipe it away, letting the sticky sweetness linger as he chews.

The entire time his icy eyes never leave my red face, sending a shiver through me.

There's something unnervingly primal about the way he consumes the fruit – as though it's a display of power rather than a simple act of indulgence.

But the dance ends too soon, and Leona releases me – my limbs back under my control, feeling heavier than before. "Your lady is glaring at us. You better get back to her."

Before I can process the dismissal, Mara appears at my side, her arm slipping through mine again. "I hope you're not stealing her away from me," her tone is teasing but there is an undeniable undertone of possessiveness.

Leona's smirk returns. "Just ensuring she experiences all the night has to offer."

Does Leona know I'm special to them too?

Mara's gaze narrows, but she doesn't argue. Instead, she leads me back to the bar, handing me a refreshing glass of water instead of another wine. "You're doing wonderfully," she praises. "Just remember, you're here with me."

Her lips brush against mine again – this time more deliberate – and I find myself leaning into the kiss as the world around us fades away.

When she pulls back, her golden eyes are bright with satisfaction. "I am so glad you accepted the attendant position. I don't think this night would be nearly as fun without you," she murmurs, stroking the length of my exposed back.

I don't know what to say, so I simply lean in for another kiss and let her steal the rest of my breath.

Chapter 34

We continue our passionate embrace in the corner. Heat builds between us even with the protective ring on my finger. When Mara pulls back, she looks hungry as she looks over my flushed face.

"It's been too long since I've felt a human girl come undone in my hands. What do you think? Can you help me remember the feeling?" she purrs, running a hand low on my hip.

I nod mesmerized, and her eyes glaze over with seductive haze. I lean in for another kiss, but instead of meeting me, she slinks behind me.

"Perhaps, if you ask nicely, our prince would be up to joining us?" she says the words with a melodic hum against my neck, and I feel a spark ignite in my core at the suggestion. The thought of Mara and Sylas in one encounter – their heavenly bodies orbiting around *me* – makes my mouth dry with want.

My eyes struggle to follow her pointed look at Sylas. He is magnificent, lounging on the throne slightly above the rest of the room. He watches the two of us with hungry curiosity. He's entirely relaxed, molded into the symbol of his power. The smallest smirk tugs at the corner of his lips once he's decided he likes our closeness.

"Go," Mara commands with a gentle push in his direction. His head angles slightly, eyes wandering over my body- like he's considering me in a way he hasn't let himself before. My lips part, air pumping faster as I shuffle insecurely towards him. It takes longer than my confidence lasts to finally reach him.

"Do you have something to ask me?" his voice is knowing; his slackened posture draws my eyes down to between his parted thighs at eye level. The idea of seeing him in bed – touching him, *tasting* him – sends desire clenching through me. I nod, looking up at him beneath my lashes.

He leans forward, resting his elbows on his knees.

"Well?" he coaxes. The proximity is so intimate, even in a crowded hall. I flush, unsure of how to even begin the proposition.

"Where's your father?" I blurt, unable to breach the question I truly want to ask.

His smile falters, but he doesn't pull away. "He's left for the evening. More a fan of reading than revelries. But we both know you're not here to ask that."

They are folk. It doesn't mean anything serious to them. It's just fun. I tell myself, thinking of their casual nature. The reminder solidifies my melting resolve.

"Right. Mara and I were wondering if – um…" I manage to begin, trailing off as his dilated eyes undress me right here.

"If what?" He teases, his gaze lowering to my lips before moving back up with a forced confusion contorting his perfect brow.

He is enjoying the tension, building it purposefully thicker with every move he makes. It's tangible enough already, but he's going to make me ask him anyway – not giving me any way out.

"Do you want to join us. Tonight. In her bed." I breathe between each segment of the request, barely biting back hyperventilation by the end.

His answering smile is fiendish, making me squirm. "Are you *choosing* me?"

I freeze. Recalling the way he'd kissed me in his study – the way his hands felt as they held me against him.

"I want you to choose me."

Then I breathe, "Yes."

He plants a zealous, promising kiss against my lips before I can finish the word. The weight of his crown presses against my clammy forehead at the contact: a reminder of who he is and how dangerous this moment really could be.

But it only intensifies my need for him all the more.

His kiss is slow and exploratory, tasting of wine and fairy fruit. The accompanying hand behind my head locks me in place just long enough that I wonder if he'll push for more. But he releases me, a whine escaping my lips at the sudden withdrawal of his touch.

"Give that to my betrothed, and tell her I'll find you both at day break," he says, eyes severe with the command. "Go warm the bed for me."

I melt under the promise of his words and bow, before turning back toward Mara.

She's standing at a high top table, talking with Leona – who leans conspicuously on it for stability. Her head is barely turned towards me, when I close the distance between us.

My lips find hers as Sylas's did mine, savoring the differences in their kisses. Her lips are plusher, letting me take the lead and deepen the kiss.

I feel her smile against me, as she leans in, raking her fingers through my hair.

"I guess I'm off to find some fun of my own," Leona mumbles, slurring slightly as she turns away.

A heartbeat later, a splash of cold liquid hits the side of my heated face, jolting me back to reality. Mara and I break apart, and I gasp as the sharp scent of wine fills my nostrils. My hand flies to my cheek, wiping away the drops coating my face.

"Oh, shit," Leona's voice comes from below. I look down to find her sprawled on the floor with a puddle of wine. She's tripped over the hem of her too long, vine tangled gown, her glass now empty and shattered at my feet.

"You're lucky that only got on her," Mara clips as she glares down at Leona. On the floor, Leona avoids her gaze, embarrassed as she scrambles to her feet.

"I'll fetch some servants to clean this up," Leona offers hastily, brushing herself off. But Mara shakes her head, her golden eyes narrowing.

"Look at Valerie. She's drenched," Mara snaps. I glance down at myself, noting the dark stain spreading across the middle of my dress – wine soaking in to clinging uncomfortably to my skin.

"I can clean it up," I offer, trying to diffuse the tension.

I don't want to ruin my chance with Mara, even if that means helping Chase's attacker in the process.

Leona's dark eyes flick to me, wide and pleading, before darting back to Mara.

"Very well," Mara relents. "Valerie, clean this up and then yourself. I'll accompany Sy to my chambers later. Wait there for us."

"Yes, Miss," I reply with a quick curtsy, already bending down to gather the broken glass. My relief is immediate, knowing I'll get the chance to freshen up and prepare before our encounter.

As I begin cleaning, the cool air and the task at hand help sober me up. The reality of what I've agreed to sinks in, and my hands pick at the glass with less confidence.

But there's no time to dwell. Our expected encounter grows closer with every shift of the moon, and I know better than to keep them waiting if I

want the chance to do this at all.
   I'm going to need another drink.

Chapter 35

After disposing of the last soaked napkin, I find myself hesitant to leave the revelry. The night is so young, and sobriety is dousing my excitement – self conscious anxiety warring with my want.

What if they expect me to… perform well. How many bedmates have they each had?

A bar near the exit beckons me with a single open stool right in the center of the space. Tall folk flank either side of the stool, their attention focused on company facing away.

A perfectly invisible spot, just what Eddie would pick for me.

I don't let myself think of what she'd say about my *other* actions tonight, as I plop onto the upholstered stool.

I don't even need to call the bartender. The human behind the counter looks to be at most twenty years old, not even old enough to drink back home. The irony isn't lost on me, but I know deep down he's been here much longer than his youthful appearance suggests – just like the rest of us. His nod in my direction tells me to go ahead and order.

"Give me the hardest thing you can," I joke, though I'm not entirely sure it's a joke. My nerves are frayed, my body drained with a mix of anticipation and fear. I need something to steady me – to give me the courage to follow through with what's coming next.

The bartender steps away for a brief moment before returning with a single shot glass and a bottle of something dark. "This should set you up well," he quips with a conspiratorial wink, before walking off to tend to an empty handed pooka – antlers gilded with filigree – at the far end of the bar. I pour the first shot and down it before I can think.

Whiskey.

The liquor is a bitter surprise in a world of such sweet, palatable flavors. I struggle to swallow it down. But once I do, the sting feels right – a physical distraction from the emotional mess inside me. The relief is fleeting though, and all I see are Sylas's icy eyes as he watched me dance earlier.

When I look over to the throne to catch another glimpse, he's disappeared. Mara has taken the seat, a devious smile on her face as she lays across the bark armrests.

They're two of the most powerful beings in the entire kingdom, and I'll have them in a way most humans could never imagine in just a few hours.

I chase away my growing nerves with another shot. This one goes down easier, my body accepting the burn with a welcome shiver.

"If they can have fun, then so can I," I mutter to myself.

Before I lose my momentum, I pour and empty a third shot. My exhale is harsh as the bitterness slides down my throat, the burn lingering in my nostrils. The alcohol mingles with my blood faster than expected, and I set the glass down with more of a clatter than intended. My limbs feel leaded – insubordinate – but no one seems to notice or care.

A strong, heady giddiness replaces the rising doubts that had begun to destroy my desire. My cheeks flush as I fight the urge to plan my next move too obviously.

I deserve a chance to dance again before I go, I think, a smirk tugging at my lips.

My heart flutters at the thought, and I wipe under my eyes – certain some errant sweat has smudged my borrowed makeup from Mara by now. My next breath is heavy, the alcohol making every move heavier in a way I know the magic of the music will alleviate.

"Let's have some fun," I straighten in my seat. But there's still a hesitancy in my limbs – a whisper of doubt in the back of my mind after Mara's command to not venture far from her side tonight.

Do I really want to go out there?

My attention drifts from the life and vibrancy out in the crowd back to the dark bottle – the promise of liquid relief still waiting inside. I take stock of my current state: my stomach is warm, my mind is floaty. But I could use a little more of both. I giggle to myself and reach for the whiskey.

The uncapped bottle is already tilted, when I notice the glass has somehow disappeared. My eyes dart around, flabbergasted by the missing cup I had set down only a moment before.

Did I drop it?

I narrowly avoid hitting my head against the bartop as I lean down to look underneath. The glass isn't there either. My head swivels back to the bartop, and I spot it – or at least an identical one – in front of one of the revelers sitting to my side.

I let out a relieved "phew" and try to guide the glass back toward my territory. But a tan hand juts out, snatching it before I can make my move.

"Heyyyy," my voice is whinier than intended.

"How is it that you get in the way so often?" Prince Ciaran's voice is clipped, his tone dripping with disdain as he looks down his strong nose at me. My blood turns to ice instantly, the dark makeup around his green eyes making them even more lethal than normal. The gilded cuffs over his ears accentuate their elven shape – the crown he wears doing the same to his severe brow.

Wrong prince to find me.

My jaw is slack with offense as I watch him hand the bartender my glass. The bartender pries the bottle from my grip as well, an apologetic smile plastered to his lips. I don't have the coordination to fight for it long.

"Where's Starling?" I slur and look around – the effort to focus is too much for my eyes.

"They're in the library avoiding this party like a smart attendant should. Are you even old enough to drink?" Prince Ciaran doesn't look at me as he speaks this time, his eyes flashing to Mara on the throne – looking for my babysitter.

I grumble under my breath "Yes, I am."

But he doesn't seem to care. His indifference is infuriating as his attention drifts to the bottles lining the bar. His profile looks bored, putting me below even his contempt now.

"I'm thirty-five," I jab louder, wanting some sort of reaction from him. The words are hard to form, the alcohol loosening my tongue and dulling my sense of self preservation.

Good.

I spin away from the bar at his continued cold shoulder, ready to seek out more welcoming company on the dance floor. But when my feet touch the ground, I find it rushing up to meet me. Too late, I realize I've tripped over my numb legs.

"I recall you've been here seventeen years. So you're eighteen, if my math is correct. Which it is," Ciaran scolds, snatching my arm to prevent me from slamming my face into the floor. My neck whips forward in a way that should hurt, but I'm too drunk to feel it.

He lets go once I've steadied myself, as if touching me burns him. Then he preens himself, adjusting the drape of his raven hair and the hem of his sinuous sleeve. "Well I'm triple your age. As are Sylas and Mara and quite a few of the sidhe you seem to have drawn the attention of, funny enough." His arrogance is enough to set my fuse alight.

"Yeah, it's hilarious. Rub it in. This is your world after all, *Your Highness*." I bow with mocking sarcasm as I recall the honorary status of his title. He turns away with an eye roll, like his retaliation is still too much attention to waste on me.

Maybe a sober Valerie would react differently, but drunk Valerie won't let him win.

"Why are you even talking to me right now? You seem to be very forgiving of such a lowly human for someone who hates me," I poke. I know it's dangerous. But it feels good to speak without fear for once.

His smile doesn't reach his intense green eyes when he turns back to me. It's unsettling, the way he slithers close – matching the snakelike appearance of his outfit. His lips almost brush my ear as he speaks, purposefully crowding me in with his juniper scent.

Even so close, I have to strain to hear him over the crowd and my slowed cognition.

"The royalty here has decided that they deem you worthy enough to keep close. And though I find you to be a complete waste of their eternally available time, the responsibility falls to me as a councilor of this court to advise you *not* to dance yourself to death," he says, his voice low and venomous. He pauses, letting the words sink into my alcohol drowned mind. His olive hand comes to rest on my shoulder – a gesture that looks casual to anyone watching – but feels like a threat to me.

"So yes, *human*, I hate you. If it were up to me, you wouldn't exist here. None of your kind would. But it's not up to me. And as an ambassador of another court, keeping you out of trouble can be used to my advantage later. Got it?" he spits, the force of his words punctuated by the way he shoves me away. The malice in his sneer is unmistakable – and for a single breath – I'm sobered by the cruelty of his words.

He's as manipulative as Starling warned.

Color drains from me as I realize what I've just done. He barks a laugh at what must be a terrified look on my face.

"Any other questions I can answer for you before I continue my night with less desperate company?" he asks, tone sweet as though he'd offered me another drink.

I shake my head, my throat too tight to speak. His eyes flash again to Mara before landing on me one last time.

"As expected. I'd tell you to stay away from us, but we both know you're too pathetic to even try," he snarks. The disinterested veil falls back over his demeanor. He mumbles as he pushes past me to leave. "I don't have time for this."

But before he can make any distance, the entire room erupts. A deafening boom shakes the crowded hall, and a blinding flash of light explodes from the dance floor. The force of the violence hurls us to the ground, the room spinning as screams replace the magical music.

Chapter 36

Intense heat presses against my skin like a thick damp blanket –
suffocating – as I struggle to collect myself. Instinct sends me upright, my
head swimming as I search for the source of the explosion.

The once grand ballroom is now a nightmare of flickering orange light
and billowing smoke. A fire roars from the center of the room, forcing ash
and an acrid stench into the air that makes every choked breath end in a wet
cough.

Shadows dance wildly in the chaos, disorienting my already unfocused
vision. I blink away the concussed haze, my hands trembling as I survey
myself for injuries. Tiny specks of blood pepper my arms and legs, but the
misting of red on the surrounding furniture tells me it probably isn't mine.

Don't think about it.

I realize I'm on the floor, still beside the bar. Shards of glass cascade
around me like jagged rain as the room settles. Tiny scratches prickle
across my exposed skin – more exposed than before – as I notice the tears
and burns riddling my gauzy dress. I try to steady myself, a dull ache
radiating through the side of my body that slammed to the ground moments
ago.

When I try to brush the debris away, a much sharper pain bites into my
palms. I flip them toward me and discover deep gashes along the
undersides of my hands from cushioning my fall. I hiss as the blistering
heat lashes at the raw flesh. Through the haze of alcohol and fear, the pain
wills me into motion.

Get up. Now.

I force myself onto wobbly legs. The alcohol dulls most of the pain,
but the adrenaline is sharpening my focus enough to know I need to get out
of here before I can't breathe.

My head whips around, my heart pounding as I take in the devastation.

Prince Ciaran and the bartender are gone. The revelers who had filled
the hall just moments ago are either vanished with them, stirring back to
consciousness with me, or won't get the chance to decide.

My eyes scan the less fortunate, searching faces… or what's left of them – for any I recognize. Limbs are detached and slung on the floor like offal. Chunks of meat and fabric cling to furniture as the only evidence a person once existed there.

A disgusting relief washes over me as none seem familiar. But then I see her: a human girl with horror sealed to her features. Her body is twisted at an unnatural angle as black char replaces pale skin and her extravagant escort's robe.

Violet: the girl so many years ago that backstabbed my barrack friends. *So this is where she ended up.*

My head angles away quickly, bile rising in my throat as a reeking odor hits me. It's the same unmistakable scent as when my neck was branded, but magnified tenfold. The nausea spurs me on.

As I shuffle towards the exit, Leona struggles to her feet at the side of a mangled attendant. The merrow girl is burned like Violet on the side furthest from Leona – like she had thrown herself over the sidhe in one last act of loyalty.

A steady drip sounds through the thunder of the rolling flames, pulling my stinging eyes to the center of the room. I spot a thin line of glowing red dribbling between the cracks of the marble tiles near the dance floor. My strained eyes follow the trail towards the dais along the glowing grid, and a horrified cry rips from my throat when I see the source.

Mara.

She lies near the base of the tree throne – the epicenter of the explosion – where all casualties radiate outward like petals from a grotesque bloom. The titanic fairy fruit tree stands eerily tall after the blast, even as flames lick hungrily at its gilded trunk.

Mara's once vibrant golden gown is drenched in glowing crimson. Her ginger hair fans out around her, singed clean to the scalp on the side closest to the fire. Her face – frozen in a wide eyed mute scream – looks almost alive. Too aware for someone so utterly gone. But then I feel the sting of a bargain broken, and I know there's no life left behind. The sight is so horrifically wrong that I can't look away.

"No!" I howl, voice swallowed by the crackling flames and distant screams. My legs move on their own, carrying me to her discarded form.

She was going to help my friends.

I stumble over debris, my hands slipping as they scramble for purchase. They're slick with blood – whether mine or someone else's, I can't tell. When I reach her, I collapse to my knees, my breath coming in shallow, ragged gasps that don't fill my lungs.

"Mara," I choke out, voice breaking. I reach for her hand but freeze. It… isn't there.

Her arm dissolves from the elbow into ragged ribbons of pink meat, the edges charred and blackened.

A low groan rips my attention away from her. My head twists to see Prince Sylas on the far side of the room, his pristine white robe now torn and bloodied. His face is ashen, blue eyes wide with dumbfounded shock as he takes in the devastation. His concuss haze clears on Mara. He looks like a lost child: regal composure stripped away.

"Save her," I plead between sobs. He doesn't respond, locked on Mara's lifeless form. I want to say something – to offer some kind of comfort – but the words won't come between the sobs and the gulps of smoke-spoiled air.

"We need to get out of here," Leona shouts hoarsely. Sylas finally looks at me, his composure returning. He nods, stiff and mechanical.

A few others are hobbling toward the exit, shouting warnings that the fire is growing. I rise next to Mara one last time, unable to offer her the help she was offering me.

She was kind to humans, I won't ever forget that.

"Valerie," Prince Sylas's voice cuts through my mental eulogy. I turn to see him holding out a sooty hand. His face is caked with glowing blood, but his eyes are steadier than I expect. "Come on."

I take it. Leona follows a step behind. Together, we make our way toward the exit, picking over debris and bodies as we go. The heat is unbearable, the stench only worsening as the flames reach more casualties. But I keep moving, one step after shaky step.

Sylas leads us through the untouched passages of the castle interior, the gleaming fireproof marble a safe haven after the devastation on the other side. The fire's roar fades behind us, replaced by the distant wails of the injured ahead. Sylas's grounding grip on my hand drops when we reach the looming doors to the king's garden.

"Continue on to the others, I need to find my father," Sylas commands us both. Neither of us has the energy to challenge his decision, simply continuing our shuffle towards the moonlit sanctuary.

Chapter 37

The king's garden, a once living masterpiece of lush greenery and vibrant blooms, now serves as a grim refuge for the survivors. Folk and humans huddle in separate clusters, but everyone's faces are streaked with ash and tears – every set of eyes are hollow with the shock of the carnage we've all just witnessed.

I drift toward the human camp, my eyes downcast. My skin still crawls with the sensation of Mara's broken bargain as escorts and servants check on one another, their voices a chorus of shock and relief that disguises my sniffling. The sound of their sincere reassurances only deepens the ache in my chest.

I miss my friends… my real friends. The ones who feel like family.

A fresh wave of tears spurred on by regret, alcohol, and crashing adrenaline track down my cheeks.

"Valerie, thank god," a voice breaks through my grief, and suddenly strong arms wrap around me. I hug back instantly, clinging to the warmth and solidity of another person. Tears wet my shoulder as the hugger's head rests against me. "I'm so glad you're alive."

I'm pulled back at arm's length, and blink, struggling to focus. Chase's bruised face comes into view, his brown eyes wide with relief at finding me. But I can't offer sentiments, my mind is still trapped in the image of Mara: her mutilated body, her lifeless face, the scent of her burnt hair.

Before I can sink deeper into despair, a commotion draws our attention. Sylas emerges through the thrown open doors he'd left us at. He's changed into a cleaner, simpler outfit. He moves with purpose, pushing his way to a small fountain at the garden's center. The sound of trickling water is jarring amidst the chaos, a cruel imitation of the blood spilling out of Mara.

I shake away the vision.

He scoops water into his hands, splashing it against his face in a futile attempt to wash away the devastation. Then he climbs onto the fountain's edge, his presence demanding an audience even in his disheveled state. The survivors turn to him slowly, murmurs fading into a desperate silence as we all await his words.

"Everyone," Sylas begins, his voice heavy with emotion. "The Unseelie rebellion launched an attack against the kingdom tonight. But they failed in their reported goal: killing me."

A ripple of shock passes through the crowd.

Unseelie Rebellion?

I can't recall anyone *ever* speaking of an uprising in the kingdom. Not Chase. Not Mara or Sylas… not even my Unseelie friend: Starling.

My arms tighten around my trembling self as I scan the crowd – the human faces around me just as confused. Then I look to the royalty across the garden, landing on Ciaran and Leona. Ciaran's expression is circumspect, his arms crossed as he watches Sylas intensely. Leona leans heavily on him – her dark skin streaked with darker bruises. Her gaze is just as unsurprised by Sylas's words.

They knew about an Unseelie rebellion?

Sylas opens his mouth to continue, but something to his side catches his eye. A hush falls over the crowd as another figure steps forward: King Anders.

He looks just like Sylas.

I've seen him in passing at revelries and in my studies, but this close he is a towering presence – his blonde hair gleaming in the moonlight, his face stony with authority. Even Sylas steps down from the fountain's edge, bowing his head in deference.

The King's voice resonates to the back of the crowd, carrying across the garden easily as he replaces Sylas on the edge of the fountain. "Tonight, we were tested. But as my son has said, we are not so easily broken. This attack was delivered through a horrific explosion, leaving only innocents to bear the brunt of their violence."

The crowd stirs with a mix of fear and unease. The King's gaze sweeps over us with inherent authority. "They attempted to remove Sylas – my only heir – from the line of succession to destabilize my reign. But instead, they have created an opportunity: a chance for us to come together, to rebuild, and to grow stronger."

He pauses, icy eyes landing on his son, whose jaw is clenched tight. "Sylas has proven himself a true leader tonight. He has shown resilience and sacrifice. Offering a pledge. One that will ensure the stability of our court."

The King gestures for Sylas to step up beside him. The prince does with overt respect for his father – who places a hand on his shoulder. "Prince Sylas's betrothed was killed in the attack. And he agrees with me that although Mara can never be replaced as an individual, she must be replaced as a figure."

A few outcries of uninformed courtiers make the rest of us jump. I swallow my offense before it can show on my face.

Mara's body isn't even cold, and they're already talking about replacing her?

Beside me, Chase stiffens. His face – normally healthily flushed – goes entirely grey. "Mara's… dead?" His voice is brittle. His hands tremble at his sides, and I can see the weight of the news physically crashing down on him.

"Chase," I say softly as I reach for his arm, but he doesn't hear me. His eyes are fixed on the king with a mix of disbelief and panic.

The callousness of the king makes my brow furrow. I glance at Sylas – unsure if his gaze lands on me or if I'm imagining it – before he nods to his father in acknowledgment.

"This new union will not only strengthen our future but also send a message to our enemies," the king continues. "We are not afraid. We are not defeated. We will rise from the ashes of this attack, stronger than ever before."

The crowd erupts into applause, though the sound feels hollow to me. I look around, taking in the faces of the survivors. Some look hopeful, others wary. But all I can think about is Mara and how she's being tossed aside – her memory reduced to a political footnote.

The injustice of it burns in my chest like another fire.

Chase's hands ball into shaking fists. "They're just going to replace her?" he reiterates, his voice low and trembling. "What happens with us?"

I squeeze his arm. "I know. We'll stick together."

My heart aches for him – for all of us – but I don't know what else to say.

He shakes his head, his eyes glistening with unshed tears. "She was the one who pulled me to my current station."

I can feel myself losing him and tuck myself closer – trying to keep the pieces of him together with force. "Me too."

The king steps back, and Sylas takes his place once more, his voice stronger now. "We will rebuild. We will heal. And we will ensure that those responsible for this attack face justice. I vow a wedding between myself and another bride before the next equinox."

Half a year.

The collective shock hangs in the air for a breath. Then applause breaks out, more enthusiastic this time.

But I feel nothing but disgust. Mara deserved more than *this*, more than being erased so quickly.

As the crowd begins to disperse, Sylas steps down from the fountain and approaches the others I recognize. His expression is unreadably composed. But that lost look is still in his eyes, and I find myself creeping closer.

Leona leans into Prince Ciaran in a mirror of how I must be with Chase. "Mara…"

Sylas's face falls. "I know. She didn't deserve this. But we have to give the people something positive to distract themselves with, or it'll be worse for the kingdom in the long run."

"What about us?" I gripe before my sobering mind can rethink the trivial question amidst the enormity of everything else. I shrug out of Chase's grasp when he refuses to get closer to Leona, approaching the shellshocked group alone.

Sylas hesitates, his gaze unable to meet mine for a moment. His face is schooled into cold determination by the time I join their circle. None of them shoo me away or make off color comments for once.

"Now, we *all* move forward," he says slowly. "You will move into my attendant's chambers. I will take on Mara's deal with you, if you'll accept it again."

I don't know what to say to that.

The thought of returning to my friends – of escaping this hell and never leaving the safety of the laundry again – is undeniably tempting. But when I look at Sylas, I see his hazy eyes mist over, like he knows which way I'm leaning.

He's about to be forced into a political union – to shove away his grief over Mara and become an example of the West's strength. The thought fills me with a sympathy that borders on agony. It overwhelms my own needs and solidifies my decision.

"I accept," I say firmly. Not a heartbeat later, I feel the magic pulse our bargain into place. "But what about Mara? And Alistar? Or Chase?" I gesture behind me to where the boy still stands.

Sylas smiles faintly, though it doesn't reach his eyes. "We will grieve. Give her a proper funeral and the respect she deserves. And then you will help me pick a new bride. Alistar will heal, he'll take her rooms for himself. And Chase… he can join you as a companion. Think of it as a gift of gratitude for accepting the bargain again."

I nod, my heart stitching itself back together with the promise of a new future to prepare: a bigger job to do. We stand in the moonlit garden, watching the glow of the fire through the windows as water nymphs begin battling back the blaze.

As much as I want to believe Sylas's words, I can't help but wonder if we're truly ready for whatever change has just been forced upon us. But I turn back to Chase, lifting my head a little more as I approach him with the bittersweet news.

Chapter 38

The night of Mara's funeral is the most beautiful and heartbreaking night of my life… so far.

A week passes after the attack. Though the region begins to rebuild, open wounds still mar the psyche of everyone who was there that night. The main hall gleams as if untouched by tragedy, its damage repaired with speed only magic can produce. The trunk of the breezy fairy fruit throne has been repainted a vibrant gold over the scorch marks. But the empty spaces left by those we lost – courtiers, staff, nameless servants I passed innumerable times – are harder to paint over.

New faces drift through, their wide eyed presence a fragile attempt at renewal. However the absence of the more veteran members lingers like a shadow no sparkling rainbow chandelier can dispel.

A bitter cold has settled over the land, draping the world in a blanket of snow far too early in the season. The gardens we step into are now a stark, deafened expanse of white, like the land itself found the remaining greenery too offensive for the memory of the fallen.

As we reach the edge of the maze, a funeral pyre of fragrant wood and dried oleander rises like a monument. Mara lies atop it, her body shrouded in blush silk that stands out in the monochrome. It is cradled gently by the full moonlight above. I know what lies beneath the shimmering fabric: charred, broken, and incomplete. But I choose to remember her as she was – golden and full of life.

Sidhe – dressed in somber hues that betray their usual opulence – form in a semicircle around the pyre. Their breath comes in visible puffs in the cold, clouding the space. The humans among us wear simpler attire, but the grief etched into our faces is just as overt.

I haven't seen most of the royalty since the attack. Moving mine and Chase's belongings into Addie's old quarters has kept us occupied – my continued studies to be the future king's attendant taking up the rest of my spare time. But as I imagine Alistar sorting through Mara's possessions as he moves into her chambers… His is a fate I wouldn't wish on anyone.

Chase stands tall beside me for the ceremony, his lanky arm linked with mine. Since Mara's death, he's become my platonic anchor: a steady presence in the chaos of everything changing around us. It's not just new staff and a new room to adjust to. I have a new prince to attend to… Though he hasn't called on me yet. The door between ours and Sylas's chambers remains sealed shut.

Alistar stands closest to the pyre, his shoulders hunched against the cold. His copper hair – so like Mara's – is unkempt. His face is pale and drawn with remorse for having ditched that equinox night. Sylas stands beside him, a hand resting on Alistar's shoulder in a gesture of quiet support. The prince looks as regal as ever. But there's a heaviness in his eyes: a weight that even his royal bearing cannot conceal.

The ceremony begins with a mournful melody, sung by a selkie clad in dark seal skin.

The sound is haunting, cutting through the muted crowd the way only magic can. One by one, the mourners step forward to leave offerings on the pyre: jewels, flowers, tokens of their affection for Mara. Sylas is the last to approach, slow and thoughtful. He places a small, intricately carved box on the pyre.

"You were my light," he says simply – devastatingly. "And though you're gone, I will see your dreams fulfilled."

The pyre is lit once he steps back, the flames catching quickly as it melts the fresh snow. The pink shroud curls and blackens as the fire consumes it, the pleasant smoke of burning wood and flowers covering what I know would be the stink of her burning flesh without them.

Don't think about that right now, I chide myself.

The crowd begins to disperse as the sun begins to crest the horizon. Chase and I linger, watching the flames dance against the bleak gray sky.

He eventually retreats indoors too. But I stay, unable to leave Mara alone.

She was sunlight. She shouldn't be left in the cold.

I stay until the pyre is reduced to embers, the chill seeping into my bones enough to make me shake.

She is gone. Really, truly gone.

"Valerie."

I turn at the sound of Prince Sylas's voice: the first time he's addressed me in the week since her death. He stands a few feet away, his blue eyes shadowed as he looks over me. He looks… diminished – smaller than the imposing prince I've come to recognize. The sight of him like this makes me wince.

"Yes, Your Highness?" I address with a deep bow. I feel relieved with the address. I've wanted to give him my condolences, unable to do so with etiquette dictating I wait for his approach.

He steps closer, his boots crunching in the snow. "Stay with me today."

There's a vulnerability in his command that I've never heard before: a rawness that makes my chest ache. I nod, not trusting myself to speak.

He reaches out, his smooth hand brushing against mine, and I let him take it. His fingers are as cold as my own – grounding me as he leads us back indoors. I don't let myself think about the last time he held my hand: dragging me out of the burning hall the other direction.

We walk in silence – the only sounds accompanying us: the crunch of snow beneath our feet and the distant howl of the wind. We walk together as they're replaced by the clips of shoes on marble and the hushed discussions of the dayshift servants.

His chambers are warm when we arrive, the fire in the hearth stoked bright already. He releases my hand to shrug off his cloak, tossing it over a chair before sinking onto the edge of the bed. I remain near the door, shifting my weight uneasily. He looks up at me.

"Come here."

I hesitate.

He is your prince. You're his attendant. Get used to being alone with him.

Then I cross the room and sit down next to him as ordered. Sylas sighs, leaning back on his hands, oblivious to the tension riddling my spine. "I keep expecting her to walk through the door," he says quietly, his gaze fixed on the fire. "To scold me for grieving so long or tell me to cease the dramatics. She always knew how to put me in my place."

I smile faintly, though it feels more like a grimace. "She kept us all in our place."

He glances at me. "You remind me of her, you know."

The words catch me off guard. I blink at him, unsure of how to respond. "I… do?"

He offers a small, sad smile. "You have the same light." He looks away, his voice dropping to a whisper. "It's why I was so quick to keep you as my attendant. After she…"

His morbid words cut short, but I know what he's thinking.

After she died. After he lost her.

I don't finish his sentence. That was always her job.

I swallow hard, my throat suddenly tight at the memory of her. "I miss her."

"Me too."

I don't know what to say to that, so I just shrug. I reach over and take his hand, lacing my fingers through his.

He looks down at our joined hands before squeezing mine gently. "I took my time to respect her memory. But moving on is going to be difficult."

He shifts then, lying back on the bed and pulling me down with him. I go rigid, unsure of his intent. But he doesn't try to kiss me or paw at my body. He simply angles my head until it finds its way against his chest.

This feels wrong without Mara. I think, but don't dare voice the thought. Not when he's finally letting me in.

He traces idle circles on my wool covered back for long quiet minutes. It feels nice, and I sink into his embrace. His heartbeat is steady – a comforting rhythm that soothes me as much as his lavender scent – making my eyelids heavy.

"I am grateful you asked me to come here, I've been worried about you," I mumble against his chest.

He doesn't respond, but his grip tightens ever so slightly. We lie there in silence as the sun shifts, my barrack trained eyes tracking nearly an hour of us curled together. It feels like we're in a bubble suspended in time – where nothing exists but the two of us and the weight of everything left unsaid… and undone.

After a while, he speaks again, mostly to himself. "I will be fine. I should have let you in sooner."

As the fire begins to die down in the hearth, I feel his breathing even out, his body relaxing as sleep finally claims him. I stay awake a little longer, listening to the soft sound of his inhales and exhales and the occasional steps of a servant in the hall. My mind races with thoughts of what tomorrow will bring – of how we'll navigate this fragile new dynamic between us. But for now, I push those worries aside and let myself sleep in his arms.

I fall into a too detailed dream of everything my body wishes Sylas would do to it: his tongue, his hands, his… everything.

When I awake with a jolt, I'm too flushed, my breathing too strong for the quiet evening I've come back to. I shake the dream from my mind. But the haze of desire doesn't dissipate as quickly.

I look around, and see him seated at his desk – his head bowed over a stack of papers – letting me sleep.

My heart speeds as the dream clings to the primal parts of my mind. It's heat seeps into my waking thoughts. I'm standing, staring at him still focused on his work before I even realize what I'm doing.

I bet he tastes even better than my dreams.

The thought isn't my own, or maybe it is. I don't know. All I know is that I *need* him.

His blue eyes widen as I approach, but only for a blink. Then his expression shifts into a slow, apologetic smile.

"Evening," he says, smoothly. "Did I wake you?"

A shiver of carnal want runs through me with the sound of his voice. My body moves on its own until I'm standing so close his head cranes up to meet my eyes. His gaze darkens as he takes in my flushed face – my heaving chest.

"I need-" I start, but the words catch in my throat. Instead, I reach for him, my trembling fingers brushing against his sharp jaw, and he leans into my touch in a mirror of how my dream began.

"Valerie," he murmurs, but this time it's either a warning or a plea.

I don't care which.

I lean in, pressing my lips to his. The moment we touch, it's like magnets pulled together. His hands are on me in an instant, tugging me down into his lap, his mouth hot and demanding against mine. I melt into him, my fingers tangling in his silky hair as I kiss him with desperation.

"I don't care," I moan against his lips. "I don't care if you're a prince and I'm just your attendant. Even if it's just tonight. I just… I need you, Sylas."

He stills, his hands tightening on my waist as he pulls back to look at me. His eyes search mine.

I think he's going to give in, to let me indulge this one reckless want. But then his gaze drops to my hand, my eyes follow.

There's no ring.

His jaw flexes, and he reaches for my hand, pulling it between us.

"Where is it?" he barks.

He's so beautiful.

"What?" is all I can pant before I'm trailing a line of kisses down his porcelain neck – trying to convince him to forget the ring.

Just let me have this, I beg with my hips – grinding against him.

"Valerie, focus," he grits out, ripping me away with more force. My eyes stay locked on his kiss-swollen lips as he speaks. "Where is your ring?"

"The ring that would ruin all the fun?" I groan, squirming just to feel his hard body against mine. The friction sends electricity through me. So I do it again. And again.

"The glamour can slip while I sleep. That's why you need the ring," he grumbles to himself as he stands up – careful to balance me – before storming back to the bed.

"I don't want it, not when everything feels so easy without it," I whine at the loss of him.

The sight of him: angry, hot, in bed right in front of me: has me stepping up behind him. To my dismay, he ignores my rubbing hands, my lips on his skin, as he pulls the sheets apart.

"Sylas," I hum his name. "I know you want me too."

He turns back to me, and my body buzzes as his hand wraps around my wrist between his legs. I blink, upset but accepting, when instead of kissing me, he slides the ring back onto my finger.

The moment it's in place the glamour lifts, and I'm hit with the full mortifying force of what I've just done. Horror floods through me as I scramble back, my face now burning with shame instead of lust.

"I don't know what happened," I stammer, shrinking away from him. "The ring has never slipped off before."

"It's okay," He stands, eyes guarded as he watches me retreat. "I told you I want you too. But not like that. Not when you're not yourself."

I shake my head. "I shouldn't have stayed in here. I shouldn't have said those things. I didn't mean them."

"You *did* mean them," he challenges.

He's right.

I can't look at him. I can't bear the way he's looking at me – like he knows every secret I've ever tried to hide.

"I need to go," I dismiss myself, already reaching for the door.

He doesn't protest when I cross back to mine and Chase's room and lock the door between us.

Inside, Chase is still tucked into his bed – his breathing slow and even – lost in a much more serene dream.

I build another wall between myself and the world, locking myself in the bathing chamber. My clothes come off with some effort, my sweat making them cling uncomfortably. Then I step into the bath, the cool water doing little to douse the heat still coursing through me. I scrub at my skin as if I can wash away the memory of his hands on me – his lips against mine.

At least he stopped me, when I couldn't stop myself.

By the time Chase stirs awake, the moon and stars are fully out. I'm dressed in my attendant uniform – my hair pinned neatly the best I can – my face carefully composed.

"Evening," he mumbles, rubbing his eyes as he sits up.

"Evening," I echo, voice steady despite the shame raging inside me. He doesn't notice anything amiss. Though I can't help glancing at the ring on my finger more than once, ensuring it's still there as I finish making my bed and organizing my half of the room.

A soft knock at the door pulls me from my busy work. I open the door just enough to see who's there.

A human servant stands in the hallway. They look familiar, though I can't quite place them. Their blue eyes are wide as they take me in, their gaze drifting over me and into the room behind me before they finally speak.

They must be new.

"*You're* Prince Sylas's attendant?" they press skeptically.

"And your uniform is stained," I tilt my head towards some brown blotch on their collar. They pale when they notice the spot. "Though I don't think you're here for us to comment on each other's condition."

They blink, then straighten. "Dinner tonight for the council *and* their attendants," they say, their tone more respectful. "Formal uniform dress. In the dining hall at midnight."

They hand me an invitation.

"Understood… and be careful out there. Humans are rare at this level," I reply, closing the door and releasing the servant back into the tower with the vague warning.

"What was that?" Chase yawns from his bed.

"That," I sigh, "was a royal decree. Mourning time is over. We have to get our asses back in gear."

I crawl into his bed, shimmying between his warm arms as he protests my cold intrusion. We lie there for a while – neither of us ready to face the night ahead. But eventually, the scurrying sounds of traffic in the hall grow too loud to ignore. We rise and dress, finding the more tailored and luxurious of our uniforms to keep to the dress code.

I notice more human servants than in the past as we head for the royal dining hall – the vacancies left by lesser folk giving us a chance at higher levels of servitude at an unprecedented rate.

Chapter 39

I've never eaten in the *actual* royal dining hall before, Mara took her meals in more intimate settings leading up to the autumn equinox. The novelty sends a thrill of excitement through me as Chase and I step into the already thriving atmosphere of attendees mingling. A rich aroma of roasted vegetables, spiced wine, and sweet fairy fruit greeting us when the actual company doesn't.

The counselors – all glittering, radiant sidhe – are mostly seated with a few empty bottles of wine on the table between them. The attendants – a small smattering of satyrs, merrows, and other folk – still cling to the perimeter, their training too ingrained to be erased with one week of relief from duty.

I'm still the only human attendant, I realize.

Even with the cool divide between the nobility and the rest of us, there's a welcoming warmth of a too large hearth as we venture further in – lit and bright to drive away the chilling weather. I notice the long table is set enough for counselors *and* attendants with polished silverware and crystal goblets.

"It's not often the royalty let others at their table. I wonder what's changed," Chase says under his breath in a teasing tone. My eyes drift to Sylas, engrossed in conversation with Princess Balora.

*Did he do all of this for **me**?*

I shake the idea from my mind, and find my seat at the table arranged with artful, edible displays. Chase and Starling flank either side of me. I'm grateful for their buffer from the other attendants and their incredulously shot looks in my direction.

I pluck pastries and hors d'oeuvres from the central trays, double checking every piece for fairy fruit. I keep my focus on my food as conversation picks up around me – my attempt to blend into the crowd failing spectacularly.

My two friends discuss books they've read over my head. I slump to give them better access to each other.

If it takes bad posture for them to finally become friends, I'll take it, I think.

Sylas sits at the head of the table in his usual velvet embroidered finery, his presence making me hyper aware as always. There's a brightness in his eyes that hasn't been there since losing Mara. Alistar sits to his right, his expression and mourning garb still swallowed in darkness. Balora – clad in jewel tones that show off her olive skin and bright green eyes – is across from him, laughing sharply at something Sylas whispers in her pointed ear. Ciaran is next to his sister in matching opulent regalia, and Leona is across from him with real gold braided into her coiled hair. The tableau of royalty gleams gilded and untouchable – back to their usual perfection after the funeral.

The less prestigious counselors – eight in total – fill the remainder of the sidhe side of the table, listening intently to the conversations at the head of the table. They offer comments and jests in the quiet moments, jumping at the chance to be included.

Other attendants follow our lead to take their seats. Too many unfamiliar faces fill the vacancies left a week ago. I don't bother with the small talk that begins to pick up.

Who knows who will be here in another week.

"A fortnight," Sylas announces abruptly, cutting through the chatter along the table mid meal. "That's when I'll host the first revelry in the search for my bride."

A hush falls over the room, his words settling over us like too much snow on the hedges outside. I glance around, taking in the shocked reactions.

"Two weeks?" a counselor named Evelyn says. "That's… soon."

Sylas nods confidently. "I don't have the luxury of time. If I'm to marry within the next two seasons, I need to ensure my choices are well considered."

No one argues with him. No one would want to be in the position his father has placed him in. The tension is unbearably palpable.

I can feel Chase stiffen beside me, his fingers tightening around his wine glass. Starling leans back in their chair as they glance at their assigned prince.

"We'll need to make a list of potential matches," Sylas continues, more businesslike. "You all will assist in this matter. That's why I called for this dinner. To prepare you *all* for the next steps."

His eyes dart to me for the briefest check-in, but more than a few heads follow his line of sight. I lift my chin under their scrutiny.

There's a murmur of agreement around the table from the councilors and even some attendants, though no one seems particularly enthused with the task.

Leona leans in towards Sylas as she pours another heavy serving of wine for herself. "If we're making a list, we might as well start with the obvious." She lets a pregnant pause follow as she sets the bottle down. "Princess Margaret and Lady Giabella of the North, for sure. And, oh, let's not forget Prince Ciaran. You could make his title actually mean something."

Sylas smirks, clearly amused by her choices. "Your input is noted, Lee."

Ciaran sets his own empty wine glass down with a sharp *clink*, before he plays with the gold cuff over one ear. "What about yourself?" he suggests to Leona, his voice dangerously sweet. "Mara's out of the way, and you're still unmarried. Don't you *want* to be a part of a ruling family?"

The room goes deathly quiet with the mention of the dead. Sylas's eyes flash with rage as his knife stabs his meal. "Careful, Ciaran."

"Oh, okay, so I have to take hits, but I can't return them? Got it," Ciaran snaps. "Let's be honest. This whole thing isn't about a distraction for the people. This is about Sylas securing his kingship before another attack."

My eyes flick to Sylas, who just rolls his icy eyes. Then to Starling, who is trying very hard to hide the hurt in theirs.

Leona lets out a cackle, her wine glass sloshing as she gestures toward Ciaran. "Oh, please. Don't act like you wouldn't do the same, if you actually had a throne to claim."

Ciaran turns his sneer on her, his hands clenched into fists on the table. "You should stop right there."

"Should I?" Leona shoots back, her voice rising as she leans forward. "You're a bastard. You'll *always* be a bastard, even if you know how to fuck your way into getting the upper hand on occasion."

I expect Sylas to intervene, but he's lounging in his chair, watching the exchange with detached amusement… as if this is *exactly* what he wanted by sitting them so close together.

"Enough," Ciaran growls, pushing back from the table. "I'm not going to listen to this drivel anymore."

Leona stands as well. "Oh, don't run away now. We were just starting to speak some *real* truth."

Ciaran storms out, Leona not more than a few paces behind him.

The table erupts into heated debate about which spurned lover is right. Then Sylas raises a hand, drawing most of the attention his way.

"Let them work it out," he commands dismissively.

I exchange looks with Chase, who appears as stunned as I feel. "I think I'm siding with Leona on this one," he grumbles.

Starling is now smirking into their wine glass, clearly enjoying the drama with insider knowledge.

"Any juicy details to share?" I venture. They take a big gulp before shrugging.

"Ciaran's just great at court drama," they hedge. "He bargained with Leona's aunt in the East. She is sending four ships to back his king stepfather's trade dispute with the Unclaimed Isles. Everyone believed he'd finally propose as part of the agreement after about *fifty* years together. But it wasn't specified that way in the wording of the bargain. So now she's pissed."

An elated sound escapes me at the truth behind the fight and I swallow a large portion of my own wine.

As the conversation picks up again, I can't help but notice the way Sylas's gaze keeps drifting to me. There's a new energy about him: a readiness to move on. It's as if the announcement of the revelry has lifted a guilt off his shoulders, allowing him to focus on the future instead of the past.

But he's going to be getting married, and I'm never going to be an option. Don't entertain the thought, I protest against the flutter of my heart every time his eyes meet mine.

The laughter around the table grows louder as we empty more bottles and trays. I try to focus on my own dessert by the end, but it's all too overwhelming.

Alistar, emboldened by the atmosphere, leans close to one of the few humans in servant navy clearing an empty tray from the center of the table. His lips curve into a sly smile at the girl's hesitancy.

"You look hungry," he coos, holding out a piece of fairy fruit. "Why don't you try some?"

The servant freezes with wide eyes, and I recognize the look. I glance down just long enough to confirm it: she doesn't have a protective ring. My heart lodges in my throat as I watch her part her lips obediently. Alistar's eyes spark with glamour as he drops a small chunk of the red flesh into her awaiting mouth, letting her lips suck the juice off his finger. The servant's expression shifts from fear to confusion at the flavor.

"Good girl," Alistar chuckles. "It's not so bad, is it?"

Starling – who's been watching the exchange with growing anger – slams their hand down on the table, startling me from the display. "What in the Dagda's name are you doing?"

The royals are too distracted by the now doomed servant to care about the attendant's disrespectful response. Alistar offers a wicked smile as he stays trained on his prey. "Having fun. You should try it sometime, Unseelie."

Starling stands, their chair scraping against the floor. "You're all barbaric," they mutter just loud enough for me and Chase to hear before they stalk out of the room. Alistar runs a tender bronzed hand through the servant's hair, feeding her more fairy fruit as the others laugh and cheer.

Chase stands up – quickly following Starling – but I cannot move. I watch in horror as the servant's delight under all their attention turns to distress, her body going rigid. She claws at her throat, mouth agape for air she cannot find.

She's choking.

My heart speeds as I look around the table, waiting for someone to do something. But no one moves. Sylas just stares at his crumb covered plate with stony focus. The other attendants ignore her writhing as they pour more wine into waiting cups. Until finally, the girl collapses to the floor – still and curled in on herself as she succumbs.

The royals' laughter fades, turning to other conversations. Alistar sighs, gesturing for the angel-winged guards to remove the body. "Well, that's unfortunate," he says disturbingly casually as she is dragged away. "I suppose the fun's over."

The others murmur in disappointed agreement, and I feel a wave of nausea wash over me.

They don't care.

To them, that servant's life was nothing more than a fleeting amusement.

I cannot stay put any longer, rising from my seat without care for the heads that snap to my quick dismissal. I leave for the safety of my chamber.

On the staircase – out of line of sight of an audience – panic closes my throat.

I need to get to my room. Then I'll be able to breathe or breakdown.

I wander up and down stairs, eventually finding my way back to my room after taking a few wrong turns in my disorienting spiral. There's a moment where I debate running for the front gates – taking the chance that I can make it out there long enough to find help or the portal home.

But I know that's just a fantasy.

Besides. Chase is right, sticking by Sylas may make him more sympathetic to humans. It seems to be working already.

When I finally reach my chamber, the prince himself is waiting in the space between our doors. My feet slow on approach, looking at the grim lines in his face.

"Alistar shouldn't have done that," Sylas mutters, not lifting his eyes to meet mine for once.

Is that shame? I wonder,

"No, he shouldn't have. Someone should have stepped in," I agree with a wavering voice. He nods, his shoulders drifting down with the weight of my condemnation.

"It's just been so hard on him: losing his only sibling. I was too relieved to see a smile on his face again, I didn't want to be what took it away," he confesses softly.

My heart feels a need to go to him – to relieve the guilt and sorrow pulling him down after celebrating new plans only moments before.

So I do.

Even when the ghost of the dead servant begs me not to.

I approach him, wrapping my arms around his waist, and give him a hug. He rests his chin on top of my head, his arms cradling me in a way that feels like an apology. We stay like that for a long, unspoken moment.

When he finally pulls away, there's a glint in his eye that I can't quite read. He looks me over once. But then he steps back – suddenly more guarded.

"Come in here with me," he orders, nodding toward his door. "We need to talk."

I go still at his formal tone, then follow him into his chambers anyway. The room feels quiet – intimate – but not in the way it did before.

It's more serious now.

He gestures for me to sit on the chaise by the lit hearth, and I do, folding my hands in my lap. He doesn't sit too, though. Instead, he paces for a moment – wearing a hole in the floor with his hands clasped. He finally stops in front of me.

"It's been a week," he declares. "I need to know: are you still okay with our bargain? I wanted to give you time to recover from the shock of everything."

I look up at him, searching his ethereal face for clues about his motives for the conversation. There's a tension in his jaw – a shadow in his eyes that wasn't there before. I wonder if it's Mara's absence that's weighing on him… or if it's something else entirely.

He feels bad about the servant girl.

"Yes," I answer steadily despite the turmoil inside me. "I'm still okay with it. I just am not sure when you'll need me to lie."

His gaze flicks away for a moment before returning to mine. "Does it matter?"

"It doesn't really, I guess," I agree, then clear my throat to banish the weakness in my tone. "As your attendant, I'll do whatever you need me to."

He exhales sharply, running a hand over his down turned mouth. In the moment, he looks almost vulnerable, and I feel a pang of sympathy for him.

He's lost his betrothed and was still giving me the chance to walk away too.

"I've heard about an Unseelie Rebellion a few times now," I say carefully, watching his reaction. "Some of the citizens seem… concerned about it."

Sylas's jaw flexes. "Unseelie sympathizers of the Tyrant King, according to my spies," he elaborates.

I lean forward with the hint of truth. "What do they want?"

"Revenge." The word is a snarl. "They don't rely on the same magic as us. When my father and the other rulers defeated the Tyrant, they didn't just kill him – they shattered his hold on our magic. Released it back into the world for us to use." His eyes meet mine, glacial and unyielding. "The rebels believe that they thwarted some grand chance for the Unseelie to control what is now the Cardinal Kingdom."

A chill creeps down my spine. "So they're attacking the courts?"

"Not just attacking." Sylas hesitates, choosing his next words with intent. "They're *hunting*. Anyone with Seelie magic is a target. Sidhe are the most magical. Hence, the most targeted."

I think of the explosion that killed Mara – the way the rebels planted their dirty work on the throne specifically. "What about the humans and Unseelie that die too?"

His gaze darkens. "Collateral damage. They see the humans in our care as 'tainted' by Seelie. The repentant Unseelie in the castles are seen as traitors. I imagine they'd purge every last one of you too if they could. Then they could take the Otherworld entirely once we're all dead."

The vision his words conjure makes my blood run cold.

"That's why you're rushing the marriage," I realize aloud. "You need a queen – an heir – power to combat the rebellion that only the king himself holds."

Sylas doesn't deny it. "They're well hidden among the servantry, even here. My father doesn't care to stop them *before* they attack. He thinks it would be bad for relations between our kinds if we started interrogating Unseelie servants without overwhelming proof."

My mind flashes to Starling. *There's no way they're part of a rebellion. They **saved** me and had every chance to hurt me when we were alone in my room… right?*

"I think it's a necessary evil," Sylas cuts through my doubting thoughts. The unspoken truth is clear: not all Unseelie are rebels, but enough of them are to make them *all* potentially dangerous.

I reach for his hand without thinking, my fingers threading through his. "Then we'll get you that queen and heir."

He studies me for a long moment. "My needing a new bride doesn't change how I feel about you," he proclaims. "But right now, we have a job to do. And you're going to be instrumental in helping me see it through."

The words sting more than I expect them to, but I push the feeling down.

This is what I signed up for. This is my role. I'm his attendant, even if he's hinting that I'm somehow more.

"Of course," I say, voice steady despite the ache in my chest. "As I already said, I'll do whatever you need."

He nods, his gaze lingering on my quivering lip before he turns away. "Then your first assignment as my attendant is to oversee preparations for the revelry in search of my bride."

I stand there, suddenly overwhelmed by the task. "Yes, Your Highness."

And with that, I step out into the hallway, closing the door behind me. The pain in my chest doesn't go away, but now it's joined by mounting dread as I realize what I've agreed to do.

Chapter 40

I pore over Addie's notes in the dim library, her looping letters barely decipherable: another noble feud to remember – another poisoned chalice to avoid. My fingers tighten around the quill I'm adding amendments with.

Lady Seraphine (councilor!) cannot be seated within sight of Lord Rakan after the incident with the firewine (??). Princess Margaret will refuse to dine if placed near anyone who has an alliance with the Southern royalty. The Duke of Greenbriar (East, not North) requires three separate wine glasses-

A shadow falls across the page.

"Planning for war already?" Starling's pitying voice cuts through my annotating as they drop into the adjacent chair. Their red eyes dart to my taut brow. "You look like you're about to set the parchment on fire."

I drop the quill and rub my temples. "I don't know the first god damned thing about royal revelries."

"Obviously." They pluck the notes from in front of me. "Which is why you're lucky Chase and I enjoy containing disasters."

As if summoned, Chase slides into the seat on my other side, the scent of spiced wine clinging to his tunic. "Tell me you've at least tripled the guard rotation," he says without preamble.

I blink. "What?"

Starling's claws tap against the table. "The rebellion. Or did you think pretty garlands would foil another assassination attempt?"

They're definitely not part of it, then.

But that relief is only doused by a different cold realization. *The explosion that killed Mara... The same could happen again. To Sylas. To any of us.*

"I-"My voice cracks. "The security plans are with the captain of the guard. I haven't-"

"Give me that." Chase snatches my attempt at a seating chart from under my elbow, scanning it. "You're lucky the courtiers have loose tongues in bed. These placements alone will get someone killed."

"And we need to vet every servant," Starling adds. "Especially the new ones."

Too many new ones after the explosion.

I square my shoulders when I feel myself begin to slump. "I'll speak to the guards about doubling the minotaur patrols on the ground level."

Chase exhales sharply. "We need-"

"More than just flower arrangements," I discern in an irked tone. "Understood."

Over the next week, the preparations take on a more purposeful approach.

I walk the perimeter with the seraphim captain of the guard each night, memorizing every hidden alcove where an attacker might lurk. Starling teaches me the basics of runes and magic charged crystals that might pose a threat. Chase drills me on the most volatile relations in the court until I can recite them in my sleep.

The main hall transforms under our watchful eyes.

Not just with garlands and gilded table settings, but with subtle protections: a rare exception for salt to be mixed into the candle wax by Belladonna to disrupt rogue magic – a discreet exit route woven by dryads behind the floral displays.

Two nights before the revelry, Sylas finds me adjusting the branches of his throne for optimal sightlines. He gently takes the pruning shear from my red stained, gloved hands. "You've thought of everything."

Not everything, I want to say. *Not how to settle my nerves when I imagine another explosion. Not how to quiet the voice in my head that whispers this might be the last time I see you alive.*

Instead, I bow. "The guards are positioned. The grigs know to stop playing music at the first sign of disturbance to give humans a chance to run too."

Before he can respond, Lord Rakan appears in the decorated archway. His hungry eyes linger on the two of us before he bows a smooth show of respect to Sylas.

"I was hoping I might accompany His Highness to the welcome dinner tonight," he suggests in a honeyed voice, eyes flashing with excitement to the prince's.

Sylas blinks once, before he composes himself into regal indifference.

"Of course." He turns back to me. "Don't stay up too late."

I bow, and turn away as he takes Lord Rakan's arm. I give the last set list of songs to the bard, visit with the chef to assure they have all the needed ingredients for the menu, and double check with the bartenders that they have specialty brews in stock.

It's still a revelry. It still needs to be fun.

Then I retreat to my quarters for a well earned sleep.

Sylas's chambers glow under the door as I pass, the air conspicuously thick with the scent of Rakan's perfume and pleasure. I avert my eyes, my brain far too preoccupied with party preparations to focus on his bedroom company.

He's sidhe. It's what they do.

When I wake again, Sylas is in the threshold between our rooms.

"My Prince?" I grumble, still half asleep. He steps back into his room, a softness in his eyes as he takes in my sleep rumpled appearance.

"Chase and I are narrowing down the potential matches, thought you might want to help," he explains, leaving the door ajar as he retreats fully.

I blink – unsure if I imagined the fondness in his voice – then crawl from my nest of pillows.

Sylas and Chase are seated around his desk, far more casual a sight than I expected. I take the open spot between them: a sprawling collection of names and descriptions spread out before us.

"Since when do you take my companion's opinions into account?" I question.

"Chase knows the courtiers better than anyone, Mara saw to it that he was well taken care of for his work." Sylas answers simply.

Chase fills the wine glasses between the three of us with a proud smirk. "And all that pillow talk is finally paying off. I just wish she was here to see it."

Chase is a spy?

It makes sense – *perfect* sense. But the thought had never crossed my mind before.

At least he uses it to help me too.

I think of the way he fixed my seating arrangements. Grateful that he's on my side through this.

"To Mara," I offer, raising my glass shakily. The other two clink in toast and we get down to business.

"Princess Margaret," Sylas says, tapping her name with a thoughtful expression. "North Court. Intelligent. Ambitious. And – according to my father – 'not entirely insufferable.' High praise, coming from him."

Chase takes a sip. "Other than her claim to her own throne and the headaches she'll cause over Valerie, she seems perfect."

What?

Sylas hums at the reminder of something lost on me. "I think she could be swayed if needed."

My hands flail with my interruption. "What headache? Over *me*?"

Sylas angles his glass at me purposefully. "Yes, you. Margaret doesn't like humans at such a level of servitude as you're in."

"Oh."

I take another sip of my wine, when the answer is so blatantly obvious.

We continue down the list, my stomach twisting as I read through them. Lady Xayah, Lady Isolde, Lady Seraphine: each one is more accomplished and poised than the last. It's hard not to feel out of place looking over them, even if I'm just here to help.

"What about Lady Elise?" I ask, trying to keep my tone neutral. "She seems pleasant."

Chase raises an eyebrow. "Pleasant? That's your assessment?"

I shrug, avoiding either of their eyes. "She's graceful, well spoken, and clearly interested in Sylas. What more do you need?"

Sylas leans forward then, resting his elbows on the desk. "I don't know, Valerie. What do *you* think I need?"

The question catches me off guard, and I feel my cheeks flush. "I'm not the one marrying her," I jab, my voice sharper than intended.

Sylas laughs, breaking the tension as he retreats back in his chair. "Leona, South Court. Ruthless, practical, and – from my memory – an excellent dancer."

"Sounds like a match made in heaven," Chase says dryly, avoiding his history with her. "You do love a good dance."

Sylas sighs. "I do. But I'm thinking my scope of potential matches is missing some… light."

I look at my drained glass, my heart racing.

What does he expect me to do? Play along? Pretend I don't know this is just a game to him?

Sylas leans over to me when I don't engage, his presence

overwhelming as he hovers just out of reach. "What do you think? Should I be looking to add a little *fire* back into my life?"

I freeze, my pulse quickening as his hand boldly plays with my too long hair in allusion to the color.

"I… I don't know," I stammer, suddenly frazzled.

Chase finishes his glass, clearly enjoying the show. "I know what my answer would be."

Sylas smiles victoriously. "I think we know hers as well."

I exhale shakily when my nerves stay frayed.

*I hate how much his attention affects me. Even with my ring – even knowing we are planning his **wedding** to a sidhe I'll never measure up against.*

But before I can defend myself, there's another knock at the door that blends into the endless stream of knocks the past week. A brownie servant steps up. "Your Highness, Lady Giabella has requested a walk through the gardens with you. She's waiting in the courtyard."

Sylas finishes his glass before straightening his robes. Then he rises from his chair. "Duty calls," he acquiesces. He glances at me with promise in his eyes. "We'll continue this later."

I nod when words fail.

He leaves Chase and I alone in his room.

For a moment, neither of us speaks. Then Chase refills his wine glass and fixes me with a knowing look. "So, you hearing wedding bells yet?"

I glare at him, cheeks burning. "Don't be ridiculous."

"Am *I* the one being ridiculous?" he teases. "Because it sure looked like he was ready to propose to you right there."

I shake my head. "It doesn't mean anything, they all like messing with us."

Chase leans forward, his expression serious for once. "It will only make him pity our human plight more if you were the queen. Just saying."

I bite my cheek, the words warming my chest more than I'd like to admit.

"But that's not realistic," I say finally.

I know how the folk are – their whims and desires so fleeting. My human heart begs me to not let it break so willingly.

Chase nods. "You're not in the human world anymore. Reality here can be surprising."

"He has much more strategic options," I challenge. "And I'm more than content being just his attendant."

He stands, stretching lazily as I shut down the conversation. "Well, just his *attendant*. I don't know about you, but my eyes hurt from staring at all this paperwork. I'm going to bed. You should too. Big night tomorrow and all that."

I let him lead me back to our room, but he stops short in the doorway. I bump into him, about to say something snarky before my breath catches at the sight inside.

A dress – a cascade of midnight blue silk embroidered with silver thread – looks like a piece of starlight on my bed. The bodice is fitted, the neckline daring but elegant, the sleeves sheer enough to catch the draft of the open door. It's the kind of dress meant to turn heads – to command attention.

A note sits atop the fabric, the wax seal unmistakably Sylas's. I crack it open with shaking hands.

Valerie-

For your tireless efforts in preparing the revelry. Wear this, and let the court see the one who orchestrated its beauty.

-S

My fingers tremble as the note falls to the floor.
This is way too much.
Chase whistles ahead of me. "Damn. That's not just a 'thank you.' That's a confession."

I run a hand over the layers, my fingers gliding under the smooth fabric without calluses in the way anymore. "It's a trap."

"Is it even a trap, if you see it coming a mile away?" He flops onto his bed, grinning. "It's not like he's subtle about what he wants."

"Exactly." I pick up the dress and hang it in my closet, out of sight. "I'm an *attendant*. Not a guest. Not a-"

Not a potential bride.

The words stick in my throat.

Chase's smile fades. "You think wearing it would send the wrong message."

"It would send *a* message," I mutter, closing the closet door carefully. "And I'm not sure I'm ready for what that means: trap, confession, or otherwise."

I reach for my usual attire: a simple tunic and trousers with silver trim. It's modest, unremarkable. *Safe. Invisible.*

Chase watches me set it in place of the dress. "You're really not going to wear it?"

"No." I smooth the fabric over my sheets, avoiding his gaze. "The revelry isn't about me."

Chapter 41

The night of the revelry arrives before I can convince myself to change my mind about the dress. I step out my door in the attendant's uniform I chose, mentally going down my list of jobs.

No dancing. No drinking. No mingling. I cannot get distracted, I am there to observe and keep notes of who Sylas spends time with. Nothing more.

"No dress?" Sylas asks, his voice curious as he steps out of his door next to mine. He's in his favorite white robe, about to step off to the atelier for his outfit tonight.

I glance down the length of myself at the royal blue matching tunic and pants, fidgeting with the quill in my hand.

I thought the chiffon looked nice, I think.

"No, I prefer brighter blues," I say instead, my voice steady despite the jolt of him stepping closer. "This is who I am. Your attendant. Not your… whatever you think I am."

His lip curves slightly before he turns away. "That's fine. Wear what you want. I'm just relieved you'll be there."

And as he strolls away from our chambers, I shake the idea of changing into the dress from my head – focusing instead on creating an easy to follow chart in my notebook.

I make my way to the main hall as I write. It is alive with music and laughter already, three weeks almost to the day from Mara's passing. Judging by the crystal chandeliers now gleaming – and freshly polished marble floors that I had the servants clean *again* – no one would ever suspect the tragedy that happened here so recently.

I stand near the edge of the room for a while, my hands clasped tightly on my notebook. I keep my posture perfectly straight as I battle away thoughts of Mara and explosions from my mind.

Be invisible. Watch and listen, I remind myself right before Prince Sylas is announced.

When he steps into the space, I admire him from this safe distance. His skin is dusted with gold to bring out every defined angle of him. His eyes are lined with kohl that makes them too bright as they sweep over the crowd. And his hair is intricately braided with golden flowers into a crown atop his head. The robe he's draped in is a patchwork of blues, tied along the sides to show off his body.

He's so perfect. Why am I keeping him away again?

As the night goes on, it's harder than I imagined to maintain my composure – especially with Sylas at the center of the entire affair. He charms and flirts with every potential match who crosses his path. He's allowing them all to fawn over him, as if he knows how much it gets to me.

I watch him across the room, arm linked with a sidhe woman with white hair and eyes like frost.

She's stunning.

They all are.

This one is Princess Margaret of the North Court. I skim my notes for a refresher.

First in line for her own throne.
Mara's second cousin.
Does <u>NOT</u> like me.

I recall Mara's trip to her mother's harvest celebration: the entire reason I was alone long enough for Sylas to kiss me and make his intentions clear. The whole reason I almost took both of them to bed the night that Mara…

Not right now.

Margaret's laugh pulls me from the memory, the sound like tinkling bells. I look up long enough to see her lean in closer, her hand resting lightly on his arm. Sylas doesn't pull away.

I look down again, my chest feeling too tight.

It doesn't bother me. Sylas is my prince, nothing more.

I jot down the affection as a positive in her chart.

"Hey," a friendly voice pulls me from my seething. I turn to see Chase, slightly off balance with too much wine.

He's dressed in matching royal blue to my own, his sandy hair too wild for the clean cut set. "You look tense."

"I'm fine," I correct, forcing a smile. "Just doing my job."

He eyes me with incredulity, before turning that same look toward

Sylas and Margaret a few feet away. "Your job is to stand here and watch him flirt with every eligible noble in the realm?"

I bristle at his tone but keep my voice even. "My job is to attend to him. Whatever that entails."

He studies me without subtlety. "If you were *really* attending him, I don't think you two would have made it to the revelry."

I stiffen. "I don't know what you mean."

He smirks. "Of course you don't."

"I'm starting to regret taking you on as a companion-"

"Valerie," Sylas calls across the room. "Come over here."

My eyes flick to Chase, who gives me a mocking bow before stepping back into the crowd for his own company. Taking a cleansing breath, I smooth my uniform pants – feeling ridiculous next to all the beautiful gowns – and make my way to Sylas's side.

"Yes?" I keep my tone neutral, angling my notes so no prying eyes can see them.

He smiles, though it doesn't reach his eyes. "Margaret was just telling me about her private estate on the phoenix ash plains. I thought you might find it interesting."

I force a polite bow, turning to her. "That sounds lovely."

She gives me a cool, appraising look. "You must be the human attendant I've heard so much about. How… unique."

He talks about me with them?

I bite back a retort, keeping my composure. "It's an honor to serve the prince."

Sylas chuckles, his hand resting lightly on my lower back. It sends electricity through me, but I ignore it. "Valerie is more than just my attendant. She's become quite special to me."

The folk can't lie. Does my bargain to lie really mean that much to him? Or does he mean… something else?

Margaret's forced smile falters, her eyes bouncing between us – unsettled. "Is that so?"

"Indeed," Sylas's tone is formal, but his grip on me tightens ever so slightly. "Now, if you'll excuse us, I think I'll grab another fairy fruit."

He leads me away, his hand still on my back. I feel eyes on us as we push off the crowded floor. Once we're out of earshot, I lean in to whisper. "What was that about? Doesn't she hate me?"

He smirks, his eyes glinting with amusement. "Jealousy is a powerful motivator. I wanted to see how she'd react to me putting you above her."

I stop in my tracks, reeling. "You used me to make her jealous?"

He shrugs unapologetic. "You're not going anywhere. They need to know that. And *you* need to know that."

I do know that. But it doesn't make this any easier, I think bitterly.

"Prince Sylas," a melodic voice sings. We both turn towards another potential bride approaching: this one wearing a sheer dress that reveals all of her ample curves. Her dark hair looks like flowing mahogany – her eyes like molten honey. She's inhumanly gorgeous – obviously – and the way she looks at Sylas makes my stomach twist.

"That's Lady Giabella: North Court. Friend of Princess Margaret. Hates the South Court and probably me too," I fire off in his ear as she closes in, skimming my notes quickly for the facts.

"Giabella," Sylas says, his smile widening with the reminder of her identity. "What a pleasure."

She curtsies gracefully. "The pleasure is mine. I was hoping you might join me for a dance."

Sylas glances at me, innocently. "Valerie, would you mind?"

I shake my head, forcing a bright smile. "Of course not, Your Highness."

He offers the lady his arm. As they walk away, I feel a pang of jealousy hit me deep.

I hate this.

I retreat to the edge of the room, my hands clenched as I try to scribble notes about the two matches we just encountered. Chase is there again, leaning against a pillar with two glasses of wine in his hands. He offers me one.

"Still fine?" he asks, mocking.

I glare at him, ignoring the glass. "What do you want?"

He shrugs, taking a sip from his own. "Just making conversation. You look like you could use a drink."

"I'm working," I say through gritted teeth.

"Of course you are. And how's that *working* out for you?"

I don't respond, my gaze drifting back to Sylas and Giabella. They're dancing now – movements graceful and perfectly in sync. She laughs at something he says, her hand testing the lean muscle of his shoulder.

They look happy together – like he doesn't have a care in this exorbitant world.

And why should he? He's a prince. He can have anyone he wants.

I swallow hard, forcing myself to look away. Chase is watching me with too much sympathy now, all mockery gone from his face.

"You know," he downs his glass before setting it on a passing serving tray. "You don't have to stay. You could go to bed. I'll cover for you."

I nod, dejected. "I owe you one."

"Consider us even for giving me a safe room to sleep in," he brushes off the offer, as he takes my notebook and begins jotting down his own observations and opinions.

Chapter 42

I sit at my desk, attempting to make a pros and cons list of every possible match. But my stomach sinks as three potential brides rise well above the others.

Princess Margaret.

Princess Balora.

Lady Giabella.

They're all beautiful. They all come out equally, when weighing their power, wealth, and lineage. Knowing how small the pool is only makes me feel like a decision is closer than I want it to be – like I can pretend that I'm also one of his potential brides, so long as the selection process isn't over.

A knock at the door pulls me from my charts.

"Busy," I bark, returning to my sheet.

But when the door opens, it's not Chase or a servant as I expect.

Prince Sylas steps inside, his party regalia gleaming even in this small space.

He's perfect – as always – but there's a disheveled quality to him now. The attention of the revelers has left him frayed at the edges in a way he rarely lets himself be.

He closes the door behind him with deliberate intent, the lock clicking into place. My heart skips a beat as I rise to my feet.

It hasn't even been half the night. Why is he back already?

"I was hoping to find you alone in here," he says urgently, his breathing uneven.

My fingers grip the corner of the desk for support with the intensity in his tone. His eyes – his total focus on my every move – sets me on high alert.

"Your Highness, if this is about me leaving the revelry-" I begin, trying to diffuse the tension.

"In case you cannot tell, I left too," he interrupts bluntly.

He's supposed to be selecting a new bride. There's a whole party full of beautiful sidhe vying for his attention – who can offer him alliances, power, and legacy.

It twists my gut to imagine them all competing for his attention – their hands on him – their lips promising things I never could.

So why is he here in my room, looking at me like this?

"I don't know if this is a good idea," I say, my voice trembling as I recognize the same desire in his eyes from our stolen moment in his study and at the autumn equinox – right before we lost Mara. It makes mine drop to the floor in retreat.

He crosses the room instantly, his boots nearly touching my bare feet. "I don't care if you think this is the worst idea in the world. I wanted to see you."

I lift my gaze again reluctantly, struggling to stay focused as his lavender scent envelops me.

"What can I do for you?" I choke out, throat tight with him mere inches away.

His eyes shift past me for a moment, lingering on my lists of names. "Do you think she should be one of those three?" he asks, a smirk on his lips as he absorbs my charts and data.

No, I think you should choose me, I think.

A blush betrays my answer as I stare at him, unable to give voice to my ridiculous truth. He reaches for my hand in my flustered state, his fingers closing around my right wrist. Electricity shoots up my arm where he's holding me, bringing my hand to his soft lips.

The kiss is featherlight against the knuckle – a whisper against my skin – but it sends a shiver through my entire being.

"I need to know. After all we've been through," he murmurs. "Do you trust me?"

Do I trust him?

I think of the way he's kept me safe after Mara's death – the choices he's entrusted me to help him make for the court's future.

But trust isn't the real issue.

It's the cost of that trust – of wanting him knowing I'll never truly *have* him. I will always be one misstep away from becoming just another forgotten lover in the prince's long life ahead.

Like Mara.

But I could help humans if I agree. Maybe even the innocent Unseelie like Starling… I just need to let myself try this.

I can't speak, but I nod.

His eyes darken as he twists the silver ring on my finger.

"What are you doing?" I hiss, not pulling away even when my pulse spikes.

"What I've wanted to do since the moment I saw you in the atelier. But I will only do it if you tell me you want me to." His pupils dilate as he plays with the ring – turning the piece in small circles to gage my body's response as he teases it further off the digit.

"If we do this, I want it to last." My words are shakier than I'd like, feeling the ebb and flow of his glamour as I set my boundary.

I sway on my feet, my thighs trembling as he pulls me closer towards complete vulnerability to his power. I squeeze my eyes shut, focusing on steadying my breath.

"Oh, Valerie," he leans in to purr against my ear, sweet wines warming his words. "The moment you tell me you're mine, I'm never letting you go."

It's exactly what I need to hear – the truth that lets me know whatever is between us is more than just a fling.

"Take it off, let me be yours then," I command.

I prepare for the overwhelming urge that will come when he does remove the ring. It must be visible on my face. Because as soon as I build up my guard, he slips the jewelry from my finger.

I can't look as he pockets the ring, nor as his hand cups my chin. My mind flashes to our very first meeting in the atelier: our instant connection – his thumb on my lip.

Just like that night, his hand guides my head up.

"Open your eyes for me, pet," he hums.

I obey, willing to do any and every thing he asks of me at this moment.

His lips part, holding back words… or waiting for mine. We stand there, memorizing each other's features on the precipice of whatever comes next.

"Sylas, I-" I gasp, but he silences me with a hard kiss, his mouth crashing against mine with a hunger that mirrors my own. His arm wraps around my waist, steadying me as I melt into him.

For a moment, I let myself forget the marriage and the politics, I forget the danger and the fact that I'll never be his first choice.

He is all encompassing, his kiss probing with a pent up need that I gladly match. My hands rest on his adorned shoulders, feeling the tension in his muscles beneath the fabric – erasing where Giabella's had just been.

Every fantasy and memory I've dreamt about pales next to the real thing right now: the softness of his touch contrasting the hardness of his body. Lavender and mint mingle with the fairy fruit on his tongue, creating an intoxicating taste that I lap up.

I feel his finger trace the scar where my brand once was on my neck, his touch curious as he continues to kiss me with a rhythm that leaves me breathless.

Is he thinking about the night he saved me?

The thought spurs me on, and I press into him, battling for dominance in our kiss. He pulls me back just enough to break the kiss. Our mingled panting is the only sound in the room as I stare up at him.

"You've been mine from the moment you stepped through that portal." His words are rushed. "I'm done staying away from you. Tonight, I'm going to make sure you know *exactly* where you belong."

I need him more than I need to breathe.

I drag his face back to mine, earning another sound from him – this one softer, almost a sigh. The fire in me burns hotter, knowing I have this effect on him.

His sure hands slide down to lift me. My legs instinctively part to straddle him, feeling his length press insistently against me through the fabric of his finery. When he begins trailing kisses along the flushed skin of my neck, a shiver racks my entire body.

My back is to the bed. I know where this is headed as I grind into him. Excitement coils tight in my core when he bites my collarbone, then soothes the sting with a slow, deliberate suck – marking me as his.

"Sy," is the only word I can conjure.

He steps forward, inching us closer to the bed. But then, unbidden, my mind claws its way back to reality.

Are we really doing this?

The prince came to me – despite the politics and expectations weighing on him – he came here. To *me*.

The thought makes my hips still, and he pauses, mistaking my disbelief for reluctance. His hands release me, and I fall the short distance onto the bed, the cool sheets a stark contrast to the heat of his body.

The space gives me a moment to breathe – to think – but his presence looms over me with expectation.

"Valerie," he says with guarded coolness, though his eyes burn. "Is this what you truly want?"

I swallow hard, my heart racing as I look up at him. He's a vision, his robe now untied and slipping from his shoulders to reveal the hard planes of his body. My gaze drops lower, taking in his excitement.

He's *ready*, waiting for my consent.

"Yes," I assert: shaky but sure. "You're just… this is just… overwhelming."

The moment the words leave my lips, he's on me again. His mouth captures mine in another eager kiss. His body presses against me, the friction of my clothes against his hardness drawing a moan from my throat. I'm suddenly too warm – too confined and desperate to feel him without barriers.

His lips sear down my neck again, and I relish in the way his teeth graze my skin this time. My hands fumble with the fabric of my top when he sucks another mark onto me.

"Wait," I gasp, pulling away just enough to tug it over my head. He watches – eyes dark with hunger – as I finally free myself from the garment and toss it aside.

His lips find mine again, and this time, I bite his lower lip, instinct driving me to claim him as he's claimed me. His hands roam my body with possessive confidence.

"I think of you everyday," he murmurs against my skin, his voice rough with desire. "Imagining what it would be like to have you in my bed just like this."

His confession sends a shiver through me, stoking the fire in my core until it's unbearable. I struggle to remove the rest of my clothes, my hands clumsy as I push my trousers down and kick them aside. Finally, I'm as bare as he is, and the sight of him above me – his body poised and ready – steals my breath.

"I've tried to fight it, but I feel the same for you," I admit.

He doesn't hesitate. His knees push my legs apart, and I feel him against my heated core – the promise of what's to come sending a thrill through me. My body hums with his glamour, every nerve alight as he angles himself and pushes into me in one smooth, practiced motion.

I cry out, the sensation overwhelming: like water after a desert – food after a famine. He fills every part of me completely until I can't think anymore. I arch into him, my nails surfacing blood on his shoulders.

"I've fantasized about you making that sound beneath me," he growls, his forehead resting against mine as he withdraws and thrusts again: deeper this time. His eyes are wild – locked on mine – and I can't look away. He rolls his hips as he adds, "Every damn day, I've imagined you like this: falling apart for me. While you've been right next door. Just out of my reach."

A wicked smile curves his lips as I moan again, the sound escaping me despite my attempt to stay quiet. The triumphant look in his eyes builds a tension deep inside me, coiling tighter with every thrust. His hand slides down my side, fingers tracing the curve of my waist before gripping my hip, forcing me to take his entire length.

"This is where you belong, got it?" he orders against my ear. "Coming undone. In my hands. You're *mine*."

He sets a rhythm, his hips rolling against mine mercilessly. I meet him every time, my hands gripping his shoulders for something to anchor myself with.

When he shifts, I gasp as pleasure sparks through me: more intense than before. His voice is honeyed and low as he mixes the glamour with true emotion. "That's it, just let go."

Pleasure crashes over me in waves, my body tightening around him as I cry soundlessly into his chest. His movements grow more erratic as he chases his own release. His body soon shudders above me – his hands gripping the sheets by my head as his breath comes in ragged bursts.

Then he stills.

For a moment, we are frozen with shared shock. Then his hand strokes my forehead with aching tenderness.

"I knew you belonged here," he whispers again. His voice is softer this time, but no less certain.

We stay like that, our hearts pounding in unison as he lays on top of me. Then, slowly, he withdraws and rolls to the side. I close my eyes, savoring the warmth of him beside me. But the moment is fleeting. He rises from the bed, and I feel the loss immediately: a cold settling in his absence.

My eyes snap open as he takes my hand over my head, sliding the silver ring back onto my finger. The glamour's pull fades. Mortifying clarity washes over me along with a blush that spreads from my cheeks to my chest.

"Don't," he warns as his eyes sweep over me. "Don't be embarrassed. Your body knows what it wants. When that ring is off, you come alive for me. I can feel it."

He leans down, his lips brushing my ear as he adds, "If you were to remove it right now, I'd gladly take you again and again. But I have to return to the revelry, and you need to sleep. So keep it on until I say otherwise."

His words make me laugh – nervous and flattered all at once – even as he steps back and begins to dress. I watch him, my cheeks burning as he ties the laces of his finery without trouble. He shifts before me back into the cool, composed prince I know.

I bow my head, my heart still racing as he slips out the door and back to the party.

Alone, I lie back on the sheets, the scent of him lingering potently. My body feels heavy, my mind clouded with exhaustion and second thoughts.

Well, I think, closing my eyes as I breathe him in, *Chase is going to have a field day with this one.*

Chapter 43

My eyes open lazily, greeted by rays of sunlight slanting through the windows at an angle I don't normally see anymore.

It is well past noon.

I prop myself up on my elbows, feeling sore in parts of my body I haven't used like this in a long time. A deep inhale brings the memories of last night flooding back: my heat, his fervor. My eyes scan the room, but there's no trace of him now, of course.

The only evidence of our encounter is the smudges of blue and gold paint flecked across my blankets and the faint discoloration on the sheets between my legs.

There's no way I'm making a servant clean this.

I feel relieved to find Chase's bed empty and scramble to hide my guilt before he makes his way back. I drag myself to my feet. Methodically, I strip the covers off, folding them for easier transport.

As I work, Sylas's words replay in my mind:

"You belong here."

I gather the blankets – my movements more organized than my thoughts – and set them aside. Pulling a simple cotton frock over my head, I head out to clean the mess while the tower is still mostly free from curious eyes.

The castle feels different in the daylight – ethereal in its own way. The metals gleam brighter. The colors are richer. The marble and stone reveal textures and details my eyes rarely catch in the dim chandeliers of night.

It's a strange beauty: one I'd almost forgotten.

As I make my way to the private laundry room in this tower, I hear faint shuffling down a side hall, but otherwise I'm alone. I'm grateful the revelers are still asleep, leaving the space deserted.

I scrub away every trace of last night, hanging the sheets to dry in the plentiful sunlight that streams through the windows. The work is soothing, until the heavy wooden door thuds behind me.

I jump – expecting to greet some eager servant – but the figure is out of any uniform I recognize. They are cloaked in a blue hood, their face hidden.

"Hello," I try politely to greet them, but the intruder doesn't respond. They don't even pause, instead crossing the room to disappear through another side door, juggling a stack of papers in their gloved hands.

What's their problem?

I shrug off the strange encounter. But as I turn back to my work, I notice a single sheet of paper left behind on the floor. Curiosity gets the better of me, and I scoop it up.

It's a map: a blueprint like the one I was once given by a satyr attendant. But this one is even more elaborate, dictating secret tunnels that overlap and connect areas I never knew were linked in the castle.

My jaw drops as I study the labyrinth built into the castle's bones – my old laundry barracks just a tiny fraction of the true vast network.

This information feels too important to leave lying around.

I open the door the visitor had just passed through, catching a glimpse of them in the distance.

"Hey! You dropped this!" I call, trying to sound polite and disarming. But the figure doesn't come back – only quickens their pace – disappearing around a corner.

"Well, I tried." I grumble.

I console my bruised ego by returning to the laundry. It isn't until I catch a glimpse of my reflection in the soapy water that everything clicks.

I look… insane. My hair is a tangled mess, half of it sticking out at odd angles while the rest is knotted at the nape of my neck. Blue and gold smudges discolor my skin, and my neck is littered with love marks from Sylas's mouth.

No wonder they fled.

I grimace as I realize how obvious my state must be to anyone who sees me.

Go take a bath, I scold myself, leaving the freshly hung sheets to dry.

I debate whether to leave the blueprint in the laundry room, in case the visitor retraces their steps. But the information feels too critical to abandon where any rebellious servant could see it.

Tucking it under my arm, I head back to my quarters.

Chapter 44

I've spent most of the evening rearranging the room – like I can erase the evidence of Sylas's presence so thoroughly that no one would ever know he was here. But no matter how many times I adjust the pillows or straighten the sheets, the memory of him lingers in my guilty eyes.

I find one of the few turtleneck shirts in my closet, the drab blue wool a bit scratchy as I retrieve it from the corner. I pull it over my head, checking my reflection.

No visible mouth marks, I console myself. *Though maybe the turtleneck itself is more obvious...*

The door to the bedroom opens, and I step out of the bathing chamber in time to see Chase and Starling standing there – their faces a mix of curiosity and amusement as they balance a tray piled high with far too much food.

"Look who's finally unlocked the door," Chase says with mock awe.

"We were starting to think you were in trouble," Starling adds, their tone less amused as they step inside. "But then we heard the rumors and figured you just needed some rest."

I feel fire in my cheeks and wave off their words. "It's not what you think," I say, though I don't even believe the words as they leave my mouth. I flop on my bed as they set the tray on our shared desk.

"Oh, please," Chase jumps onto his own bed with a portion of roasted vegetables. "Everyone knows Sylas ditched the party to come here. The real question is: how was it?"

I groan, burying my face in my hands. "Can we not do this?"

"Absolutely not," he counters, as Starling settles onto my bed beside me, sliding a plate of pastries my way. "Spill."

There's no point in trying to hide it from them.

They're the only friends I have up here, and they'll find out eventually anyway.

So I settle in, picking at the offering as I reluctantly begin.

"He just – he came in here. Asked me if I trusted him, ripped the ring off my finger, and had me falling apart in about five minutes. It was intense." I leave out the most intimate details, but the looks on their faces tell me they've already filled in the blanks.

Chase grins. "I *knew* it. I knew he wanted more than just to sleep with you. Otherwise, he could've taken that ring off any other day and had his way. He actually cares about you."

"Oh, does he?" Starling's tone is more biting. "You know he's still going to marry someone else, right? And she's still his *attendant*. He just doesn't want to make things more complicated than they need to be to get her in his bed."

My eyes widen at Starling's bluntness. But the accusation isn't entirely unfounded. "He told me before that he wants me to choose him. Maybe he does mean for us to be something more."

We sit there, talking and laughing about the rest of the party as we finish the meal. Chase and Starling seem closer tonight – lingering stares and excuses to touch each other. But I don't push, wanting them to grant me the same privacy.

"Ciaran's probably looking for me by now," Starling excuses themselves, red eyes shifting to the window to gauge the moon's placement when I raise an eyebrow at their hand on Chase's knee. "We should head to the lounge."

I'm not entirely sure I'm ready to face Sylas again, but I know I can't avoid him forever. So I let the two drag me down into the hall, where the court is already alive with more drinking and dancing – like last night's party never ended.

We enter an intimate lounge tucked in an alcove of the main hall, and I immediately notice Sylas sprawled on a couch, his presence magnetic even in such a relaxed state. A few crowned heads surround him, their laughter carefree. His eyes meet mine, and the rest of the room fades away. Then he gestures to the empty spot beside him.

My stomach drops.

It's unorthodox for me to sit with them – normally keeping with my fellow attendants along the wall – but I know better than to refuse.

I make my way to the couch, ignoring the curious glances and comments behind gilded hands as I take the seat beside him. Chase and Starling linger near the edge of the room, watching us too.

"Well," Leona says, her voice dripping with sarcasm from her perch across the low table. "Look who's joining the court."

"Enough," Sylas clips in warning. "I won't have anyone disrespecting my attendant."

The small circle's mood falters at his tone. I feel suddenly self conscious, my flush fortunately covered by the turtleneck sweater. I focus on my hands – trying to blend into the furniture – picking at my nails as his fingers absently play with a strand of my hair.

"You see the throne over there?" he asks me suddenly, angling his chin towards the large golden throne.

It's impossible to miss, I think.

"The giant tree chair?" I joke instead.

"It's been growing ever since my father freed the Cardinal Kingdom," he explains.

I don't know why he's telling me this, right now, amidst his friends.

"Oh, that's fascinating," I offer politely.

He smiles, leaning conspiratorially towards me in front of everyone. "Fairy fruit trees usually only bear fruit for a season or two before they begin to wilt. This is one of only a few that has eternal – season defying power. They say eating its fruit gives the consumer equally impressive power."

"That's where you get *your* fruit, right?" I prompt, suddenly more engaged.

"Only my direct bloodline may take from it," he confirms. "Probably for the best that my future bride is forbidden from doing the same."

My heart flutters at his words, the meaning not missing me.

He's just messing with you. It's what they do.

"Although," Alistar interrupts our stare off with the word. "There are a few missing after the break in."

"What do you mean 'the break in'?" Sylas asks sharply, his hand stilling in my hair.

"Just what I said," Alistar replies equally short. "Someone got into the archives today. It's clear they were looking for something. But they also got ahold of some of the fruits from the throne tree."

Sylas's jaw tightens. I can see the wheels turning in his mind. "Any idea who it was?"

"Not yet. But the guards are looking into it."

The table erupts into speculative whispers of a dark cloaked figure and their hidden motives. My eyes shoot to Sylas, but his expression is unreadable. I want to tell him about my encounter in the laundry room.

But Prince Ciaran interrupts.

"Enough about the archives," he drawls, voice cutting through the chatter. "I have a much more important topic to discuss."

The conversations deaden, all eyes turning to him. He stands with purpose. I feel a knot of unease form in my stomach.

"My birthday is coming up," he says with a devilish smirk.

There's a murmur of congratulations around the table. Ciaran holds up a hand, silencing them.

"Lorelei and Moore have offered us their summer cottage. About a two days' journey from here. If we leave at nightfall tomorrow, we'll make it in time to celebrate there properly," he continues, his gaze flicking to me pointedly before returning to the rest of the table. "With it being so close to Unseelie lands, it's not recommended for humans to come. Which is why it's the perfect spot to celebrate."

The chatter dies, and I feel my face fall. I hadn't expected him to be so outright with his disdain in front of Sylas.

"If that's what you want, then we'll make it happen," Sylas says coolly. "Pull exclusively folk servants for the trip, and we'll return in a week's time. I expect to bring my remaining potential brides along."

The table turns from hushed conspiracy to loud excitement at the journey ahead. I can't look at Sylas, even when he nudges me.

"Hey," he says softly as he holds out a hand. "Come with me."

My lip quivers against my will. "Of course."

The conversation picks up even more as he pulls me to my feet, the group debating the logistics of the week and the pleasures they might indulge in.

He's already leaving me behind. Perfect.

I find myself pacing my chambers once we make it back, unable to settle. Chase and Starling don't make an appearance – opting for their own adventures – leaving me even more alone to listen as Sylas oversees the final arrangements for the trip. Servants scurry to pack trunks, guards organize carriages, and the nobles lounge in the halls as they await the week-long retreat.

I feel detached – useless – amidst it all.

That should have been my job as his attendant.

I remember Flora orchestrating Mara's trip to the North. And my stomach drops remembering that neither are here anymore.

Sylas is busy until the beginning streaks of dawn find the horizon. I've nearly resigned myself to not seeing him before he leaves, when there's a soft knock at the door between our rooms. My heart skips a beat before opening it.

Sylas stands guiltily in the doorway. He's already dressed in his riding attire, but there's an apology in his eyes that I catch.

"Can you come in here?" he winces.

I step into his room past him. He closes the door behind us, shutting the world out.

"I'm leaving in the evening," he finally breaks the silence I refuse to.

"I know," I lash, my voice barely containing the resentment.

He steps closer, his gaze searching mine. "I didn't want to go without seeing you."

I look away. "You've been busy organizing. I get it."

"Listen to me." His voice firms. He reaches out, tilting my chin up so I have to meet his pained eyes. "Just because I've approved this trip doesn't mean I'm pushing you aside. Do you understand that?"

I want to believe him, but the doubt lingers as a stubborn ache in my chest. "I know you don't want me to lie to you." is all I can say.

He sighs, running a hand down the length of my hair. "I know how it looks. But this isn't about you and me. It's about keeping the court healthy and happy. If I don't play my part – if I don't maintain these alliances – everything falls apart."

I nod, though the words only worsen the ache.

Of course I understand. I've always understood. It's why I didn't want to get closer to you, I think, holding back the words that would only sting us both.

His hands come to rest on my hunched shoulders. "You're special to me, Valerie. Uniquely so. This trip doesn't change that."

I want to argue – to tell him that it really doesn't feel like I'm special if he's so quick to drop me for this trip – but the look in his eyes stops me. There's a slight gleam in them, expecting me to fight him on this.

"I don't want to lose you already," I breathe, fear slipping out.

"You won't," he vows with matching vulnerability.

And then he kisses me, his lips capturing mine with a desperation that I believe. He sweeps a hand down the length of my side, claiming me with nothing but his fingers.

I let him slide the ring off my finger again – my self doubt slipping away as his glamour floods my senses. It amplifies every touch, every breath, every heartbeat. I melt against his solidity, my hands tangling in his flaxen hair, pulling him closer to erase the space between us entirely. He ignites a fire that burns through me, scorching away my doubts until there's nothing left but him and this moment.

We don't speak as we move to his bed, our hands and lips saying everything words can't. His tunic falls to the floor, followed by my uniform, each layer discarded like the walls we've kept between us for too long.

His fingers trace the curve of my spine, sending ripples of pleasure through me as he guides me down onto the bed. He lays back, his eyes dark with desire as he coaxes me to climb on top – to take control this time.

I do, my hands braced against his chest as I move over him, my breath hitching at the way he fills me completely. His hands grip my hips, urging me to set a fast pace. But it doesn't last long before he flips us – his strength effortless as he pins my arms above my head – his grip verging on painful. He drives into me with a force that steals my voice, deeper than last time. My back arches as pleasure overwhelms me.

We find our release together, the world dissolving into a haze of heat and light. But I don't let him slip the ring back on my finger when I come back to myself.

Not yet.

Not when I can still feel the echo of his touch – the way he whispers my name like a secret prayer.

We come together again and again, each time slower, more intentional, worshiping every inch of each other. He takes longer to find his release each time, my nails digging into his skin, his breath hot against mine.

When I'm finally exhausted – body trembling and spent – I let him return the ring to my shaking finger. The cool metal is an unwelcome reminder of the now sunlit world outside this room: one I try to ignore as long as possible.

We lie tangled together – his arms protectively around me – his heartbeat steady beneath my ear. I let his lavender ground me when my mind spins with what we've just shared.

"I'll be back before you know it," he murmurs against the top of my head, his fingers tracing lazy patterns on my bare skin.

"I'll miss you," I confess.

He presses a kiss to the crown of my head. "This isn't forever. It's just a week."

I know he's right. This trip is necessary, and he has responsibilities I can't fully understand.

But it doesn't make the coming separation any easier.

We stay in bed for a long time, neither of us willing to break the spell. But eventually, Sylas sits up.

"I should go," he says, though he makes no move to leave. "There's still a lot to do before tonight."

I sit up as well, tugging the blankets over my chest. "Okay."

He slips out from the covers and pulls on his clothes quickly. I watch him, memorizing every detail. When he's dressed, he turns to me, his gaze achingly soft.

"Take care of yourself while I'm gone," he orders. "And don't overthink things. This trip doesn't change anything between us."

I nod, though I'm not sure I believe him. "Be safe."

He smiles – a small, fleeting thing – before leaning down to kiss me one last time. And then he's gone, the door closing softly behind him.

I know I won't see him again before he returns in a week.

I lie back in his sheets, staring at the ceiling, my mind trying to mesh this warm, loving version of Sylas with the cold Prince of the West Court. I decide that sleeping in his room while he's gone will help me remember that he's kinder when he's mine.

Is this why Chase stayed in Mara's room when she went to the North?

The thought jolts me, but I shake it off. I turn onto my side, an ache low in my abdomen: my only companion as I drift off to sleep.

Chapter 45

When I wake past sundown, the castle feels eerily quiet. Sylas and most of the court left at dusk for the Southern royalty's cottage – leaving the attendants and servants to slack off.

I'm sure it's a lavish trip to the beautiful mountains that separate the West and South. It will definitely be full of exciting drama and unforeseen stories to come.

But I won't know until they're back. Because they left us humans behind.

I curse Starling's prince for taking my new found stability from me. I am aware that I don't need Sylas to dote on me. It's not practical to expect him to explain his every move as the literal prince of this region… but none of that pacifies the hollow ache in my chest that burrows deep as the night stretches on. I shuffle into my own room when I start to get too lonely – only to see that Chase has also vacated the space for the night.

"It's going to be a long week," I groan.

To distract myself, I throw myself into work. Sylas's impending marriage looms over everything. And though I hate the thought of him with someone else, I know it's inevitable.

So I sit at my desk – notes spread out in front of me – and refine my list. I focus on each match's strengths and weaknesses, their alliances and ambitions.

Margaret, with her power and cunning. Giabella, whose beauty is matched only by her practicality. Balora, whose family controls the oceanic trade routes encircling the entire continent that the Cardinal Kingdom is situated on. I write until my hand cramps – until the names blur together – until I can almost convince myself that this is just another way to serve the crown.

*But it's not. It's **torture**.*

I set the pen down, angry that I'm still comparing myself to them and in desperate need of a real honest talk.

While I appreciate Starling and Chase, they're too removed from my experiences – not understanding my perspective as someone new to this whole royal court thing.

I wish I had other outsiders to talk to.

And then – with overwhelming contrition – I realize I do.

Maddie, Lilia, and Eddie. It's been months since I visited them.

I look to the window and know it's far too late to head down to the barracks tonight. But I make the mental note that I *will* go to them tomorrow.

So until then, I decide to neglect my work for a long relaxing bath in Sylas's private tub. I lock the door to his room, and strip down to nothing, untangling my wild hair as I settle on the rim of the too-large porcelain bowl.

There's enough room here for both of us, I think with a smirk.

The bath takes much longer than mine and Chase's bath to fill and heat. But once I've slid inside and am able to relax every muscle without touching the sides, I decide it was worth the effort.

It's as I'm floating there that I feel a sharp pain in my gut – faint – just a few strikes like stuck gas. I freeze, ready to react more overtly. But nothing else happens, and I go back to my relaxing soak.

Once the worst of my tension softens, I sit up and see a slight pink discoloration between my legs in the clear water.

The sight jolts me.

I haven't bled in seventeen years. Not since coming to the Otherworld.

The magic here suppresses that part of my biology – that much is clear. But I try to rack my brain for other reasons for blood and pain in *that* region.

Sylas and I were… enthusiastic before he left. Was he too rough?

I crawl out of the bath and towel off, adding a small wad of cloth to my underclothes before I dress in a loose attendant's uniform.

I don't tell Chase the juicy details of overdoing it when he finally returns to our room around daybreak – his clothes askew and mouth in a hard line. I pretend I don't notice the dark circles under his eyes nor the way he closes the door too hard.

We're both having a bad night it seems.

I bury the concern for us both deep down, focusing on my excitement of getting the chance to visit my friends downstairs in the evening.

Chapter 46

When the sun touches the horizon – the universal barrack signal of a shift change – I decide it's time to see my family below. I collect the basket of filling foods I called in from the kitchens and eagerly sink to the main hall, finding the correct stairs that take me lower without issue now.

But as I descend, the castle's lower levels no longer feel familiar the way they once did. The grime is even more obvious than I remember – mustier than my last visit. My nose wrinkles as I take each step, until my eyes water with a gag.

I hold a napkin scented with lavender oil – one I *had* planned to give as a gift to Maddie – over my nose to stifle another wave of nausea, before I even reach the minotaurs.

The bovine brutes don't shake me down this time for treats, letting me go with the lavender scent of Sylas raising my status like any other title.

My boots click against the uneven stone: a sound that feels out of place in this grimy tunnel even to my own ears. I clutch the woven basket I brought in my free hand, careful not to jostle the thoughtfully arranged display too much.

It's a small offering, but one I hope will ease the guilt gnawing for how long it's been since I visited.

I hover at the last step above the actual barracks, my eyes adjusting to the dim light with only the dusky skylights above. The sight of them forces me to confront every way I've changed since I was pulled upstairs.

I've grown accustomed to the opulence of the upper levels – to the warmth of fires that never die out. Down here, the cold seeps into one's bones. The darkness feels alive, pressing in from all sides like I've been swallowed whole.

"Val?" a voice breaks my musings. My head angles down a passage to see Eddie emerging from a nearby doorway. Her face is wide with surprise. "What are you doing down here?"

I snap the napkin from my nose and offer a small smile, holding up the basket. "I brought food. The royals are away for the week, so I thought I'd visit."

She steps closer, her eyes scanning my face. "You look… different."
Her tone is laced with awe. "Healthier. Happier."

I feel a flush creep up my neck. I know it's true. The regular meals and
rest have cleared my skin and banished the dark circles under my eyes.

"I'm just taking care of myself," I say, brushing off her comment.
"Come on, let's find Lilia and Maddie."

We make our way to the cramped room I once shared with my friends.
The sight of it stops me short. The bunks are still too small, the air still too
tainted, and the walls still too close. But Lilia and Maddie are also still
there too, sitting on a bunk just like I remember them.

They look up as I enter, polar opposite reactions warping their faces.

"Oh my god!" Maddie clambers from the cot to pull me into a bear
hug. "I was starting to think we'd never see you again."

"I know," I return the embrace just as tightly, ignoring the odor that
clings to her. "But I told you, they can't keep me away."

Lilia rises more slowly, her unenthused eyes taking in my appearance.
"You look well," she accuses. "Life upstairs agrees with you."

"It's a different type of work," I say, setting the basket on the cot –
shoving my offense at her tone aside. "I brought you something better than
they feed you down here."

The three of them gather around the basket, their hands grabbing
eagerly for the food. I watch as they scarf it down, my heart aching at the
sight of their swollen joints and calloused hands.

I've brought them a taste of my new life – but it feels like a cruel
reminder of the divide carved between us. They devour the offerings with a
desperation that makes my face fall.

*When was the last time they ate something that wasn't scraps? Was it
the last time I brought them food?*

"You can keep the basket too," I try to offer, but they exchange
confused glances.

*What use do they have for such a trivial thing? It's just going to take
up space.* I realize a second too late to stop the offer from leaving my lips.

"Oh! Thanks," Maddie says, her smile not reaching her eyes as she
shoves another mouthful of cheese in her mouth.

The gratitude stiffens my spine before I remember that "please" and
"thank you" are acceptable down here.

"Where's the new roommate? Art?" I ask, suddenly remembering the newcomer I saddled them with a week before leaving. Maddie's eyes shift to Lilia.

"Ash," Lilia corrects with a guarded tone, "They've been moved up too. A messenger, supposedly."

My mind flashes back to the servant at my door – giving me the invitation to Sylas's dinner.

They *had* looked familiar.

Holy shit. That was Ash.

"They were picked over you all?" I ask, confusion coloring my tone. Eddie shakes her head.

"We decided that we need to stick together, and they were only calling for one new messenger. They jumped at the chance," she explains.

I nod, and a heartbeat of silence passes as the unspoken "*just like you*" remains unsaid.

"How are things up there?" Eddie asks between bites of bread. "Still playing attendant to that fae lady?"

I tense.

They don't know about the attack?

I debate telling them the truth – then scold myself for feeling such hesitation around them. They're the first people I ever trusted in this life. They are the ones who kept me safe for so many years.

But they have so much more pressing matters to worry about.

"Mara is dead," I say before I can talk myself out of it.

They all pause, and I'm met with a skeptical beat of shock.

"What?" Lilia asks on behalf of them all.

"At the autumn equinox, there was a huge revelry." I relay the information as clinically as I can to hide my sadness. "Some rebellion group set off a bomb on the throne. It was meant to kill Sylas. But he had stepped away, leaving Mara up there. I want to say the final count was over twenty dead. Mostly servants."

They exchange more excited looks at the violence against our perceived imprisoners.

*If only they knew the ones attacking us were **worse**.*

"Sylas? The prince, right? You're on a first name basis?" Eddie asks, plucking the one slip up from my story.

I force a casual shrug when my pulse leaps into my throat. "He took me on as his attendant once Mara died."

More dumbfounded shock presses down on them, and I clear my throat.

"Valerie. You are not the prince's attendant, shut up," Maddie laughs.

I can't meet any of their eyes as I continue. "I'm not *just* his attendant. I took a bargain with him: to keep that position as long as I lie on his behalf."

"Val…" Eddie warns, her hand hovering just off my shoulder, suddenly afraid to touch me with the truth revealed. Like I'm not the same girl she spent a decade beside.

"I did it for us. Mara had agreed to bring you guys up to work under me, but then she *died*. I plan to ask the same of Sylas. It's just been so complicated with helping him pick a new future queen and our relationship and-"

I just fucked up.

"Your… relationship," Eddie lets the words roll over her like they're brand new concepts. My face crumples as I shake my head, but it doesn't erase my admission.

"It's nothing, don't worry. Everything is consensual and I'm safe. I'm trying to convince him that humans are worth more than life in the barracks. I'm doing it for all of us," I try to smooth over what I know they must be thinking, but it only makes it worse. Maddie sucks in a breath through her teeth as she surveys my face.

"Valerie. Sleeping with the prince. That's like the exact opposite of safe," she gently grabs my hand.

Lilia's dark eyes narrow slightly – sensing more – but she doesn't press. Instead, to my shock, she changes the subject. "The other attendants? Are they treating you well?"

A long exhale escapes me as I take her offered out. Though the look on Eddie's face tells me this isn't over yet.

"Mostly," I say, the scar on the back of my neck tingling at the omission. "It's… complicated. But I've made a few friends. I think you all would get along."

As they finish the meal in uncomfortable silence, my feelings as an outsider only grow. I am undeniably just a visitor in a home that was once my own. I notice the way they glance at the changes I can't hide. My hands are soft now – my nails clean and filed. My uniform tonight is simple but finely made, a far cry from the rough spun fabric they still wear.

But before any more scrutiny can be put on my transformation, the moment is shattered when a pech in a dirty uniform appears at the door, his shoulders squared with the confidence of a higher level guard.

"You've been down here too long," he drawls. "Time to go."

I bristle, my anger flaring at his intrusion.

I'm so done with these power tripping guards picking on my friends, I think.

"I'll leave when I'm ready," I counter.

His eyes narrow as they flick to Eddie. "Be careful," he warns. "She might be untouchable, but you're not."

The words hit me like a slap. I look at Eddie and the fear in her eyes, feeling a surge of guilt.

"No. Wait. I'll go," I pacify, standing to leave. "I didn't mean to-"

"It's fine," Eddie interrupts, but it's obvious that she's lying. "Just be careful. Up there *and* down here."

Her words stick in my mind as I leave them behind and track down the guard I had just overstepped. I give him a sharp look and a promise for one of Sylas's nice wines in exchange for forgetting my transgression and leaving my friends alone.

He agrees, and the bond pulses in place.

Then I climb the stairs, the miasma dissipating with each step. I breathe easier when I spot the rainbow chandelier on the third level of my ascent, and turn the corner to continue higher.

Chapter 47

With no company and empty hands, the dull, persistent ache in my stomach makes it hard to focus. I press a hand to my lower abdomen, wincing as I retreat to Sylas's tower. I don't know what's wrong, only that the pain is sharp enough to make me feel like it's time to seek help.

But it's too embarrassing to approach Starling, who always has a cure. And I don't know if I'm allowed to call upon a healing witch without Sylas's approval.

I rack my brain for any other options, and realize – as my finger absentmindedly spins the ring on my finger – that there is another magic wielder here. And I still wear the ring I got from her.

Maybe she'll have something to help.

I try and recall the twists Chase took me through that first night as an attendant. The way there is confusing and I double back many times. But by some miracle, I find the door in a tower belonging to the king himself.

She answers on my first knock. If I hadn't just decided to make the journey, I'd assume she'd been waiting by the door for me.

"Finally," the boggart mumbles, letting me in.

Maybe she was waiting for me.

The space is just as dim and cluttered as I remember: shelves crammed with jars of unidentifiable herbs and trinkets that glow with magic. The stumpy creature perches on a stool, her fingers returning to a pile of dried clippings that she must have been sorting before I arrived.

She glances up as I stand there, her eyes shining in the light like Starling's sometimes do – and I freeze.

Unseelie. But she's also helping humans. She can't be part of any rebellion.

"Out with it," she rasps. "What's wrong with you, human? You look pale."

"I'm not feeling well," I admit. "I've got this pain, and I don't know what it is. I thought maybe you'd have something to help."

"You're the prince's attendant?" She asks, sniffing the air around me.

I nod.

She studies me for a moment, then hops down from her stool with a grunt. She rummages through a cabinet behind her, pulling out a small satchel. "Here," she thrusts it at me. "For the pain. Brew it and drink it all at once. It'll taste foul, but it'll work."

I take the satchel and open it, eyeing the deep purple herbs inside. They have no aroma, when I bring it close for a curious sniff.

The boggart waves a hand dismissively and reaches for something on the counter: a small, tan fruit flecked with spots. She takes a bite – red juice dripping down her fingers – and sighs contentedly.

"Fairy fruit," she says, catching my curious gaze. "Nothing like it in any world. Sweetest high you'll ever know… for the Seelie, at least. I just like the taste."

I frown – intrigued – having never had a folk so openly discuss the stuff with me. "And the trees only last half year?"

"The orchard on the outskirts of the gardens is in constant turnover," she smacks her lips. "Beautiful place, but not for the likes of *you*. Humans can't appreciate it properly. Too much magic. You all get lost in it." She fixes me with a stern look, suddenly aware of the secret she's just revealed. "Don't go pestering the Seelie about their precious fruit now, girl. Just avoid it and keep to your own kind of trouble."

But my mind is already turning over the information, more questions rising to the surface. "I won't," I lie, tucking the satchel under my arm. "And in return for this-"

She grunts, already turning back to her herbs as she cuts me off. "Give me a single tear from your eye, then *go*."

I comply, sniffing the onion she shoves under my nose to coax the watery eyes needed. She captures the tear in a vial, then I slip out of the room before she thinks to ask for more.

I'll have to ask Starling what I really just gave away there.

Because a tear cannot possibly *just* be a tear up here.

As I make my way back to Sylas's tower, my thoughts linger on the orchard and the forbidden fruit. I wonder if all of the trees are as titanic as the throne, or if that is another side effect of its eternity. If the trees only last for a few months, the fruit *must* be delicious to have them so dedicated to maintaining a constant supply.

I make it back to my room in time to find Chase and Starling quietly sitting on his bed. My intrusion seems to be a welcome one, as neither looks particularly enthused with the other.

I excuse myself to change clothes and brew my herbs. The kettle in Sylas's room does the job – heated over the hearth with the purple sprigs inside. I pour the tea into a cup and down the contents in one gulp before overthinking everything. The taste is bitter and earthy as I choke it down.

I grimace.

But almost immediately, the sharp jab of the pain begins to dull. "So much better," I whisper in relief.

I clean out the kettle and cup, setting them where they belong before turning back to my room.

I'll talk to Sylas when he's back. Make sure we're more careful.

I open the door again to a tense hissed conversation that halts the moment I interrupt.

"Do you both want to help me look over Sylas's matches?" I awkwardly offer. They both agree way too animatedly. And I refuse to engage with whatever drama they're involved in right now.

So, we migrate to Sylas's room. Chase stokes the fire in the hearth, brightening the room to better see the stacks of parchment on Sylas's desk: the ones that contain my notes on his three remaining choices.

They're probably all over him right now.

I shove the thought away, knowing that it's their right.

I'm the one who's out of line trying to claim him.

The room feels too quiet – too still – as we sit there with our thoughts, no one quite up to confessing their real focus.

"I just don't know why he cares so much about me." My frustration breaks the feigned tranquility of us all pretending to read. My fingers trace a blotch on the parchment – the ink smudged from where I'd nervously tapped my quill before Sylas found me mid-revelry that first time.

Starling rolls their red eyes before they speak. "With peace and love, I don't think he does. I think he just likes that Mara picked you. And you made it a bit of a challenge to follow through."

I narrow my eyes at them, but there's nothing but honest concern as they look back at me. Their words sting – not because they're cruel – but because they might be true. I think back to my visit with my barrack friends earlier – the way they'd looked at me like I wasn't Valerie anymore. My rounded face, my softer hands, the way I spoke so familiarly about our imprisoners: all of it had felt like a betrayal to them.

And maybe it was.

I flinch at the memory still so fresh in my mind.

"Sleeping with the prince is the exact opposite of safe," Maddie's voice echoes in my head. I feel her phantom grip on my hand; I see her big black eyes filled with worry. Even Eddie – usually so on my side – had looked at me like I wasn't the person she'd shared so many nights in bed with.

"My friends in the barracks think that too," I admit, ashamed. "They think I'm too close to Sylas."

Chase snorts crossly, tossing his neglected report on the desk. "And? What's wrong with that? If the prince wants to keep you warm all day, who's to stop him? Or *you*, for that matter."

Starling shoots him a glare, their lips pressing into a thin line. "It's not that simple, Chase. You know it's not. Valerie's in a dangerous position. If she gets too close to Sylas, she could be a target. You saw what happened to Mara."

I hadn't even considered that, I think with new fear. But Chase interrupts my thoughts before I can explore them further.

"Oh so they should just completely ignore their feelings then?" Chase jabs. "Valerie's smart – she's loyal. And she's got more heart than half the people in this castle. If Sylas's too stupid to see that, then he's the problem. Not her."

I blink, surprised by the intense defense. Chase is usually so casual – so carefree – but now he's sitting forward, brown eyes locked on Starling like he's ready to fight.

Starling doesn't back down. "I'm not saying her feelings are invalid. I'm saying Sylas isn't capable of protecting her. Not in the way she needs him to be. He's a prince, Chase. He's been raised to see people as pawns, not equals. And if Valerie forgets that, she's going to get hurt."

"So what?" Chase snaps. "She should just shut herself off? Pretend she doesn't feel anything? That's not *living*, Star. That's just surviving."

I don't think they're talking about me anymore.

But I hold my tongue – curious to see this play out.

"And surviving is better than getting your heart broken… or worse," Starling fires back, their voice rising in a rare show. "You think Sylas is going to protect her if things go south? You think he's going to choose her over his crown? Over his duty?"

"Maybe he will!" Chase shouts, slamming his hands on the desk. "You don't know him. You don't know what he's capable of."

"And you do?" Starling scoffs. "Because you've spent so much time with him? Because you're such an expert on the inner workings of the royal family?"

Chase stands, his chair scraping against the floor. "At least I'm not so damn cynical that I can't see when someone's actually trying to get to know me!"

Starling stands too, their face inches from Chase's. "And at least I'm not so damn naive that I think sleeping together again is going to solve all our problems!"

Both of their next words die in their throat with the slip, the tension between them sparking like a live wire. I watch frozen as they stare each other down – their breaths coming fast and heavy. And then – as if fate itself couldn't stop him – Chase grabs Starling by the front of their tunic and pulls them into a kiss.

It's fierce, *angry*, like he's trying to prove a point. Starling stiffens at the contact, their clawed hands flailing in the air, before they grab Chase's face and kiss him back just as hard.

I look away, my cheeks burning. But I can't help the small smile that tugs at my lips.

Of course they'd end up like this.

When they finally break apart, both of them are panting – their faces flushed. Chase looks as smug as ever. Starling looks like they're trying very hard to maintain an offended reaction as they wipe at their mouth.

"Well," I drag the word out, breaking the tension. "That was… something."

Chase grins, running a pale hand through Starling's dark hair. "Yeah, well, someone had to shut them up."

They roll their red eyes, but there's a hint of a smile on their lips. "Valerie, do you want to go for a walk? It's way too warm in here."

"Oh, it's going to get a lot hotter," Chase teases as he pulls Starling back towards our room by the tunic he still hasn't fully released. Starling feigns terror, clawing jokingly at the door jamb as they disappear.

I rise to my feet, smiling despite myself. I snag my wool cloak, deciding a walk is *exactly* what I need to end the morning.

Chapter 48

The dark morning air nips at my cheeks as I step into the king's garden – the crunch of frost covered grass beneath my boots the only sound in the stillness. The world feels hushed – the earth itself hibernating for the coming winter.

Above, the sky is a deep, endless gray.

No stars tonight.

I pull my cloak tighter around me, my breath visible in the cold.

I hadn't planned to come to Mara's pyre sight. But between the squawking gryphons in the aviary and the dryads arguing over hedgemazes – everywhere else was too cacophonous for me to think.

I wish I could ask for her guidance.

I'm not alone though, as I step towards the sight.

Alistar stands at the edge of the clearing, his frame silhouetted against the browning trees. He's wearing a dark cloak – hood up against the cold to show just the roundness of his nose – his hands tucked into his pockets. He doesn't turn as I approach, but I know he's aware of me.

They always seem to be.

"No birthday celebration?" I speak first.

He glances over his shoulder, his expression stuck between melancholy and relief at my appearance. "Celebrations are for the joyful," he says heavily. "Besides, I wanted to see the garden again before the snow buries it for good until spring."

I step closer, my boots sinking into the frost kissed earth. The garden is nothing but a shadow now: the flowers gone, the trees revealing branches that claw at the sky. But there's a quiet dignity in its emptiness that feels fitting for the setting.

I can mentally picture Mara's pyre not too far from where we stand now, the complete unreality of sending her body away from this world.

"It's peaceful," I murmur, more to myself than to him.

Alistar hums in agreement, his gaze fixed on the same spot. "The winter solstice is a month away. Did you know that?"

I nod. "I've heard the servants talking about it. They say it's a time for reflection. For honoring the past."

"It is," he agrees wistfully. "I'm planning a tribute to Mara. Something small to remember her."

"That's a beautiful idea. She would have liked it."

He turns to me then, his eyes searching mine. "I think she would have liked to be here more, but it's the best I can do."

The words catch me off guard, and my eyes drop like the leaves from the branches around us.

"I wish I could have known her better," I say quietly. "She was only in my life for a few weeks, but she changed so much for me."

Alistar's brow softens – just a little. "I wish you could have too." He pauses, his gaze drifting back to the empty spot where we said goodbye. "She was extraordinary. Kind, but clever. She had a way of seeing people. *Really* seeing them. She believed in Sy – in what he could become. She believed in you too."

I frown, confused. "In me? But she barely knew me."

He smiles a ghost of a smile. "True, but she knew you had potential."

My heart skips a beat, but I don't let the surprise show. "I'm not special, Alistar. I'm just… me."

He turns to me fully now with absolute sincerity. "You are, though. Sy sees it. Mara saw it too. You've become unique among your kind."

I want to argue – to tell him he's wrong – but the certainty in his voice stuns me.

He can't lie.

Instead, I ask, "What do you mean, I have potential? I'm unique?"

Alistar's smile returns, but it's frustratingly cryptic. "You'll see," he teases. "Stick close to Sy. And when the time comes, I'm sure he'll explain everything."

"Explain *what*?" I press, frustration creeping into my voice as much as hope. "Alistar, if there's something I need to know-"

"It's not my place to tell you," he interrupts gently. "But it's what Mara would have wanted. For you. For Sy. For all of us."

I stare at him, my mind racing. There's something he's not saying – something *big* – and it's maddening. But I know Alistar well enough by now to know he won't budge. His loyalty to Sylas is too strong.

"You're infuriating, you know that?" I growl, only half joking.

He chuckles warmly. "So I've been told." He embraces me in a quick hug that makes me stiffen. "Just trust me. And trust Sy. That's all I ask."

My stomach is a knot of unease as I hug him back. "Okay. I'll try."

He steps back with a relieved breath. "Good." He glances at the sky, then back at me. "You should get inside. It's too cold out here for you."

"What about you?" I counter.

He smiles again, but it doesn't reach his eyes. "I'll stay a little longer. I like the cold. It reminds me of our childhood up North."

I offer a bow and a knowing smile. "Goodnight, Alistar."

"Goodnight, Valerie."

I turn and walk back toward the castle, the weight of his words settling over me like a second heavier cloak. As I reach the door, I glance back. He is still standing there – a solitary figure in the frost covered garden – his gaze now turned upward toward the cloudy sky. And a silly thought crosses my mind.

Maybe Mara sent him out here today to be the guidance I wished for.

Chapter 49

The rest of my week consists of sleeping, letting Chase and Starling have our room, and trying to pick between Sylas's matches. Though deep down, I know who I truly want him to pick… and she isn't anywhere on the paper.

He'll never pick me. He needs a sidhe to be his queen. I'm just an attendant that keeps his bed warm, I humble myself when the daydreams of him choosing me are too painfully easy to imagine.

"Hey," Chase calls from our room's door, pulling me from my self-pity at Sylas's desk. I glance up, seeing Starling linger behind him, pointy chin resting easily on his shoulder. "Let's have some fun, it's our last night of freedom."

He holds up a bottle of nice wine in invitation. I smile, setting down the quill to join them back in our room.

We down it quickly. Then another.

I let myself forget the weight of responsibility coming back tomorrow. Laughter becomes easier as we decide to pilfer the kitchen for some early morning snacks – completely against protocol.

But the idea of sneaking in feels so much more fun than ordering them to the room.

The kitchen level is quiet as we slip inside, the heavy wooden door creaking softly closed behind us. The antics feel almost like my old life, like we're back in the human world sneaking around and causing trouble.

With few nobles around to serve, the kitchen hobs have vanished for the last night of light duty –likely causing their own brand of mischief as we are doing now. But the space is still warm from the ovens – sweet with the scent of freshly baked pastries – drawing us to the most promising corner in our search for stolen goods.

"I can't believe we're doing this," Starling gripes as they peer around the corner ahead. "If we get caught, Ciaran will *not* be kind about it."

"Relax," Chase slurs, grinning as he pushes into the kitchen properly. "Sylas and Ciaran are gone. Who's going to catch us? The pastry chef?"

"Yeah," I cackle. "We're two attendants. If anyone's getting punished for this: it's Chase."

We stifle communal laughs at my joke. The corner is dim, the only light coming from the dying embers in the ovens. But it's enough to see the counters lined with trays of pastries – their golden crusts glistening. My stomach growls at the sight.

"Okay, grab what you can," I whisper, already reaching for a flaky croissant.

Chase snorts, shoving an entire tart into his mouth. "Too late," he says around the pastry. "I'm already winning."

Starling plucks a small fruit tart. "You're such an idiot."

"An idiot with excellent taste in pastries," Chase retorts, grabbing another tart and holding it out to me. "Here, Valerie. Try this one. It's amazing."

I take the tart, biting into it carefully. The crust is buttery and flaky: the filling sweet and tangy. "Okay, that's incredible," I moan. "What's in it?"

Starling shakes their head at our enthusiasm. But they're laughing now, their usual sharp edges softened by the warmth of the moment and the drink in our systems.

For a while, it's just the three of us, laughing and eating and pretending like we don't have a care in the world.

It's nice. Normal. Something we've never gotten to share.

But then Chase pauses, his hand freezing halfway to his mouth. He looks down at the pastry in his hand, his expression shifting from amusement to horror.

"Uh, guys?" he says, his voice suddenly tight. "What kind of jam is this?"

I lean closer, squinting at the pastry in the dim light. The filling is a deep, almost bloody red – with tiny chunks that glisten like jewels. My stomach drops as my nose recognizes the smell.

"Chase," I caution in a trembling voice. "That's… that's fairy fruit."

The color drains from his face, and he drops the pastry like it's burned him. "No, no, no. Tell me I didn't just eat that."

Starling bends down to study it, their eyes wide with panic. "How much did you swallow?"

"I don't know!" Chase barks. "A bite? Two? It was savory, I didn't even think about it until after I swallowed!"

"Shh!" I cut in, glancing at the door. "Keep your voice down!"

"Keep my voice down?" Chase repeats, incredulously. "Valerie, I just ate *fairy fruit*! Do you know what that does to humans?"

"Yes," I snap as my own panic rises. "I do. But freaking out isn't going to help."

Starling grabs Chase by the shoulders. "You're going to be fine. We will fix this. Right, Valerie?"

I don't answer right away.

I remember the few examples from the barracks, and the servant girl at dinner a few weeks ago.

But she choked. She didn't even have time to develop the hallucinations.

"You need to try and throw that up. Right now," I say as soon as the idea comes to me.

Chase rolls his shoulders in determination. "Now there's an idea," he mutters before shoving his fingers down his throat in a desperate attempt to trigger his gag reflex.

It's successful, and relief floods me as globs of fleshy jam splat onto the floor.

"Okay – if anything's going to fix this – that's it," I breathe, patting him on the back. "How do you feel?"

"I feel… fine. Normal. Maybe a little lightheaded, but that's probably just the panic," Chase answers, wiping the bile from his lip.

Starling lets out a sniffle, their usual composure cracking as they pull Chase into a tight hug.

"You moron," they spit, their voice muffled against his shoulder. "You absolute fucking dumbass."

Chase hesitates for a moment before wrapping his arms around them. "Hey, it's okay," he soothes. "I'm fine. I feel fine. It's going to be okay."

I watch them together, feeling powerless.

"We can't tell anyone," I warn. "Not yet. We'll figure out what to do."

Starling pulls back, their red eyes glistening. "Agreed. We keep this between us. For now."

Chase nods, though his face is still pale. "Yeah. No one needs to know. Not until – not until we know for sure."

We sit in the silence for a while, the shock of what just happened numbing us. The pastries sit forgotten on the counter, their sweetness now tainted by the bitter taste of fear.

"I didn't mean to ruin the night," Chase mumbles.

"You didn't ruin anything," Starling counters defensively. "Just don't do it again, okay?"

Chase manages a weak smile. "Deal."

I force a smile too, though my stomach is still in knots. "Come on," I stand, brushing the crumbs off my pants. "Let's get out of here before someone finds us."

We clean up as best we can, leaving the kitchen as quietly as we came. But as we walk back to our chambers, the laughter and lightness of our earlier haze is gone, replaced by a heavy forced muteness. I glance at Chase – his eyes horror-struck but face composed – and wish I could put on an equally convincing mask.

Chapter 50

The snow falls again on the evening of Sylas's return, blanketing the world in a pristine white that glows faintly under the moonlight. I am grateful Chase seems to be ok. Though I leave him and Starling alone in our room as I wander to steady my nerves.

*What if the week off made Sylas realize how ridiculous his affection for me really was? That I'm **not** as special as he thinks I am?*

I find myself in the main foyer, my arms crossed as I watch the small courtyard through the frost kissed windows. The sound of hooves on cobblestone echoes through the night long before Sylas's carriage rolls into view.

It appears far ahead of the rest of the caravan, its ornate design setting it apart. Two pegasi's hooves clack in a rhythm that spurs my heart faster. The doors swing open. And he steps out – his presence dominant as always.

Two disheveled sidhe follow him, making my stomach drop. Their laughter is muted by the glass between us as Rakan and Seraphine lean on him: drunk and carefree. They're breathtakingly beautiful – elegantly effortless as a trio. I feel like a shadow in their presence.

See, he's already moved on.

But then Sylas's eyes find mine through the window. His gaze softening with enough relief to make me second guess my assumption.

He says something to Lord Rakan that makes him pout. But he lets him go, Seraphine shrugging out from under his arm with an equal displeasure. I step back from the window as the doors to the courtyard swing open, the cold rushing in with him. His coat is dusted with snow – his cheeks flushed from the chill – but he looks as regal as ever.

He strides straight over to me.

"Valerie," he says warmly, a contrast to the icy chill still clinging to him. He doesn't give me a chance to respond before his lips are on mine. The kiss is brief but ardent: a silent declaration that removes all doubt of our status. When he pulls away, his eyes search mine. I see exhaustion lurking beneath his usual confidence.

"I need a moment with my attendant," he announces to the lingering pair who have drifted in behind him.

"Of course." Rakan's tone is kinder than his eyes as they rake over me.

Sylas takes my hand and leads me towards our tower, directly into his room. He closes the door behind us, the click of the latch signaling his desire to get me entirely alone.

Chase and Starling must already be asleep, I think with relief at the empty space that greets us.

Sylas shrugs off his frosted cloak, tossing it onto a chair before turning to face me. His eyes are worried now, the commanding mask he wears for the court gone.

"We need to talk about Margaret," he prompts. "She was displeased that I have a bargain with you. She made it quite clear that she expects me to dismiss you if I were to choose her as my queen."

I hide my sudden panic behind crossed arms. "And what did you say to that?"

He steps closer. "I told her that wasn't an option. That you're not going anywhere." He reaches out, his fingers brushing against my goosebump riddled arms. "But it's more than that. She's not the right choice. She's too rigid. Too controlling. I can't have someone like that by my side."

I swallow hard, trying to ignore the way his touch makes my skin spark. "So what does that mean? You're dismissing her?"

He nods resolutely. "Yes. She's out. But that leaves us with two options, and the court will start to question my intentions if I don't make a decision between them soon." He pauses, his hand dropping away. "I need you to help me navigate this."

I blink, surprised by the truth. "You want my help with the final decision?"

"I want you to get to know them, ensuring I don't make a mistake," he confirms.

The room feels too small suddenly. I take a step back, trying to steady my thoughts. "I'm just your attendant. I don't know if I'm the right person to-"

"You're not *just* anything," he interrupts. "We have a bargain. And you're as important to my future as any bride will ever be."

His confession hangs between us: fragile and flattering.

I want to remind him of all the reasons that I can't be this close to him… but the look in his eyes stuns me.

There's a vulnerability there – a crack in his usual ice – and it's enough to make my resolve waver.

"Okay," I concede.

He steps closer, hand cupping my face as he leans in. His lips find mine in a kiss that's softer than any he's given me before.

"You're thinking too much," he teases roughly against my mouth. "Let's fix that."

We move to the bed, I let him hastily strip away both our clothes. But when he reaches for my hand, I don't let him take off my ring.

He cocks an eyebrow. I drop to the floor before him – unfastening his belt to answer his unasked question. He sits on the edge of the bed, eyes dark as he watches me. I feel his nails gently scratch my scalp as he collects my hair, guiding himself to my waiting lips.

"Just like the first time I saw you," he hums as his fingers twist in my hair. "Perfect on your knees."

Then he pushes himself past my lips. His grip on my hair tightens just enough to make me whimper, and I feel him twitch in response. My eagerness – as I suck in my cheeks – spurs him on, his hips moving with an intoxicating rhythm. He murmurs my name as I take him deeper, his voice desperate with need.

He stills before my jaw gets sore, but doesn't find his release.

With a dominant tug on my hair, he pulls me back onto the bed so I'm on all fours. He shifts behind me in one fluid motion, hands sliding down to my hips as he pumps into me from behind. The angle is intense, and I cry out in a broken moan.

He leans over me, his lips brushing against my neck as he purrs, "I missed that sound."

I can't reply, my mind too hazy with the sudden rhythm. He chuckles before kissing the nape of my sweaty neck. I collapse forward, letting him set a punishing pace as he drives into me over and over again. His movements grow more frantic quickly – his grip on my hips bruising as he chases his release.

His body shudders as he finishes deep, pulling my head back to kiss me as he does. I curse at the way my knees fail to keep me upright.

He supports my entire weight without complaint, his arms wrapped around me as we catch our breath. He withdraws once we both recover, and we collapse together onto the bed. I stare at the ceiling, my mind racing with the memory of my blood in the tub.

I should tell him to be more gentle.

There's space between us, as I think, that wasn't there before. I can feel it in the way he touches me – in the way his kisses linger just a little too long on my shoulder.

He readjusts beside me, his hand brushing my sweaty hair away as he surveys my face. "You're distant," he observes. "What's wrong?"

I swallow hard. "Nothing. Just thinking."

He props himself up on one elbow to look down at me. "About what?"

I feign composure, completely unprepared for this conversation. "I had some pain. Some bleeding while you were away. I think we need to be more… gentle."

"I don't want to cause you unnecessary pain. Have you not been ready when we-"

I shake my head, cutting off his words. My cheeks flush with the question, even as I lie naked in his bed.

"I've been ready. And I don't feel any pain whenever we're together. It was just the one time, after we kept going… and going. I think if I take the ring off, we need to be careful." I can't hide the smile on my lips as his eyes gleam with the memory.

"Of course. I want to make sure you're healthy, no matter how passionate we get." He brushes away another nonexistent hair from my face, lingering on my jaw as his eyes bore into mine.

Even if I didn't know he can only speak the truth, I would believe him.

"Ok then, maybe we can try again without the ring this time," I smile, perking up.

"You're insatiable," he says with a laugh against my lips as his fingers find the band on my finger.

The glamour has us tangled until the peaking sun on the horizon calls us to sleep.

Chapter 51

I wake alone in Sylas's bed, the sheets still warm where he'd slept beside me. The lavender scent of him lingers on the pillows.

Fading sunlight streams through the parted curtains, signaling the start of another busy night. On the bedside table, a tray awaits: fresh fruit and a pot of mint tea. Propped against the teapot is a note in Sylas's precise hand.

Interviews today. Balora at midnight, Giabella after.
Be yourself: your honesty is what I need.

No signature. No endearment. Just instructions, as if I'm still merely his attendant and not the human who'd spent the day being ravaged by his mouth.

My stomach twists. *Be myself.*

Which version? The one who dutifully records every flaw in his potential brides? Or the one who wants to scribble "*neither*" across the page and present *herself* as the only viable option?

I dress carefully in a high necked tunic in deep blue: the shade Sylas prefers. My fingers work deftly to detangle the mess of curls he so generously tangled this morning.

When I'm finally done preparing myself and my questions for the matches, it's near midnight. I bring my journal to Princess Balora's chambers.

They are a study in orchestrated wealth. The walls are lined with maps of trade routes throughout the entire Cardinal Kingdom, the shelves heavy with ledgers and samples of rare minerals. She sits behind a carved desk: her posture rigid, her green eyes sharp as broken glass.

"So." She taps a polished nail against the arm of her chair. "You're the human whose caught Sylas's eye."

I keep my expression neutral. "I'm his attendant, Your Highness. My name is Valerie."

"Mm." Her smile is all teeth. "Ciaran told me what you are."

A flush creeps up my neck. *Of course he did. And he's wrong.*

Balora leans forward, her voice dropping to a conspiratorial whisper. "Let's be plain, shall we? You don't want him to marry me."

"My opinion doesn't matter," I say smoothly.

"I hate that humans can lie." She smirks. "But I'll play along. Ask your questions."

I glance at my notes, though I've memorized what I want to ask. "Your family controls the Southern trade routes. Would you prioritize those alliances over Sylas's existing ones?"

"Obviously." She flicks a hand, as if the answer is trivial. "The West needs our ships. Our minerals. Without us, they're vulnerable and without buyers. My family's power will always take priority."

I jot down: "*Arrogant. May undermine Sylas's authority.*"

"And your thoughts on human servants?"

Balora's lip curls. "They'd be mostly removed. My family court has few humans on its staff. Those who have proven *useful* and *willing* to work. Lesser folk would fill the positions vacated."

My quill presses harder into the parchment. "*Openly prejudiced. Risk to staff morale.*"

She watches me write, her smirk widening. "He'll choose me anyway. My family is too powerful to refuse."

I force a smile. "We'll see."

Then she stands, gesturing towards the door. "We will."

I don't hesitate, rising with a formal bow. The door clicks shut behind me. I exhale sharply, rolling my shoulders to release the tension Balora's hostility had coiled there. The stairs are blessedly empty even as midnight deepens. I adjust my grip on my journal – the damning notes about Balora safely tucked inside – when a familiar voice calls out.

"Fancy meeting you here."

Chase rounds the corner, his arms laden with a teetering stack of books. The titles catch my eye – *The Alchemy of Fairy Fruit*, *Magical Botany of the Unclaimed Isles* – before he shifts his grip, nearly sending the top three volumes tumbling.

I dart forward to catch one before it hits the floor. "What are you doing with all these?"

He shrugs. "Starling's latest obsession. Something about cross breeding fairy fruit for a potential cure." He jerks his chin upward, toward

Ciaran's chambers. "You know how they get when they're deep in research."

I do.

"And Prince Ciaran just lets you waltz in with armfuls of books?"

Chase's smile doesn't waver, but something else passes his eyes. "We have an understanding."

I know better than to press.

Handing back the book, I glance at the moon outside the window. "I should go. Lady Giabella's expecting me."

"Ah, the saintly Lady of the North." Chase adjusts his grip on the stack. "Think she'll fare better than the princess?"

"She's... kind."

"Kind." He snorts, eyeing me pointedly. "The weakest possible trait in a queen, according to court gossip."

I stiffen. *He still wants me to actually go for it.*

Before I can retort, he's already stepping back, the moment broken. "Don't let me keep you," he throws over his shoulder as I watch him disappear up the stairs.

I find Lady Giabella's door down a level below Balora's. It is a stark contrast to the princess's: warm and inviting, filled with poetry and half finished embroidery. She greets me with a kiss on both cheeks, her golden eyes crinkling at the corners.

"Valerie! I've heard so much about you from Alistar." She presses a cup of tea into my hands. "Chamomile. Good for nerves."

I blink. "I'm not nervous."

"Aren't you?" Her smile is knowing. "Interviewing the sidhe who might marry the prince you love?"

The tea scalds my tongue as I choke. "I- that's not-"

Giabella pats my knee. "It's alright. I'd feel the same."

She does actually seem *kind*. Genuinely, infuriatingly kind.

I scramble for my questions. "You grew up with Lady Mara. How would you honor her legacy?"

"By not replacing her." Giabella's voice sobers. "No one could. I'd simply try to be my own version of a queen."

"*Humble. Wise.*" I write, then cross it out. Too glowing. Sylas might actually *like* that.

"And your thoughts on human servants?"

"Oh, I adore them!" She clasps her hands. "They've the most fascinating perspectives. Why, just yesterday, one told me-"

I jot: *"Overly familiar. May cross necessary boundaries."*

Giabella tilts her head. "You're not writing that, are you?"

"Professional discretion," I mutter.

She laughs, bright and musical. "Mara told me you fit in well up here, she was right."

My heart stutters with the mention. I school my face neutral, and tuck the quill between the pages before closing the book.

She's trying to flatter me.

"I think I've asked enough questions for one afternoon, I'll return if I have anymore," I conclude, standing with another bow before making my escape.

"Of course! I'll keep the tea warm for us," she offers. And though I don't turn back, I can hear the smile on her lips.

Back in my chambers, I stare at the two reports laid out on my bed. Chase is still with Starling, giving me ample time to focus on my two options. Balora's flaws are glaring, and Giabella's are nitpicks at best.

I crumple the parchment with a curse, the answer becoming glaringly obvious.

*It should be Giabella. She'll let me stay, **and** she will be sympathetic to humans.*

The door between our rooms opens without warning. Sylas steps just inside, taking in the sight of me: hunched on my bed with the papers. "Well?"

I lift my chin. "Balora's oppressive. Giabella's a saint."

"And?" he coaxes. "I have a council meeting next week. I'd like to bring a proposal for a bride as one of the topics on the agenda."

"And I don't think either is right for you." The words spill out in a rush.

Sylas's lips twitch. "No?"

"No." I shake my head, my pulse roaring in my ears.

Stop talking, I command myself.

But I don't.

"You need someone who understands the court but isn't enslaved by it. Someone who challenges you. Someone who..." I trail off. But I know he won't let me get away without answering.

"Who what?" He steps closer, looking down intensely.

"Who wants *you*," I bear my entire heart. "Not your crown."

The silence stretches with my hand finally shown. Sylas plucks the reports from my bed and takes them to the desk.

"You're serious," he asserts, settling into the study chair next to me. "You truly believe you could be queen."

"You said yourself that I belong up here. That I am special. My ability to lie could be very useful at your side." I lift my chin, as I recite his own words back to him.

He looks back at my notes, reorganizing them in a rare show of restlessness. "My father would never allow it. And besides, do you have any idea what they'd do to you?" He continues, not meeting my face. "The moment you took the crown, every highborn sidhe with a drop of royal blood would see you as an usurper. And that's not even factoring in the rebellion."

A hurt stabs my chest, but I hold my ground. "You'd protect me."

"Not from poison in your wine. Not from a blade in the dark." His gaze finally lifts, eyes freezing. "I watched them do it to Mara. To a dozen others before. I won't let them take you too."

The reasoning hits exactly as intended.

"Then why let me hope?" My voice cracks. "Why show me the aviary? Teach me the histories? Make me think I'm special?"

"Because you *are* special." He is out of the chair in a blink, hand cupping my cheek as his thumb brushes away a traitorous tear. "But some doors aren't meant to be opened. Not like that."

I search his face for the lie, but of course, he can't lie.

"Then what am I to you?" The question claws its way out of me.

Sylas exhales, long and slow, before pulling me to my feet. "Mine," he murmurs against the top of my head. "In every way that matters."

His next kiss – when it finds my lips – is a brand of its own. His hands map my body like a territory to be conquered. When he lifts me into his arms, I don't resist. When he lays me on the bed, I arch into his touch.

"Let me remind you," he hums, sliding the ring from my finger as he shuts out my doubts.

This is the truth he offers. Not crowns or vows, but heat and hunger and the sweet, suffocating weight of his body pressing me into the mattress.

"You'll stay by my side," he breathes between the moments where pleasure blurs into something dangerously close to love. "Not as queen. As something *better*."

I gasp as he moves inside me. "What's better than queen?"

His laugh is hopeful, his lips trailing down my throat. "The one a king relies on above all others. I need you, Valerie Harlow."

The words are honeyed poison. I *know* this. And yet…

When he whispers "Imagine it." I do.

When he hums "You're the one I need." I believe him.

And when he spills into me with a shuddering breath – his fingers tangled in my hair – I forget to ask why he never made me get another brand if I'm to be his human pet forever.

Chapter 52

We continue our dance around the topic. I spend most midnights with Giabella, sipping tea and learning about Mara's life.

She explains that Mara and Alistar were orphans, taken into the North Court by Margaret's family as a show of sympathy to their fellow sidhe nobles.

I had no idea.

Mara would have left another child motherless in the name of duty, I think, remembering her tears and confessions of her plans before the autumn equinox.

I visit Balora's parlor on the few times her schedule allows… it's much less inviting. And neither of us pretend the visits are for anything less than me noting her flaws. She dismisses me after a few questions every time.

I wake to Sylas already gone one evening, my ring left on the side table.

Council meeting. Right.

I dress and clean up the room a bit before venturing out for some meaningless duties to fill the hours before his return. The castle corridors are tense as I move through them, seeing to it that Sylas's favorite wines are ordered in reserve and the fairy fruit pastries have been sent to the oven for his after meeting snack.

My arms are laden with fresh linens for his chambers, when I find Starling in the lounge – a half empty bottle of wine in their claws.

I raise an eyebrow at their uncharacteristically flushed cheeks. They don't turn to look at me.

"Ciaran gave me the night off. He's negotiating well," they grumble as they tip the bottle back.

"And I assume that means Sylas is *not* negotiating well?" I guess. Their answering shrug confirms my fears.

Maybe that's why Balora's been so dismissive. She's not as allied with Sylas as she pretends to be.

"Well, thanks for the warning. I hope Chase's night is going better."

They wince on Chase's name before I turn, and I hasten my pace away before I can overthink what that might mean. I eavesdrop on servant conversations during my trek back to the room, piecing together segments of a heated council meeting. My toe catches on the stripped sheets still by the door in his threshold, earning a yelp as I stagger into the room.

Servants are slacking. I'll have to tell the overseeing brownie.

After tucking the fresh linens, I begin straightening the space: organizing his correspondence, aligning quills in their holder. My fingers pluck a sealed letter bearing the South Court's crest. I tuck it at the bottom of the stack.

The door swings open without warning.

Sylas's usual grace is replaced by visible burnout. His discarded jacket draped over one slumped shoulder. He doesn't acknowledge me at first, going straight to the decanter to pour himself a stiff drink.

"Rough council?" I venture, keeping my tone neutral.

He downs the glass in one swallow. "Ciaran nearly has my father convinced to reduce the human intake by half. He wants to replace them with paid folk laborers, but our region cannot afford that right now."

I freeze.

"That's... good, isn't it?"

His gaze snaps to mine, incensed. "For whom? The humans left behind will be worked to death."

The truth of his argument – his care for those of us still here – reframes the entire debate in my mind immediately.

"Dinner is ready when you are," I change the subject. "Would you like me to-"

"Some silence." He rubs his temples.

I nod, slipping into my chamber to give him time to cool down. I look over my notes on both potential queens, the news of Ciaran's success making me doubt my choice for the kinder of the two.

Fewer humans. More burden. Maybe kindness isn't the virtue I thought it would be.

He needs someone strong at his side – someone with real authority.

When I return, Sylas is standing at the window, biting his nails. The sight is so unguarded – so nearly human – that it steals my breath.

"You okay?" I ask slowly.

He doesn't move.

I step closer – my hand hovering over his shoulder – debating whether to touch him or not. "Sy?"

"Snapping at you wasn't right." The words are raw, stripped of their usual command. "I'm just stressed over the implications for the realm as a whole. For the *humans* as a whole."

"I understand." My hand makes contact and nudges him towards the bed. "Let me help you relax."

He allows me to tend to him, discarding the rest of his clothes while I busy myself arranging the dinner tray so I don't stare.

My eyes snag on his body anyway.

He crawls onto the freshly made bed, his muscles tensing before they relax on the soft expanse. I crawl next to him, my fingers plucking a piece of carrot to feed him.

"You still want quiet?" I murmur, coaxing him to open his mouth.

He takes the bite, then sighs as I press my thumb to his lower lip. "No, I want to know which match you really think I should choose."

I take a bite of my own, using the moment to choose my next words carefully. "Giabella would be kind," I admit, as I pluck a grape off the bunch. "She'd let me stay. Maybe even advocate for *more* humans. But..."

"But?"

I feed him more, so I can continue talking.

"But Balora's ships control the mineral trade. Her family could strangle the West Court's economy if slighted." The words are a sour truth. "And with the human intake halved, you'll need every advantage to keep the economy stable."

Sylas looks at me – long and hard – before his head tips back against the headboard. "You're arguing for Balora."

"I'm arguing for your *throne*." My eyes rake over his chest, tracing the muscles. "Even if it means I'll spend the rest of my days dodging her venom."

He lifts his head slightly, just enough to catch my gaze under heavy lids. "You'd really endure that? For me?"

"I'd endure worse." The admission slips out before I can stop it.

I reach for another morsel, breaking the silence that tries to descend. "You should decide before the council reconvenes. Balora won't wait forever."

Sylas watches my face instead of my hand. "No," he agrees at last, accepting it. "She won't."

We don't speak again as I feed him, the tray emptying quickly. Neither of us mentions the fact that he still hasn't chosen a bride after a full week of avoiding it – nor the fact that every time he slips my ring from my finger, I feel like he's choosing *me* over either of them.

Chapter 53

A few nights of constant meetings and passionate mornings later, I find myself with Chase and Starling in our room while the royalty negotiate in consistently zealous debates.

Sylas still hasn't declared a choice, and even *I* am getting nervous about it. Nausea turns my stomach when I think too much about how his choices will affect my future at his side.

Balora or Giabella – venom or sugar.

But I weigh both possibilities as I sit sprawled across the floor, a makeshift picnic spread out between Starling, Chase, and me. Chase leans against the foot of his bed, a half eaten pastry in one hand and a bottle of wine in the other. Starling sits cross legged on the rug, their sharp eyes scanning the assortment of cheeses and fruits for the most perfect pieces. I'm perched on the edge of Chase's bed, picking at a plate of roasted root vegetables.

"You're quiet," Chase muses, nudging my foot with his arm. "Everything going well with Sylas's decision?"

I shrug, popping a piece in my mouth. "It's going… Whenever I think he might finally be ready to answer the question, he finds a way to get me into bed and dodge it. I still haven't gotten a straight answer out of him."

Starling tilts their head thoughtfully. "And what if he's afraid of your reaction to his choice?"

"Any answer would make me happy now," I vent. "I just don't know why he's still wasting time on me. He tells me that I'm-"

"That you're special," Chase interrupts, grinning. "Yeah, we've been over this. And my stance remains the same." He pauses, stumped before the memory surfaces. "If you're both consenting, and he thinks there's some intangible great thing about you, there's nothing wrong with enjoying the attention. Maybe even using it to help *all* of us out. Right, Star?"

Something feels… off as he speaks. Not glaringly obvious, just subtle enough to make me notice.

Starling rolls their red eyes, not noticing what I do. But before the old fight can be revived, the door is shoved open with a force that makes all three of us jump. Prince Ciaran strides in as cold and bitter as the winter descending. Behind him, Sylas follows – taking in the scene with shameless amusement.

"Starling," the ambassador prince barks. "You're needed."

Starling blinks, clearly caught off guard. "Now? I'm in the middle of-"

"*Now.*" His tone leaves no room for argument. He doesn't even address Chase or me, already turning on his heel back out into the hall.

Starling sighs, setting down the piece of cheese they'd finally settled on. "Fine. But this better be worth it."

They shoot us an apologetic look before following, the door shutting politely behind them.

"Someone's in a mood. What's his problem?" Chase grumbles.

"Ciaran's problem," Sylas answers, stepping further into the room. "Is that he's upset about my choice of bride."

I freeze, the piece of potato halfway to my mouth. "Your... Bride?"

Sylas nods, his expression unreadable. "Yes. I've made my decision. It's Giabella."

Time stills while I process the words.

Giabella. Not me.

Chase replies when I don't. "Giabella? The one without a crown?"

Sylas head bobs once. "Yes, Chase. The one without a crown."

I set my plate down, my appetite suddenly gone. "Why Giabella?"

*Why not **me**?* I think.

Sylas's gaze shifts to me, his eyes softening. "Because she'll be kind to you and agrees that you can stay by my side. She also doesn't have a throne of her own she's potentially in line for, which means she can focus entirely on my needs."

His needs.

I think of her in his bed – the promise of an heir to be written in their wedding vows.

He was never going to pick me, he told me as much. Don't be irrational.

Chase lets out a low whistle, the tension between Sylas and I lost on him. "Well, isn't that romantic. But let me guess: Ciaran's pissed because it's not his sister?"

Sylas smirks. "Balora was his first choice. But she's... complicated. And I need someone who won't complicate things further."

I frown. "But Giabella. She's not just your pick because of me, right?"

Sylas steals a bite off my plate. "Everyone has a role to play, Valerie. Including me. Including her. Including you. She knows we have a bargain, and she supports us. It's not the only reason I picked her, but it's the most important one to me."

I want to push back. But with Chase sitting by me – ever the peacemaker – he breaks the tension with a grin.

"Well, I for one think Giabella's a great choice. Nice hair, easygoing, no court back home to rule. What's not to love?"

Sylas chuckles, only ratcheting my tension. "I'm glad you approve. I hope Valerie can do the same in time."

I force a smile, but my mind is still reeling.

Sylas. The future king. Giabella. The future queen.

And *me*, caught somewhere between them, trying to figure out where I fit in all of this.

Sylas steps back out the door, one lithe hand lingering on the handle. "You'll see this was the right choice."

"I'm sure I will." The consolation feels hollow.

Then it's just Chase and me. He leans heavily against the bed, blonde head pivoting around the room.

"Where's Starling?" he asks suddenly: genuinely.

I nod to the door. "They're helping Ciaran. They just left, remember?"

He blinks, his hand pausing mid reach for a pastry. "Did they?" He shakes his head, a faint smile tugging at his lips. "I think I was just distracted by these delicious pastries,"

His tone is light, but there's an uncertainty in his eyes that makes my stomach tighten. I watch him carefully, my smile faltering as he looks genuinely unsettled by the lost memory.

I don't know for sure that he's infected by fairy fruit. It could be nothing. Maybe he's just tired. Maybe he's been focusing too hard on Starling's research.

Every excuse falls flat as he nibbles on the edge of his next treat.

"They're amazing, aren't they?" I agree. Though my mind is already racing, trying to figure out what to do. I decide not to say anything directly to him, at least not yet.

I'm probably overreacting after learning about Giabella.

Chapter 54

I don't find private time to mention my worries over Chase to Starling. An invitation arrives addressed only to me two nights after my suspicions begin to grow. The slip of parchment Ash delivers is edged in gold. They bow and vanish before I can apologize for my previous defensiveness.

Dinner. Private lounge. Bring your appetite.

Sylas's handwriting. No mention of Giabella, but I know. *Of course,* she'll be there.

Chase slips into bed earlier than ever, and Starling finds their way to Alistar's library while I dress. I assume they're pouring over ancient texts – trying to brew Unseelie concoctions to reverse the curse of the fairy fruit.

*Maybe they **have** seen what's wrong with Chase.*

I dress carefully – to not wake the sleeping boy – in a deep blue bodice and skirt that cling to my curves, the neckline high enough to be modest but tight enough to remind Sylas of what he's denying. My fingers tremble with nerves as I fasten the silver clasp at my throat.

First night of our new dynamic.

The private lounge is accompanied by a bard's music when I arrive, the dreamy melody swirling through the air to fill what would otherwise be suffocating silence. The intimate table is set with three places. Sylas sits at the head, Giabella to his right, and the empty spot I take is to his left: a carefully arranged tableau of the new order.

Giabella is radiant in a gown of pale shades, her brown hair braided with tiny white flowers. She smiles warmly as servants bring out course after course, complimenting each dish with genuine enthusiasm.

"The seasoning is exquisite," she comments, dabbing her lips with a napkin. "You must tell the chef, Valerie."

"Of course," I answer, jotting it down on my ever present parchment.

Wedding planning: ask about seasonings for main course.

Sylas watches me, lightly tracing the rim of his wine glass. "You're quiet tonight."

"Just focused," I smile unconvincingly. "There's a lot to prepare."

"Indeed." He turns to Giabella. "The announcement will be made tomorrow. Valerie will arrange the festivities for three nights of celebration: music, dancing, the usual revelry."

Will I? I swallow down any outward surprise.

Giabella eagerly nods along. "I'd love your input on the flowers, Val. I've heard you have an eye for color as an artist."

"It's Valerie," I correct lightly.

Only Eddie gets to call me "Val".

Sylas's jaw works, but Giabella speaks first. "Oh! Valerie, yes, of course."

The kindness in her reply makes my stomach twist. *She's trying.* And it's worse than if she'd been cruel.

A satyr places a plate of potent seared mushrooms in front of me, the rich scent of butter and herbs suddenly overwhelming. My mouth waters in exactly the wrong way.

"Excuse me," I blurt, standing so abruptly my chair teeters. "I – I need a moment."

I don't wait for permission, fleeing to the nearest private washroom. I barely make it to the basin before retching, my body revolting against the rich food… or maybe just the reality of what I'm expected to celebrate. I collapse against the rim of the chamber pot, letting the cool tile floor soothe my full body flush.

"Here."

A damp cloth presses against my temple. Giabella kneels beside me, concern coloring her expression as she dabs sweat from my forehead.

"You didn't have to follow me," I mutter.

"I know." She moves to the water collection, rinsing the towel before returning to wipe at my chin. "I wanted to make sure you were alright."

She angles my face to hers, I obey without a fight. When my eyes flick up, she's watching me with something like pity.

"I'm not your enemy, Valerie."

"I never said you were."

"You didn't have to." She rises, offering me a tan hand. "Sylas cares for you. Deeply. His decision to marry me changes nothing between you."

A hollow laugh escapes me as I ignore the help up. "Except now you two will share a bed. A life. A *title*."

"Titles are just words." She tucks a loose strand of hair behind my ear, before she backs away. "Hearts aren't so easily swayed. You know our marriage is a political necessity."

I want to hate her.

God, I want to so badly.

But there's no malice in her touch, no triumph in her golden eyes as she rinses the napkin once more.

"Why are you doing this?" I whisper, more to myself than her.

"Because I remember what it's like," she says simply. "To love someone and fear they'll drift away. You're young. Your fears are understandable."

I'm not as young as I look, I scoff internally.

"You'll stay with him?" she pleads. "Even after the wedding?"

I look down at my hands: my clammy, trembling hands. "I don't know if I'm strong enough for that."

"Think on it." She drops the napkin onto the counter for a passing brownie to collect. "He needs you." A pause. "And for what it's worth... so do I."

With that, she leaves. I rinse my face with cool water, scoop handfuls of it to my lips to swish out the worst of the vomit, and then I follow her.

I need to try. If they need me, then I can use that to help the barracks somehow... right?

The dining hall feels calmer when I reenter, the candles struggling to remain lit as if sensing the shift in the atmosphere. Sylas's gaze homes in on me immediately, his fingers pausing around his silverware.

"Better?"

"Yes," I lie as I take my seat. "Just overwhelmed by the work ahead."

Sylas's eyes narrow slightly, but he doesn't press. "Then delegate. Have Chase and that Unseelie assist you, as they did before."

I force my shoulders to unstick from my ears. "Of course."

Chase isn't well, he won't be able to help this time. I think, *but I can't tell* **you** *that.*

Sylas leans back in his chair, fingers drifting to my knee under the table in emphasis. "Don't overexert yourself. I don't want you stressed over this."

The words are tender, but they land like a slap.

Stressed over this. Over *his* wedding.

"I will do my best," I hedge, picking at the remains of my meal.

Across the table, Giabella rises gracefully once she finishes her spoonful of dessert. "I have letters to send before the announcement."

Sylas releases her with a nod, and she glides from the room, leaving us to our own company. His hand drifts boldly up my thigh, fingers digging in just enough to make me jump. "Come with me," he grins.

I comply as he takes my hand and pulls me back to his room. It is dim inside, the fire already banked for the quickly approaching dawn. Sylas locks the door behind us.

"You're upset," he accuses when he turns back to me.

"I'm fine."

"Don't lie to me." He cups my face to force eye contact. "You think I don't see it? The way you flinch when I touch her?"

I pull out of his grasp, crossing my arms over my chest defensively. "What do you want me to say, Sylas? That I'm thrilled? That I can't wait to plan your wedding to another woman?"

"I want you to trust me." His frustration only encourages my own. "This changes nothing between us."

"You keep saying that but I think it changes *everything.*"

He steps into me, his long body pressing mine back against the door to my own room. "Does it?" His lips brush my ear. "Tell me you don't still want this. Tell me you don't still feel how much I need you."

I lean away, but he cages me in, his arms braced against the door on either side of my head.

"You knew this was coming," he coos, his breath warm as it mingles with mine. "You wrote down that she was the right choice."

"I changed my mind." I say, cross.

"Did you?" His smile is wolfish.

The truth sits heavy in my chest. *I knew he wouldn't pick me; I just hate that I was right.*

I should push him away. Should demand more – demand *respect.*

But the look in his eyes – that barely leashed desire I recognize well – makes my throat dry.

"Sy…" I start, but he silences me with a hard kiss.

"Enough talking," he growls against my lips.

His hands slide down my body – deft and demanding – until his fingers find the ring on my hand. He pauses, his gaze locked with mine in challenge as he slowly twists it off.

The glamour hits like a wave, drowning my doubts in heat and honeyed want.

"Better?" he teases, pressing the ring into my palm before closing my fingers around it. "Now you don't have to think if you don't want to. Just *feel*."

And I do.

I let him back me toward the bed – let him push me down. I let us both lose ourselves until neither of us can remember why we were arguing in the first place.

But later, I lie awake in the daylight. His arm is immovable across my waist. I slide the ring back on my finger, finally dissipating the last of his influence. And I become suddenly unsure if I've made a huge mistake in trusting a sidhe with my heart.

Chapter 55

I plant a kiss on Sylas's pale cheek before I slip from his bed in the evening. There are no sleeping humans or Unseelie on the other side of our shared door when I step inside.

Chase is probably just researching with Starling, I comfort myself.

Once I've bathed away Sylas's lavender and dressed in comfortable wool, I step into the hall to help the quickly growing decor team prepare the courtyard for the arriving guests.

I dictate where to set what evergreen arrangements and watch from the window with a critical eye as sprites shovel snow away from the carriage path outside. The brownies report to me when they've finished scrubbing halls. And the dryads ensure the fairy fruit will not run out before the festivities end.

With the preparations well underway a few hours later, I decide to retire to my room before Giabella and Sylas can drag me to another dinner.

They won't miss me. They'll be too infatuated with each other, I think bitterly.

Chase and Starling return shortly after I do. I can see the dark circles under both their eyes – darker than my own. They both tuck into his bed. We don't bother catching up before they drift into dreams.

I busy myself rearranging Starling's notes for clues about Chase's condition.

I can't decipher half of this. And the half I can… I don't like what I find: failed hybrids, illogical theories, the writings of someone desperate to save a loved one. I stack the pile, before turning my attention to the window and the flurry of activity far below.

Nobles arrive in the jewel toned dress of their courts. A line of carriages pulled by gryphons, pegasi, and the occasional shapeshifted pooka line the path all the way through the gates to the forest beyond. I can name almost every guest by title, court, and a passable amount of knowledge on their alliances and rivalries as they step out.

Though it all feels more like trivia than strategy when I'm up here.

A knock eventually comes, and I don't need to turn to know Sylas steps inside. His presence fills the room before he even speaks: cold and *mine*.

"You're not dressed." His voice is even, but I hear the hurt beneath it.

I keep my back to him, my reflection pale in the glass. "I'm not going."

Silence.

Then the measured click of his boots as he crosses the room. His hands settle on my shoulders, his breath stirring the hair at my nape.

"This isn't a request."

A shiver runs down my spine. "I'm still feeling unwell after dinner last night," I lie.

"I'll have the healers bring you a tea." He counters.

"Chase isn't feeling well either. I told him I'd stay with him."

His grip falters. A beat passes.

"Very well." He releases me, stepping back. "But I expect you at the revelry tomorrow. No excuses."

I wait until the door shuts behind him to exhale, my knees buckling as I sink onto my bed.

I don't know if I can do this anymore, even if it helps the other humans.

Starling stirs on the other bed, turning just in time to see my horror before I school my face neutral.

"You look terrible," they remark.

"I feel worse than either of you," Chase groans into the pillow.

I collapse back, kicking off my slippers as I change the subject. "Is Ciaran going?"

Starling's mouth twists. "He refused. Said he had 'urgent business'."

"Which means he can't stomach watching Giabella win." I venture to guess.

They scoot out of bed, and I finally notice the deep purple dress jacket draped over the chair when they reach for it. "I have to attend, though. Someone needs to represent his household."

"Be careful down there."

Starling gives me a dry look as they shimmy into the fitted piece. "It's a dinner, not a battlefield. Don't wait up."

The moment they're gone, a servant enters with a tray of light fare and a carafe of water.

"From His Highness," the selkie explains.

Chase mutters, barely coherent. "God, even gone, he's fucking here."

I pick at the bread, my appetite nonexistent. The distant swell of music picks up from below: the celebration starting without us.

Chase yawns, tossing uncomfortably in the bed. "Wake me when this nightmare's over."

I lie down beside him, staring at the ceiling. My mind chases too many questions in my life – none are wrangled into solutions by the time I fall asleep.

Starling is there when I wake, rumpled finery still on. Chase takes considerably longer to rouse as Starling strokes his sandy hair. When he does, he still seems to be clinging to a dream.

"How was last night?" I ask.

"You should have been there."

"Oh?" I prompt, suddenly more awake.

"A messenger came stumbling in, covered in mud up to his knees. Announced Princess Margaret's death right between the soup and salad courses."

Princess Margaret is dead? I think with horror.

Their claws still. "Giabella's face was-"

The door swings open between mine and Sylas's room, the creak cutting off the rest of their sentence. Sylas stands in the doorway: shirt half laced, hair unkempt.

My stomach twists at the unexpected sight.

"Valerie." His voice is exhausted as he closes the distance between us and pulls me into his arms.

"I just heard about Margaret," I gasp, feeling the tension in every part of him as he holds me against him – convincing himself I'm still alive.

"My spies have reported that it was Unseelie work. They slaughtered her caravan on their way home from her dismissal a week ago. Word took a while to reach us," he explains, pulling me back an arms length to watch my reaction. My morbid imagination flashes with what the scene must have looked like.

The graceful sidhe with eyes like frost – her family in tow. All gone with gore and malice because they dared to exist with Seelie magic.

"What does that mean for the North?" I manage to say through the gruesome thought.

He sighs as he lets his hands drop to mine. "Queen Penelope stayed behind, *alive*. She will take a new king, and they will... try for a new heir." His mouth is a hard line at the words.

Princess Margaret was born before sidhe couldn't conceive anymore. Will the queen be so lucky to survive another child now?

He continues when he sees the worry overwhelm me. "We will cancel the week's revelries, Giabella plans to travel home for the funeral anyway. Mourning will last until the Winter Solstice in a week. Then we can spend the next season planning the spring equinox and the wedding," he answers with finality.

His confidence and plan help slow my spiking heart rate. His fingers brush my fingertips – where old calluses have now gone soft in his care. I look up at him.

But his gaze isn't on me. It's probing Chase, who struggles to sit up with slow, uncoordinated movements.

"Still unwell?" He steps closer to the boy with incredulity.

Chase blinks at him, mouth working soundlessly for a moment before managing, "Just... tired."

Sylas reaches out, brushing Chase's forehead with the back of his hand. "No fever."

Starling moves between them, their voice carefully light. "Human illnesses don't always present like folk ones."

Not a lie, just not applicable right now.

Sylas's gaze softens as he turns back to me, lingering on the dark circles under my eyes. "You look pale too. Are you sure you're well?"

"I'm better today." I force a smile. "Just worried about Chase... and you."

His shoulders relax a fraction. "Focus on your own health." The dismissal in his tone is subtle, but there. "Rest. Eat. But tonight..." His finger curls under my chin, tilting my face up to his. "I expect you at my side at the mourning dinner. You were missed last night."

Then he leans in, kissing me with a sweetness that tells me he means it. He leaves a moment after, not waiting for a reply.

Once his footsteps fade to nothingness, Starling whirls on me. "We need to move him. *Now*."

"Where?" I'm already gathering Chase's lanky arm over my shoulder, my hands trembling almost as much as his.

"Ciaran's chambers." Starling hoists Chase's other arm over their shoulders with more ease. I slip out from under him in disbelief. Starling barely notices the weight change, turning back to explain. "He's with Leona all night. She's been insistent on reviewing the alliance treaties between the South and West."

Chase mumbles something unintelligible as we drag him through the bustling corridors. The crowd of servants are too busy preparing their courtiers for Northward travel for the funeral to care. Chase's feet scuff against the stone, his dependence on us growing heavier with each step.

We round the final corner, and freeze.

Prince Ciaran looms in his chamber's threshold, arms crossed, Leona squared to him. Her nose wrinkles in disgust when she follows his line of sight to us.

"What is *this*?" she sneers.

Starling doesn't flinch. "We need the room."

Ciaran's gaze locks onto Chase's pallid face, calculating for a moment. "Inside." He pushes the door open.

Leona stiffens. "Darling-"

"We can take this back to your room." His eyes rake over her in a way that makes *my* cheeks flush. She rolls her dark eyes but smiles at the suggestion.

I guess they're on good terms again.

But I don't really care about their relations, and help Starling haul Chase inside.

Ciaran catches my wrist, holding me firm as Chase slips off my shoulder again. The prince's voice is a barely audible threat. "If you value your time left with him, no one will know I'm allowing this."

Then he's striding away, an impatient Leona already sinking down the stairs ahead.

The door clicks shut, leaving us in juniper scented chambers that put me on edge. Moonlight can't penetrate the purposefully closed off curtains, hiding the extensive collection of Starling's work.

I stare at the closed door. "He just... left."

Starling settles Chase onto their prince's massive bed, claws gentle as they arrange the pillows. "I told you. Ciaran and I have an understanding."

"But he *hates* humans." My disbelief seeps into the words as I settle on the floor near the bed.

Chase murmurs something unintelligible into the sheets, his fingers twitching against the embroidered coverlet.

Starling moves to a carved cabinet, pulling out vials and bottles with practiced ease.

"Hate is a luxury. Ciaran is many things, but he's not stupid." They hold a yellow tinted potion up to the light. "He knows which debts are worth collecting."

I sink onto the edge of the bed, watching as Starling coaxes Chase to drink it. His eyelids flutter, then grow heavy, his breathing deepening almost immediately with peaceful sleep.

"What debts?" I prompt.

Starling doesn't answer at first. They tuck the blankets around Chase's shoulders with tenderness. Then they slide down to sit beside me, propped against the bed frame.

"Last winter," they say at last. "A scorned lord tried to poison Ciaran during the solstice feast after a broken bargain. I was the one who caught him before he was successful." They give me a moment to imagine it all. "I bought him the night to convince the court to oust that lord for other reasons. Then I took him out *permanently*."

Somewhere in the castle, rich laughter breaks out and we both turn instinctively towards the door. But no one intrudes.

I study Starling's angular profile, trying to picture them killing a lord. "You saved his life."

They shrug. "And he's saved mine twice before that. Practicality makes for stranger bedfellows than affection ever could."

Chase yawns in his sleep, one hand curling into the pillow. I reach up automatically to smooth his hair, shaping it back into the elegant style he preferred when he was more aware.

I swallow around the lump in my throat. "Will he...?"

"Wake up coherent?" Starling's voice is flat. "Probably not. His condition has been worsening rapidly this week. I don't expect him to be… around by solstice." They whisper the prognosis, as if the walls would steal him away from us sooner if they knew. I watch as they adjust his pillows, the hurt in their eyes forcing mine away.

Solstice. That's far too soon.

We sit in companionable silence after that, shoulders pressed together, watching the starry night out the window.

Eventually – remorsefully – I rise to my feet. "I need to go. Sylas's mourning clothes need to be steamed."

Chapter 56

The mourning dinner is a somber affair.

Black silk drapes the hall, and the usual glittering chandeliers are snuffed out, leaving the stairwells to the ghostly glow of the moon. Sidhe nobles – who remained in the West – murmur in hushed tones, their sparkling attire replaced by darker shades again, too soon after Mara.

Giabella's absence is felt in the empty chair at Sylas's right, but I take my place at his left again tonight.

He hasn't let me stray more than a step from him all evening – his fingers brushing my wrist, my waist, my lower back. Each touch is a wordless reassurance that I am safe as long as I'm near him.

When the final course is cleared and the guests begin to retire, Sylas leans down to speak against my ear. "You've kept me sane tonight."

The praise makes me smile despite the heavy atmosphere. "I'm glad I could be of service."

His thumb traces the curve of my jaw. "Come back to my chambers, we both shouldn't be alone."

I hesitate.

Normally, I would be weak to the suggestion – would cling to the fleeting illusion that I could be his one and only love. But now...

Now, I'm tired, and scared.

"Actually," I decline carefully, "I am not in the mood for... that."

Sylas straightens. "Oh?"

I keep my voice light: diplomatic. "I just want to rest after everything we've been through."

He searches my face for something, though I'm not sure what. Then – with a sigh – he presses an apologetic kiss to my forehead. "Of course we can rest. But I still want you near."

He lets his hand drift down to mine, leading me back to his room.

He actually does care about me more than sex, I think with surprise at the way he so easily readjusts his grip: not hungry now, but achingly tender.

A fire already crackles in the hearth inside, melting away the grief of the mourning dinner, my worry for Chase, and even the ever present fear of Unseelie attacks.

Sylas doesn't pull me toward the bed like I expect. He leads me to the chaise near the fire where he likes to read, his fingers lingering between my shoulders. "Sit," he commands, though it's soft.

I sink into the cushions, my body exhausted by consecutive restless days. His eyes trace the shadows under mine then drift to my slumped shoulders.

Without a word to me, he turns and strides to the door, speaking in low tones to a brownie outside. When he returns, he kneels before me, hands sliding under the hem of my skirt to ease my slippers off.

"You've been pushing yourself too hard," he says, his thumbs pressing into the arch of my foot. The touch pinpoints a tender spot, making me jerk.

"Sy-"

"Hush." His voice is firm, but his hands are gentle. "Let me take care of you tonight."

A servant enters with a tray of raspberries, dark chocolate, and a pot of mint tea. Sylas dismisses them with a nod before lifting a berry to my lips. "Eat, pet."

I part my mouth automatically, the sweetness bursting on my tongue. He watches me with an intensity that has nothing to do with lust, his thumb brushing juice from my lower lip.

"Better?"

I nod, and his tight lips ease. He shifts onto the couch behind me, drawing me back until I'm nestled against his chest. His fingers find my hair, ginger curls twining around his hands like a living flame.

"I've always loved your hair," he admits quietly, combing through the strands with reverent slowness. "It reminds me of Mara's."

The name doesn't sting the way I expect it to. Not when his touch is this doting.

"That's why you kept me, isn't it? Because I have her light?" I ask sheepishly.

His fingers still. Then, to emphasize his next words, he tilts my chin up until our blue eyes meet. "I offered the bargain because of that, but I kept you because you're *you*." His thumb traces the line of my cheekbone. "And I'll execute anyone who says otherwise."

The words should frighten me with their violence. But tonight, wrapped in his quiet devotion, they're comforting. I exhale, letting my head fall back against his shoulder. His fingers return to my hair, unraveling the braids I'd pinned up for the dinner, separating each curl with painstaking care.

"Sleep," he murmurs against my temple. "I'll be here when you wake."

And he is.

I sleep curled against him, more deeply than I have in days. His arms are still encircling me when I wake, his own breathing deep and even. For a moment, I let myself linger in the warmth – in the rare peace of his stillness being *mine* for once.

He's got a full schedule today. I should wake him.

Then his fingers twitch against my waist, and I know he's already awake.

But I don't want to leave. It's so easy to love him when it's just us.

"You're thinking too loudly," he grumbles. His nose brushes the nape of my neck, inhaling deeply. "What is it?"

I turn in his arms to face him. His face is relaxed, the gold of his lashes catching the dusk light. He looks younger like this – less like a soon-to-be king and more like the prince he still is.

"I know you're going to the atelier today," I refocus my nervous energy. "For your wedding fitting."

A shadow darkens his face – barely there, gone before I can call him on it. "Yes."

"Can I come with you?"

His brows lift in surprise.

I press on before he can dissect it. "It's just… I haven't been back since I went with Mara before the equinox. And I-" I hesitate, then lay my palm flat against his chest, over the steady beat of his heart. "I'd like to be there. At your side."

Like I hope I always will be.

His eyes brighten with understanding. "You want to see the place we met again?"

"How could I not?" A self deprecating smile tugs at my lips as I remember how I knelt before him. "You had me weak in the knees."

He huffs a sleepy laugh. "And you looked up at me like I'd hung the stars." His fingers tighten in my hair, just enough to tilt my head back. "You still do."

I don't deny it.

He kisses me: slow and savoring. When he pulls away, his voice has firmed. "You'll come. I'd want you nowhere else."

Chapter 57

After a long evening of preparing the mourning solstice with Alistar –
while Sylas debates political nonsense with the king and council – the time
comes for us to go to the atelier. I link my arm in his stronger one as we
stroll the halls, clinging to his steadiness as the memories of that first night
flood back.

The hall with his painting, the gilded hammered sign, even the
chandeliers: they're all so normal to me now when not too long ago they
were sights to behold.

The atelier hasn't changed when I open the door for him, reverting to
the more formal titles of "prince" and "attendant".

Bolts of fabric still line the walls in cascades of color. Grigs and
leprechauns move about the space hard at work. The starch and lye soap of
my past permeate it all.

I step inside behind Sylas – my chin up and my posture confident. The
stitchers bow to him as expected. But a few eyes dart to me soon after,
recognizing me as the human attendant who survived Mara's assassination:
the one the prince kept.

"Belladonna," Sylas calls, and the witch emerges from behind a shelf
of dupioni, her magic darkened fingers clutching the same pincushion I
once held for her.

Her sights land on me first. "The ginger girl." She voices the identifier
with bafflement. "Here to flirt again?"

A hot flush crawls up my neck. *She remembers.*

Sylas's hand finds my shoulder when my posture falters. "She's here to
observe."

Then he begins shrugging off his jacket just like before.

"Let's begin."

Belladonna waves her hand, and stitchers swarm with his wedding
ensemble.

The coat is liquid midnight, embroidered with silver constellations: the
same ones that will crown the sky on his wedding night. The high collar is
lined with fur tinged pink, a concession to Giabella's Northern roots. But

the cape is pure Sylas: sheer, shimmering – like ice over a winter lake – fastened with antler shaped clasps.

The White Stag, even now.

I remind myself more than once to square my shoulders as they dress him, looking over their work with awe.

When they step back, Sylas looks like a *king*. Like someone I should have never talked to, much less everything else that's happened between us.

Then his eyes find mine in the mirror. "Well?"

I step closer, drawn despite myself. My fingers hover over the embroidery: the stitches are perfect, each star a tiny reminder of his eternity. "It's… regal."

His mouth twitches. "You like it."

"I do."

"That's all I need to hear." He catches my wrist, raising the knuckle to his lips. "You'll need a dress too. One in matching shades."

Not white, I remind myself.

Though I don't know if white dress is the bridal custom here.

Belladonna clears her throat to break our stare down. "The trousers need pinning, girl." She thrusts the old pin cushion into my hands. "Hold this."

I kneel obediently as she herself lowers. Sylas exhales audibly when I look up at him, a tease on my lips as I know what he's imagining me doing instead.

Belladonna's voice is dry. "Don't move, Your Highness."

But Sylas isn't listening. His hand fists in my hair, tugging just enough to sting.

"Stand," he commands. "I didn't bring you here to kneel."

I rise, but I don't step back. The cushion in my hand is too far now for the old witch to steal from. The human stitcher with curly hair takes the thing from me, kneeling where I'd just been to assist.

Sylas barely glances at his reflection when she's done. His attention is fixed on me as I wait beside him.

"Good," he says, stripping off the coat and handing it to a leprechaun without ceremony. Then, to Belladonna: "Take Valerie's measurements."

Belladonna scrunches her face at the human girl. "Sydney."

That's her name, I remind myself.

There's a beat of silence when she stands frozen in place. Then the witch jerks her pointy chin in my direction. "You heard the prince."

Sydney plucks a journal and quill to record the numbers, her mouth pressed into a tight line. She doesn't look at me as she unrolls the measuring tape from her apron, and I know she's remembering our conversation as well.

"Be careful around sidhe... they're self serving."

I don't think she expected me to end up in such a powerful position.

I should probably say something.

It's fine, I can do it myself. Or maybe, *I don't need a dress.*

But the words die in my throat when Sylas's fingers brush the back of my neck, as he ties back my hair for an accurate measurement.

Sydney approaches stiffly. "Arms out."

I comply, lifting my arms as she loops the tape around my bust.

"Breathe in," she instructs, pulling the tape snug.

I do. And for the first time – this close – I really see how different we are.

Her nails are bitten low, her fingers calloused from work I haven't thought about in months. The scent of lye clings to her: sharp and utilitarian like life usually is here. She is human in the way I used to be before Sylas – before I learned how to survive up here without groveling.

And then I look at my reflection ahead.

My skin is smooth, my hair glossy. The cracks on my palms have softened, replaced by the blessing of Sylas's favor. Even my uniform – simple by court standards – is finer than anything anyone is wearing as a stitcher here.

I'm not like you anymore. The thought rises unbidden.

Sydney's jaw tightens as she measures my waist, my hips, my inseam. She mutters as she measures my neck. "Must be nice to play house with the prince."

Sylas watches us from the mirror with passive amusement. He sees it too: the way Sydney's fingers hesitate near my silk sleeve, the way she steps back too quickly when she's done like my newfound status might be contagious.

She's jealous.

"All done?" he prompts.

Sydney's throat works. "Yes."

Belladonna checks Sydney's scrawled numbers once over. "We'll have something made by week's end."

Sylas nods, satisfied. "See that you do."

Sydney retreats without another word, melting back into the line of stitchers. But not before I catch the look she shoots me: part resentment, part envy.

You think you're one of them now? Her eyes burn. *You're still just a human on a leash.*

But she doesn't know.

She doesn't know the way he confides in me – leans on me for support. She wouldn't understand the power I'm wielding in the hope of helping all of us humans one day.

Sylas's hand finds mine, steering me toward the door. "Happy?"

"Yes," I say automatically, and then realize I *am*.

He's brought me along as I asked, ensuring I'll have my own statement of a gown made for the wedding.

My chest warms for once when I imagine the day.

Regardless if I'm the bride or not, he's proven I mean something to him.

He smiles a small victorious smile as we return to his tower. And I notice the fresh tray of fairy fruit pastries on his end table.

Chase.

It's been well over a day since I checked in, and his deterioration was noticeably accelerating.

Are they eating?

Does he still remember my name?

"I'm going to go check on Chase, he's been holding up with Starling," I excuse myself, slipping Sylas's grip as I stay in the threshold of his room. "Afraid whatever he has might be contagious to humans."

His face falls for only a moment, before he schools it away. "Send him my well wishes."

The castle is too noisy with folk I don't recognize. I still haven't bothered to learn the new attendant's names, but they sure know mine. And they straighten when I shoot a glare at a laughing clique.

Good. They won't mess with me if they respect me.

When I find Starling, they're in the library of Alistar's tower. I don't tiptoe around my intent.

"How's Chase?" I quiz, hoping some miracle may have helped turn things around in a night.

When they don't answer, I know we're running out of time.

"I'm going to ask Sylas for some time off once Giabella returns," I continue slower. "To be with Chase... and you."

Starling freezes, their quill hovering above the journal of notes they're copying from a larger collection on fairy fruit. They turn to me then. "That will be too late. And besides, Sylas won't let you."

"He will," I insist, defiance creeping into my tone. "I'll make something up, the wedding is two months away. He doesn't need me to plan everything right now."

"That is a terrible idea," they critique bluntly. "Sylas is possessive. And when he finds out you lied to him about why you're neglecting your *duties*, he'll be furious."

I push myself up from the table, unable to bear the way they spit out the innuendo.

They're just upset about Chase. It's not personal, I remind myself.

"I'll handle it," I say, my voice louder than intended. "I just need a week off. That's all... He'll let me."

Starling doesn't respond, their attention already drifting back to their studies. Frustration burns up my neck as I storm out of the library.

The nausea hits me halfway to Sylas's chambers: a sudden, oily wave that has me gripping a windowsill for balance. I press my forehead against the cool glass, breathing through my nose until the dizziness passes.

Too much stress. Too little sleep.

By the time I reach Sylas's study, my palms are damp. He's at his desk reviewing correspondence. But he looks up the moment I enter with worry. "You're pale again. Is Chase alright?"

"He's sleeping. I'm just tired too," I lie, then force myself to step fully inside and close the door. "Sylas, I need to ask you something."

His quill stills, attentive with my use of his full name. "Ask."

"I'd like the rest of the week away from my duties."

Deafening silence.

He sets the quill down before he answers. "No."

The refusal is so absolute, it makes me bristle. "It's just a few days. The wedding isn't-"

"You'll stay where I can protect you." His voice remains even, but his knuckles go white around the armrest of his chair. "The rebellion was reported to have slaughtered Margaret's entire retinue on an open road. Do you think they'd hesitate if they found you alone? Weak?"

Weak. The word lands like a slap. My nails bite crescent moons into my palms. "I'm not some fragile thing to be protected."

"Aren't you?" He rises, circling the desk. He gestures to the hollows under my eyes. "Look at you. You're shaking. Whatever illness Chase has, you may have caught it too." He drags me into a fierce hug. "I won't lose you to human stubbornness."

The nausea surges again at his lavender, bitter on the back of my tongue. I will myself not to shove him away. "But they're all I have."

He mercifully pulls me back to arms length, his hands cradling my greening face. "You have *me*," he murmurs. "And I'll keep you safe."

He's right. The rebellion won't hold back, just because Chase is sick.

He kisses my temple, before releasing me entirely. "Tomorrow, we'll enjoy the gardens. I'll entrust planning the solstice to Alistar alone. We can take time away. Forget all of our duties while it's just us."

"Let me distract you," his smirk challenges.

Chapter 58

Life is sweeter with Giabella's too kind presence gone. The halls are lighter, like the very walls of the castle are relieved by her absence. Sylas is wholly mine right now. And maybe that's what makes this week so… special.

We spend the nights meandering the private gardens, his arm slung proudly around my waist as he points out constellations I'd never see in the human world. At dusk and dawn, we dine alone in his chambers. And in between, his teeth are at my throat as he slides the glamour protective ring from my finger and makes me forget my own name.

He's relentlessly intentional every step of the way. The gifts he wakes me with are extravagant – my favorite being a silver ring with a single sapphire.

"I've read that in your world, rings are exchanged between lovers," he explains, sliding it onto my finger beside the magic one.

It's dangerous: this illusion. But I cling to it anyway. Until the evening Giabella returns – when I wake to Sylas already dressed – his back to me as he fastens a cloak lined with silver fur.

"Stay in bed," he says without turning. "You're pale again."

I push up on my elbows too fast. The world tilts enough to make my stomach lurch. I barely make it to the wash basin before I'm retching, my body convulsing with empty heaves.

Sylas is there in an instant, his hands cool on my nape, fishing my hair away from my sweaty face. "Shhh," he soothes, as if I'm some skittish animal. "It'll pass, just like last time."

When the spasms subside, I collapse back onto the pillows, drenched and trembling. Sylas offers me a wet cloth to clean up with. "No more wine. No more rich foods until you're better." He tucks the blanket around me as I wipe away the bile.

A servant's high voice sounds at the door, "Your Highness, the Northern delegation has arrived."

He tenses at the announcement – a frustrated sound in his throat as he bends down again.

"I'll send some tea." He pacifies my wounded expression. His lips brush my forehead. "Be good."

Once he's gone, I press a hand to my aching belly… and freeze.

No.

Humans don't conceive in the Otherworld. It's common knowledge that our frozen age suppresses that part of our biology.

In that fear's absence, another more alarming possibility crosses into my mind.

What if I ate fairy fruit without knowing it? What if when he kissed me...

My next breath is labored. I cannot finish the theory, the weight of Chase's fading condition and my own mortality crushing my chest.

I need to do anything other than sit back and watch us both slip away.

The fairy fruit trees – their quick life cycle – lingers in the back of my mind like the answer to a question I don't know to ask.

If I can just see them. Maybe I can figure it out.

But I have no idea where the orchard is exactly. I remember the boggart's words – that it's on the outskirts of the gardens somewhere. But the castle grounds are a vast purposeful labyrinth.

Then I remember something even more helpful.

The blueprint.

The one the cloaked figure dropped in the laundry room months ago. I took it – thinking it might be important – and then never brought it up to Sylas like I'd planned to.

But where did I leave it?

I don't remember anymore.

I throw open the door to my room, my heart pounding with a sudden mix of hope and desperation that battles away the lingering nausea. I stay as quiet as possible, knowing I am one intrusion away from losing my privileges of being alone at all.

Sylas would lose it, if he knew I may have eaten some.

The room is exactly as I left it: my bed neatly made and my clothes steamed on their hangers. I look over my desk, finding nothing. I check Chase's unused desk and unmade bed as insurance.

I've been so distracted. I haven't visited him in days, I realize.

I shove my guilt over the boy from my mind, and continue looking over every possible nook or cranny that paper could be: under my bed, behind the vanity, in my closet.

But the blueprint has vanished.

I stare at the quietly overturned space, my stomach sinking.

I'm sure I left it here. Did someone discover it before I could tell Sylas? Panic claws at my thoughts – at the possibility of him thinking I'm part of some rebellion.

But I cast out the thought with a shake of my head.

He's keeping me safe. I'm not even Unseelie. He doesn't think I'm part of them.

"There's no time to worry now," I tell myself. "If I can't use the blueprint, I'll have to find the orchard on my own."

I slip out of my room and into the castle gardens, the bitter late fall chill magnifying my panic. The moon hangs low in the sky, disorientingly so.

I start walking along a random white dusted path. The gardens are a maze; their layout designed to confuse and delight courtiers. I've wandered them countless times before at this point, plucking snacks from branches and running confidential messages on Sylas's behalf.

But tonight, everything feels as off as I do.

The hedges seem taller; the paths incorrigibly shifting as my panic overrides any sense of direction, I turn left, then right, then left again. Circling back to my own footsteps.

The fairy fruit trees have to be here somewhere.

But as the minutes turn into hours, I begin to doubt myself. The paths all look the same, and I can't see anything but the moon above to orient myself.

I pause at a fork in the path, my frustration warming my frozen cheeks.

"Where are you?" I mutter under my breath, glaring at the hedges like they might part and reveal the orchard… or a way out in general. But they remain stubbornly still, their browning leaves rustling in mockery.

"Looking for something?"

I whirl around, my heart in my throat. Starling stands a few feet away, suspicious. Their shadowed eyes reflect the moonlight, and with it a spark of anger.

"Starling," I greet, forcing a smile. "I didn't hear you."

"Clearly," they say dryly. "You've been wandering around for hours. What are you doing out here?"

I hesitate, unsure how much to burden them with. "I just needed some air. The castle feels... suffocating."

They cross their arms, clearly unconvinced. "And you decided to get lost in the gardens?"

"I wasn't trying to get lost," I counter defensively. "I was just exploring."

Starling sighs. "You're a terrible liar, you know that? You really don't get how useful that can be for you humans."

I cross my own arms, my frustration bubbling over. "Fine. I was looking for the fairy fruit trees. I thought if I could find them, maybe I could get help. But I can't even find my way back to the castle now, so it doesn't matter."

For a heartbeat, Starling says nothing. Then they inch closer, voice dropping so the hedges can't hear. "First off, the orchard is on the entire other side of the gardens." They jab towards the north with their thumb. "Second, do you have any idea how dangerous that is? If Sylas finds out you're snooping around for the orchard, he'll-"

"I know," I interrupt, my voice too animated in the stillness of the garden. "But I can't just sit here and do nothing. Chase is going to be discovered, Starling. I feel so useless."

I see something raw and unguarded pass behind their eyes. But it's gone as quickly as it appeared, replaced by a grim resolve. "They already took him."

My arms drop. The words strike true, knocking the breath from my lungs. My mind scrambles to make sense of what they've just said, but it's impossible.

I'm too late. I didn't say goodbye.

"No," I choke out the brittle denial.

Starling's face is stony, even as tears spill down their cheeks. "Sylas figured it out when I swung by your room a few days ago with a note about his progress. But you were sleeping. He took the note himself. He had the guards drag Chase out of my bed. I just... I thought I could fix it." Their voice cracks – followed by a sob – the sound wrong and gut wrenching.

Without thinking, I step forward and drag them into a hug, my arms tightening around their shaky small frame. For a moment, they don't resist, their body sagging against mine after carrying the weight of this for far too long. But then they stiffen, their hands shoving against my chest with bruising force.

"Get off of me," they spit venomously as I stumble back. The shock inside me is replaced by a hurt confusion at their rejection.

"Starling –?" I begin, my own voice catching.

Are they mad at me? What did I do?

"You left us," they snap as they answer the question I didn't dare ask. They still won't look at me, their gaze fixed on some distant point behind me. "I've been so careful in this dungeon of a castle. *So* careful. And the one time I slip up – the one time I think I've finally found people to let my guard down with – it all falls apart. Chase is slowly dying and you left me alone to take care of him while you slept your way into a happy-enough ending." Their voice trembles, but their words do enough damage.

I wince. "I didn't know-"

"This is the last time I'm helping you, Valerie," they interrupt: cold and final. They swipe at their tears with the back of their hand, their jaw clenched. "So keep up."

They turn on their heels and walk away quickly. I follow with heavier steps – my body dragging with the crushing realization that I've lost not only Chase… but Starling, too. I barely keep pace, my vision blurred with tears and the gray scale of moonlight.

When we reach the safety of the castle, Starling doesn't look back. They stop at the door to my chambers but don't turn to face me. "Don't go out there again," they order, devoid of emotion. "Don't look for the fairy fruit. Don't talk about this with Sylas. And stay away from me from now on."

I nod, finding my throat too tight to speak. They finally give me one last look – a fleeting glance that feels more like a goodbye than anything they've said – before turning and disappearing up the stairs. Their footsteps fade into nothingness, leaving me standing alone in the hollow, dimly lit corridor.

I shuffle into my room, leaning against the closed door for support. My legs give out anyway, and I slide to the floor. My back presses hard against the cold wood. More tears come then – hot and uncontrollable – spilling down my cheeks as I let myself be consumed by the enormity of everything I've lost.

For Chase, who's gone without a goodbye.

For Starling, who walked away.

For the hopelessness of it all: that ironic, suffocating ache of being alone in a place surrounded by bodies.

I cry until my throat is raw and my eyes hurt; until the numbness returns to dull the edges of the pain. But even as the tears slow, the emptiness remains, and I'm not sure I'll ever be able to fill it again.

The sun peaks over the hills outside before I stop shaking.

My barrack friends don't understand. My friendship with Starling is ruined. And Chase... is gone.

The words don't feel real. My fingers dig into the rug beneath me, twisting the fibers until my nails sting. He can't be gone. Not Chase: with his stupid jokes and his terrible notes and the way he always stole the last bite of my dessert.

I have no one left.

A sob claws its way up my throat again. The door creaks open to my room, and I don't lift my head when his shadow falls over me.

"Valerie."

Sylas's voice is gentle.

But it doesn't alleviate my remorse. Right now, I'm too hollow to care what he has to say. I don't answer. My fingers tangle further in the rug, my knuckles bleaching.

He crouches in front of me slowly. His fingers brush my cheek, catching the damp trail of tears. "You're hurting," he observes.

A broken laugh escapes me. "What gave it away?"

His other hand brushes my ring, his touch featherlight. "I can make it better."

I yank away. "I don't want sex."

"Not like that," he clarifies, so quietly I almost miss it. His fingers skim the ring again.

My gut tells me to pull away, but I don't.

He twists the ring free, and the world shifts – dunking me into warm nothingness. The weight in my chest – the grief and guilt – melt away. And Sylas's kind face is the only thing in focus when I look up.

His glamour drapes around my mind, smoothing out every sharp thought until there's nothing left but quiet.

"Better?" His voice resonates through me.

I exhale before I nod.

And it's true. I'm not sad anymore. I'm not *anything* anymore. Just...

pliant. Content.

No more pain – no more overthinking to the point of nausea. Just this stillness for a sweet, forgiving moment.

Sylas smiles as he tucks the ring into his pocket. His fingers card through my hair, lifting my head further to meet his gaze.

"There's my girl," he murmurs. He lifts me into his arms and carries me to my bed.

I let him kiss me, let his hands wander.

"Maybe I was too hasty saying I don't want you right now," I pant as his fingers test me. He lets out a breathy laugh, kissing my neck as I let my legs fall open under his touch.

"Not right now, you're exhausted," he says against my skin. I whine as he tucks me against his chest.

"Just sleep, Valerie," is all I hear before unconsciousness pulls me under.

The rest is dreamless. Like I'm dead. And when I wake again it's with a gasp in my empty room. I stumble to my feet on instinct, my vision swimming.

I feel worse today.

The nausea from earlier surging back with a vengeance. I don't make it to a washbasin before my stomach empties itself directly onto the floor – until there's nothing left but acidic spit.

When I straighten, my reflection in the mirror of my vanity stops me cold.

Pale. Hollow eyed. *Weak.*

Just like Chase in those final days.

Fairy fruit.

The thought strikes like lightning again. It makes too much sense: the nausea, the fatigue, the way Sylas's been watching me like a hawk.

Does he know? Is that why he's being so attentive? He's making the most of my last few days?

I press a hand to my belly and shudder.

Then I crawl into bed, too tired and sick to do much of anything about it.

Chapter 59

I wake to a webbed hand shaking my shoulder.

"His Highness requests you in his study," a merrow servant delivers the order, her green hair the only glimpse I catch as she disappears before I can ask questions.

I struggle out of bed to wash the last of the vomit from my cheek. My reflection is even more ghastly tonight: dark circles under bloodshot eyes, lips chapped from dehydration.

Poisoned.

The certainty settles in my bones.

Sylas is at his desk when I enter the study, Giabella perched on the arm of his chair, her fingers busy organizing the invitations for the wedding. They both turn when I bow, and Sylas's smile drops.

"King's graces, Valerie, are you ok?" Giabella asks, a jeweled hand over her heart.

Sylas rises, crossing to me in the slow blink of my eye. His hand cups my chin, tilting my face toward the ever burning firelight. "You slept through the winter solstice memorial."

Did I really?

My face pales further. "I'm fine."

Giabella tsks. "You shouldn't overexert yourself."

Sylas's thumb strokes my cheekbone to keep my focus on him. "Tell me what's wrong."

You already know.

I swallow the retort, opting for half truths. "I... don't think I can keep being your attendant."

Sylas *laughs* – low and amused – like I've told a joke. "Bella, leave us."

She hesitates, golden eyes flicking between us, but a stern glance from Sylas has her bowing and sweeping out.

Sylas crowds me against the desk the moment the door clicks shut, his body too warm against my shivering as he places a hand on my waist. I feel magic spark at the contact.

"Now," he drags out the word in challenge. "Say that again."

His glamour wrangles my resolve into pacificity. "I want out of our bargain." I still manage to say.

His grip tightens. "There *is* no out. You work for me, I use your human ability. That's it." His hand slides to my hip. "I already told you that once you chose me-"

"I think I'm dying," I blurt.

He stills.

"Fairy fruit," I press on, trembling. "I'm weak, I'm vomiting, I-"

"*Poisoned*?" He fights a grin. "If it was fairy fruit, you'd be showing more symptoms by now." His lips brush my temple. "But you're *alive*. And I want you thriving again."

"You know what it is then." I discern. "What's wrong with me?"

"A healer will tell us." His hand drifts lower, dangerously as he tests the hem of my sleep shirt. "But first-"

He kisses me: a claim without the words. When I don't respond, he nips my lower lip, drawing a whimper.

"Remain by my side," he cautions against my mouth. "And you'll keep your freedom. Try to leave…" His fingers find my waist under my shirt, stroking slowly as he floods my senses with more and more glamour. "And I'll make sure you're agreeable. Keep you in my bed. Leash you, if I must."

My head slumps against his shoulder as the pleasure builds. "You wanted me to choose you, you don't want to glamour me into this."

He catches my wrists with the free hand when they shove at his arms, holding them above my head as he continues. "You already chose me," he corrects, smiling when I lean into his touch. "And you're mine. Which means I get to keep you healthy. Keep you safe. If that means I need glamour to remind you that you're being difficult, then I'll use it."

The knock at the door comes like a reprieve: sharp, urgent.

Sylas tears himself away from me with a growl, answering it with a "what?"

A messenger with a letter bearing the West's deer head crest stands there, petrified. "Your Highness, His Majesty requests you immediately. The council is assembled."

Sylas's jaw tightens. "Now?"

The messenger nods. "It concerns the Cardinal succession."

A beat of silence. Then Sylas turns to me with the full force of his title.

"Stay here. Do not move. If you move..." His eyes drift to my hand where the ring still hasn't been replaced.

I swallow the threat and nod.

The door slams behind him violently.

For a moment, I actually *don't* move – caught between two terrible prospects that end with me caged either way.

Cardinal succession.

Either Sylas will get his crown or he won't. And I am not sure which of those options terrifies me more.

If I have no power now, what will I be when he wears the crown?

A pet in a gilded cage – withering away as he glamours me into loving it.

Or he remains prince.

And I become the one thing he has total control over – even as I lose my sanity and potentially my life.

No. I need to get out of here.

Before I can second guess the decision, I cross back into my own room. I snatch my cloak from the chair, shove my feet into the sturdy boots that carried me upstairs the first time, and vacate the quarters in search of salvation.

Just head north.

I see the map of the Cardinal Kingdom I studied so many weeks ago – when I was Mara's attendant – in my mind clearly. The portal to the human world lies north, past the forest. And if I can just get there...

But first, I have to get out of the castle.

The tower is fortuitously quiet, with only a handful of servants milling about as the nightshift lulls. Their presence is sparse; their attention focused on their tasks. And I move like one of them, slipping past unnoticed.

I crack the door in the main hall just wide enough for my frame. The gardens stretch out before me in a barren tapestry of frost smothered blooms and green abandoned hedges. I stroll through them casually, though my heart races with every step away.

The more conspicuous I look, the more likely someone will gossip.

As I move away from the castle, a heady, overwhelming aroma pulls me forward: intoxicatingly sweet yet dangerously sharp.

Fairy Fruit.

I round a corner in the hedges, the path forks.

Left, toward the stables and the northern road to the portal.

Right…

Right, where the air grows even sweeter – where the fairy fruit trees must grow.

The logical part of me is begging "left!"

I am well aware the orchard isn't on the way to the portal. It's a detour – and more likely – a death sentence.

But if I may already be poisoned – if the fruit could already be in my veins… What's it taste like?

I head right.

The fragrance leads me far beyond the areas Sylas and I explored together, past the hidden alcoves and secluded corners we'd stolen moments of pleasure in.

A hill rises before me, its crest obscured by towering topiaries and the gryphon aviary where Sylas first approached me. The memory surfaces unbidden, a contrite twist finds my lips.

Everyone was right. I shouldn't have trusted him back then.

I hasten my pace away, shallow pants coming out in cloudy bursts as I climb. The aviary looms to my left, its inhabitants silent and watchful as they snuggle against each other for warmth. Their curious black eyes track my movements along the outer rim.

Tell him, little spies. I'll be long gone by then.

As I crest the hill, I catch my first peek of the orchard. It is much smaller than I expected for the amount of fruit consumed nightly. Maybe twenty trees in total are encircled in a fenced field. Carved into the posts of the fence are runes, and I think better than to touch the barrier.

The trees inside are unlike any I've ever seen: small, weeping willows with slender, cascading branches that sway gently in the breeze. Their leaves shimmer in autumnal hues of wheat, amber, and sepia: a stark contrast to the frost covered landscape everywhere else.

I circle the perimeter until I find the gate, unceremoniously left ajar.

Like they want someone to wander in, I think, but don't examine further.

As I breach the fence, the trees' uniqueness become more overt – not just their leaves, but the trunks and fruits themselves. They range from ivory to deep ebony. The forbidden fruits hang ripened from the branches, each one a perfect peach in matching shades. Their magic scent warps my thoughts into a new dizzying option – replacing the instinct to run with a more violently rebellious concept.

Just one more bite, and I'll never have to go back to Sylas.

It's not a bad idea… I'm just not ready to say goodbye.

Not yet.

I hold my breath as I pass within inches of the trees, letting my fingers brush the soft cascades of leaves.

I pause behind one, hearing faint voices drift on the wind: whispers that seem to come from everywhere and nowhere. They're indistinct – rambling unintelligibly under the rustling of the leaves – but they pique my defenses.

My eyes scan the area beyond the fence line: suspicious. But no one is speaking within sight. So I move to the center of the circle, using one particularly coppery tree as camouflage.

The trunk is smooth as I settle beneath it; its leaves are just long enough to tickle the top of my head. I observe the younger trees nearby, tucked safely in the center of the orchard before they become fruitful. My eyes drift up through the bright foliage and unripe fruits to see a starry sky. Clipped branches spill ruby sap between us – catching the twinkle above – adding to the inherent magic of the space. My eyes fall back to the ground and the knotty roots I prop my sturdy old boots against.

It's peaceful here. A little longer, then I'll say goodbye.

It's as I sit there serenely – deciding which fruit will seal my fate – that I see it.

Right in front of me.

A tree that isn't *quite* a tree.

Its trunk is even smoother than the one I rest against. It's too smooth. Too… familiar a shape.

A human shape.

My next breath shudders as I rise, my heart suddenly pounding in my chest. I reach a trembling hand to touch the uncanny likeness. There's give beneath my fingers – disturbing and unexpected – as if the tree has been molded around meat instead of wood.

As if the bark isn't bark at all.

*It's **skin**.*

The tree… person… body moves without a breeze.

And I lurch back, only to catch a heel on the roots and collapse to the frosted sod. The new angle is utterly horrifying. I can better make out their elongated torso – the weight of branches forcing their fingers, elbows, neck, everything that can possibly move into unnatural, agonizing angles.

My eyes lock on a partially visible face. The one hazel eye in its socket is wide – looking straight at *me*.

The remnants of a full upper lip move faintly, a gust moving through their hollow excuse of a throat attempting to call for help. It creates an almost whisper that blends with the others on the breeze.

No.

My chilled hand flies to my mouth to stifle a scream, my mind trying to make sense of what I'm seeing – what my mind is finally *letting* me see.

People are everywhere, their bodies making up the entirety of the orchard as I pick out their contorted forms. Some are more human than others: their faces recognizable, their bodies only partially transformed.

Others are fully tree-like: features caked over with bark and….

The leaves... are hair.

My hands feel irredeemably sullied, remembering how absentmindedly I'd stroked the tresses just a moment before.

The same way Sylas always strokes mine.

Is this what is happening to me? Is this what Sylas is hiding?

But he can't lie.

He blatantly told me it wasn't fairy fruit making me weak…

Right?

The paralyzing panic prevents me from remembering his precise phrasing. I rack my brain for any symptoms of the fruit: whether it be in the barracks or upstairs. I've only seen the effects up close and personal once.

Chase.

He could be here, somewhere among these gnarled mutations.

I force myself to move forward, my legs numb but determined. I scan the circle, my eyes darting from one victim to the next, searching for any sign of him. The hisses are more frequent as the tree people try to communicate with me. I catch fragments of words – *"help, please, stop"* – but they're drowned out by the rustling of the hair and my blood roaring in my ears.

And then I see him.

A figure near the center where I had sat: his body still mostly human –

his face turned toward the sky at a sickening angle. His hair is the same shade of sandy blonde, his frame familiar even in this contorted state.

My heart drops as I recognize him.

"Chase?" My whisper blends with theirs as I approach.

He's tied to a post, his arms outstretched like a scarecrow, his skin pale and slick with sweat.

Like my own.

This is my future.

Sprouts are beginning to pierce through his flesh like needling thorns. His fingers are undeniably broken, weighed down by the too long branches until they snapped with the pressure. It looks so torturous. Though his eyes are closed, his visible clouds of breath are even.

He's alive.

His brown eyes flutter open when a whine sounds in my throat. And for a moment, there's a flicker of recognition. The look brings tears to my eyes – knowing he's still in there. His lips form my name, but no sound comes out without a breeze this far in the circle.

He can't even call for help.

Tears stream down my frozen cheeks as I reach for the ropes binding him, my fingers fumbling with the knots.

"I'm here," I sob. "I'm going to help you."

"You've gotta be fucking kidding me. What are you doing out here?" an irate voice sounds behind me.

Chapter 60

I keep my back to my company, trying to free Chase. Before I can even get through the first knot cinched around his neck, an arm is around me, dragging me away.

"I have to help him!" I wheeze, thrashing against the steely grip.

The arm slings me ahead, forcing me to turn towards… Prince Ciaran.

He's cloaked in deep blue that obscures his distinctive face until he lifts his head. My entire body freezes under his sneer: an expression so lethal, I can feel my own bindings tethering me to the sod underfoot already. His disgust is palpable – as though touching me has dirtied him in some irreparable way.

A group of dryads pass, ignoring our presence.

"He ate the fruit. There's no helping him," he states flatly. "You need to get back to your prince, unless you want to be one too."

My feet instinctively steal a step back, and I nearly collide with a tree.

No, a *person* behind me – writhing in their half mutated form.

He'll tell Sylas. He'll tell him I know the truth about the fairy fruit, my mind screams.

"Stay away from me!" I shout – hands flying up between us – praying to any gods for another chance to free Chase from the too tight bindings.

"You've caused quite the scene. And if I don't take you back to Sylas now, *I* will be blamed for your stupidity," he counters bluntly. His olive hands hover on either side of my pale ones, close enough to block any attempt to get around him.

My curls whip my damp cheeks as I shake my head quickly, my thoughts a freezing mix of fear and desperation.

I need to get out of here. Away from him. Away from all of the folk.

"Don't," he warns, reading my mind or my darting eyes. "You'll be caught by someone far less tolerant than me."

Tolerant? Ciaran?

The word feels like a cruel joke. His disdain for humans is no secret. He must love it out here – the humans subjugated with such finality. I continue to search for a way out, my eyes scanning the graveyard…

orchard.

But I don't notice his attention on my ringless hand, before glamour slams into me. My body goes suddenly lax under his influence.

"There is nothing you can do to help your servant friend," his voice is paradoxically soothing and assertive as it fogs my mind. "So you will go back to Sylas. You will pretend you don't know about the fairy fruit. You will be *okay*."

"I can't go back. Not after seeing that." My voice is too flat for my violent emotions. But at least I can still speak.

Ciaran's lip curls. "You're going to have to."

"I'm sick," I confess robotically.

He goes very still, and I blink once before continuing – my horror held at bay by the glamour enough for me to finally say what I've worried about for weeks.

"I'm vomiting. I'm weak. Sylas says it's not poison or fairy fruit, but I don't know what else it could be."

The words spark something behind his eyes. Then, with a hissed curse, he seizes my wrist and drags me out of the gate.

"Don't make me-"

"*Quiet*."

His voice is in my mind; glamour presses against me with overwhelming force. It's different from Sylas's soft caress – like a fist holding my brain – one squeeze away from destroying it.

My thoughts dull at the command, but the adrenaline in my veins still wants me to run.

My limbs obey, shaky and uncoordinated: panic held hostage in his grip of forced serenity. Ciaran guides me calmly through the servant halls.

He'll tell Sylas. He'll tell him I know. He'll-

"Stop fighting it," Ciaran mutters, shoving me into his room once we reach Sylas's tower.

Starling looks up from a cluttered desk, their red eyes flicking between us. "What the hell are you doing?"

Ciaran doesn't let go of my arm. "Test her."

Test me for what?

A beat of dubious silence follows the command. Starling's gaze narrows, studying my face: my empty, *calm* face – so at odds with the despair inside me. They see the truth; their lips twist in amusement.

"You glamoured her."

"She was hysterical," Ciaran defends the decision.

Starling barks a bitter, short laugh. "Of course." They stalk to the cabinet, yanking out vials with vicious precision. "Stupid. *Stupid* human."

The insult should sting. It *would* sting, if I could feel anything right now. But the glamour smothers all emotional senses, puppeting me with artificial calm.

They thrust a vial of red liquid at me. "Swish it in your mouth, then spit it back into here."

I take the vial obediently. My hands don't shake. I dump it in my mouth without a single hesitation.

This isn't me.

The liquid is sweeter than other Unseelie brews. I swish it thoroughly, then spit it back into the vial. For a moment, nothing happens, and everyone's shoulders relax.

Then, gold – bright, unmistakable gold.

The glamour evaporates at the same time that Starling slams the rest of the bottle on the table too hard. All at once – the fear, the panic, the *horror* comes crashing back in.

"What does it mean?" I choke. My knees threaten to buckle under the weight of anticipation of their answer. "Is it fairy fruit? Am I going to die?"

"It reacts to the presence of secondary life: parasites technically," Starling explains – their face falling at the explanation. "I was trying everything I could to save him. But nothing worked."

This potion. It was for Chase.

"It means you're carrying Sylas's child," they follow up.

Pregnant?

"No. I- I can't be-" I stammer.

"You are. It's happened before," they cut me off.

My mind flashes to my conversation with Mara before her death. *"Pregnancies are exceedingly rare. Those who do manage to conceive often don't survive childbirth."*

I press a hand to my stomach, tears welling in my eyes. "I don't know if I can do this."

Ciaran's jaw is tense as he takes the vial from me, setting it beside the collection of other vials. "Are you sure it's Sylas's?"

I shoot a glare at the bastard. "Of course it's Sylas's. Whose else would it be?"

He rolls his green eyes. "I had to ask. We need to get her back. *Now.*"

Starling whirls on him. "You're not seriously-"

"What's your alternative?" Ciaran's voice is lethally calm. "Give her that other potion? It didn't work last time."

Last time?

He jabs a finger at my stomach. "He's going to look for her soon, and find her *here*. But if she's with him, our hands are clean of all this."

Starling's fists clench. For a heartbeat, I think they might strike the prince. Then they release a breath, turning back towards the papers on the desk. "She made her bed. Now she can die in it. Get her out of here."

Ciaran hauls me upright – his grip bruising as I let their acceptance of my doom settle over me. Starling doesn't look back up at me as he drags me away.

We approach my door wordlessly, the unreal truth buried beneath my shock. As I reach for the handle with a trembling hand, the door flies open.

A very angry and very present Sylas stands in the doorway. My jaw drops. It's the only motion I have time to make before his hands are at Ciaran's throat.

"Sy, stop!" I scream.

"I am the one who gives orders around here," Sylas snarls, his eyes locked on Ciaran, who raises his hands in mock surrender.

"Ciaran." His voice goes lethally cold. "Explain."

"This isn't the show of gratitude I expected," Ciaran rasps under Sylas's hand.

He can't lie, but he's also not telling him about the fairy fruit or the pregnancy.

I step forward, my voice steady despite the fear coursing through me.

"Prince Ciaran was just chaperoning me so you'd know I was safe." The half truth slips out easily, and Ciaran's answering nod corroborates it.

Sylas's grip on Ciaran loosens, but he doesn't step back. "Why did you leave?" His voice is hurt, directed at me.

I cover my hand where the ring should be as I quickly weave a new story for my absence.

"I was going to get some fresh air. You know I'm sick, but I didn't want you to worry," I force confidence into my voice.

Ciaran chimes in, calculatedly light. "I offered to escort her safely on her walk. And here we are – no worse for wear – before you decided I was up to no good."

Sylas relents, stepping back. His arm wraps around my rigid shoulders in a territorial display.

He's bought the lie.

I disguise my sigh of relief with a yawn, leaning into him as he nuzzles the top of my head. The scent of mint on his breath is another blessed relief.

There's no fairy fruit. Not right now.

"Well, if that's the case, you've returned her safely. You can go," Sylas's voice softens as he pulls me towards the door.

Ciaran nods, his bored mask slipping as his eyes meet mine. Disgust flashes in them, but I can't tell if it's directed at me... or at Sylas.

"Humans are fragile," he warns, laced with meaning. "Make sure she doesn't break."

Sylas guides me inside my room, his arm a possessive weight around my shoulders. When the door closes behind us, he spins me to face him, his fingers tightening on my arms.

"Did he do anything to you?" His voice is fierce, edged with something darker than mere concern.

"No," I say too quickly. "He just walked with me. That's all."

Sylas searches my face, his gaze fixed on the way my hands tremble. *Ringless.* I clench them into fists.

"You're lying," he mumbles to himself.

"I'm not-"

"You're shaking." His hand cinches around my wrist, right over my frantic pulse. "And your heart is racing. Did he threaten you? Did he glamour you into-"

"No," I say again, but my voice wavers unconvincingly.

Sylas exhales sharply, his grip loosening. "Then what is it?"

He wants me alive and thriving. He'll help take care of this.

"I think-" The words lodge there, choking me.

I think I'm pregnant.

But saying it out loud makes it real. Makes it *inescapable.*

Sylas waits, preternaturally still.

"I've been feeling... strange," I hedge. "More than just the sickness. Tired all the time. My emotions. Everything is too much. And I..."

His thumb brushes my arm with tenderness. "You're worried."

I nod, swallowing hard. "I think I might be pregnant."

The silence that follows is suffocating.

I brace myself for shock. For horror. For the terrible realization to dawn on him: that this shouldn't be possible – that I should *never* have been able to conceive. But he doesn't react the way I expect.

Instead, his lips curve. Just enough to make my stomach drop.

"Is that so?" he purrs, his voice warm, almost… *pleased.*

I stare at him in wide-eyed disbelief.

This isn't right.

He knows how dangerous this is. He knows sidhe pregnancies are rare, that those who carry sidhe children rarely survive them. Mara told me herself, and Sylas *has* to know.

So why isn't he afraid?

"Sy," I speak purposefully: even and low. "This is bad."

His smile doesn't fade. "We'll have a healer confirm it before we assume the worst."

"Assume the worst?" I choke out. "Sylas, this *is* the worst! Your people's pregnancies are fatal!"

"Not always," he coos, his fingers trailing down my arm. The certainty in his voice sends a chill through me.

"How can you say that?" I demand, ripping away. "You know what this means. You know what could happen to me!"

He catches my wrist before I can retreat further, cinched enough to remind me of Chase's ties. "Valerie," he drags out my name in warning. "Don't stress, it would be bad for my heir."

The taunt is punctuated by a wave of glamour drowning me, dulling my righteous fury into complacency.

"You're not afraid," I comment, my voice level now.

His thumb strokes my pulse point, satisfied to find the beat slowing. "No."

Why?

The question is trapped in the glamour, preventing me from voicing it. He drags me into another embrace, arms wrapping around me with overt care. And as he presses a kiss to the top of my head, murmuring reassurances I don't believe, one terrible thought claws its way to the surface:

He knew this would happen.
And he's *happy* about it.

Chapter 61

The knock at my door the next evening is considerate and soft, dragging me from a sleep that had been more like practicing death. My body feels heavy – my mind sluggish. Whether those both be from exhaustion or the weight of what's growing inside me? I don't really care. I just feel worse than ever.

My hand still presses against my stomach as I push myself upright, some traitorous instinct insisting on guarding the thing that will kill me.

The door opens without waiting for my response. Giabella glides inside, her gown far too formal for such a simple visit. Her smile is warm – practiced – the same one she'd given me weeks ago when I'd helped Sylas choose her as his bride.

She was always the better option, I'd told myself. *She's kind. She loves humans.*

Now, that kindness curdles in my stomach.

"Valerie," she says, voice eager. "I hope I'm not disturbing you."

I force my face blank. "You did just wake me."

She doesn't flinch. *Of course she doesn't. She's spent her whole life perfecting this performance.*

She keeps an effortless gentle curve at the corners of her lips, her eyes soften just enough to seem sincere when I meet them. She takes the chair beside my bed, her gaze dropping to where my fingers linger over my womb.

She *knows*.

"How are you feeling?" she asks with faux sincerity. "I've heard your condition has been difficult."

Condition.

Like it's just some temporary inconvenience that won't end with me drained and cold on silk sheets.

"I'm fine," I lie.

Her smile deepens. "You mustn't hesitate to tell me if you need anything. I intend to make sure you're well cared for."

The words slither under my skin. And I see why Sylas chose her over

Balora or Margaret: her easy compliance with this plan.

"I've arranged for the healer to see you shortly," she continues, smoothing her skirts. "And I've instructed the kitchens to prepare meals tailored to your needs. You must keep your strength up."

For the fetus, she doesn't say. *For the thing that's going to suck the life out of me.*

My nails dig into my palms. "How thoughtful."

Her hand covers mine, unyielding as polished marble when it holds me down. "You're a gift to the entire Cardinal Kingdom, Valerie."

A gift.

A *gift* is given freely.

I am a sacrificial offering. And she is the smiling hand that will cradle what's left when this is over.

She rises, her gown whispering against the floor like the fairy fruit trees. "Rest," she orders as she slips back into the hall. "You'll need it."

I don't move until another knock pulls me from my thoughts, and the royal healer makes their appearance. A silver streak in their hair hints at a long history here, but their face is frozen at a respectable age: a balance of fine lines and youthful glow. They're a kind faced witch named Angel with rounded ears and gentle hands. But their touch feels clinical, detached under the attempted stab of my glower. They listen to my heartbeat, measure my pulse, and ask a series of questions about my symptoms.

"Everything appears to be in order, according to records," Angel says in a reassuring tone. "But you must take care of yourself. Eat well, sleep often, and avoid stress."

No way, this is really happening.

I nod, though their words do little to ease the knot of anxiety in my chest.

"I will," is all I say.

And then they pack quickly, excited with the news. "I'll convene with the prince myself. You should sleep more."

So I do. Because I don't know what else to do.

Then the evening sun spills across the bed, too warm for the ice settling in my bones when my blood shot eyes snap open again.

I wake to the scent of honey and roses: thick, overwhelming. A feast is laid out beside me with sugared plums and warm bread dripping with butter. Gifts are piled at the foot of the bed: silks, jewels, a fur lined cloak fit for a queen.

And Sylas, seated in a new, cushier chair beside me, watching.

His smile is real. It makes me *sick*.

"Angel says you've done well," he praises.

I sit up slowly, my fingers twisting in the sheets. "I don't want it."

His expression doesn't change. "That isn't your choice to make."

The words land like a blade between my ribs.

"Mara told me," I whimper. "No one survives a sidhe birth."

Something dark haunts his blue eyes with the mention of his late bride. Then it's gone, smoothed away by that infuriating calm. "Mara was wrong about many things." His hand finds mine in the sheets, a thumb tracing my bony knuckles. "But not about *you*. She knew you'd be special," I scoff at the words, but he continues. "I have the best healers. The strongest tonics. You'll survive with my help."

"You can't promise that."

"Then I'll promise to try," he vows, and the certainty in his voice terrifies me. "I'll keep you safe. Healthy." His grip tightens, just shy of painful. "Adored."

The word is a shackle.

I yank my hand away. "You're sentencing me to death for an heir."

Sylas sighs like I'm being unreasonable. "You'll be revered, Valerie. Every court in the kingdom will bow to you. You'll never wash another sheet. Never take another order. If you survive, you'll want for nothing. Ever again."

If.

I press my palms to my stomach, nausea rising. Sylas stands, brushing a kiss to my clammy forehead.

"Eat," he murmurs. "You'll feel better once you do."

As if food could fix this.

As if anything but a fucking blade in the belly could.

He gestures in his retreat to a card left on the table at my side. And I'm left alone with the feast, the gifts, and the future I never asked for.

But I've never bothered tampering my impulses before, so I snatch the card from the table.

In honor of Prince Sylas's Western Throne secured,

You are cordially invited to dine at the royal hall this evening. Midnight. Dancing and celebration to follow.

I crumple the cardstock, my hands shaking violently with sudden rage.

No. I won't go. They can't throw a funeral before I'm even dead.

Then I eat. Not because I'm ordered to, not to save the child, but because if I am going to find a way out of this, I'll need my strength to do it. I think over my options as I bite into the first honey cake.

I could try to run. Avoid the fairy fruit and make it to the portal home.

But what then? I'll be stuck in the human world with a freakish pregnancy, somehow further from help. And who knows how time would affect me: would I suddenly be thirty-five as I should be or am I stuck at eighteen even there? Either way, I would need to pass through the portal first... and that's still another unsettled "if" about getting there.

So I change my course of thought as I pick at the berries next.

I could run to another court. Beg them to give me sanctuary... and risk starting a war if they do.

No one would gamble Sylas's wrath for one human.

So I stay here. End the pregnancy myself.

The thought stuns my jaw still. I could do it. Throw myself over the ledge of the balcony or purposefully poison myself. I could die... but I will probably die anyway.

My resolve hardens as I rub the crumbs from my hands, uncaring for the way they spread across the sheets for a brownie to clean later.

I heat the tub, sliding in to enjoy its warmth – its weightlessness – maybe for the last time.

Starling could help.

Though I know the sudden thought is futile. They sentenced me to death before anyone else even knew. And now the whole region knows how foolish I'd been – how easily I'd let Sylas ply me with kisses and twisted words.

I play with the spot where my ring used to sit – the only callus on my hand now right above its resting place.

I was so blind.

He'd plucked the damn thing off of me so often, I'd thought it meant I could trust him. Until it wasn't a trust exercise anymore. It just became expected. And then he'd use it to stop fights – potential nights off from a chance for an heir.

My rage returns anew at that last thought, and I scramble out of the suddenly too hot tub.

I catch my reflection – red cheeked, purple eyed – a pitiful excuse of a girl. My hands react before logic catches up, and I throw a decorative vase at the mirror shattering the girl.

I pluck the most wicked looking shard from the destruction.

To do what? I'm not sure yet. But it's barely in my grasp, when the door to the hall swings open. Two guards storm inside, both with bull's heads.

Fucking minotaurs, of course.

I feel the bite of the broken mirror in my hand as I brandish it between us.

Were they standing outside this whole time?

I swipe when they step closer. They deftly avoid my assault, the bloody piece slipping from my fingers to clatter against the tile floor as they pin my arms to my sides.

"Let me go! I wasn't going to do anything!" I shriek the lie.

The guards ignore my flailing as they drag me into my bedroom. I fight harder – my nails goring at their cowhide arms – but they don't flinch.

I scream until my throat is raw.

"Enough."

Chapter 62

The voice is cold, commanding. We all freeze. Sylas stands in the doorway between our rooms, his expression unamused as he steps inside.

His eyes flick to the destroyed mirror, then the dripping blood on the rug, and then to my palm. I see the rage nearly surface before his cold mask slips back into place.

"Release her," he commands evenly.

The guards drop me, stepping behind Sylas. I collapse to the bed, my chest heaving as I scowl up at him.

"I need to ask you something," I say, my voice steadier than I feel as I sit up, complying just enough so he doesn't use the glamour to *make* me.

His eyes are curious with the unexpected shift. "You're in no position to ask anything – not after the stunt you just pulled. But I'll humor you this once," he says. "What is it?"

I take a steadying breath, my hand drifting over my stomach. "How?" I question. "My… condition. Humans aren't usually fertile. How did you know I was different?"

He smiles like he's been waiting for that exact question: a cruel curve that sends more fire up my neck. "Your brand," he answers, pointing at the back of his own neck.

My brow furrows.

He laughs, amused by my confusion. "You still don't understand, do you?"

"Understand *what*?"

He prowls in front of me, standing so close I have to crane my neck to look at him. "The brand that was on your neck keeps you all sterile and under control. It's a rune, that's why it had to be removed."

The words shake the very foundation of my understanding. "You planned *all* of this."

"Of course, I did." he preens. "This is our bargain."

I shake my head, my throat tight. "But Mara…"

Sylas kneels before me, capturing my gaze as he speaks. "Mara made the bargain with you first," He speaks slowly, letting me process the words in real time. "A bargain I took on after she died. You were to be used for your human ability: your *fertility*. In exchange, you would serve as her attendant. Now as mine."

I feel the blood drain from my face. "She said she needed me to lie for her."

His smile is razor sharp. "Did she? Or did you assume that's what she meant? What *I* meant?"

I try to remember Mara's exact words.

"*You want me, because I am able to lie,*" I had guessed.

"*Nothing outside of your nature,*" she'd said.

Oh god. She never cared if I could lie.

"You were chosen because you resembled her the most out of our servantry. Because you were so easy to seduce. Because you were… convenient."

The room spins around me, and I reach out to steady myself against the bed.

He rises to his feet again as I find stability. "It was Mara's idea to get you to fall in love first. She understood humans so much better than me. I didn't think it was necessary, but after my *disastrous* attempt with the other girl… I agreed to try her method," he says.

My mind flashes back to last year – to Becca Dawson: my look alike who was bloody and running through the tunnels.

"*They'll try and use you like they were planning to use me. Don't let them.*"

I had assumed that I'd know when my bargain was called upon – that it would be something easy to outwit. I thought I would be able to find a way to keep myself and my friends safe, getting a leg up on the folk who always stand on us.

I ball my fists at how reckless I'd been, willing tears not to fall as my understanding bleeds into embarrassment.

"You were so encourageable – so ready to believe you mattered more than your body. Who was I to disillusion you?" he finishes with a hand over his heart.

"*You* told me I was special. That I was unique," I throw his words back in his face, but they seem to hurt me more than him.

"And you were. You *are*. I had those attendants cut off your brand, making you one of a kind. A personal vessel to carry my heir," he smiles as if the truth of his twisted words should make me feel better. "And Mara was right. Your eagerness made the entire process so much easier than last time. You barely needed glamour or potions… it was far more fun too," he winks on the last bit.

I want to scream again. I want to claw out his moonlit eyes and make him feel a fraction of the misery I'm feeling. But I know it's pointless.

He's untouchable while I don't have my ring.

"So that's it?" I urge, my voice breaking. "I'm just a womb to you?"

He walks back to the threshold between our rooms. "You're whatever I need you to be," he agrees. "And right now, I need you to bear my heir. Do that, and you'll be rewarded. Defy me, and…" He trails off, but the threat is clear.

"I hate you," I spit.

His jaw tightens, but that's the extent of his reaction. "This child is important, Valerie. More important than *you*. I can't let you desecrate this kingdom's future because you feel bested."

"It's *my* body!" I howl.

"But I own *your* body. As your prince and as your bargainer," he says, his tone final. "From this moment on, you're under constant supervision. The guards will ensure no harm comes to you or the heir. Even from yourself."

My mouth gapes at his cruelty, but no words come out.

"I'm protecting you," he clarifies, though his voice lacks conviction. "And the child."

I shake my head, sudden tears spilling down my heated cheeks. "You don't care about me. You never did."

He steps back towards me – his hand reaching out to brush the tears from my face – but I shrink away. His hand hovers before dropping to his side.

"You'll get over this. And then we can go back to being happy together. His voice is more command than comfort. "Get dressed, you're attending the party or I'll give the barracks half rations for a month."

Then he's gone. I sit there, my body trembling with a horrible mix of fatigue, rage, and disbelief. The guards stand at attention, their eyes never leaving me. I feel the walls of my room closing in – tighter and tighter – until I can barely breathe. A single thought screams in my head.

The barracks. He knows about my friends.

Chapter 63

The gown delivered is beautiful: a deep ruby red that clings to my frame, accentuating the nonexistent curve of my stomach. I despise how it feels like a costume – how it marks me as something I never wanted to be.

I'm halfway through styling my hair when a knock sounds at the door. The guards open it without my permission. My eyes narrow as Giabella steps into view, hands clasped and expression pleasant.

"Feeling smug yet?" I snap, my fingers still working to tame my hair. She doesn't step inside, her gaze passing over the minotaurs between us before settling on me.

"I am feeling grateful to have you in our lives," she twists. "Sylas sent me to fetch you. So here I am."

My hands drop. The braid I've been plaiting unravels. I catch her reflection in the mirror.

I should attack her, I think.

No. My friends in the barracks would pay the price.

"It must be so nice to not have to carry your own child," I grumble.

She shrugs politely. "I wish I could do it safely myself. But we have trouble even conceiving. It's a blessing that Sylas was able to with you so quickly."

I can't meet her eyes now, focusing instead on my reflection as I adjust one last curl. "Lucky him. Only had to bed a human for a few weeks to get it to stick."

She rolls her golden eyes and steps into the room for the first time, the guards trailing a step behind. "Don't be so pessimistic. You enjoyed yourself. And now it's time to repay that enjoyment."

The folk never do anything for us for free. The hardest lesson I ever learned – forgotten so easily.

"You're disgusting," I sneer, stepping around her to prove I'm only leaving because I'm ready. We both know it's a lie. Her glamour slithers into my joints just enough to stop me in my tracks.

I'm forced to wait there – pliant and still – until she catches up with a smooth smile. Then she releases me.

We walk the rest of the way in performative peace, the guards too close
for me to try and get a good whack on Giabella before they'd subdue me.

The dining hall is alive with laughter and chatter when we arrive,
everyone else too excited to arrive as fashionably late as us.

The long table laden with food and drink makes my face contort into
something ugly. Sylas sits at the head, Giabella guides us to either side of
him, her eyes gleaming with satisfaction at the fawning coos that follow
my arrival. The chair I settle in feels like a throne.

And I hate it too.

"Ah, pet," Sylas greets, grabbing my hand to lift in a quick, chaste kiss.
"We've been waiting for you."

I ignore the stares of the rest of the table as I snatch my hand away.
"I'm not your fucking pet," I growl, but my words are met with placid
laughter: my truth seen as just a joke of a lie.

The dinner keeps a jovial atmosphere, but I can't bring myself to even
pretend to participate. I pick at my food with hunched shoulders – my
appetite gone – as the guests discuss the heir growing inside me.

"I wonder if the child will have Mara's hair," Alistar muses, his voice
carrying across the table. "It would be a fitting tribute to her memory."

"Or Sylas's mind," Leona adds with a wink towards him. "Imagine the
power they'll wield."

I clench my fists on the table to keep myself from stabbing Sylas with
my fork. They speak of the child as if I'm nothing more than an
afterthought – like it's already theirs.

Giabella leans in on his other side. "I've been researching an ancient
spell: one that could ensure the child is fully sidhe, even if born with… less
desirable traits."

Human traits, I mentally correct

Sylas's eyes light up. He turns to her with a venerating sincerity. "You
amaze me, my beautiful, brilliant bride."

Beautiful… brilliant. Words he's never said to me, I think with a pang
of foolishness.

He kisses her then raises their joined hands in victory, the gesture
drawing applause from the guests. I look away, my stomach churning.

Maybe I should let it empty itself right onto the table.

Ciaran clears his throat, drawing my attention as he stands abruptly. "I
need to check on my attendant," he explains politely.

Starling.

He strides out without waiting for a response, his departure barely noticed. I watch him go, wishing I could follow – wishing I had listened to him months ago when he told me that I meant nothing to them all.

But I'm trapped here, forced to endure this grotesque theater so they don't take it out on the barracks below our feet.

The conversation continues, the guests speculating about the child's future – about Giabella's spell and the legacy it will carry. I stay mute, staring a hole through my plate as their words blur into an incoherent hum.

"Valerie," Alistar's voice cuts through the noise at some point. "You've been quiet. Is everything alright?"

I look up, meeting his golden gaze. For a moment, I consider lying and telling him how much this excites me – how much I love being reduced to a surrogate.

But I'm too numb.

"It's not," my voice is as dimmed as the rest of me. "But none of you really care."

He ignores my attempted snark. "This is a celebration for you. You should be happy. You're continuing Mara's legacy."

Happy.

The word is the cruelest possible suggestion. I force a too wide smile, though it feels like it might crack my face in two, and turn back to my plate. He shakes his head at my irreverence, before turning to others at the table.

When the funeral of a meal finally ends, Sylas's had just enough fairy fruit to hold court at the titanic golden throne. He pulls me up onto his lap, and I sit stiffly: a doll on display as he strokes my hair tenderly. I feel the tresses of whoever used to be this eternal fairy fruit tree stroke me too. But Sylas's glamour seeps through each inebriated touch, keeping me from leaning away from either.

"I saw her in the atelier," Sylas declares, wine loosening his tongue further. "Kneeling on the floor, her ginger curls like Mara's, her eyes like mine." He grins, drunk on the memory. "I knew then. She was perfect."

The court sighs, enchanted.

"Mara knew the cost of wanting a child," he continues. "She said the human had to be willing, so we began planting the seeds of romance." His wandering hands have mine twitching to smack him. "After the equinox…" His voice drops, solemn. "I knew I had to fulfill her dream. Valerie would carry our heir in her honor."

Our heir. Her honor.

Giabella presses a hand to her heart. "How poetic."

Alistar nods, his eyes glistening. "Mara would be proud."

I sit there- –compliant but dying inside – as they continue to drink and dance around us. Sylas chews on a fairy fruit, freshly plucked from the tree.

Why is this throne still alive? The thought rises, unbidden, as I watch him devour the revolting flesh. I gag when the scent hits me – memories of Chase's broken body too fresh in my mind. He shifts, nudging me to my feet.

"You may go," he excuses me without fanfare, devouring the rest of the pitted fruit with fervor.

I excuse myself before he changes his mind and make my way back to my chambers. The guards' hooves clack close behind, stifling any thoughts of running before I can even conjure them.

I try to close the door behind me, but they push their way in with folksy strength. I move to the far wall, trying to find some semblance of privacy. The tears I've been too afraid or glamoured to shed finally sting my eyes. I slide to the rug, my body racking with sobs, as a paralyzing panic steals my breath.

I'm not a person to them. If I die now, they'll just damn another girl to this fate. And I won't even be able to give her the warning Becca tried to give me.

The guards don't so much as look my way as I crawl into the bed. The stars shift a healthy amount across the sky, but I can't find composure.

"Get me the healer," I sniffle to the air, hoping the minotaur stationed in the corner can at least do *that* much for me. I hear both of them shuffle, exchanging looks without action. I groan. "Get me the healer before the prince learns that you *refused* to get them for me."

That works.

One's hooves clip out of the room immediately. And I'm left staring at the ceiling with only one pair of cow eyes on me.

If I can't escape, they can at least keep me numbed. I think bitterly. *Anything is better than this panic.*

The door opens again and I hear the concern in Angel's voice before I see it in their eyes. "What's wrong?"

"Other than my looming mortality? I can't stop panicking about it. And I don't want to be glamoured anymore," I grumble.

They hum, understanding in their tone as they shuffle through the bag of clinking glass they brought along.

"The timeline *does* seem to be progressing faster than standard human pregnancies. Maybe four to five full moons instead of nine. But you still have time before you need to panic. The pregnancy should be fairly normal until the third trimester. That's when things get tricky."

"Do you know why that is? The… danger?" I raise the question, as if the possible solution will be easy to parse.

They shrug, their eager smile faltering, "The leading theory right now is magic – sidhe magic specifically – doesn't process through humans well. Our bodies can't quite handle it."

"But then why don't they just have their own children. Why is it dangerous for them too?" I press, frustrated.

"Because magic isn't some infinite resource for the Otherworld. And it's spreading thin after a century of our inclusion," they roll up their sleeves to show lines of runes inked into their skin as proof of our collective sin. "New sidhe life comes in the form of cannibalizing the host nowadays. They believe since our inclusion caused the magic drought, *we* must be the ones implemented in the fix. But I will do everything in my power to make sure you survive. I've already started stocking up on potions and supplies for the big arrival day," their eyes crinkle again, genuinely assuming the words soothe me.

But they don't, and their smile falters under my glare.

"Well, I'll leave you with this, and I'll be on my way. Take a spoonful, once a day with tea."

Angel sets down a large bottle on my side table with a *thud.* Then they leave the chambers without looking at me again.

Days turn into weeks with the help of the healer's tonic, and I stomach the sickening parade of false smiles and hollow kindness without vomiting again.

Every morning, a new gift appears at my bedside: silken robes, clothes for the unborn child… a sealskin cloak that looks alarmingly familiar. The courtiers buzz around me like flies, their voices dripping with saccharine concern.

"How are you feeling, Valerie?"

"You must rest, girl."

"What an honor this is for you."

I let them fawn.

Because every time I show any spine, I hear the gossip in the halls afterward: the allusion to reprimands dealt to the humans in the barracks below.

Eddie. Maddie. Lilia.

So I let them do whatever the hell they want with me. Which – more often than not – is another gaudy baby shower with another group worshiping Sylas's *clever* plan.

He controls it all at my side with prideful eyes and satisfaction at my obedience. He doesn't touch me – not like before. Now, his affection is gentle displays that come in the form of a hand on my shoulder at dinner or a kiss to my temple in the gardens.

All to prove to his court how *grateful* they are for my sacrifice.

Giabella is worse, somehow. She hovers constantly – her fingers always brushing my arm or my back – checking for signs of failure.

"You look thin," she coos one afternoon, her grip tightening on my arm enough to drag my attention from the bard's tale. "Eat something."

I chew the sugared figs she pops between my teeth, swallowing them untasted.

Eventually, a half-hearted knock comes at my door while I'm hunched in my chair that overlooks the gardens.

Starling stands in the threshold, their claws tucked neatly behind their back. The guards block their path, but they don't move, red eyes scanning the length of me.

It's been weeks since they've shown their face. And I feel a spark of indignation at their sudden appearance.

"Let them in," I order flatly.

The guards hesitate, never having dealt with me receiving a personal call before.

"*Now.*"

Starling strides in, all calculation. They don't speak at first, their gaze sweeping over the opulence of my prison, snagging on the potions lined up like more guards on the dresser.

Finally, they look at me. "You're still alive."

A laugh claws its way up my throat. "For now, unfortunately."

They shift uncomfortably. "I didn't-"

"Care?" I finish for them, my smile brittle. "That Sylas was using me? That he'd kill me for an heir? That I was just another *stupid* human who fell for his lies?"

Their jaw tightens. "I tried to warn you."

"Not hard enough."

Silence.

Starling exhales, running a clawed hand through their raven hair. "I was upset."

The words hang between us – too little, too late.

I focus on my fingers curling around the edge of the bed. "Get out."

"Valerie-"

"You wanted me to die," I drag out the last word. "Now you'll get your wish. But you don't get to stand there and pretend you care."

They press closer. The guards inching the same amount in response. Starling's face falls as they approach. And I see something in their reflective eyes – something like pleading.

"I've brought a gift. Courtesy of Becca," they extend a closed hand towards me.

My brows furrow at the name, *Becca. The girl who looked like me. Who died before they could do to her what they've done to me.*

I open my mouth to question it, but Starling clears their throat, cutting me off.

"She used this to help her *end* the bad decisions she'd made last time," they say slowly.

Last time. This is what Prince Ciaran was referring to.

I'm not sure the guards catch their meaning – if their brains are more bovine than simian – but I do.

End the pregnancy. Die by a blade to the throat like her instead of screaming while Sylas wins.

Then they speak louder, "You're not just thinking about yourself anymore. You're thinking about that life inside you and what it means to the entire Cardinal Kingdom. This can be *very* helpful with that."

I sniff away unexpected, hormonal tears as I extend a pale hand to take the vial. Their dark clawed ones are cool as they hold mine with both of theirs.

"It's up to you, but it's what I would do in your circumstance," They give me a squeeze before dropping their hands and striding out of the room.

I sit there for a long time, staring at the green, toxic liquid in the vial. My thoughts become a chaotic mess. And as much as I try to convince myself to swallow it – to not overthink things – I can't do it.

I still feel like there *might* be another way to end this nightmare and survive.

Chapter 64

I continue in my uncomfortable play of normalcy with the prince for more days. For more *weeks*. Until it's nearly the spring equinox and it's been three months since I discovered the truth… I think.

I'm not sure how much longer I'll be able to remain compliant, but I've lasted this long.

I can last a bit longer. Just until this thing kills me and no one else gets punished for it.

It's like I'm waiting for something – for an answer to appear or a savior to reveal themselves and sweep me away from here. But nothing happens. No one saves me.

Not unless I count the vial that will lead to my death.

And tonight, I find myself sitting in the greening gardens with nothing but my boots, a stupid lavish dress, and a wool cloak. The air is hard to breathe as the sickly sweetness of fairy fruit drifts in every now and then, the victims flowering more with the nearing spring.

I hate that smell. I hate it more than anything.

Every time I catch a whiff, I think of Chase: his laugh, his teasing, the way he made me feel like I wasn't just a stupid child.

And now he's one of them.

The stone bench beneath me leeches my warmth as I sit near the north edge of the garden, my hands clasped tightly in my lap. Sylas is beside me, his presence colder than the winter chill. It cinches the cold knot of dread in me until I can physically feel it. He's been watching me all night, his piercing blue eyes searching for cracks in the mask I've been wearing since Angel gave me that potion.

He doesn't believe I'm happy, even as I smile and accept the gifts and compliments with grace.

And why should he? I'm not.

"You've been quieter than usual tonight," he observes. He reaches over, brushing the curl from my face that's always in the way. The gesture is tender – almost loving – making my skin crawl. "Is something bothering you?"

I force my most practiced sheepish smile, turning to meet his gaze. "Just tired, so much attention drains me almost as much as the heir."

He studies me for a moment, unconvinced. "You know you can talk to me. About anything."

Anything except the fact that I know your precious fairy fruit is made of people. Except that I would rather be gutted than carry your child to term, I think.

"I know," I say instead, my voice light. *Too light.* "I'm fine, really. Just… tired."

And I am. I've felt exhausted more and more as I feel the growing life start taking mine. I'm asleep more than I'm awake, distracting my waking hours with big meals – more hungry too.

Sylas's fingers trail along my too pronounced jaw, tilting my face toward his. The kiss he presses to my lips is a test more than true affection. When he pulls away, his thumb lingers on my bottom cracked lip, his eyes darken.

"I know you know, Valerie."

My heart stutters.

"What?" I try to sound confused.

But he chuckles as he gestures to the horizon. "You've been so good. The gryphons alerted the handlers of your little stint in the orchard," he drawls. "You have kept quite the tight lip after your discovery. It's almost impressive."

*He knows… he knows I **know**.*

I force myself not to flinch as his hand drifts to my middle, his touch featherlight over the slight swell that's begun to show.

"Do you know why those trees exist?" He probes.

I can't speak, stunned silent. But I shake my head.

He continues, conspiratorially. "They release the magic stuck inside you. They make it a palatable experience to recycle the life you steal from us, while we allow you to live here. A way to pay your dues when fate decides its time."

"Magic isn't an infinite resource," I parrot Angel's explanation, my speeding heart making the thing kick.

Sylas beams approvingly when he feels it. "It's my destiny to fix the flow of magic for us all, every seer in the realm has determined as such."

"Because you were born the same night the portal I came through appeared?" I venture to guess, vaguely recollecting the journal entries from my self-study as Mara's attendant.

He nods once, proud. "My father cultivated the most efficient fruit from these novel trees. He is so proud of them. But they require too much oversight – too much enforced secrecy to convince humans to continue eating the fruit. Once I'm king? There will be more… opportunities to test other solutions." His hand drops to my limp one. "And you, my dear, are the first successful pioneer of one of those opportunities."

Those damnations, I amend.

The crunch of boots on the gravel path halts his monologue. We both turn.

My next words die in my throat.

Eddie.

Here. Now. Dressed in royal blues instead of laundress muslin, her dark eyes burning with quiet fury.

"Eddie," I whisper, the name slipping out before I can stop it.

Her gaze flicks to mine, just for a heartbeat, but it's enough. Twenty years of shared survival pass between us in that look as she stands behind us, caught in the same gilded trap that snared me.

Sylas's thumb strokes my wrist, checking my heart rate. "It took a while to find your lover. But with Chase gone and you unable to fulfill your attendant duties, I knew she'd be the perfect stand in." His voice is light, amused at the wide eyed surprise on my face.

Eddie bows at his explanation. The movement is flawless – the perfect picture of obedience.

But I know her.

"An honor to serve, Your Highness."

I glance down just long enough to see the protective ring on her finger, and I force my shoulders to unstick from my ears.

She's not glamoured.

Sylas smiles like he can't see the tremor in her hands that I do. "Eddie was so eager to take over your duties. Weren't you?"

Eddie's jaw clenches. "Yes, Your Highness."

Liar.

She'd rather scrub table runners until her hands bleed than serve at a sidhe's side. Which means only one thing: she's here because he bargained with her – because he *knew* this would keep me cooperative.

And suddenly, Starling's vial becomes the worst solution.

Becca used this to end her bad decisions.

But Becca didn't have an Eddie. Becca didn't even fall into this trap – she was just forced. She had nothing to lose.

And I... can't do that to Eddie.

Sylas's words cut off my thoughts. "Eddie will attend us at dinner tomorrow. Won't that be nice?" His fingers set a curl in my hair.

"Lovely," I choke out, pretending the sound comes from excitement rather than guilt.

I've just exposed her to the whims of the folk in a way she's never had to deal with before.

His fingers are warm, but the touch feels bitingly cold. "I want you to be happy. Not just pretending."

"I am happy," I lie through my teeth. "I have you, don't I?"

He leans in, his lips brushing against mine in another test. I kiss him back this time – because if I don't, he'll know something's wrong.

When he pulls away, he looks at me with that perfectly composed face. "You're mine, Valerie. Forever. Never forget that."

"I won't," I whisper, the sound too similar to the whisper of the trees.

He stands, offering me his hand. "Come on. Let's go back to the party. It's getting far too cold."

I take his hand, letting him pull me to my feet, and avoid Eddie's agonized face as he leads us inside.

The main hall is alive with revelry still. Sylas leads me to his corpse of a throne, his fingers laced through mine. The courtiers part before us merrily with too bright smiles and too deep bows.

Eddie follows at a distance. Seeing such performatively elegant posture on her usually slack person is strange. She takes her place with the other attendants on the wall – Starling among them, their face carefully blank as they track Ciaran on the far side of the room.

Sylas guides me down onto the arm of his throne, his hand settling on my thigh. "Look at them," he murmurs, his lips brushing my ear. "All of them, waiting for the heir."

I smile weakly, my fingers tightening around the stem of a goblet he forces me to take. The tea is sweet like the false compliments dripping from every noble's tongue.

Across the room, Eddie's hands tremble as she avoids the attention of Lord Rakan, only flinching when he leans in to proposition something in her ear, but otherwise staying safely invisible.

The way I should have.

Sylas's thumb strokes circles on my knee, his touch growing bolder as the night wears on. The more he drinks – the heavier his hands become: trailing up my side, toying with the laces of my dress.

"You're perfect like this," he purrs, his voice thick with fairy fruit and desire. "Undeniably mine."

It gets harder to fawn believably.

I catch Eddie's eye across the hall and see helpless wrath in them, though the rest of her is masterfully relaxed.

Sylas nips at my earlobe. "Come to my chambers tonight. I've missed your touch."

It's not a request.

I turn in his arms, pressing a hand to his coiled tight chest. "The healer said... it might not be safe for the heir. Not in this state."

His grip tightens disapprovingly.

I lower my voice, letting it tremble just the way he likes. "I want to. But what if something happens? After everything…"

I begin to worry that he'll push when his jaw flexes. Then his hand falls away. "You're right." He sighs, waving me off. "Go rest. Take the attendant with you."

Two minotaur and Eddie follow me out. To my surprise, the guards remain stationed *outside* tonight when we push into my room.

My chambers are still dark with dawn nowhere in sight, when Eddie and I slip inside. Neither of us moves to light a candle. I lean against the door, enjoying the serenity of the space with her for a long tension-easing breath.

Her face warps with the buried rage as she stabs the kindling in my hearth. "I can read lips, Val. I heard everything."

My stomach drops.

She stalks forward, her voice a hiss. "You still let him touch you like that?" Her hands flail at her sides.

"It's not like I have much of a choice," I scoff, gesturing around the room just as wildly. "I fucked up. I know that. But I didn't ask for this."

Her face falls.

"I don't know what I'm supposed to do." Tears spill down her cheeks, cutting through the carefully constructed mask of anger. "I want to be angry with you. I *am* angry with you… but I can't watch you die."

The words unravel me.

I cross the room in two strides, pulling her into my arms. She collapses against me immediately, her shoulders shaking with silent sobs. We sink to the floor together, clinging to each other like it's the last time.

It might be.

"I have a way out," I murmur into her hair. My fingers drift beneath my pillow above where Starling's vial rests. "A toxin from a friend. It would… end the pregnancy."

Eddie pulls back, her puffy eyes searching mine. "But?"

"But they'll kill us both if I take it." My thumb brushes the tear track on her sunken cheek. "I won't do that to you."

"You won't?" she blubbers in relief.

And as I stare at the woman I love – at the fear she's too proud to name… I realize that Sylas's already won. I won't terminate this pregnancy. Not if Eddie suffers the consequences for it too.

She sees the resolve harden in my eyes and opens her mouth to say something. But I speak first.

"The wedding is in a week," I force steadiness into my voice. "Once Sylas and Giabella are married, their attention will shift to their own moment in the spotlight. I'll have space to think of a real way out." I squeeze her hands. "And until then… we have each other."

Each other. Alone in the quiet between guard rotations. Stealing moments in the dark together again. She exhales, her forehead resting against mine. "You're really going through with it for me?"

"Yes." The truth tastes bitter, but I sell it with a smile. "For us to have a chance. Now help me out of this damn dress."

Her hands tremble as she unlaces my gown, her calloused fingers skimming the curve of my spine. She leans in, her lips brushing the shell of my ear.

"I missed the way you order me around," she jokes, and the tease in her voice makes me bolder.

I guide her palm around front to the slight swell of my stomach, erasing Sylas's smooth touch with her familiar, rougher one. Her breathing picks up as she traces slow circles, her thumb dipping low on my hip.

"You're so soft now," she whispers against the back of my neck. Her kisses trail over my shoulders, spinning me around. She pauses at my collarbone. "But you're still Val."

I arch into her as her mouth finds the sensitive spot beneath my ear, the one she's known for seventeen years. Her hands are careful, relearning the new landscape of my body: fuller chest, the taut stretch of skin over my hips. When her fingers slip between my thighs, it's with a question in her touch.

"Please," I whine, tangling my hands in her coiled cropped hair as I say the word only allowed between trusted humans.

She takes me apart slowly once we move to the bed, her mouth hot on my skin, her fingers moving in languid strokes that build like a rising tide inside me. Every kiss, every shuddering peak is a secret between us: a language Sylas will never speak.

When I shatter, it's with her name on my lips and her arm locked around me, holding the pieces together.

Then I return the favor, flipping her onto her back and kissing a fervent trail down her dark skin, glistening with sweat before I even reach my goal.

My hands slide down her torso, mapping the familiar planes of her – the taut muscle of her stomach, the barely there hair leading me lower – before hooking my fingers into the waistband of her trousers.

She arches off the bed with a choked laugh, helping me tug them free, her heated eyes never leaving mine.

"Still impatient too," she mutters, but the tease falters as I drag my nails lightly up her inner thigh. Her legs fall open, and I kiss the inside of her knee, then higher, savoring the way her muscles tense under my lips.

When I finally close my mouth over her, she gasps, her hips lifting off the bed. My tongue strokes with muscle memory in the way that always undid her. She tastes like home – like safety and sleepless nights. I moan against her, the vibration wrenching a broken sound from her throat.

She comes apart with muted cries. Her thighs clamp around my head – I work her through it, gentling my touch until her eyes refocus.

When I finally crawl up her body, she drags me into a searing kiss, tasting herself on my tongue. Her strong arms pull me closer.

As dawn finally begins to streak the sky, there's no Sylas, no pregnancy, no mortality: just her skin against mine, her heartbeat thundering in time with my own as she curls around me.

Somewhere beyond these walls, Sylas plans our deaths. But here, in this stolen moment, we are finally alive and together.

Chapter 65

We sleep tangled together that day, Eddie's arms wrapped tight around me, her breath warm against the back of my neck. For the first time in weeks, I feel something like safety – fragile and fleeting – but there all the same.

Evening comes too soon.

Golden hour spills through the curtains, gilding the drifting dust motes as Eddie helps me dress. We run through the schedule as I finger comb my hair.

"Library after breakfast?" she questions, her voice low enough that the guards outside won't hear.

I nod. "I need to tell you something."

I guide her towards the library in what is now Giabella's tower, once we've eaten and I've taken my potions and tonics. It's fortuitously empty tonight. We settle at the table Starling and I formed a tentative friendship around, hidden between towering shelves of ancient texts. Eddie's knee bounces restlessly as she watches me, waiting.

Once the guards have grown bored and meander towards the outer stacks, I quit stalling.

"The fairy fruit," I begin, my voice barely above a whisper. "It's not fruit."

Her brow furrows.

"It's *people*, Eddie. Humans. Like Chase-" My voice cracks. "I made a friend up here. He ate a pastry with the stuff in it by accident, and they took him. They turn into *trees*. That's why it drives humans mad. It transforms them from the inside out so the folk can eat the magic stuck in us."

Her face goes grey. "No."

"I saw it," I assert. "I saw *him*. Half turned, tied to a post. They're all there, in the orchard. All the humans who ever ate the fruit go there, and die after like six months once they run out of magic."

Eddie's hands fly to her mouth in stunned silence.

Then, we hear footsteps.

We both freeze as a shadow falls across the table.

Starling stands at the end of the aisle, their eyes sharp, their mouth curved disapprovingly. Eddie leans forward, blocking me from their line of sight.

Starling ignores her, looking straight through her. "Miss Valerie," they lilt. "Walk with me."

It's not a request.

Eddie's fingers tighten on my arm, her doubt palpable. I squeeze her hand once, before standing and slipping from her touch.

"Of course," I acquiesce.

They offer their thin arm, the gesture deceptively courtly. As I take it, Eddie's terrified gaze digs into my back.

The moment we're out of earshot, Starling drags me faster. "You're reckless. Telling her that."

"You were listening."

"I was *waiting*." They pull me into a secluded nook, their voice dropping. "Do you have any idea what the king would do if he knew you were telling others about the orchard?"

I stiffen. "Are you going to tell him?"

Their grip bruises, before they release me.

"No, I won't. But you had a way out of all this," they growl. "I gave you the vial. Why didn't you take it?"

Eddie's face flashes in my mind: her fury, her fear.

"Because Sylas would kill Eddie too," I admit.

They huff a laugh. "Sentiment. How very *human*." They lean in even closer, a petrichor musk clinging to them. "You won't survive the birth just because you think you're *special*. We can't help you that much. If you drink the vial now, at least you have a chance."

A desperation seeps into their tone as they retreat back.

We can't help. Not *I* can't help. Which means…

"You're with them," I breathe. "With the rebellion."

Their lip curls until I see a fanged tooth. "Don't be absurd, I'm a court attendant." But their gaze flicks to the library at large, ensuring we're alone.

They didn't say no.

"Then what does it matter to you if I take it or not?" I press.

"Because Ciaran wants the West's throne," they snap. "And I'm tasked with making that possible."

Shock pales my already sallow face, and they shake their head –
shaking off the slip – before continuing. "Sylas's line ends with him. And
right now, you're part of that line."

The words are too cold and ruthless for the friendship I thought we
once shared. Their fingers brush the hilt of a dagger tucked strategically
under their tunic, showing me the blade that may have been there the entire
time I've known them.

*Have I ever even **known** them?*

"You *want* me to die."

They don't deny it. "There'd be less loose ends that can talk if you
did." They glower at my swollen stomach. "Your lover doesn't have to go
too, if you *stop* telling her things and take the damn vial."

I meet their gaze with the idea. "And what do I get out of it? If I take
the poison instead of letting the heir make it to term?"

A slow, cruel smile replaces their sneer. "A chance to fuck over Sylas.
He'd lose the court's favor as he searches for rebellious Unseelie he will
never find. Ciaran would get the crown that can help my people. I could go
on, but you get it."

Their people. The Unseelie. The pieces click together.

The Unseelie rebellion wants to remove the sidhe and humans without
mercy. Sylas mentioned it had something to do with magic.

They want all the magic in the Otherworld for themselves.

Prince Ciaran wants everyone distracted enough to take a throne out
from under a rival's nose, since he isn't in line for the one in the South
Court and wants real power.

And Starling – an Unseelie attendant to a Seelie usurper – comes out
winning either way.

My voice hardens. "Do what you must. But I won't damn Eddie with
my choices."

Starling's face opens with surprise before it closes again. "That's
unfortunate." Their fingers brush the dagger's hilt once more before
concealing it again. "For everyone involved."

They slip away – quieter than they appeared – leaving me standing in
the alcove with stress soaked hands. I take a moment to compose myself,
smoothing my dress and schooling my features into something neutral
before returning to Eddie.

She's exactly where I left her, her eyes narrow incredulously. "What did they want?"

"Nothing important," I lie. My fingers trail over the book spines on the nearest shelf, before plucking a brightly illustrated one. "Look. _How The Realm Was Saved_. I read this when I first got up here."

Eddie frowns but takes the book when I extend it to her. "Why this one?"

"Thought we could start planning the nursery," I say delicately, stacking two other children's books in my own arms as the minotaurs lumber into view. My heart speeds when I spot the folded parchment hidden between the pages of the book in Eddie's grasp: the detailed map of the Cardinal Kingdom I'd slipped there months ago, before everything fell apart. "Sylas and Giabella will be pleased if I contribute before the birth."

If I even make it that long, the grim truth seeps through my placid smile.

Eddie's eyes don't soften. But she nods, ignoring the way my lip falters. She knows me too well to argue.

As we retreat down a flight of stairs, my mind races. The map shows everything: the castle layout, the orchard, the portal back to the human world. A legacy hidden in plain sight – for when I'm gone, and Eddie has nothing left to do but get away from here.

The thought is a small comfort as we reach the nursery. My pulse thrums against my ribs, when Eddie reaches for the door.

"Actually, I… forgot something in my room," I say the lie when I think of it, not breaking stride as I tug her back to the staircase. "Pregnancy brain."

The guards follow, so uninterested in my comings and goings that they don't question me.

We trek all the way back downstairs, across the main hall, up Sylas's flight, and to my room. I close the door behind me, leaving a cautiously concerned Eddie and the guards outside. I cross to the wardrobe overwhelmed in superfluous silks and furs, my fingers clawing a small tunnel into the very back. I tuck the map inside with a silent prayer that it won't be found. Starling's still full vial finds a place alongside it.

For Eddie. When I'm gone.

The gifts are back to a mishap of pastel tones just as the door creaks open. Eddie leans against the frame, her arms full of the remaining books, her eyes weary.

"Ready?" she asks, too casually.

I wave the book with a grin, tying a random capelet at my neck like it was my purpose for our return. "Let's go charm the future queen."

The nursery is all pale woods and enchanted mobiles when we enter; I haven't stepped foot inside until now. The air prickles with the tingle of magical offerings from other kingdoms.

Giabella stands by the window, her golden eyes bright as she arranges a collection of rattles on a velvet lined tray.

"We've brought gifts," I alert her to our presence.

She turns with a sprawling smile. "Valerie," she coos, gliding forward to press a kiss to my cheek. "I'm so pleased you've come to see the nursery. I was just telling Sy how lovely it would be if you took more interest."

Her fingers cradle my stomach: possessive and proud. I force a sheepish smile, gesturing to the books Eddie and I carry. "I thought these might be nice additions."

She takes one, her smile widening as she reads the titles. "How charming!" She tucks them onto a shelf between a jeweled music box and a set of ivory teething rings. "We will have to read them together when the heir is born."

We.

Eddie's breathing changes beside me. I reach for her hand, squeezing once before pulling away.

Steady.

Giabella doesn't notice. She's too busy tracing the spine of *Lesser Folk and Their Families*, her voice dreamy. "Perhaps we'll name them after one of our fallen. Mara would be fitting, don't you think?"

My stomach twists. *Mara.* The reason I'm in this nightmare to begin with, instead of tucked in the barracks with Eddie.

"Very," I concede.

Giabella beams, mistaking my compliance for enthusiasm. "I knew you'd come around," she pats my arm. "You're as strong as Mara thought. She'd be so proud of you."

Before I can respond, a small brownie appears in the doorway, bowing low. "The healer is waiting in your chambers."

Eddie exhales beside me, letting out the breath she's been holding.

Giabella waves us off. "Go, go. We'll have plenty of time to plan later."

The guards shadow us back. Angel waits by the bed.

"Undress," they instruct, already rummaging through their herb heavy satchel.

Eddie helps me with gentle fingers, untying the laces of my gown. The healer's magic prickles against my skin as their runed arm flickers to life – examining me for things I don't bother trying to understand.

"The fetus is strong," they announce at last, stepping back. "But you're weakening faster than expected."

Eddie's face falls.

The healer doesn't meet my eyes as they pack their tools. "Get some more magic sources in your diet: mushroom caps and jackalope are in season. There's nothing else to be done right now, but we will keep looking into our options."

When they're gone, Eddie turns to me in morbid defeat. "You're dying."

"I know," I admit, less distressed. My hands paw through the pile of gifts stuffed into the wardrobe where the map lies tucked away. "But I'm not dead *yet*."

She locks the door behind me, my resolve harder than it's been all week as I feel a sense of acceptance wash over me.

I'm going to die. But Eddie doesn't have to.

The map crinkles as I pull it from beneath some furry monstrosity of folk fashion, spreading it across the bed so I can explain it properly.

"Look," I tell Eddie, tracing the lines with my finger: the garden borders, the orchard to the north, the portal home marked with a star not much farther. "Memorize the route to the portal. Then burn it. When you leave, don't stop at the fairy fruit, no matter how tempting the curiosity is."

Eddie's hands tremble as she takes the parchment. "What-"

I press the vial into her palm before she can finish. "And if they do to you what they did to me before you can escape," I say, holding her gaze fiercely so she understands, "Drink this. Don't hesitate. Don't tell anyone."

I don't let her speak. I pull her into me, my arms tight around her waist – probably *too* tight. But she doesn't complain.

She's shaking.

I kiss her. Hard.

It's heartbreak given form. It's the banned salt of tears – hers or mine – I can't tell. I pour every ounce of regret – every shred of longing into it. Because this is the last time. This is the last night we'll have before the wedding preparations have Eddie running errands and me stuck in revelries. Before I'm nothing more than Sylas's pretty prop until my body gives out.

Eddie whimpers against my mouth, her fingers digging into my hands on her waist, holding them tighter.

The door opens. Sylas's triumphant laugh drifts through the room. "I wondered where you'd gone tonight."

Eddie tries to break apart, but I hold her tight. I won't give him the satisfaction of seeing me flinch. I keep one arm locked around her hunched shoulders as I turn to face him.

He lounges in the doorway, goblet in hand, his eyes bright with delight. "Don't let me interrupt," he teases.

"You already did," I bristle.

His grin widens.

He loves this: my defiance and Eddie's fear. "Enjoy your gift," he says into his wine. "After the wedding, you'll be at my side. The court needs to see how humans *thrive* under my rule."

My eyes narrow. "How inspiring."

He chuckles again, pushing off the door frame. "Those hormones are making you irrational. Maybe up the dosage on your herbals."

He pulls the door closed.

Eddie sags against me. "He's not going to let us do this again. Not if it's interfering with his plans."

I press my forehead to hers. "I know."

And then I kiss her again, because there's nothing left to say.

Chapter 66

Winter's grip loosens tonight, but the chill still nips at my skin as I sit by the window, staring out at the fading light.

It's been colder since they forced Eddie into a glorified errand runner. I don't get to see her other than when the healer visits… and never alone.

The knock at my door is insistent. I don't turn, assuming it's the guards or another servant with another invitation to an event I won't refuse. But when the door creaks open, I hear Starling's voice.

"Come for a walk with me."

I whirl, surprised to see them standing there, claws tucked into the pockets of their attendant's uniform. Their red eyes meet mine, and for a moment, I see the guilt in them.

"Why are you here?" I demand, searching their waistband for another dagger. Even though I can't see one, there's doubt that they're unarmed. They step inside, closing the door behind them. The guards don't bother intruding anymore; I behave.

"Because I've had time to think," they offer.

I look back down to the gardens – the hedges beginning to green again. "I should have listened to you," I grant, a hand rubbing over my too stretched middle. "Back when it was Mara's library. I should have been more careful."

Starling doesn't respond immediately. They step closer, breaching the rug. "Yes," they agree. "You should have. So if you've ever learned a lesson, it's that: listen to me."

I glance at them, searching their face for some hint of what they're thinking. Their expression is wary. But the way their eyes dart to the door – I can tell there's something more.

"What do you want from me?" I ask, my voice noncommittal in turn.

"A walk," they say simply.

The gardens are quiet, the air crisp when we reach the spot under my window. Our footsteps crunch softly on the gravel path, the guards trailing behind us, far enough to give the illusion of privacy but close enough to remind me I'm still a prisoner. Starling walks beside me, their hands still in their pockets, their gaze fixed on the path ahead.

We reach the clearing where Mara's pyre was burned months ago.

Good riddance, you demon, I think.

The ground is still scarred, the earth uneven. But tiny shoots of green are beginning to push through the thawing soil.

Life returning, even here.

We pause at the edge of the clearing, my arms wrapped tightly around myself as best I can. "I thought this place was beautiful the first time I saw it." My breath forms a faint cloud. "Now it just feels… haunted."

They step closer to the patchy sod, their boots sinking slightly into the softened ground. "It has to be by now."

I glance at them, still entirely composed.

"Why did you want to talk to me now?" The question slips out before I can stop it. "Is it pity? Because if it is, I'll take it. I just need to know."

Starling turns to me, their red eyes disgusted. "Pity?" they repeat, sharply. "You think I'd waste my time on pity for *you*?"

I flinch, taken aback by their harshness. "Then why?"

They sigh, running claws through their dark hair. "Because I know what it's like to feel trapped," they confess, their voice softer now. "Because it's what Chase would have wanted me to do."

The words sting more than I expect. I look away, my throat tightening. "I don't know what to do anymore. Every time I try to fix things, I just mess them up more. My intuition is broken."

Starling doesn't respond immediately.

"You don't have to know," they eventually counter. "But you should stop trying to do it all on your own."

I shake my head, tears pricking at the corners of my eyes. "I just – I wish I could start over. Somewhere far away from this court and my shitty choices. I want a new life where I'm not the only thing between a monstrous future king and a rebellion that I think *might* have a point in wanting us all dead."

Starling's gaze homes in over their shoulder at the guards – who are currently chewing on the hedges. When they speak again, their voice is barely audible: a whisper meant only for me. "What if I told you there might be a way out?"

I freeze, my heart skipping a beat. "What do you mean?"

Their eyes dart to the guards again before returning to me. "There. Is.

A. Way. Out," they say slowly, each word measured. "But you will not like it."

I stare at them in disbelief. "No. They'll kill Eddie if I leave."

Starling huddles closer, pretending to protect me from the chill. "There's a way to escape your situation that won't be traced back to you *or* to Eddie. A way to leave this life behind. But it would mean giving up everything… potentially."

I swallow hard, my pulse picking up. "Including the heir?"

"*Especially* the heir."

The thought of ending the pregnancy – of defying Sylas and his cruel court – fills me with a mix of fear and sick excitement.

"I'll do it," I eagerly agree. "I'll do anything to get out of here as long as it doesn't implicate anyone else. I've heard Sylas's ideas for his reign, and we can't let him do that."

Starling studies me with sobering intensity. "Are you sure? There's a chance you'll die, but it won't be while delivering his child." They clarify.

I nod, though my hands tremble when the heir kicks in objection. "I don't care. I'm sure."

They exhale slowly in a relieved, strong cloud. "Alright. You've just bought every human in this court another chance for a better future."

A better future? If the Unseelie win or Ciaran becomes king?

I open my mouth to challenge the idea, but they're already turning away. "We should head back," they say louder, wanting the guards to hear. "It's late, and the wedding will be overwhelming tomorrow."

I walk with them back toward the castle, my mind spinning with possibilities. The guards fall into step behind us. As we walk, I can't shake the feeling of unease that settles over me.

If I die escaping, it's better than dying for Sylas's cause.

When we reach the castle doors, Starling pauses, their hand resting on the handle. They glance at me. "Remember," they say quietly. "This is for the future of the Otherworld."

Then they're gone, disappearing into the shadows of the castle, leaving me standing there with my thoughts and the cold, overwhelming presence of the guards.

Chapter 67

Sylas strides into my chambers unannounced the evening of the wedding, his excitement tangible in a way that makes my skin crawl. I sit by the window, staring out at the thawing gardens like I've done mindlessly for days, but his reflection in the glass forces me to turn and face him.

"Valerie," he says my name warmly for once. "I have wonderful news."

I don't respond. I have nothing worth saying.

He steps closer, his pale hand reaching out to stroke my hair. I jerk away before he can touch me. His smile falters for a moment, but he quickly recovers.

"You've made it to the third trimester," he says with reverence. "It's a milestone worth celebrating. We're honoring you at the grand feast after the wedding ceremony tonight."

I stare at him, unblinking.

A celebration. For me. On their wedding day.

The irony is almost too much to bear.

"I don't want a celebration," I decline.

Sylas's smile doesn't waver this time. "Nonsense. This child is progressing as expected, and you've done so well to stay healthy too. You deserve to be celebrated."

*I **deserve** to be left alone,* I think rebelliously. *I deserve to be treated like a human...*

Then I realize with indignation that I *am* being treated like a human here: something to be used and discarded.

He steps back, gesturing to a servant who has been waiting quietly by the door. Her brown eyes widen as she looks at me.

Sydney. The stitcher from the atelier.

I look away, shame filling me as I see the shock on her face.

She recognizes me too.

Then, she holds up a gown of shimmering fabric that draws my eye right back. The dress is exquisite: a rich, royal blue with silver embroidery that catches the light at all angles.

"I had this made for you," Sylas explains pridefully. "You'll wear it tonight. Everyone will be there to honor you by wearing royal blue: your favorite color."

I look up at him, unmoved by the gesture. "I don't want to wear it."

Sydney drapes the dress onto my bed, then takes the silent standoff between me and Sylas as a chance to make her escape.

Take me with you, I beg.

His jaw tightens, but he keeps his tone light. "Valerie, don't be difficult. This is a special occasion. You'll look beautiful."

That's the first time he's ever actually called me beautiful.

I want to scream. I want to tear the gown to shreds and throw it in his face. But I know it's pointless. And someone else will pay the price for it.

So I nod, my hands clenched on my belly.

"Good," he says, his smile returning. "There's one more thing."

I brace myself, my stomach twisting.

"Your other friends from the barracks, they will be serving at the celebration," he mentions casually. "I thought you'd appreciate seeing them again."

My breath catches.

Lilia. Maddie.

The thought of seeing them again – up here – fills me with a mix of longing and dread.

"Why?" I probe.

Sylas shrugs. "I thought it would make you happy. But remember, this is a *formal* event. You'll need to be on your best behavior."

The warning in his voice is clear, and it makes my blood run cold. If I misbehave, they'll be punished.

Personally.

I nod again.

"Good girl. I'll see you at the wedding."

He turns and leaves.

I'm left alone with the guards and the gown until a knock at the door jolts me from my unfocused stare. I realize I have no idea how long I've just sat here, but my neck protests as I angle towards the door.

I groan and rub the muscle – uncomfortable in my own body. I'm dreading the evening more and more with every carriage I catch sight of below. The minotaurs open the door, and a small selkie steps inside – fresh faced and curious eyed – her seal skin draped over one shoulder like a sash. When she sees me, her curiosity turns appalled.

"You're Valerie?" She forces a polite lilt.

I nod mechanically.

"I'm Tara," She bobs a bow. "I've been assigned to help you get ready for tonight."

I don't fight her. It's not her fault.

I sit obediently as she brushes out my rats nests with gentle efficiency. She hums softly under her breath as she works: a tune I don't recognize. The sound soothes my spiking rage when I realize it's a glamour she's using to keep me still.

She adds powders and concoctions to my face, her touch light and precise. She has an artist's hand, hiding my permanent scowl with a professional finish.

When she's done, she steps back to admire her work. "That's enough for tonight."

I turn to my reflection in the mirror and barely recognize the girl. The dark circles are gone, replaced by a faint glow that makes me look almost well rested. My hair is gathered into an elegant twist, loose strands framing my blushed face. But my eyes are still hollow – haunted.

Tara helps me into the gown Sylas dumped on me. The fabric is tight against every part of me I wish it wasn't, the silver embroidery scratchy against my sensitive chest.

It's beautiful, but it feels like a cage designed to keep me from getting away.

"You're all set," Tara bows again, stepping back. She hesitates for a moment, then adds, "Good luck."

I wave her off. I don't trust myself to say anything nice. The minotaurs are waiting outside. And I'm almost offended that they're my only guides to the main hall.

If they're going to pretend this is an honor, at least do so where the guests in the halls can see.

But as we walk, they guide me past the staircase that would take us to the party sight. Instead, we continue… north. North to the aviary of snitching little beasts. North toward the fairy fruit trees desecrating the gardens.

I find myself at the edge of a glamorous crowd, my blue gown a cruelty. It matches the extravagance of the courtiers too well, making me blend with the sidhe in a way that makes me disgusted.

I'm nothing like them.

Eddie is stationed near the perfunctory dais, her hands clasped behind her back, her face carefully blank. Starling lingers on the periphery, their crimson eyes never acknowledging my appearance.

Sylas waits at the center of it all – resplendent in Belladonna's work. He looks every bit the king he'll soon be.

It would be so easy for another bomb to go off right now.

But nothing happens. And Giabella appears as expected.

The crowd parts for her like water, murmurs rippling in her wake. She wears no veil, her hair long down her back. Her gown is composed of sheer embroidered lace, azure crystals shifting with her movements as if dusted with the last snowfall of the season.

She steps up beside Sylas to complete their ritual in front of every Cardinal court's ruling family.

No priestess presides, their word binding and true without the need for a third party. Sylas extends his hand, a small chunk of gemstone in his grasp.

Giabella places hers atop it.

"For your hand in marriage, I offer you my strength," Sylas says, his voice carrying across the garden. "My crown. My future."

Giabella's reply is just as measured. "And for your hand in marriage, I offer you my loyalty. My cunning. My legacy."

A beat.

"Do you accept?" Sylas asks.

Giabella's lips curve. "I accept."

The magic pulses tangibly between them as they squeeze the gemstone between their hands. The bargain is sealed, when a glow begins to emanate from the small thing

That's all it takes? Where's the kiss or I Do's?

The guests break into thunderous applause, but I protest by looking away. My fingers twitch toward my stomach, where the heir – *his* heir – shifts restlessly.

You're next, the fairy fruit trees whisper on the breeze… or maybe that's just the obvious next step in the back of my mind.

A servant brushes past me, her tray laden with goblets of wine. When she turns, she bears Maddie's carefully neutral face as she serves Alistar and Rakan. Lilia is nowhere to be seen when I begin combing the crowd for her.

Then Sylas turns his crowned head, his gaze finding me instantly. His smile stops my search, hoping desperately that at least one friend has dodged his trickery.

You're mine, his face says. *Until the day you die.*

Chapter 68

The main hall is alive with music and laughter, the revelry spilling out into the gardens with guests dressed in their finest – all shades of blue and silver: the West Court colors.

The royal blue I once loved sends a shot of disgust through me right now. It's everywhere: draped over tables, woven into garlands, shimmering on the guests like a sea of sapphires. It's supposed to honor me, but it feels like a mockery: a reminder that I'm their incubator for five or so months until they get what they really want.

The place is decorated *exactly* to my specifications for the wedding – other than the added color.

And I. Hate. It.

The spring blooms I was so proud of procuring now make me nauseous with their overwhelming sweetness. They tuck into every corner, their fragrance cloying against the bold perfumes of the nobility.

The crystal table settings I insisted on are too bright, their light reflecting ostentatiously off the silver filigree that adorns every surface.

I stand by the exit of the room, the gown making it too uncomfortable to sit. The fabric is heavy, pressing down on my shoulders. The train is too long – the neckline too low. The embroidery scratches at my skin like a thousand tiny needles.

I can't wait for tonight to be over.

I can feel the eyes of the guests on me, their gazes lingering as they gossip behind their hands. They don't see me. Not really. But I offer shy smiles and respectful inclinations of my head when necessary, swallowing my gripes only to keep my friends safe.

The music swells, a lively tune that sets the guests spinning across the floor, their laughter ringing out in melody. But the sound grates my nerves, each song nothing more than a personal dirge.

I glance down at my hands, pale and trembling against the rich blue fabric of my gown.

This might be the last time I ever attend a revelry.

And I'm at the center of this one, a living, breathing symbol of every wrong choice I've made this year.

Sylas finds me after exchanging more private gifts with Giabella, gifts that he'd never give *me*: a confession of love or some sort of family jewel. His hand rests possessively on my lower back as he prods me into the crowd. "The rest of the night is about us," he murmurs against my ear as the glamour removes all sense of fear and disgust.

I relax, my skin singing at his touch. "Of course," I sigh.

He doesn't acknowledge my compliance. He's too busy basking in the attention, his smile radiant as guests approach to offer their congratulations. I smile and play the part of the grateful bearer-to-be under Sylas's influence. But inside, somewhere, I'm screaming.

Maddie is stationed near the banquet tables, her uniform crisp and her posture practiced. My heart wants to ache at the sight of her, but I can't feel anything right now.

She belongs in the barracks, laughing and bickering and living life untouched by the cruelty of this level of the castle.

I catch Lilia's brown eyes for the first time, her gaze knowing when my face falls.

No. Not her too.

She gives me a small nod that I can't do anything but blink at. The understanding in the gesture is somehow worse than any contempt she could hurl at me.

Lilia subtly nudges Maddie when they cross paths, her eyes following Lilia's line of sight to me. Then they drop, avoiding me entirely.

But I see her dark hands lighten around the tray she's holding. Her shoulders stiffen, battling away a volatile reaction she knows she can't have here.

I want to run to them – to apologize for everything and beg their forgiveness. But Sylas's glamour is strong, dulling my thoughts into placid compliance.

I'm happy here. Why would I ruin that?

Sylas's hand tightens on my back, his touch deliberately possessive as I fight the influence. He leans down to murmur. "Your friends look uncomfortable. Perhaps they're not used to such grandeur."

His tone is teasing, but my broken fury rears its head enough to fracture his hold on my mind. I force myself to keep smiling, though it feels like a grimace. "They're not used to being around all of you," I say, my voice low to hide the rising spite.

Sylas chuckles. "They're lucky to be here at all. Most humans never set foot in a room like this."

And if I step out of line – if I do anything to disrupt his carefully constructed illusion – they'll pay the price.

So I glance back at my friends once more, my chest tightening as I absorb their strained expressions. Lilia's gaze is still on me with quiet intensity. Maddie is staring at the floor, her lips pressed into a thin line.

Sylas's hand slides down to my waist, guiding me further into the room as he drops all glamour from my mind – purposefully this time.

"Smile, Valerie," he commands sweetly. "This is your celebration, after all."

I force another betrayal of a smile. The grig's music continues around us, tugging at my limbs. The dancers and courtiers mingle in line for the fairy fruit buffet. But no amount of grotesque spectacle can banish the way my friends look at me like I'm a stranger –like I've become something they don't recognize.

And maybe I have.

Chapter 69

The night drags on, each moment more degrading than the last. Sylas keeps a constant, leashing grip on me, to the point that I begin to question if he's using magic to keep his hand glued to my back.

He keeps us at the center of everyone's attention, his bright smile drawing everyone to us with the hope of the heir. His gaze pierces me occasionally, cold eyes reminding me to play my part.

I force a smile that keeps him satisfied, nodding at the guests who approach to offer their congratulations.

But inside, I'm still screaming so hard I can't think straight.

I need air.

I turn – intending to ask Sylas if we can step outside for a moment – when I see Starling.

Their small shoulders stay squared with me, even while they stand sentinel with the other attendants on the edge of the crowd. I catch their red eyes and feel a flicker of hope when their pointy chin tilts in acknowledgment.

Maybe they're here to help.

Sylas introduces me to another visiting dignitary that I don't bother learning the name of. When my eyes slink back to the line of attendants only seconds later, Starling is missing.

My head whips around until I spot them surprisingly near – predatory as they stalk silently closer.

"Valerie," they greet as Sylas ignores the Unseelie attendant.

He's too involved in the story of Mara's plans for me again, waving the now revealed truth like the banner of red flags I was too blind to see it for.

"Starling." My voice is equally low, as their eyes narrow on my rounded belly. "I've been waiting for you."

I've been rotting all night in this stupid dress, my mind corrects.

They reach into their coat, a dark hand closing around something I can't see in their waistband. Instinct screams at me to run. But my feet stay rooted to the spot, Sylas's hand on my back keeping me in place.

Are they going to force the vial down my throat? Right here in front of everyone?

"You said you wanted to get out of this," Starling says as they take another step closer.

I nod, my throat tight. "I did."

Their gaze meets mine with desperation and resignation all at once. "This is the only way."

Before I can react, they move.

The blade is small but sharp. I only catch a glimpse of it, as it reflects the chandelier's rainbow light. It doesn't feel real when it enters me.

I gasp: a wet, tearing sound in the back of my throat.

My hands fly to my stomach, fingers sinking into the hot, sticky wound…

Too deep. Way too deep.

My hands come away glistening. The blood pulses around the blade in thick, rhythmic spurts – splattering the floor like spilled wine.

But I'm supposed to escape?

"Starling –?" I choke out, unable to process the attack. Their face is blank as they wrench the knife free and stab again.

Lower.

This time, I feel it when the steel parts muscle, gristle, and womb. A shriek rips from my throat, raw and animal, as they drag the blade sideways – unzipping me until suddenly…

I feel something heavy fall out of me.

More than my blood and viscera.

I look at the drenched floor to see… a *shape.*

Small. Twisted. Half formed.

Oh no.

My breathing turns into ragged, wet hitches of disbelief. The room tilts. Around me, the revelry has frozen. A nightmare of slack shocked faces drop filled goblets of wine that join my lifeblood on the floor.

Starling is gone before I can find enough air to scream again, disappearing into the crowd like this is somehow the help they promised me.

The pain is everywhere as my mind catches up: a burning, tearing agony that radiates from my abdomen and spreads all the way through my limbs.

My hands are coated with blood – the distinct metallic filling my nose as I press my palms uselessly against the gaping divide. Pink slimy entrails poke out, and I whimper as I try to hold them inside.

I can't breathe – can't think – can't do anything but feel the cold creeping into my bones and the heat against my hands.

Giabella kneels in the pooling blood, her wedding gown soaking crimson. She lifts the thing that fell out to the light. A fetus dangles from her fingers – slick and translucent. Its tiny limbs are curled like a plucked spider. A thin, blue veined sac clings to its skull, still tethered to me by a glistening cord.

I retch.

Sylas's arms lock around me, dragging me against his chest. His voice is a roar. "Healer! Now!"

His grip is steel, holding me together at the waist as I convulse.

Blood floods my mouth. My vision fractures.

"The rebellion isn't taking anyone else. Not during my own fucking wedding," he growls.

It wasn't the rebellion. I want to say. *It was a friend.*

But it doesn't matter, I can't form words anymore.

Giabella turns the fetus over, inspecting what should have been its face.

"It would have had his eyes," she murmurs.

The last thing I see is Giabella tossing the fetus onto the floor again next to me, sighing with frustration as my vision blacks out.

This is it. This is how I die.

The thought crashes over me like a wave, drowning out the chaos of the solstice.

I'll never get rid of the fairy fruit for Chase. I'll never go back to the human world. I'll never make up with Lilia or Maddie…

I feel my body jerk, spine bowing as my remaining insides slop onto the floor in a wet, steaming heap. But I mercifully can't feel it; everything is cut off with a honeyed warmth.

I don't know if its Sylas's glamour, a healer's herbs, or death itself – but the pain is gone now. There's only the distant thud of my heart, slowing with acceptance and death.

This isn't so bad.

I feel Sylas's lips press to my temple. "Shhh," he whispers through the syrupy haze. "Just sleep."

Yes. Sleep. That sounds like a good idea.

Epilogue

She dunks me again, my Eddie.

Oh great.

I know I'm still stuck in a dream because Eddie is a colossus hunching over the napkin that makes up my world – the one floating in the sea of an impossibly large basin. Furthermore, her thick rubber gloves don't mesh with this old world, and her wrists… I know those swollen joints would never be so animated.

But she is full of fury – scrubbing the linen I cling to – trying to drown me like any other stain.

She scrubs and she curses and she calls *me* a stain.

Her fiery eyes are the only warm thing in this cold water.

"I'm not a stain! It's me: Val!"

Eddie's hands pause, listening intently.

This hasn't happened in the dream before.

"Yes! Eddie, I'm here!" I shout again.

But she shakes her head and scrubs again.

She murmurs my name – thinking of me in some way – though she will not say it louder.

"Good riddance," she grumbles.

But she doesn't mean it. She has the same calluses that once kept me safe. I look down at my hands, clinging to the linen as she swirls it in the basin. They are smooth – not a finger print nor scar blemishes the surface now.

Uncanny.

Eddie – for all her incensed scrubbing – hasn't thrown my world of a napkin away. I don't know how I know, but if this napkin disappears I know I will follow it into nothingness.

So I hold tight when she dunks us and jabs me with the bristles.

Lilia comes, a watery silhouette above the surface as I hold my breath

"Still at it?" Her flat tone is muffled beneath the water.

Eddie does not turn. They are both so good at being invisible.

Lilia's dark eyes watch me. I risk waving one hand, almost lose my grip, then return to my clinging.

She knows.

Not what I am, but that I am something more than just another stain to be cleaned away.

"Be careful," Lilia warns.

Eddie counters with a sarcastic laugh.

Lilia leaves another dunk later.

Then my love stares into the water, deciding she's lost this battle today. She wrings out the only thing I have left and drops me in the pile to be ironed.

The dream usually stops here…

It always restarts when my napkin touches the peak of the mountain of linens – and I find myself holding on as she dunks me in the basin again.

But this time, when I'm atop the pile, Eddie grabs another napkin.

Huh. Maybe the dream is almost over.

But the thought barely forms before the world blinks – rewinding – and I am holding my breath in the basin again.

I debate letting go, exhaustion lulling me towards that serene nothingness.

But if I let go, that means I will never be more than the gullible girl who got tricked: a story barely worth remembering.

My fingers dig into the linen more determined, a tear in the fabric forming under my grip for the first time in this cyclical hell.

The End